Don Prophet
a novel

Erik Simon

ISBN-10: 0-9856619-0-9
ISBN-13: 978-0-9856619-0-8

Published by Beef and Barley

Book design by Sheepscot Creative

DonProphet.com
WeAreBeefAndBarley.com

For Nen

CONTENTS

For Brianna Culp of Tuttle, Pennsylvania, the doubts came early. Age eleven, to be exact, on a sunny July morning during Vacation Bible School. All grades K - 6 had joined together to begin the day with prayer and song, as they did every morning that week, and while "Jesus Loves Me" was never a particular favorite of Brianna's (she much preferred the upbeat tempo of "Jumping Jacks and Jesus" and the no-holds-barred rhyming hilarity of "Sinners Must Die, Here's the Reason Why"), the song proved especially bothersome to her that morning. All during the subsequent activity, crafts, during which she and her classmates made paper-sack puppets of children from countries where it would be most fun and challenging to go on a mission (Brianna went with Botswana), she could not shake her qualms. Finally, when her sixth-grade class joined with the fifth graders to head outside for some dodgeball, Brianna tugged on the hand of Kay Fugate, the thickly-built, pleasant, matronly teacher of the fifth grade.

"Kay," Brianna said, using her first name because the Fugates were close friends of the Culp family. "In 'Jesus Loves Me,' we sing, 'Little ones who here belong / They are weak but he is strong.'"

"We sure do, Brianna," Kay said, calm and smiling, as if warmed with reassurance that her own children were safe with JC. Kay and Brianna stood to the side in a darkened foyer where the other kids all walked hurried and loud toward the light at the other end, which was the door to the outside. "And isn't it lovely?"

"Yeah," Briana said, "but I thought of something this morning that kind of bothered me."

"What's wrong, Brianna?" Kay lightly rubbed the young one's bony shoulder with her soft, thick hand.

"The little ones belong because they're weak and he's strong, but if he's so strong, how come he ended up nailed on a cross by his enemies? All the real strong people I know, it'd be hard to nail them to a cross."

"Oh, Brianna," Kay said, smiling beatifically, stroking Brianna's long brown hair. "Jesus wasn't crucified because he was weak. Being crucified was part of the plan all along."

"If that's the case," Brianna said, head cocked, "then why does it matter if he's strong or not?"

"Honey," Kay said, "these are really good questions, but why don't we go out and play some dodgeball before we miss out on all the fun." Brianna did as Kay suggested, but she didn't have any fun. She was too concerned. After all, the question was ultimately one of Brianna's own safekeeping. How safe was she belonging in the hands of a guy who wound up nailed to a cross?

Later that day, in the early and warm evening, Brianna sat to dinner out on the large front porch with her mom and dad. The menu was hamburgers her father had grilled, Tater Tots her mom had baked, and a green Jell-O salad with little square chunks of canned pears. Her mother was a squat woman who had the solid, barrel rotundity of one who'd been fat her whole life and, of necessity, had simply learned how to wear it well. But Glenda Culp had not been fat her whole life. Her first twenty-three years she was a petite beauty, a cheerleader and homecoming queen candidate, and she'd gained the weight during her difficult pregnancy with

Brianna, much of which she'd spent confined to her couch. During delivery, she hemorrhaged horribly, almost losing her newborn and her own life, and it was that experience that turned Glenda so resolutely to Jesus. She never did lose the weight because once you had the continuous comfort of Jesus in your life, who really cares if you're fat?

"Mom," Brianna said, waiting with her arms to her side while her mother stood to cut her burger in half. "I asked Kay Fugate some questions today at Bible School about Jesus being crucified."

"That's so good," Glenda said, setting Brianna's plate of food before her. "Kay is such a sweet person. I'm sure she had some wonderful answers."

"We didn't really get to all of my questions." Normally, Brianna hated when her different foods touched, but she was so preoccupied that she didn't bother moving the stray Tater Tot that had rolled against the Jell-O.

"What else do you want answered, honey? Maybe I can help?"

"Kay said Jesus' crucifixion was planned all along. If that's the case, why do we treat Judas like he's such a bad guy? I mean, if the whole thing was planned, wasn't Judas just doing what he was supposed to do?"

Never a deep thinker, Glenda was frankly cowed by her daughter's theological precocity. She chewed the first bite of her hamburger vigorously, trying to come up with some kind of answer, any answer, but failing, she hurried to take another bite, stalling for time and pointing to her full mouth as the reason why she couldn't answer at the moment.

But Brianna pushed on. "And I don't really get why Jesus had to die for my sins in the first place. I mean, Pastor Markey is always saying how we're all born sinners. If that's the case, then that's not really my fault, is it? So it's kind of like the whole game's rigged to put Jesus in charge. And besides, aren't you and Dad always telling me to take responsibility for my own actions? Well, why do I need to do that if Jesus already died for my sins two thousand years ago, especially when Pastor Markey says that I'm already a sinner just by being born?"

Glenda Culp ceased all chewing. Her mouth was full, but she was simply too horrified by her daughter's questions to go on chewing. She didn't think little Brianna's questions were outright blasphemy, but she sensed it was all headed that way, and all she could envision was the final result: a strung-out, teenaged daughter regularly pumped full of heroin and the sperm of various men. Glenda had yet to meet an overly smart woman who wasn't, to some degree, a slut. So seeing such a future for her own daughter, she did the only thing she could do on that warm July night while her family supped on the spacious front porch: she cried. A fat tear rolled from her fat eye down her fat face, quickly followed by another, and before she slipped into a full-bore crying jag, she rose with effort from the table and padded across the porch to the front door and inside, her mouth still full of food.

Brianna turned to her dad, a wiry insurance salesman with pale, almost grayish, skin and a jaw chiseled and hard as a Norwegian fjord. His brown hair was thick but short. Brianna wasn't that surprised that her mom didn't answer her question. She was plenty old enough to have an inkling that her mother wasn't a particularly bright woman. She was a bit surprised, however, at how emotional it had gotten. "What about you?" she asked her dad, who couldn't have been less ruffled by all that had just happened. "Do you know why?"

"You know me, honey" her dad said, calmly. "I don't really give all of that stuff too much thought."

"You mean you don't believe in Jesus?" she asked, strangely undisturbed by the idea, which, until she'd voiced it that moment, she'd never really realized was an option.

"Oh, I don't know. I guess I just don't really care." Four years ago, even four months ago, Sam Culp might have answered differently, might have nurtured a façade, a lie, for Brianna's sake.

4

But he could clearly see that she could handle the truth now and would see right through anything that wasn't. Not The Truth, of course, because he laid no claim to that, but his truth, the truth of how he saw things.

And Brianna could handle his cavalier take, but she was confused on one thing. "Why do you even bother going to church, Dad?"

"Honey, when you're older, and you're married, you'll realize that it really is better to pick and choose your battles." Of all the things said and heard that day, that last comment of her father's was by far the most cryptic.

Brianna's questions and doubts didn't fade. In fact, in time, they proliferated and grew more intense. They caused a pain deep in her soul common to all of those who pursue the Lord in earnest. They plagued her waking hours and, at night, they made sleep difficult. Relief was coming. Release. She didn't know it, and initially she'd misread the signs, succumbing first to a false messenger of hope and wisdom before the real thing came along. But in time, she would be righted, and her questions would be answered.

Don Prophet was on his way.

ERIK SIMON

THE MISSION

ERIK SIMON

"What's the obsession with suffering?"

Thus spoke Don Bollinger, a hefty, heartland teddy bear of a guy, loud but not bellicose, smart but not arrogant, girthful but not obese, witty, rumpled and earnest. His hair was a ripe strawberry, his skin an unripe one, his voice a resonant bass instrument. He was watching TV, a televangelist. He watched them often, and though this particular preacher was not Barry Gladwell, the silver-haired, silver-tongued evangelist Don thought of as his primary nemesis, it was nonetheless a well-groomed, adroitly-cadenced preacher almost every bit as adept as Gladwell at herding legions of gullible sheep. At that moment, he was preaching about how much Jesus suffered for us, and of course he was preaching in tears. In ranting at the TV, Don was speaking to no one in particular, though his girlfriend of almost two years (cohabitating for a year) was somewhere in the apartment rumbling about—sounded vaguely like the bedroom.

"Suffering was pretty much the least of what Jesus did," Don continued. "He was hardly the only person in the history of the Roman Empire to die on a cross. Hell, he wasn't even the only one that day." Somewhere in the overstuffed storage space of Don's brain sat a box of information (name, date) of some Roman general who crucified as many as one thousand of his enemies in one day, but Don couldn't locate the box right now, and given that he was only mid-rant, he didn't think it was a good time to stop and hunt, especially since Gretchen, his improbably named Chinese-American girlfriend born and raised on the other side of the Manhattan Bridge in Chinatown, had just entered the room: the tangible appearance of some semblance of an audience decimated the luxury of a pause.

"And even if it was a bad couple of hours up there on the cross," he proceeded, his volume lightened but his ranting tone intact, "spending eternity alongside Yahweh wasn't a bad payoff. I bet my eye teeth millions of souls in those third-world cesspools that pass for countries would be more than happy to trade a few hours of nail-driven hell for an eternity of bliss at the right hand of ultimate power."

"Don," Gretchen interjected, serious-faced. "We need to talk."

"Dying on a cross in the course of six hours is bad?" He'd heard Gretchen, of course he'd heard her, and he didn't begrudge the interruption since he had offered something of a pause (he'd had to swallow to get some saliva under control), but he was on a roll and not about to stop. "Try starving to death in Ethiopia over the course of a year. Try cashing out with dysentery in Indonesia or Thailand, literally shitting yourself to dehydration and death over an ungodly amount of time. Try four years in Auschwitz with no afterlife bonanza or ten years in one of Uncle Joe's gulags. To any of those folks, six hours on a cross would sound like a weekend in the country."

"Don, please, we need to talk."

"Hell, those three days of kidney stones I had would rival anything Jesus had to deal with on his last day as a mortal."

"Don!" Gretchen yelled, her last resort. Short and thin but with thick thighs and defined arms, like one of those stocky gymnasts from Don's Midwest, Gretchen did not like the sound of yelling in confined quarters; she'd endured too much noise in the cramped shoebox of an apartment in the cramped neighborhood of her overpopulated childhood. But when she had to she would and could reach decibels that rivaled those of her slobby, stentorian beau. "Enough!"

"Sorry, Gretch. You know how I get when I watch these guys."

Gretchen knew better than to ask Don why, if the televangelists got him into such a lather, he ever bothered watching them. She knew why: He needed to. Sure he hated them, the whole pack of them, but he couldn't live without them. They were his heroin. Actually, they were more akin to cigarettes, for he never slunk to an abandoned warehouse to shoot up or free base the Jesus freaks. They were simply a seamless habit of his life, something he turned on when he had a few minutes to kill, something he watched with his morning coffee, something he'd resort to after sex. Every now and then they preached him into a rant like what he'd just delivered, but for the most part when Don watched, he kept a private counsel, sometimes actually agreeing but most often shaking his head or tsking now and then, occasionally offering a word here or there, a succinct rebuke or speculative rebuttal. That's what Don was doing when he watched them—he was formulating arguments. God knows why. Don said he did it to keep on his theological toes. Debating roadwork, he sometimes called it. Gretchen didn't mind. In fact, she found it appealing. So many of the people in New York City their age (hovering around thirty) were so goddamned affected that Gretchen could barely abide them—the stylish glasses, the dark clothing, the pseudo-intellectual critiques of something on HBO. Don was never affected. Don was never anything less than wholly earnest. Whatever his yen for televised theology was, it was sincere, and that's what made it bearable, even endearing.

"Don, I need you to turn that off for a minute." Remote dangling from his hand, Don flicked its aim at the TV to mute it, but he didn't turn it off. Gretchen sighed and strolled over to the ladder-back rocker in the corner of their cozy, wood-floored living room. The way Don had his thick, pale legs splayed on the couch, there was little chance of her squeezing in on it; it was more a love seat than a couch. His feet were atop the heady magazines scattered about the glass-topped coffee table. His calves were thick and pale as newborn pigs.

"You're not getting ready to break up with me, are you?" he asked.

"No," she said sharply. "Why would I do that?" In the shrug of his response, Don sneaked a peek at the tube: the camera had panned to include untold numbers of the congregation, so many crying and shaking their heads.

"Don, I don't know how to say this, but I need you to get a job."

Don's heart skipped a beat. In a way he knew this day was coming, but it was still a difficult set of words to hear. In fact, it was the last thing in the world he wanted to hear. Radically so. "A job," he said with breathy defeat. He dropped the hand holding the remote from the back of the couch to the worn and variously-stained seat cushions. Puffy thud. Simultaneously he dropped his massive head back and stared at the plaster ceiling. "A job."

"Not forever," Gretchen hastened, as if softening the blow of having just told him she thought they should spend a little time apart. "It's just, well, I thought I could take care of everything for us for a while, and I could, I did, but things, as you know, aren't really working out the way we'd hoped and, well, I need some help."

"But what about my copy?" Don said, still staring at the ceiling, knowing the answer to the question but not wanting to go down without a few token swings. Don wrote catalog copy for an academic textbook publisher, a nice sideline of bit work but nothing that he could survive on. It paid well but was very sporadic—one week of work four or five times a year. "I bring in some pretty good money writing copy."

"I'm not saying you don't," she said. "And I'm not blaming you, either. After all, the arrangement was my idea. It's just that—look, neither of us wants to admit it, but we both know things aren't developing the way we thought they would, and for now, until something changes, I need you to go get a job."

It wasn't that Don was lazy. Far from it. A product of the heartland (a small town in Southern Illinois, Jerseyville), he'd been sweating his ass off in one type of field or another since he was nine years old—walking the rows of thigh-high soybeans in drone-like malaise to pull out the weeds; stepping over the sharp and crunchy ankle-high spikes of mown hay to chuck the bales onto a tractor-pulled wooden rack; fighting his way through corn taller than him to pull out the tassels, the corn initially wet with dew in the chilly mornings just after sunrise when the work began but soon dry and painful as the leaves cut against the skin from mid-morning until quitting time just after noon. And that was just the beginning of the litany of ass-chapping odd jobs he'd had to endure. So it wasn't that he was lazy. It was just that in the past six months he'd finally gotten a taste of rising each morning to spend his day at work he *wanted* to perform, which for Don was writing, and what he dreaded was not so much the effort required of his forthcoming job, whatever it might be. It was the inanity of it, the ennui, the sense of purposelessness with which it would suck the vim right out of his existence.

"I feel really awful about this, Don."

"No, it's not your fault."

And it wasn't her fault that he had to go back out and get a job. It wasn't anybody's fault. It was just the way the world was.

"Genius. Genius." That's what Muriel Davidson, one of publishing's top agents, said in reference to Don's first novel, *The Letter Why*. They sat in Puccello's, a dim, airy Italian restaurant in Midtown just a few blocks from Muriel's office. Muriel was short and thin with short and thin gray hair and a face incongruously smooth. Don suspected some surgery there, but you could never be sure, and really, who cares? Muriel, or more accurately, her list of authors through the years, had won it all, and in multiples: Pulitzers, PEN/Faulkners, National Book Awards, Bookers, two Nobels, even an Oscar. She also represented a poet whose books actually made a profit—the Holy Grail of publishing. Muriel had been so successful for so long that ten years prior to this lunch with Don she'd stopped taking on any new clients. But when *The Letter Why* came into the small empire of her agency, the book, after its first read, was immediately dropped onto her desk. Muriel read the book in one sitting and, upon conclusion, wept silently for a multitude of complex reasons.

"Let me tell you something about me, Don," she said as they sat at a tiny patio table on a warmish September afternoon, bottle of Chardonnay and basket of bread between them. "When it comes to the business side of books, I have done it all. It stopped being about accomplishments for me a long time ago. I'd retire tomorrow if there was something else I gave a shit about doing. But there isn't. And so only one word has to come to mind for me to take on a new project: important. For ten years that word has not popped into my head with anything new, but it did with your book. It screamed in my head. I read your novel, and the minute I finished it, one word came to mind: important. You've got the book of a lifetime here, Don," she said, gesturing at the table as if the manuscript lay between them, which it didn't.

Muriel reached into her roomy black purse and pulled out an elegant package of dark European cigarettes. Don watched her light one and said, "I couldn't care less, Muriel, but I'm not sure you can be smoking that here."

"Fuck Bloomburg," she said at the end of a long inhale and exhale. "Mayors come and go. Literature is eternal. Who the fuck is Fiorello LaGuardia today? That airport might as well be named after some chef for all people know."

The small, dark, heavily-accented waiter came and took their order and made no mention of Muriel's cigarette. He refilled her wineglass before he left.

"So you think you can sell this book?" Don asked.

"Let me tell you something, Don." She pointed at him with the two fingers between which she clutched her dark cigarette. "Take me out of this business and this city, I wouldn't last a day. Fifteen years ago I bought a house in the country. I spent one night there and put it on the market the next day. I'm not saying it wasn't lovely. I'm saying it wasn't me. No cement, no Muriel. Paris is even too bucolic for my tastes. So I know this city, and I know publishing, and what I know is you've got a gold mine with *The Letter Why*. You've got a literary bestseller. You not only wrote a great novel. You wrote your ticket."

Don almost wept. How long had he waited to hear such words, and not from his best friend or girlfriend but from someone whose opinion had been validated by years in the business, someone with real muscle and chops. "So what do you want me to do?" he asked.

"I want you to do two things," Muriel said. "First, we need to sign a contract so I can begin to represent you immediately. Delay's not my forte. I want to messenger this manuscript to an editor at Scribner before this evening's martini has touched my lips." Muriel reached again into her massive black purse and withdrew a manila folder from which she pulled out a contract—one page.

Don read it. It was really much simpler than he'd ever imagined such a contract would be. "Should I take this home and go over it with a lawyer or something?" Don asked. By lawyer he meant Gretchen. No way could he afford a lawyer, but when it came to business, Gretchen was a tough and savvy little spark plug, and he sought her counsel in all fiduciary matters.

"No offense, Don, but this contract ain't *Ulysses*." Muriel reached into her purse and pulled out a pen. "I can't imagine any lawyer can make it any clearer for you than it already is."

Don bowed to the logic, took the pen and signed. "Okay. What's the other thing I need to do?"

"You got another in you?"

"Another book?" Don asked. Muriel nodded. In fact, Don did, or at least an idea for another book, another character to pursue. It was something he'd been rolling around in his brain for a few months now. "Yeah, I've got another book I'm ready to start," he said.

"Then start it. Immediately. If you've got a second one ready while sales for the first are soaring, the deal we may be able to get may top everything I've ever done before, and I doubt I need to tell you how impressive some of my numbers have been."

Go start another book. It was music. Sweet, sweet music. He could not believe he'd heard it. Neither could Gretchen.

"She said what?" Gretchen shouted, which she probably wouldn't have done if the store weren't empty, but it was, and who knows, maybe she would have shouted even if there were a couple of customers. She worked on the Upper East Side in a shop that sold glasses, top-dollar stuff, the sunglasses and prescription specs that the rich and famous buy. She was the store manager and also its top salesperson. She'd gone to

Cornell and majored in sociology, but only after she was just weeks away from graduation did she realize how idiotic the field was. "I don't remember a fucking thing about any of it," Gretchen often said, "probably because none of it was worth remembering." So she came back to the city and got a job at the glasses counter, and five years later she was manager and had been now for an additional five years. It was an immaculate place, blond wood floors, high ceiling, clean lines and colored geometry everywhere—lemon and lime cushioned boxes for chairs, paintings of pastel octagons and hexagons, an oversized mobile of various metal trapezoids. And the air inside, so clean—Don teased Gretchen about how the store bought bottled air from Norway and had it shipped in.

"She said for me to get cracking on my next book."

Gretchen squealed and leaped into Don's arms. Literally. She wrapped her legs around his waist and said, "This is fucking incredible." It was no strain for Don to hold Gretchen in such a fashion, he being a mammoth, she a chimp. Don knew they were an odd looking couple, but far from the oddest walking hand in hand in this town. "I knew this was going to happen for you. I just knew it."

So Don started his next book, working title *Funnel Cloud*. But it came hard because he lacked energy. He was still working at the time, at Meyer and Levy, a small investment firm on Wall Street. It was a job he'd started six months before as a temp, and they kept him on because his boss, a middle-aged trader fatter than Don, said, "You're a funny son of a bitch, Bollinger. I need funny around here. Not nearly enough of it." So Don was kept on for his wit, and now it was getting harder for him to find the energy to write while working full time.

Then came the springlike yet chilly night in late April. Don and Gretchen sat in their living room, each reading, Don a novel and Gretchen a magazine. The windows were opened halfway, a compromise for early spring and late autumn when

Don wore shorts and a T-shirt around the pad while Gretchen was in jeans and a sweatshirt. That's what she was wearing that night, a maroon hooded sweatshirt with C-O-R-N-E-L-L emblazoned in white, block letters across her flat chest. Don's old, dingy T-shirt didn't quite cover his girthful, strawberry-haired abdomen. Gretchen set her magazine in her lap; the page facing up contained a picture of some bat-like creature hanging from a tree in the Amazon rain forest. "I think I'm ready to cut a deal, Don," she said.

Don peered over the top edge of the novel he was reading. "Speak."

"You quit your job and keep the copywriting gig. You contribute what you can with that, and I've got us covered until you sell your book and get your advance. Then you pay me back for the months I covered, and we move forward with the old arrangement. What do you think?"

Don peered unmoving for a few moments. "Leaning toward no."

"What do you mean leaning toward no? It's a fair deal."

"Not if I don't sell the book." Gretchen made a scoffing noise as if that were the least likely scenario the future might unveil. That aside, Don also didn't like the idea of someone else paying his way. He was a Midwesterner—hale, hearty, and independent, the first to offer a helping hand but the last to extend one in need. Heartlanders were huge. Per capita Don figured they had to have become the fattest people on earth. They'd swallow just about anything with glee, especially if it were fried, but not a handout.

"I'm not sure I'm cut out to play the role of sponge, Gretch."

"Sponge my ass, Don. You'll be bringing in some money with your copywriting."

"Hardly enough to matter."

"Look, Don," Gretchen said in a new tone, quieter, more serious. "*I* need you to make this deal with me. For the past six months you have been absolutely miserable to live with. I don't even like coming home to you in the evenings anymore. I'm willing to go six or so months with this deal, just so you're not miserable and I don't dread coming home to the guy I'm living with."

"Yeah, but Gretch, you don't understand. This book may not sell."

"That's a risk I'm willing to take. This really could be your chance for the big time, and everyone who's ever made it big will tell you that at some point he had to take that big gamble, the one that all of his friends thought he was crazy to take. Well, this is your big gamble. This is your time to take that crazy risk."

"But it's not me taking the risk, Gretch. It's you."

"Like it or not, Don, the moment I decided to move in with you, our fates became intertwined, even if only temporarily. You're my chance, too. I grew up in Chinatown squalor with three siblings and two parents in an apartment big as our kitchen. I'll never be more than lower middle-class by standing on my feet all day selling glasses to rich people. This is as much my chance as it is yours, and I'm willing to invest. I'm willing to take that gamble."

"Are you proposing marriage, Gretch?"

"What are you talking about?"

"Your talk of our inextricable bond sounds awful permanent."

"It's a business arrangement, Don. If you get a fat advance on that second novel because of sales on your first, don't think a chunk of that isn't coming my way."

And so it was: a business arrangement. Since he'd been dating Gretchen, Don had spent plenty of time in Chinatown. He'd supped on not a few conches and sea cucumbers (he still didn't know what the hell they were, but they went down easier than the bird's nest soup, made from regurgitated bird spit; how the hell do you even harvest that? he wondered) with Gretchen's folks in the larger apartment they'd moved into after the kids departed, and even though Don couldn't understand a word her parents said, and they couldn't understand him, he always left their place knowing one thing for sure: these people knew how to stretch a dollar to miraculous lengths. In business, growing up, Gretchen sat at the table of masters. A business deal, that's what she was offering. Sure she loved him, but this was still business, separate from love.

"All right," he said, "It's a deal."

"Jesus Christ," Gretchen said, getting up and heading into the kitchen to make some tea. "I cannot believe how hard you made that."

He finished out the week at Meyer and Levy but saw no need to give them two weeks' notice since he was still just a temp. "If you make some real dough, you better invest it with me," his boss said in between bites of some breakfast food suffocated by melted cheese. So Don had his deal and lived his dream of a life spent writing, a dream of mornings and afternoons dancing and wrestling in the flutter and sludge of words, a dream, six months and a pile of rejections later, abruptly cut off, a dream whose deferment became his own private devastation.

"Newt Gingrich. Newt fucking Gingrich," Don said to Stephan Pancier, an American-born Haitian reared in Bed-Stuy, Brooklyn, with a college degree from, improbably enough, Brandeis, where he went as a Posse Scholar, one of hundreds plucked every year from the inner cities and dropped onto campuses embarrassingly white, all of it funded privately by a bevy of philanthropists. Steph was medium-height, dark, and, as Gretchen and other women had assured Don, scrumptiously handsome. He also flirted with renaissance man status, which is one of the key reasons Don numbered him among the few whose company he sought. At Brandeis, Steph majored in comparative literature *and* the classics, but he was equally well-versed in foreign film, college football, American jazz vocals, American political history, baseball, musical comedy, tobacco and Bette Davis. "Ms. Davis may be the only genuinely self-actualized woman this country has ever produced," he was known to say at parties, sometimes sincerely, sometimes just to elicit, and then gauge, reaction. When Don asked him how he became, at such a relatively young age, so knowledgeable in so many subjects, Steph said, "Growing up in Bed-Stuy, I found it prudent to spend the bulk of my time indoors. And we were too poor for cable." He owned a high-end cigar bar in Prospect Heights that served espresso to patrons who stayed to smoke, and that's where Don met him a few years back, having strolled in one chilly Saturday. Steph sat on a stool behind a glass-encased counter reading a new biography on Disraeli. Bing Crosby sang and scatted over the speakers into the dim store with two exposed brick walls and heavy, leather furniture. "You read with the music on?" Don said by way of greeting. "Only nonfiction," said Steph. "Fiction and poetry demand silence." Don nodded approvingly. "My soul requires a cigar. What do you recommend?" Steph studied him for a moment, even leaned over the counter to consider Don's shoes. He sat back down. "Everything about your being screams Padron Anniversario, but something tells me you don't have twenty-five bucks to throw at cigars."

"That something speaks the cold, hard truth."

"Then let's go with a Gloria Cubana Series R, Number 5." Don nodded, and they'd been bound friends ever since.

"Even Newt fucking Gingrich can get a novel published, but I can't—silly little historical novels that aren't even historical. They're these bizarre Civil War what-ifs, alternative takes of the South winning that he probably masturbates to as he writes. Am I the only one who thinks it's a little weird that the most blindly and virulently patriotic citizens, the Southerners, are the same ones who go to bed every night wishing they'd have kicked America's ass a hundred and forty years ago?" Don shook his head. "Newt fucking Gingrich."

It was night, and they ambled along the Promenade on the edge of Brooklyn Heights, confronted by what Don thought was easily the most spectacular view of Manhattan—all the lights from Wall Street to Midtown, the lights of four major bridges, the black of the East River, the green glow of Lady Liberty. One of the things Don disliked about living in the city was that he rarely got to see the stars, and even if he did see them, it was never the crystal panoply of, say, a night on the New Mexico desert but rather a depressing tease of a dimmed handful here and there. But the lights of the city from the Promenade were a formidable consolation prize.

"What's amazing to me about America," Don resumed, "is that once you're a success in one field, you're automatically eligible to start near the top of any other field. Eddie Murphy makes a couple of funny movies, so he gets to go be a rock star and record a few albums. Cindy Crawford has a great body and face, so *Good Morning America* sends her to Colorado to do some mindless piece about skiing, and now she gets to put "journalist" on her resume. Tom Arnold just marries someone famous, and the next thing you know he's got his own TV show. I mean, come fucking on."

"Mike Healy came into the shop the other day," said Steph. "You know Mike?" Don shook his head. "Mike's a classically trained actor. Grew up in Oklahoma, went to Yale for drama, studied Shakespearean technique over in London. I go to all of his shows because he asks me to. They're always two-bit, unpaid productions in some converted warehouse over

here in Brooklyn or some closet triple-off Broadway in the city.
Shows aren't always so great, but he is. I've seen him flawlessly
pull off six different accents. Last February he was Vershinin in
a pissy little production of *Three Sisters*, and his farewell to
Masha was the most poignant lover's farewell I've ever seen.
Anyway, he was in the shop the other day, and he'd just got
back from another audition, one for a commercial, and he was
as low as low can go. He said he knew he wasn't going to get it,
and I asked how he knew, and he said that you always know.
You just do. Then after one of those long sighs of resignation
he said, 'George Steinbrenner has gotten more acting work this
past year than I have.'"

Steph ceased, and Don waited for more until he realized
that Steph, in fact, was finished. "You took that long to tell a
story that only corroborated everything I've said the last five
minutes?"

"Thought you might gain solace from the commiseration."

"Defeat gets no comfort from fellow losers. That's like
saying all the Romanovs were tickled to death about their
execution because the whole family was there to share it."

"All right, so fuck off, Don, I was trying to be nice. What
do you want me to say? Ninety-nine point nine percent of the
world has to live with the fact that life isn't going the way
they'd hoped. The mass of men lead lives of quiet desperation.
The only difference with you is that it isn't so quiet. Hell, you
think I'm giddy about planting my black ass on a stool behind a
counter to peddle tobacco ten hours a day six days a week?"

"I thought you loved your life. You're running your own
business."

"Oh, it's not bad. Just a lot more sitting around and
paperwork than I ever dreamed it'd be. I'm just getting restless
and bored. Feeling the need for something different. Some
kind of change."

"So take a month off. Go to Paris or Barcelona or something. Marty can run the store." Indeed, Marty could. He was Steph's right-hand man, his only employee beyond a few part-timers who helped on weekends. Marty was a Bay Ridge Italian ten years older than Steph who was, in Steph's own words, "the ablest assistant a second-tier entrepreneur could find."

"Oh, I'm fine. I'll come out of this rut. Maybe I just need a girl. The point is you can't get wrapped up in your own defeats. You think you've got it bad? Talk to the family of three in Baghdad that was a family of six four days ago until one of our misguided bombs took out Daddy and Auntie and big brother Ahmed."

"That kind of comparison holds no water with me." For Don, relativism like that was usually spurious at best. It really was apples and oranges or, in this case, apples and olives. Yes, the genocide in Darfur was absolutely horrific, and Don was quite glad that he was neither starving in the African heat nor running for his life across the Sudanese desert, but since he was born in Alton, Illinois, and raised in Jerseyville, it was irrelevant to compare his life to that of a Dark Continent refugee. Or an Afghan villager. Or a Baghdad amputee. Rather, he measured his success against those of comparable talent and education in the U.S. of A, and with that more appropriate metric he was hard pressed not to conclude that thus far, the fates of the world were screwing him pretty good. "You're going to have to offer me a better sop of solace than that."

"Yeah, well, sops of solace aren't my forte. Among the black man in America, there aren't deep reservoirs of sympathy for any injustice served upon a white guy."

"I've certainly no rejoinder for that."

Don angled his saunter over to the wrought iron railing preventing would-be suicides from leaping into the rush of traffic on the Brooklyn-Queens Expressway about thirty feet below. He scanned across the deep and deeply dark waters of the East River to the manifold sparkle of lower Manhattan—all those colors, all those lights. He would rarely, if ever, admit it publicly, but he did not miss the World Trade Center towers. The problem with admitting that was that he knew people would immediately infer that he was glad they were gone. He was not, by any stretch. Though he was, at best, only midway on his life's journey, he was reasonably confident that by journey's end, 9/11 would go down as one of the worst days in his life. He stood on the roof of his Brooklyn brownstone but four miles away and had gotten up there early enough to see the second plane fly into the second tower. Surreal was the best word he could use to describe it. He had an unobstructed view of both towers, and the plane crashing into the building somehow didn't look real, looked more like a video game. He was not the only one on the roof. His neighbors were also up there, as were the residents of adjoining brownstones—a whole street of brownstones with a handful of people on top of each one. Their mood was almost giddy, Don not excepted. Somewhere deep in Don's consciousness was the idea that something terrible was happening and a good number of people were already dead, but still there was a certain sense of excitement that he was watching something spectacularly rare. There wasn't a lot of fear, not yet at least, because that early into the morning neither Don nor anyone around him knew why it was happening. The term al-Qaeda had not yet made it into the national dialogue. It was still just an unbelievable scene to behold. More amazing than anything else was the amount of black smoke pouring from the towers. Words fail to describe just how much smoke there was and how black it was. It was selfish, Don admitted, but he was glad the wind was blowing south that morning, pushing that smoke away from him. Then came the collapse of the towers, first one, then the other, and the mushroom cloud of ensuing gray smoke was every bit as awesome and terrifying. By then someone had come running up with information from the TV, and al-Qaeda was now in the dialogue, and Don was scared. And he sat down on the roof of his brownstone when that first tower fell, and all the giddiness he'd heard and felt gave way to a numbed and overwhelmed silence. The people on his roof were silent, the people on the adjacent roofs were silent, and the only noise beyond the chain of sirens was a long, tortured scream, a howl of anguish, despair, fear, grief and full awareness from some man on some roof somewhere in his neighborhood.

So no, Don was not glad the towers fell. All the instruments agreed that the day they fell was a bad, bad day. As was the next, and the next after that. And the smoke lasted for months. And the smell lasted for months, an alloyed odor of an electrical fire and burning flesh. It was two months before he could concentrate on anything, six months before he felt somewhat relaxed on the subway again, and over a year before he felt safe in crowds. That said, he still never liked the towers. At night, viewing them from the Promenade, he thought they looked like two glowing dicks among the glittery pubic hairs of all the surrounding buildings. Don didn't know squat about architecture, but he knew a thing or two about pride, and he simply didn't see the sense of the architectural pissing contest all these cities were having. Was there really a point of this international one-upsmanship of tall buildings? How high was humanity going to go before one of these buildings tipped just enough to break off at the top? Granted, these architects and engineers knew their business, but human error was hardly rare, especially with projects pushing into the unknown. Even now there was talk of coming back with towers taller than the ones knocked down. For what earthly purpose? Don wondered if anyone would ever step in and say, even quietly, "It's not really necessary, guys. Nor particularly wise." And maybe utter something about pride going before the fall. Literally. The

Tower of Babel tale offered some relevant commentary on all of this.

"If you really want to publish," Steph said, "you should write a memoir."

"Ain't that the God's fucking truth."

Don could not believe the profusion of memoirs in contemporary society, all of these self-pitying screeds of "terrible" or "awful" or "heartbreaking" childhoods written by people who, frankly, were doing pretty well in life, at least well enough to get paid to write a book about their lives. It never ceased to amaze Don how tenured Harvard professors or international celebrities could still find a room in the successful condos of their lives to bitch about. He'd spent enough of this lifetime hearing about people who felt "uncomfortable in their own skin" during their teenage years. Who the hell among us didn't feel uncomfortable at thirteen? The difference was that while most of us muddled into uneventful lives of struggle that were average at best, these people went on to highly successful careers wherein they could still somehow imagine they were slighted during their formidable years, enough so to matter, enough so to imply that life's scales might still not be tipping in their favor. And all of them, of course, had one lousy parent, usually the father. But given that these people turned out to be such successes, didn't said bad parent do something right? Or was every success utterly self-made these days? And then there were those rehab memoirs of the rich and famous. Let's see, life offered you every opportunity or advantage or incredible breakthrough possible, and you responded by freebasing heroin for twenty years, and now you want us to know just how tough it all was on you? Don longed for the memoir by the laid-off steel worker with three kids whose wife died of breast cancer. Or the journeyman electrician with no health insurance paralyzed from his car accident with a drunk driver. Those would be memoirs worth reading of slights not imagined. To

Don it seemed we were establishing a society in which personal responsibility was, like the sea turtle, slowly disappearing, and the more toys and prizes you owned, the less responsible you could be.

The only books that Don reviled more than the legion of memoirs were all the self-help books on bookstore shelves these days. Faux spirituality. If these televangelists were the hucksters from the Right, and they were, then these New Age self-help authors were their spurious counterparts from the Left.

"I need a gimmick," Don said.

"Gimmick?" Steph said.

"You know, something like canoeing the Mississippi, although that's not nearly gimmicky enough. Something like hang gliding around an active volcano or scaling the Golden Gate Bridge in protest of air pollution. Just something. If you can get a gimmick that's provocative enough to garner some decent publicity, then you can go *do* or *be* whatever you want. That Bobbitt guy got his dick cut off by his wife, and all of a sudden he's making movies. Granted they were porn, but it was a foot in the door. Traci Lords and Sylvester Stallone got their starts in porn. Maybe I should start publicly sodomizing dead cattle. That would get some publicity."

Steph laughed. "Careful. You're treading on Paris Hilton's turf. She's already cornered the unabashed whore market."

"But sodomizing dead cattle is still unmined."

"For now. She's only in her twenties. The older she gets, the more creative she's going to have to become. Just like Bette Davis saying you need to take supporting roles once you turn forty."

Don laughed. "The unabashed whore routine would never work for a fat common Joe like me anyway. That kind of thing works only for an heiress."

"Or a scholar," said Steph. "I can see a chemistry professor pulling that off, too."

Don nodded then sighed. "I cannot believe I've got to get a fucking job. Again." No, he could not believe it, and part of him refused to accept it. His mental gears were grinding. Don Bollinger was not joking when he said he needed a gimmick.

Don didn't go job hunting right away. Initially he had a decent-sized assignment of copy work, and that took a week, but after that a malaise set in. He was so loath to drag his ass out in search of some obnoxious job that he would not do it; he couldn't even bring himself to phone the temp agencies he'd last worked with and let them know he was back on the market. He pretty much spent these sparkling autumn days in Brooklyn doing one of two things: Watch televangelists and go to Steph's tobacco shop and have a cigar, drink coffee, chat with Steph or Marty or any of the random customers. But that was something he'd do only late afternoon or early evening. He liked to be out of the apartment when Gretchen returned for the day. By then he'd been in the apartment all day long, so it was then that he felt a need, mentally and emotionally, to get the hell out. He also needed an audience, even of one, just to vent a little because invariably he'd been watching those televangelists all day long.

They became something of an intense study for Don, the televangelists, as if he were cramming for a final exam. He'd watched hours of them before, hours, but never consecutively, and watching them back to back to back offered him fresh insights. He'd never before really processed the numbers. Oh, he knew they were popular—that's why they were on TV after all—but now he began to digest just how many televangelists there were and just how many followers each had. In his youth it seemed, like the auto industry, there were just the big three— Falwell, Swaggart and Bakker—but now there were dozens and dozens, each with thousands upon thousands of followers. They didn't preach in churches; they preached in auditoriums. The numbers boggled the mind.

Regarding form and content, Don noticed that there were three camps. The first pitched tent in the land of the shamelessly money-driven, preachers so obviously in it for the lucre that it was effortless to spot. These folks almost always spoke of just money, either the money you should send them or the money you will indubitably make if you just believe in them, a belief you can verify by sending them money. These guys (and they were almost always guys, although a few women were making inroads) never ministered on anything akin to helping the downtrodden or even saving your soul. Stuff and nonsense, that. And if you did send them money, their tokens of appreciation reaffirmed their philosophy: you'd get a fake dollar bill with a picture of Jesus instead of Washington or a gold-plated keychain with the dollar sign superimposed over the cross. And all of these money preachers relied on the same scripture: For instance, they would cite Deuteronomy 8:18: "You shall remember the Lord your God, for it is He who gives you power to get wealth." To which Don would draw and fire his own retort of cold, hard Deuteronomy, 18:20: "But the prophet who presumes to speak a word in my name which I have not commanded him to speak, or who speaks in the name of other gods, that same prophet shall die." (Don was wont to add "motherfucker," at the end.) Or another straw passage of scripture they loved spinning into their own personal gold was Proverbs 11: 24 - 25: "One man gives generously and ends with more. Another stints on doing the right thing and incurs a loss. A generous person enjoys prosperity." No matter how distant their financial goals lay, they could always find the scripture that would help get them there.

What was shrewd about these money-preachers was that in the final tally, what they were really preaching was a comfort

Christianity. It was about putting your faith in Jesus so that you could have a better life, and if your life didn't get better, it was because your faith was weak. Thus, there was all avoidance of scripture pertaining to how difficult it is to live a life carrying the cross. At no time did they mention Jesus' dictum about it being easier for a camel to pass through the eye of a needle than it is for a rich man to get into the Kingdom of Heaven. Never was there a mention of Jesus commanding a rich man to sell everything he owned, give the money to the poor, and follow Him. No meek inheriting the earth on these shows. Following Jesus was the easiest thing in the world, according to this camp, and if you did it right, you would intuitively know which stocks to invest in. And if you picked the wrong stocks, well, that's because your faith was too weak.

The other camp of evangelists Don labeled the Salvationists. They were old school, the traditionalists, the ones that seemed to be genuinely, if misguidedly, concerned about your salvation. (Among these two types were many different species, but for now Don was largely interested in the general phyla.) These guys rarely referenced money, and never in their sermons. When they did make their fiduciary pitch (for all of them always made some pitch for money), it usually came at the end of the show: it was brief, it was in a setting different from where the sermon was given, often a nondescript office during an obviously separate time, and it was often linked to a specific purpose—trees for Israel or Bibles for Uganda or bicycles for the children of Zimbabwe so they had transportation to that thatch-hut church ten miles from home. No doubt this batch of preachers was skimming enough off the top for a good living, but at least there was the pretense or even genuine goal of helping others. It was these old schoolers that Don preferred. They were more entertaining. They were capable of saying the craziest things. They could be outlandish beyond parody. They would use a game show format to answer who might be the anti-Christ, or they would have a special segment titled, "The End Times and the Apocalypse," that included games and prizes. These old schoolers had no qualms with consigning the majority of humanity to an afterlife of Hell, whereas the money guys never dangled such unpleasantries above their flock. And while the money-guy ministry had gone global and included preachers from Australia, England, Korea, Japan, Kenya and a number of other countries, these Salvationists still tended to be the good old-fashioned Southern white male. For Don, there was something comforting in that. His hometown, though in Illinois, was closer to Memphis than Chicago, and though he was raised a soft-edged Baptist, he'd gone to his share of Pentecostal services, even a few tent revivals, so the zealous Southern televangelists with their theology of fear were no more than some of the voices echoing from his childhood.

And in the third camp, all by himself, stood Barry Gladwell, the king of Jesus TV. He was able to fashion a theology that mixed the best of the money guys with the best of the Salvationists. It was, like steel, an incredibly tough alloy, and sometimes Don couldn't dent it. Another reason Don preferred the Salvationists was that they actually provided theology, meaty God talk that Don could sink his teeth into and try to tear apart. But Gladwell's theology was in a class by itself. Some things he'd said Don had still found no credible argument against. Some things he'd said Don actually agreed with. His very existence was a marketing miracle. His air was Southern, but his accent was the no-accent of Iowa, and his appearance was the sheen of Southern California. He was tall but not gawky, thin but not skinny, handsome but not unapproachably so. His age was anywhere from forty to sixty, Don just wasn't sure, and his smooth baritone had just enough humanity and occasional rasp to keep from sounding even remotely fake. He could put forth an alliterative riff that would make the blackest of rappers green with envy. He was king. He reigned supreme. And during his moments of apogee, he even filled Don with awe.

But it wasn't Gladwell that Don was watching that warm afternoon in early October when Gretchen surprised him by coming home from work early; it was just some Salvationist.

"Hey," Don said, slumped on the couch, struggling with the immediate need to give his full attention to her. The Salvationist on the tube, a skinny little sawed-off Cajun with a last name like Daribeaux or Fobisheux (Don had never seen him before) had just told his congregation that all of those who have coworkers of the opposite sex need to find another job as soon as possible since, "scientific studies have proven that once you work two hundred and fifty hours with someone of the opposite sex, you are guaranteed to have an affair with that person." Don especially wanted to focus his mind on a rant that addressed the numerous forms of idiocy tucked like crawfish in the muddy bank of that statement, but he knew he needed to give his undivided attention to Gretchen right now. "What are you doing home early?" he asked. "You sick?"

"No, I'm not sick," she said, moving toward the counter that divided the living room from the kitchen area. It was topped with a glossy, beige Italian tile, miniature little squares, and the sound of Gretchen's keys was quite pronounced as she dropped them with a jangly clatter onto the tile. She laid her large black purse next to the keys.

"Honey, what's wrong?" he said, not getting up but at least sitting up, removing his legs from splayed on the coffee table and planting his wide, white, hairy feet on the floor. He wore old gym shorts, no socks, an orange T-shirt dully bright, like a road construction sign that's been in the elements for months. "Are you sick?"

"Don, I told you, I'm not sick." Don was chastened. He sat straighter. She rarely slid into this biting snap of a tone, and almost never with him. He wondered if her quick anger was partly responsible for his finding her incredibly sexy right now. It probably was, but the white blouse didn't hurt, ditto the jeans. Don thought shorter women, like Gretchen, always looked better in jeans than a dress or skirt.

"This is incredibly difficult for me to say, Don, so I need to just say it without any interruption." She had not moved away from the counter, and she would not look directly at him, just off to the side or down at the floor, as if at cue cards. "Three weeks ago I asked you to go out and find a job. I not only asked you. I told you I absolutely needed you to. Since then, you haven't done one thing about getting a new job." She paused to gather herself, and Don, uncomfortable, jostled. Gretchen held up her hand. "I told you: no interruptions." Don hadn't been about to interrupt, but telling her that would have been an interruption, so he remained mum. He wished he'd have turned off the TV. The sawed-off Cajun was prancing feverishly all over the stage, and Don struggled not to watch beyond the sidewise glance when Gretchen wasn't looking.

"Now, I know some of this is my fault," she continued. "I can't possibly imagine what I was thinking when I made that deal. I think I was a little drunk with all the talk and possibility. And for what it's worth, I'm not even worried about you paying me back for any of the last six months. But what bothers me so much is that since you finished that copy two weeks ago, you have done nothing, I mean nothing, about finding a new job. I kept giving you some time, thinking any day now you'd go ahead and start. I mean, I'm not completely callous to the situation. I know how devastated you were. Are. But days kept passing by, and you kept doing nothing, which surprised me more than anything. Even if things didn't go your way, how could you sit around doing nothing all day long, day after day? It's kind of sad. Actually, not sad, pathetic the way you sit around and just watch those televangelists. And by the way, turn that fucking thing off," she said, gesturing toward the TV. "I see you stealing glances." Don immediately complied.

"So I realized that in order for something to change, something had to change. Nothing changes if nothing changes."

"Which of your helpless twelve-step friends did you pick that hollow cliché up from?" Don said, unable to bear being confronted by recovery jargons.

"Now's not the time for you to be ridiculing others for helplessness, Don."

"I bet it was Amber."

"It was Amber. We had lunch."

"That bitch can't go a day without stumbling upon a new addiction she's prey to."

"At least she's got a job." Don was cowed by that retort. "Anyway, I'm giving you one month to find a job. One month. If, by the end of the month, you don't have a job, I'm going to have to ask you to leave."

"Wait. You're going to break up if I don't have a job in a month?"

"I didn't say that. I didn't say break up. I said ask you to leave."

"Which pretty much strikes me as the same thing."

"Not necessarily, although I will admit it'd be tough for a homeless, jobless slob to keep my heart captured." At this point, the gravity of it all finally got to Gretchen, and she cried. She brusquely wiped away a tear as if angry for displaying such weakness. "It's not that I don't love you. I do. Although God knows why. At lunch today, Amber even said she had no idea what it was I saw in you, and I was hard-pressed to come up with some concrete rejoinders."

"Fuck her. If it weren't her old man who she's constantly blaming for all of her problems, that sniveling bitch wouldn't be able to afford an apartment in Davenport, Iowa, let alone the one she's got in the Village."

"That's basically what I told her."

"You nailed her on her old man paying for everything?"

"Not in so many words, but I did tell her to fuck off. And I did tell her you have some incredible qualities that make you unlike anyone else I know. And I do love you. Still, all that love ain't paying the rent, and call me hard-hearted on this, but I've been without money before, and I've been without a boyfriend before, and I know which of the two is easier for me to live without. I do love you, but I need someone to help me cover the rent, and if it can't be you, then it's got to be someone."

"You don't mean another guy, do you?"

"No, I don't mean another guy. I just mean a roommate who can pay some bills. Get it?"

Don did get it. Like a fist to the gut, he got it. So he nodded his assent—numbly, reluctantly, he nodded his assent. And early the next morning, as soon as Gretchen got out of the shower, Don got in. He couldn't remember the last time he'd showered first thing in the morning. He didn't begrudge Gretchen's ultimatum—she had to do what she had to do, they weren't married after all—but he felt overwhelmed and almost suffocated by how everything had turned out, so as he and Gretchen bobbed and weaved around each other in the bedroom, a parry of preparation for the day, he was unable to respond to her questions and comments with more than a nod or grunt. And when he walked out of the apartment ten minutes after her, he felt ill-equipped to face the day ahead.

Terrific Temps was located on 41st Street between Madison and Park. The first time Don had gone there a couple of years back, given the moneyed name of the cross streets, he was expecting a pretty swank and spiffy office, but it wasn't that at all. It was located in a tall, tired, gray building with battered revolving doors and dusty, lusterless granite floors in the lobby. Dark too. It stood in the middle of the block, surrounded by other tall buildings, so the aura was one of cold and constant sunlessness, an aura of a dingy soul. Even as fresh and resplendent as was the October morning two years later when Don was making his return to the work world (and even Don, down as he was, had to admit it was one of those perfect autumn days in New York, fresh, clear, bustling, romantic, hectic, escapist, colorful, breezy and bright), 41st Street between Madison and Park was still shadowed and bleak, like Bartleby's Wall Street. But Terrific Temps was the agency where Don got most of his work back in his temping days, so it was logically the first place to go now that he was back in the market. Besides, Don liked the four guys who ran the place, Brooklyn-born and -bred good-hearted smartasses who all, except one, lived on Long Island now. The ancient elevator wheezed and lurched him up to the fourteenth floor.

"Donny," one of them shouted as he walked into the office. Don had forgotten his name. One was Regis, one was Paul, but given that they were all cut from the preposterously same cloth, he never could remember who was who. The other two's names he never remembered enough to even forget since he didn't much deal with them. "What the hell are you doing here?" he asked with his arms spread in that universal gesture of comedic perplexity. "I thought you went off to be Stephen King."

Don had forgotten that he'd told these guys the good news then, but he wasn't too surprised since he'd told almost everyone in his orbit. Now he was sorry as hell that he had. "Oh," Don said, sidling to the chair next to his desk, "things didn't really work out as planned."

"Join the fucking club." The two shook hands in slap-smacking fashion before Don sat. "This economy's so bad I'm about to register with a few temp agencies myself."

"Not exactly music to my ears," Don said.

"You didn't hear me singing it, did you?"

The other one that Don knew hung up his phone at his desk toward the back. "Donny," he shouted. It was the one with the mustache. Paul. That one was Paul, Don remembered, making the one next to him Regis.

Don sized up Paul. "You've lost some weight."

"Thirty fucking pounds and still counting. If I weren't married I'd be getting laid all the time." Regis and Don laughed.

"Donny here's looking for work," Regis said.

"Thought he went off to be Stephen King."

"Don't one of you guys have at least one bone of individuality?" Don asked.

"What's your individuality gotten you?" Paul said. "You're back here begging work from us."

"And don't think that doesn't suck," Don said.

"You think that sucks," Paul said, "wait till you see what we have to offer."

"That bad, huh?"

"For you, worse," Regis said. "If I recall, you didn't bring a lot of marketable skills to the table, and you're not exactly the receptionist type that any business is dying to show off at its front desk."

"I can write," Don said, and Regis gave a short laugh and shake of the head. Good writing skills. Who needed those? He could also think analytically and read intelligently and even converse dazzlingly, but again, what entry level position called for any of that? The places where an anonymous slob like Don could get hired for fifteen to twenty an hour needed easily identifiable skills, which usually meant quick dexterity among the multiplying array of computer programs out there in the business world, and Don had precious few of those. A Word document was about as far as Don could ride that horse, although with aching slowness and a lot of fits and starts he could fake his way through an Excel spreadsheet.

"I'll do what I can for you, Don," Regis said, "but you'd be wise to register at half a dozen other agencies while you're out and all dressed up." Don's dull yellow tie lay sodden and lifeless as a string of drool down his blue shirt, also dull. His collar was as soft as Kleenex. "You might even inquire at every fast-food place with a 'Help Wanted' in the window, and I'm not kidding."

Don knew things had gotten bad, but he'd not realized they'd gotten that bad. What the hell happened? A couple of planes flew into a couple of symbolic towers, and the economy tumbles along with the buildings? Really? Good Christ, how does an event that covers just a few square miles throw off the largest economy in the world? Is the world really that interdependently fragile now? Don was scared that if he sneezed too hard, he might raise the price of grain by one cent over in Kuala Lumpur.

He went to a couple more temp agencies that morning; Regis had recommended he do so, yes, but he'd been planning to anyway. One was on Madison Avenue and 46th, a high-end outfit whose jobs paid a minimum of twenty-five dollars per hour. Don had never registered with this company before, and the moment he stepped into the office, he knew this place was not for him. It hemorrhaged swank all over the furniture, the carpet, and even the applicants sitting lined against the wall, attractively shaped and perfectly postured and dressed in clothes he was a long way from being able to buy. How the hell does a temp afford Brooks Brothers? "Can I help you?" the cute blond receptionist said from her glossy wooden desk. "Not in this lifetime," Don said, cryptic even to himself. He turned around and left. He spent the next couple of hours registering at some more middle-class agencies around Midtown. The hiring agents there didn't explicitly tell Don that there was no work for him, but they didn't have to. Their eyes and their lackluster attitudes said it all.

He found some solace in a couple of slices of pizza. Back home in Jerseyville, it was Pizza Hut or nothing, but every other block in this town offered pizza so good he always felt blessed when he ate it. He had three slices then headed back out into the city and walked south.

How did it come to this? he wondered as he sauntered down Seventh Avenue, his belly full, his heart a tad elevated. No matter how depressed he might be, walking the streets of New York always lifted his spirits. Seven years he'd been here now, and he still got a romantic tingle when he was in Manhattan—the canyons of architecture along the avenues, the harried bustle of everyone. No element of this city ever bored him, and it simply had too much energy to allow him to sink into a full-blown depression. And yet, he was pensive.

He was not only flummoxed by how pathetic a position he'd gotten himself into, he was also baffled by the seemingly insurmountable wall between those who succeeded in whatever field and those who did not. He'd seen those successful people. The city was crawling with them. They were in Midtown, the Village, the Upper West Side, the Lower East Side, Wall Street, everywhere. You'd be walking along Fifth Avenue to the Guggenheim, and bam!—there was Barbara Walters. Or you'd pop into a bookstore near NYU just for the hell of it, and on your way out, bam!—there was Dustin Hoffman, peeking at the titles in the display window. Go to a Broadway show and three rows in front sat that chick from *The Wire*, a character actor whose name you didn't know but whose face you'd seen enough on screen that now, in person, she seemed familiar enough to go up to and say hello. But it wasn't just the famous. It was also the unfamous who nonetheless oozed success—the moneyed guys in silver Armani suits all over the city, the sleek women in business suits getting out of limousines. How the hell does it happen for someone? That was an agony particular to living in New York. All the success it offered was always so damned close no matter where he stood that he just couldn't fathom his inability to gain it. He simply couldn't identify what needed to be conquered between him and it. At the end of the day, was it no more than dumb luck, plain and simple?

He let out a roaring groan. On the impossibly busy intersection of Seventh Avenue and Thirtieth Street, all of those pedestrians and all of those vehicles and all of those stores selling electronics or incense or jewelry or clothes or handbags or costumes or pizza or mirrors or whatever, he let out a full-throated groan of anguish and frustration, not even breaking stride to do so. And because it was New York, a few in the immediate bustling throng surrounding him looked over to investigate, but no one else broke stride either.

By the time he got to Washington Square, Don was a sweaty mess. His soft shirt collar was softer and wet, the T-shirt underneath his frumpy Oxford was soaked, and his underwear had gained five pounds in water. His feet didn't feel so hot either. He'd just walked three plus miles, and though by definition living in New York meant you walked a lot, it had been a good while since Don had walked more than a handful of blocks in one shot. And even then it was in sneakers, not the cheap, brown dress shoes, thin-soled and inflexible, he was sporting today. His dogs were barking. He bought a bottle of water from the Pakistani or Bangladeshi or whatever the hell he was vendor at the corner of the park where he entered on University Place and made his way down the diagonal spoke of asphalt toward the center. His aim was a bench on the other side where, for some reason, it always seemed quietest. Kids screamed and laughed in the playground off to the right, old folks sat quietly observant in sweaters and coats heavier than the day called for, and someone down near the fountain in the center was shouting into a microphone about something, but someone was always shouting about something in this park, this town. Probably those black kids from Queens doing their acrobat routine, Don thought. He stopped to take a massive drink of water.

Don got to the center area, near the fountain that was dry today. The shouting wasn't the black gymnasts from Queens. Over to the right, toward the Arc d' Triomphe knock off, a middle-aged Korean man in charcoal slacks, a glaringly white Oxford and dashing orange tie, stood atop a three-foot plywood pedestal, his waist level with the heads of half a dozen minions surrounding him, all Koreans of various ages, the men in dark slacks and white Oxfords, the women in long skirts, pale blue, with white blouses. The pedestal Korean spoke into a portable microphone while his minions passed out small Bibles to passersby. It was no secret to Don that Koreans could be pretty damned nutty about Jesus. It was the one Asian group that had a couple of their own shows on the evangelist channels, and they had a wild-eyed fervency that could make a Georgia Baptist seem slack on devotion. Don actually feared the day the walls around North Korea came down, letting the gospel in there. Those people were already deranged enough by the absolute brainwashing of their cult-like dictator. Toss some Matthew and Mark into the void at the center of their misshapen lives, and those sheep were going to become some rabid mammals. Don moved closer to the Koreans.

"Witchcraft. Sorcery. That's what you find in Harry Potter," shouted the pedestal Korean with not one hint of "l" in his "r's." Must be second or third generation, Don thought. "And if Harry Potter isn't the spawn of Satan, then someone please tell me why in all of those books there is not one mention of our Lord and savior, Jesus Christ? Not one." Good Christ, what is it with Harry Potter and these people? Was that little fictional wizard really a threat to their God? They weren't even very good books. Don tried to read the first one, just to see what all the fuss was about, and he couldn't make it past fifty pages. Some hipster at some idiot party Gretchen dragged him to asked him if he'd read Harry Potter, and Don said that he didn't read children's literature. "Oh, but it's not children's lit," she said, gooey and excited. "Yes," Don said, "it is."

"And don't tell me reading is good for our children," the pedestal Korean continued. Don now stood about ten feet away. One of the Korean women offered him a Bible, but he made no motion to take it. He just stared up at the speaker while the Korean woman stood with her arm outstretched, Bible proffered. "It's only good if they're reading the right books. The Good Book. Because the minute you open a young mind too wide, you give Satan all the room he needs to just walk right in."

"Hey. Hey you," Don shouted in a reflexive action that surprised even him, his voice stentorian and resolute, starting deep within his bowels, moving past his diaphragm and out his throat, gathering along the way all the rage and frustration that was his day, his life. "Shut up."

The pedestal Korean, either too aswirl in the vortex of salvation to hear the shout or too familiar with the random noise of the city to think the shout was meant for him, continued with his preaching, but the Korean girl next to Don did pull her Bible back to her person and took a few steps away. "And once you let Satan into a mind so precious, so young—"

"Hey!" Don shouted again, louder, angrier. "Preacher man! You!" This time the pedestal Korean did stop speaking, and he slowly turned to Don. "I said, shut up." All the Koreans passing out Bibles ceased their activity and turned to watch the scene unfold. "It's a children's book, for God's sake," Don shouted, not abating at all in volume or rage. "A children's book. How could that possibly hurt anyone?"

"Because," the pedestal Korean started, but Don was having none of it.

"No!" Don shouted, even louder, striding toward the pedestal and taking the microphone from the Korean's loose grip, not because he needed it in order to be heard but simply to get it out of the Korean's hand. Nonetheless, now that he had the microphone, he decided to go ahead and use it, casting his voice far and wide. "I said shut up! The Gospel of Mark, chapter seven, verse fifteen, says, 'There is nothing outside a man which by going into him can defile him.' In other words, it's not a story from without you need to fear, especially an overrated children's story. It's your own black heart from within you need to fear, that we all need to fear. So please, until you know what you're talking about, just shut the fuck up!"

A large number of people in the surrounding area threw up a cheer. Don heard them, but the applause didn't fully register as he handed the microphone back to its owner. No sooner than he did, though, the pedestal Korean brought it to his mouth and was on the verge of some retort. Don violently reached forth and grabbed the microphone and shouted into it, punctuating each word: "I. Said. Shut. Up!" The surrounding crowd then gave up a huge cheer—all the people on the big circle of benches around the fountain area, the shirtless NYU students playing hacky sack in the dry fountain, the mothers with their babies in strollers, the professionals in ties or dresses, the handful of vendors, even the ripe and scraggly homeless— all of them gave Don a fun, happy, raucous cheer. Don surveyed the ovation and smiled.

Don Bollinger had his gimmick.

"A prophet?" said Gretchen, incredulous. She stood at the sink, her head cocked sideways in confusion, while Don sat across the room on one of the stools at the kitchen counter, showered and powdered at the groin and smelling fresh as May. He was as excited about his idea as he was the array of Arab food he'd picked up on the way home, food that sat in aluminum and plastic containers before him—falafel, hummus, kibbe, pita, fattoush. Gretchen leaned back against the counter, framed by the two-basin sink. "What do you mean a prophet? A prophet for what?"

"A prophet for God. You know, like Isaiah or Ezekiel." Gretchen had no immediate response, and Don could not refrain from tossing in "Habakkuk."

"Are you out of your fucking mind?"

Don was not to be daunted. He wasn't even upset by her response. "I cannot believe you don't see the potential here. All across America there are huckster evangelists making a name for themselves by preaching fire and brimstone and idiocy. I'm going to preach a message for the thinking man who believes or who wants to believe."

"Which, correct me if I'm wrong, I'm just a pagan Chinese girl here, is pretty much what every mainstream minister or rabbi is already doing."

"Yeah, but I'm going to make some noise about it, Gretch. I'm going to bring down the house. I'm going to take these charlatan evangelists on toe to fucking toe, and people are going to know who Don Prophet is."

"Don Prophet?"

"The name came to me on the subway home. Isn't it perfect?"

Gretchen regarded Don as if she had no earthly idea who, or what, he was. "I cannot believe you think this is a fantastic idea."

"And I cannot believe you think it isn't. How many great ideas looked bat-shit crazy at first? What about the naked cowboy?" Don was referring to the golden-haired guy built like a professional wrestler who walked around Times Square in all kinds of weather wearing just bikini underwear, cowboy boots and a Stetson hat, carrying a guitar. "He must be charging tourists twenty bucks to pose in a picture with him. He's making a fortune. And what about that chick who paints herself green and stands still for hours in Washington Square posed as the Statue of Liberty? Have you seen how many dollars she collects in the basket at her feet?"

"Yeah, but that's New York, Don. People expect crazy shit in New York. It's partly what tourists pay to come see."

"But in New York I'd be just one more crazed evangelist. I have to go out there," he said, sweeping his arm westerly in a grand, operatic gesture. "I have to go where I'm not already there."

Gretchen put her face in her hands. She did think this idea was crazy, but crazy in the kind of way that made Don what it was she loved. After all, a crazed, declaiming prophet in the mode of the Old Testament taking on the televangelists? There was a big something to like about that. And Don struck her as exactly the right guy for it. In fact, if she were given the power to hold auditions all across the land in order to cast the role of a latter day Jeremiah, she was pretty confident it would be Don she would choose from among the multitudes. It *was* a good idea. She loved its zest, its originality. And these uber-Christians had gotten out of control—way too powerful and overconfident. Someone needed to take them on, even if only in gimmick combat. And Don was that ideal someone, and as much as anything, Gretchen was simply trying to process the fact that her own little life was attached to someone who fit that bill. Still . . . she pulled her hands away from her face and spoke in a calmer tone. "I still don't understand how you're going to make money from this."

"I'm not making money from this, per se. I'm making myself a name. I'm getting publicity with the act. Then, once I've got the name, I make the money, ideally in the form of a book contract." Don could sense she was coming around.

"How are you going to afford this trip? You can't even pay your half of rent."

"Actually, I can pay my half of rent." His half was seven hundred and fifty dollars. The day's mail sat in a pile on the counter, and he pulled out the envelope that held his check for the recent copywriting.

"You could have just told me your check came in," Gretchen said. "I hardly needed the drama and graphics to believe you."

"The check buys me one more month in the apartment and leaves me a thousand dollars to take my ministry into America."

"A thousand dollars won't get you too far."

"Farther than you think. We plan to camp and eat cheap—buffets and such. America's full of them."

"We?" Gretchen said with the obligatory raised eyes.

"Steph's coming with me, at least for a couple of weeks."

"You talked Steph into coming?"

"He wanted to come. It was his idea."

Don had been so excited by his prophet idea that when he got off the subway in Brooklyn earlier, having just had his revelation in Washington Square, he went straight to Steph's cigar shop, knowing Gretchen wouldn't be home for a couple more hours. He had to share it with someone. The two stood across from each other over the glassed-in counter, a few patrons over in the small lounge area smoking cigars. Steph gave his undivided attention as Don related the entire afternoon in painstaking and exquisite detail. Don finished, and the two stared at each other in silence before Steph inhaled deeply, exhaled, sucked his teeth and said, "It's not the craziest idea I've ever heard."

"So you think it'll work?" Don said, calm, as if negotiating a contract.

"Not at all. But it's still not the craziest idea I've ever heard. Where all are you going with your act?"

"Not really sure. Just going to get in the car and see where the winds take me."

"You're not going down South, are you?"

"Two schools of thought on that. Go down South because that's where all the real crazy evangelists are, so I know I'll have someone to fight. Don't go down south until I've got my act honed. It's the big leagues down there."

"So even if you do go down South, you're not going there initially."

"Not initially, no. I'll start out heading west, like every other pioneer."

"Then why don't you let me tag along, at least for the first week."

"You really want to come?"

"Look, D., it's not my first choice for a vacation, but what the hell. I have been itching to get away, and I've never been west of Philadelphia."

"No one from out here has."

"And the conversation will be good."

"You realize there won't be much time for sightseeing."

"Just traveling new states will be sightseeing enough for me. And hey, if your gut's right on this, I may catch a miracle or two. Or at least a good fight."

So yes, Steph did want to come, but not because he was a great believer in Don's idea. Don, though, kept that to himself because he almost had Gretchen across the goal line. "And with Steph along, we'll be able to keep in touch," Don added, hoping that might be the coup de grâce. Don might well have been the last person in America who didn't have a cell phone. Sometimes that posed a problem for Gretchen, such as when she wanted to call him at the last minute for a change of plans, but for the most part it was another element of his individuality that she liked. Don didn't have a cell phone because he didn't want one. He didn't want to be "mobile." He didn't want people to either reach him whenever they wanted or think they had that kind of access to him.

Gretchen shook her head. "I cannot believe that the man I have thought most seriously about marrying is about to spend our last month together out on the road with a Brooklyn-born black guy trying to pick a major fight over religion."

"Don't be so sure about that last month together thing."

"Amid everything you've just told me, Don, it's the one thing I am most sure about."

Most boyfriends at this point would have crossed the room to console their lovers with comforting words and tender gestures that quite possibly would lead to some lovemaking. (Don was so vivified and confident that his manhood felt reasserted, and he did plan on banging Gretchen later, if she'd have him.) But with the exception of Gretchen, he was probably the least sentimental person he knew. Nostalgic, yes. He was easy prey for a dose of nostalgia now and then. Just the smell of the first cool day in autumn launched him into reverie for the autumns of his youth—bobbing for apples and hayrack rides and decorating the class float for the homecoming parade. But sentimental? Not a shred. Which was why Don didn't cross to console her. He merely pointed his finger at her and said, "Ye of little faith." Then he plucked a falafel ball from the half dozen before him and popped it into his mouth like a bonbon.

Four days later, on an unseasonably warm October morning, there was no gooey affection or teary sentimentality between Gretchen and Don. She stood on the steps of their brownstone stoop wearing brown corduroys and a pink T-shirt. Her arms were crossed. "I sure hope you enjoy camping with Don," she said to Steph, who leaned against the hood of Don's doubleparked blue Hyundai while Don finished loading the trunk. "I got a hunch it's you he's going to be living with when his fat ass gets back to Brooklyn." Steph smiled, but Don maintained his focus on packing the suitcases, tent, sleeping bag and pillows. The cooler of beverages and snacks he'd already put in the back seat, within easy reach. He laid his Men's Warehouse pinstripe suit flat atop the luggage. "You never know if the occasion might call for one," he'd told Steph, who refused to bring one for himself.

"Or who knows, Steph," Gretchen continued. "Maybe I'll let Don keep the place so I could move in with you."

Don slammed shut the trunk door. "A typical American confusing her Asians," Don said, striding now toward Gretchen. "It's the Japanese who love black men, not the Chinese."

"Asshole," Gretchen said, smiling. Steph laughed.

Don reached her and gave her a kiss on the cheek which she didn't reciprocate but didn't avoid. "You've got one month to get a job," she said.

"Won't need either the job or the month."

"You are fucking crazy."

"No prophet has ever been fully sane."

"Idiot," she said as she descended the steps and joined those on the sidewalk headed toward the subway for another day at work.

Don and Steph got into the car. "I got a hunch this won't take more than a couple of weeks," Don said as he started the engine then steered onto the roads headed toward the George Washington Bridge, headed toward Interstate 80 West, headed toward America to pick a fight on behalf of a smarter God.

ERIK SIMON

THE MEETING

For Brianna Culp of Tuttle, Pennsylvania, the doubts came early. Age eleven, to be exact, on a sunny July morning during Vacation Bible School. All grades K - 6 had joined together to begin the day with prayer and song, as they did every morning that week, and while "Jesus Loves Me" was never a particular favorite of Brianna's (she much preferred the upbeat tempo of "Jumping Jacks and Jesus" and the no-holds-barred rhyming hilarity of "Sinners Must Die, Here's the Reason Why"), the song proved especially bothersome to her that morning. All during the subsequent activity, crafts, during which she and her classmates made paper-sack puppets of children from countries where it would be most fun and challenging to go on a mission (Brianna went with Botswana), she could not shake her qualms. Finally, when her sixth-grade class joined with the fifth graders to head outside for some dodgeball, Brianna tugged on the hand of Kay Fugate, the thickly-built, pleasant, matronly teacher of the fifth grade.

"Kay," Brianna said, using her first name because the Fugates were close friends of the Culp family. "In 'Jesus Loves Me,' we sing, 'Little ones who here belong / They are weak but he is strong.'"

"We sure do, Brianna," Kay said, calm and smiling, as if warmed with reassurance that her own children were safe with JC. Kay and Brianna stood to the side in a darkened foyer where the other kids all walked hurried and loud toward the light at the other end, which was the door to the outside. "And isn't it lovely?"

"Yeah," Briana said, "but I thought of something this morning that kind of bothered me."

"What's wrong, Brianna?" Kay lightly rubbed the young one's bony shoulder with her soft, thick hand.

"The little ones belong because they're weak and he's strong, but if he's so strong, how come he ended up nailed on a cross by his enemies? All the real strong people I know, it'd be hard to nail them to a cross."

"Oh, Brianna," Kay said, smiling beatifically, stroking Brianna's long brown hair. "Jesus wasn't crucified because he was weak. Being crucified was part of the plan all along."

"If that's the case," Brianna said, head cocked, "then why does it matter if he's strong or not?"

"Honey," Kay said, "these are really good questions, but why don't we go out and play some dodgeball before we miss out on all the fun." Brianna did as Kay suggested, but she didn't have any fun. She was too concerned. After all, the question was ultimately one of Brianna's own safekeeping. How safe was she belonging in the hands of a guy who wound up nailed to a cross?

Later that day, in the early and warm evening, Brianna sat to dinner out on the large front porch with her mom and dad. The menu was hamburgers her father had grilled, Tater Tots her mom had baked, and a green Jell-O salad with little square chunks of canned pears. Her mother was a squat woman who had the solid, barrel rotundity of one who'd been fat her whole life and, of necessity, had simply learned how to wear it well. But Glenda Culp had not been fat her whole life. Her first twenty-three years she was a petite beauty, a cheerleader and homecoming queen candidate, and she'd gained the weight during her difficult pregnancy with Brianna, much of which she'd spent confined to her couch. During delivery, she hemorrhaged horribly, almost losing her newborn and her own life, and it was that experience that turned Glenda so resolutely to Jesus. She never did lose the weight because once you had the continuous comfort of Jesus in your life, who really cares if you're fat?

"Mom," Brianna said, waiting with her arms to her side while her mother stood to cut her burger in half. "I asked Kay Fugate some questions today at Bible School about Jesus being crucified."

"That's so good," Glenda said, setting Brianna's plate of food before her. "Kay is such a sweet person. I'm sure she had some wonderful answers."

"We didn't really get to all of my questions." Normally, Brianna hated when her different foods touched, but she was so preoccupied that she didn't bother moving the stray Tater Tot that had rolled against the Jell-O.

"What else do you want answered, honey? Maybe I can help?"

"Kay said Jesus' crucifixion was planned all along. If that's the case, why do we treat Judas like he's such a bad guy? I mean, if the whole thing was planned, wasn't Judas just doing what he was supposed to do?"

Never a deep thinker, Glenda was frankly cowed by her daughter's theological precocity. She chewed the first bite of her hamburger vigorously, trying to come up with some kind of answer, any answer, but failing, she hurried to take another bite, stalling for time and pointing to her full mouth as the reason why she couldn't answer at the moment.

But Brianna pushed on. "And I don't really get why Jesus had to die for my sins in the first place. I mean, Pastor Markey is always saying how we're all born sinners. If that's the case, then that's not really my fault, is it? So it's kind of like the whole game's rigged to put Jesus in charge. And besides, aren't you and Dad always telling me to take responsibility for my own actions? Well, why do I need to do that if Jesus already died for my sins two thousand years ago, especially when Pastor Markey says that I'm already a sinner just by being born?"

Glenda Culp ceased all chewing. Her mouth was full, but she was simply too horrified by her daughter's questions to go on chewing. She didn't think little Brianna's questions were outright blasphemy, but she sensed it was all headed that way, and all she could envision was the final result: a strung-out, teenaged daughter regularly pumped full of heroin and the sperm of various men. Glenda had yet to meet an overly smart woman who wasn't, to some degree, a slut. So seeing such a future for her own daughter, she did the only thing she could do on that warm July night while her family supped on the spacious front porch: she cried. A fat tear rolled from her fat eye down her fat face, quickly followed by another, and before she slipped into a full-bore crying jag, she rose with effort from the table and padded across the porch to the front door and inside, her mouth still full of food.

Brianna turned to her dad, a wiry insurance salesman with pale, almost grayish, skin and a jaw chiseled and hard as a Norwegian fjord. His brown hair was thick but short. Brianna wasn't that surprised that her mom didn't answer her question. She was plenty old enough to have an inkling that her mother wasn't a particularly bright woman. She was a bit surprised, however, at how emotional it had gotten. "What about you?" she asked her dad, who couldn't have been less ruffled by all that had just happened. "Do you know why?"

"You know me, honey" her dad said, calmly. "I don't really give all of that stuff too much thought."

"You mean you don't believe in Jesus?" she asked, strangely undisturbed by the idea, which, until she'd voiced it that moment, she'd never really realized was an option.

"Oh, I don't know. I guess I just don't really care." Four years ago, even four months ago, Sam Culp might have answered differently, might have nurtured a façade, a lie, for Brianna's sake. But he could clearly see that she could handle the truth now and would see right through anything that wasn't. Not The Truth, of course, because he laid no claim to that, but his truth, the truth of how he saw things.

And Brianna could handle his cavalier take, but she was confused on one thing. "Why do you even bother going to church, Dad?"

"Honey, when you're older, and you're married, you'll realize that it really is better to pick and choose your battles." Of all the things said and heard that day, that last comment of her father's was by far the most cryptic.

Brianna's questions and doubts didn't fade, but she did learn to shield her mother from them. Still, because her mother insisted the family attend church every Sunday, except in instances of illness, Brianna's questions proliferated. "How can the Father, Son and Holy Ghost all be the same thing, and why is that even necessary? In Matthew, Mark and John, Jesus is carrying his own cross, and in Luke, all of a sudden some guy named Simon of Cyrene shows up to carry the cross. Explanation, please? And could someone tell me what the Apostle Paul is even talking about fifty percent of the time?" Her questions didn't remain confined to one testament. "Let me get this straight: Jacob deceives his father, royally screws over his brother Esau, and yet it's Jacob that God prefers? David has a guy killed so he can sleep with the guy's wife, and God still lets him be king? God kills David's baby as punishment? Really?" Most of the questions she asked only silently in her head, but every now and then she'd voice one to an adult she thought might have an answer, and rarely did she get an answer, never a satisfying one. She grew frustrated. She deeply wanted her questions answered. She never stopped believing, but the longer her questions went unanswered, the harder it became to retain her faith and to even know what her faith was in.

The issue came to a head a year and a half later, the autumn of Brianna's eighth grade. A full-fledged junior high student, Brianna had developed a somewhat saucy tongue, and her fluency in profanity sometimes slipped out during emotional exchanges. (Though again, never with her mother: Brianna knew that her mom was not only dim, she was also fragile, and an adroitly thrown cuss word from her own mouth might send her mother into paroxysms. For all of Brianna's confusion and errancy, she was never less than a decent-hearted person.) She sat one September morning with a dozen or so other junior high students in her Sunday school class. The teacher was Jim Drayer, a handsome, thin and confident lawyer who never shied from letting people know just how much money he gave the church, though he couched the boasting in humility—"God has so blessed me to be able to do this," kind of thing. He was taking a few weeks to teach a five-part series to the kids on the Ten Commandments, concentrating on their various ramifications and their applicability in current society. "We want to use the letter of the law," he said, "to get at its spirit, its essence." The class was in the second of his five weeks, and Jim was detailing the many ways that humans could place other gods before God. Brianna raised her hand.

"Mr. Drayer, I need to back up a minute and get a few things straight. I'm confused on some things."

"Go right ahead, Brianna."

"First off, how many years after Noah did Moses come?"

"Well, we can't be sure, and I certainly don't know, but it was many hundreds of years." Jim, though devout, was not a strict fundamentalist.

"Last week, you told us that God gave Moses these Ten Commandments so that human beings would know how to behave."

"That's correct. Humanity needed guidelines, some general principles and basic rules."

"Prior to the commandments, humans didn't have them?"

"Not really. No."

"Well then that's my question. How could God destroy the world during Noah's time because everyone was misbehaving so badly when it wasn't until hundreds of years later with Moses that He finally let them know how it was He wanted them to behave in the first place?" Her tone was neither sassy nor victorious; winning wasn't what this was all about. Jim, an able lawyer, knew when to keep silent, and now was one of those times. He had nothing close to an answer. Brianna, in a tone of thinking out loud, as if she were walking along by herself, continued: "I mean, flooding the whole world because people were breaking rules they hadn't even been told about seems like a real asshole thing to do."

Her peers gasped. And then they laughed—at least the boys did. Sure they might get scolded, but hey, it wasn't every day that someone—a girl, no less, and one of the prettier ones—said "asshole" in Sunday school. Brianna had blurted the word because she was so deeply aswirl in the vortex of her thoughts, but the word did emerge with a tinge of righteous anger. It *was* kind of an asshole thing for God to do. But now that she was no longer lost in her own thoughts and mild indignation, she began to process what she'd said, as well as some possible ramifications, and a new dread pressed on her undeveloped chest. "I am so sorry, Mr. Drayer," she said, knowing she was going to have to atone early and often to wiggle out of this one. She didn't care if she got in trouble with Mr. Drayer or even Pastor Markey. (Although really, what could either of them do? It was more the possible effect on her reputation that bothered her. It was important to Brianna to be thought of as a nice girl, which is what she was.) She also didn't want this getting back to her mother. "I really didn't mean for those words to come out like that," she said, the boys around her still tittering. "It's just that I'm so confused about the Noah story. Everybody always focuses on the rainbow promise at the end, as if a rainbow makes it okay that God just wiped out millions of human beings, a lot of them children, just because they weren't doing what He wanted them to do. And then when you started with the commandments last week, you know, their purpose and essence—"

Mr. Drayer closed his eyes and held up his hand. He'd only half-registered, half-heard, Brianna's running plea, but even that half was enough. "Brianna, please," he said. "It's okay." His low, smooth voice was calm. "I'm not upset by your curse word. In the context of your legitimate question, it actually seemed quite appropriate. And your question is shrewd and insightful. What bothers me most is that I really have no answer for it." And Mr. Drayer really was deeply disturbed. Any kind of defeat did not settle comfortably on his shoulders. He told everyone that for the remaining ten minutes, they could talk quietly amongst themselves. Meanwhile, he sat deeply pensive while Brianna sat in quiet torment at her inability just to get some answers. Her anguish was palpable, but it was a darkness before dawn. Relief was moments away.

Almost a year before, Pastor Markey announced his wish to retire. The church immediately established a search committee for a new minister, and over the last few months, a couple of them had already visited, one making a very fine impression (his soprano wife wowing with a solo of "How Great Thou Art" didn't hurt his case any), the other not having as strong and positive an impact. Today, the third and final candidate was preaching, Pastor Clay from a small town in northern Wisconsin. Brianna gave the prospective minister no thought as she dragged herself listlessly to the sanctuary and sat between her mother and father where they sat every Sunday— twelfth pew back, all the way to the right, her dad on the edge where he could more easily gaze out the stained glass window when it was opened. The window was tall and narrow and one of six in a row; it showed two bearded apostles casting a fishing net.

"I am so blessed to be with you all here today in Tuttle," Pastor Clay said after he'd been introduced by Bill Fugate, Kay's husband and head of the search committee. "Back home in Wisconsin, we're already scared of the upcoming winter, even though it's only September. And besides, deep down, every one of us Packers fans suspects that the Steelers really are a superior team, so it's good to confront these fears on the enemy's turf, as it were." Pastor Clay knew his crowd. That comment drew not only a tempered ripple of laughter from among the parishioners; it also drew an early nod of collective approval. Even Brianna was drawn from her semi-despair. She'd never before heard anyone joke so lightly and pleasantly from the pulpit.

"My name is Paul Clay," he continued, "but I really would prefer if you all just thought of me as Paul. And if that's a bit too familiar for your tastes, Pastor Paul works just as well." His tone was comforting, comforted, his entire air light and easy. He was a thin man, not especially tall, handsome with short but thick sandy blonde hair. Brianna just noticed that unlike every other preacher she'd ever seen before, he wasn't wearing a robe. His suit was light blue, his shirt white, his tie a playful orange paisley thing.

Pastor Paul held up the church bulletin, the cover of which featured the photo of a maple leaf on grass, fallen but green, and a line from one of the psalms. "I know this lovely bulletin has the order for today's service but I'm going to go ahead and switch things around a little if I can." He pulled the bulletin down. "Jesus says that in order to enter the Kingdom of Heaven, we must all be as children, so I want to start today's service with our children's sermon. And by children, I mean even you high school kids. I know, I know, you hate church because it's way too boring, and you don't want to come up front now because you're waaaaaaaay too cool. But since I am a stranger in a strange land, just this once do me a favor and come on up. There's some little kids who think it'd be really cool to sit next to you."

A few parishioners glanced around, disconcerted, but Pastor Markey, sitting on the spacious altar opposite the choir, had a pleasant, approving smile, and much of the congregation nodded and smiled as parents of varying ages orchestrated the migration of their children toward the front pew kept empty for the children's sermon. Glenda turned with a fun face to Brianna and nodded that she should join the children, and Brianna rose to do just that. Pastor Paul had a charm, a magnetism, and Brianna had no hesitation in joining him up front. She'd completely forgotten about cussing at Mr. Drayer a half hour earlier. Pastor Paul clipped the small microphone to his lapel and walked down the three red-carpeted stairs toward the front pew that was now filling up. The high school students did come, as did the junior high kids and all the others. There were so many children that Pastor Paul had the youngest sit on the floor. Clair Jacobson, the two-year-old daughter of Brian and Margaret, did not want to sit on the floor in her new yellow dress, and Brianna reached out her arms, gathering the child to sit on her lap.

"I know that some of the things we speak about in church can be real, real confusing," Pastor Paul said directly to the children, and though his voice was amplified through the microphone, it was quiet, intimate—just for the kids. "Jesus walked on water. Did he really? Jesus fed five thousand people with two fish and five loaves of bread. Really? The first shall be last and the last shall be first. Huh?" With perfect theatricality, Pastor Paul scrunched his face in confusion, like a little kid, and the children before him giggled. Brianna smiled at little Claire giggling on her lap. "Well, what I want to tell you today is that in order to accept Jesus Christ as your personal lord and savior, you don't have to understand everything we talk about or everything in the Bible. It's okay for some of it just to not make sense. Heck, there's parts of the Bible that still don't make sense to me. And that's okay.

"How many of you have a stuffed animal at home?" he asked in a sudden change of tone, perky and peppy. Many of the younger children raised their hands. Pastor Paul leaned over and mock whispered, "See all these bigger kids sitting around you? They all have stuffed animals, too, but they're too cool to admit it in front of everyone." The younger kids giggled, the older kids smiled, and Pastor Paul stood straight and resumed a normal voice. "How many of you give your stuffed animals a big old squeezy hug at the end of the day?" All of the little kids raised their hands again. "Can you show me that hug?" Pastor Paul wrapped his arms around himself as an example. The little children squeezed themselves with glee. "Tighter," Pastor Paul said, and they complied, giggling. "Tighter," he said, scrunching his face to emphasize just how tight, and the children squeezed tighter. "Good," he said, unwrapping and dropping his arms, the children doing the same with big, delighted sighs. "Now, whenever I say something to you about God that doesn't make sense, or when Pastor Markey or your parents say something to you about God that doesn't make sense, or when you read something about Jesus that doesn't make sense, or when you come across something really confusing in the Bible—that part that doesn't make sense, I want you to squeeze it as hard as you do your stuffed animal. Don't run away from it. Squeeze it. It's called embracing the mystery. God is more than okay with us not understanding everything, just so long as we don't use that as an excuse to push things away. Because someday, after all of that squeezing, what you don't understand will make sense. I promise. So, for practice, everyone who just doesn't understand how Jesus raised Lazarus from the dead, how he took an old dead man and made him alive again, just hold out your arms—" here Pastor Paul acted out what he suggested, all of the younger kids, and some of the older kids (Brianna hypnotically among them), playing along—"let that story into your chest, and squeeze." Those participating squeezed. "Good." They relaxed their squeeze, dropped their arms.

Pastor Paul took a few steps over to the large, wooden baptismal font behind which stood a thin circular table that came to his waist. He carried the table out and set it down in front of the kids. On the table stood a glass pitcher of water, a canister of sugar, and a packet of Kool-Aid. "How many of you kids have heard us talk about the Holy Trinity before?" Brianna was so fully entranced now that she threw her hand in the air along with the toddlers. "Pretty confusing, isn't it, when we talk about the Father, the Son and the Holy Spirit all being the same thing, huh?" The children nodded, and Pastor Paul leaned forward again to confide in his mock whisper. "I got news for you. It's confusing to your moms and dads, too, even if they don't admit it." He stood straight and positioned himself behind the table.

"Here's a way to think of it all that might make some sense. Let's say this pitcher of water is God, the Father. Actually, it's a pretty good symbol for God since we do need water in order to survive, and I think we need God to survive." Pastor Paul picked up the packet of Kool-Aid and shook it back and forth before he tore open the top and poured the powder into the water, saying how the Kool-Aid represented Jesus. (The Kool-Aid was cherry-flavored, red, allowing for easy association with the blood of Christ.) He then dumped two measuring cups of sugar into the pitcher, noting that it represented the Holy Ghost, before he stirred together the familiar concoction. He set down the spoon and held up the pitcher, high enough for a shaft of sun coming through the large, circular stained glass of Jesus as a boy petting a lamb to catch the Kool-Aid, making it a fiery, impressive red.

"You see how we mixed these three distinctive ingredients into the pitcher?" he asked. "The contents of the pitcher now, the Kool-Aid, is just one thing, but we all know it took three distinctive components to make that one thing. And we all know those three components are in there, even though we see this as one. And we all know that take any one of those three components away, you'd have something that wouldn't be very good, something you wouldn't want to share with others, something you wouldn't even want for yourselves. Does that make sense?" The children nodded, enlightened, and many adults nodded approvingly. Pastor Markey up on the altar had a huge, relaxed, relieved smile, as if he could resign in ease, knowing his flock would be ably attended by this new shepherd from Wisconsin.

Pastor Paul lowered the pitcher but remained holding it. "So, kids . . . of all ages—" he scanned the adults and, of course, got an approving chuckle from many of them. "Anytime you hear us talking about the Holy Trinity, the Father, the Son and the Holy Ghost, all being one, and you get a bit confused, wondering how that's possible, just think of this pitcher of Kool-Aid." He nodded warm-heartedly. "Now," he said, leaning down toward the kids with an excited smile, "who wants to drink some of this Kool-Aid?" The kids squealed with glee as they raised their hands. Not Brianna, though. She was reverent, relieved and awed. She remained silent, but she, too, raised her hand. She, too, wanted to drink the Kool-Aid.

It had gotten warm inside the Hyundai. After they crossed the Delaware River on I-80 into Pennsylvania, Don took the first sort of backroads highway he could find, one headed south. They rode on that two-lane highway through heavily wooded, mountainous terrain, the mountains the older, smaller, gentler variety of the Appalachian range, not the jagged, severe peaks of the Colorado Rockies Don had come to think of when he thought of mountains. The trees on both sides of the road were tall, some of them just barely beginning to turn—nascent smudges of pale yellow—but enough of the sun still found its late morning way into the car to make it warm. Don had his window open, but not very wide. Steph had *The New York Times* splayed on his lap, and too strong a breeze had made it impossible to keep the pages still enough to read. Don could have turned the air-conditioner on, but using the air-conditioner in early October in Pennsylvania struck him as obscene. Don came of age in the eighties when humanity was learning that it was zapping a hole in the ozone. Granted, it appeared we'd taken care of that environmental issue, but having lived through that and understood its ramifications, Don succumbed to the air-conditioner only under extreme circumstances, much like old folks who survived the Depression refusing to toss into the trash a potato old enough to have grown sprouts. Don didn't even know if air-conditioners harmed the environment like they once did, shooting off Freon with a Wild West recklessness. They probably still did. But even if they didn't, he couldn't justify using the air-conditioner in Pennsylvania in October. Miami, Houston, Phoenix, sure, you could make a case. But Pennsylvania, no.

"I really had no idea Pennsylvania was this beautiful," Steph said, looking out the windows.

"In its own way, most of the country is this beautiful," Don said.

"Have you seen most of the country?" Steph said, snarky, as if actually seeing most of the states between New York and L.A. was barely possible.

"I have," Don said. "Forty-seven states I've traveled, and each one a splendor in its own right."

"What are the three that are missing?"

"Hawaii and Alaska, of course. And Arizona. I have no idea how the hell I've missed Arizona, but I have. The Grand Canyon is not only a big hole in the ground, it's also a huge void in my life. I've seen many of the finest sites America has to offer, but I've yet to see arguably the finest, the pinnacle, the apogee. Maybe now I should just wait to visit it with my son, should my loins ever bring one forth."

"Why the ethereal tone, D.? We're talking about traveling."

"Busted," Don smiled. "I was just sort of tinkering with tone and diction for this prophet stuff. Propheteering, I'm tempted to call it. The word works on a couple of levels then."

Steph thought about it for a moment. "It is catchy and clever," he said, "and it does get to the heart of things. But the double entendre might only work if the words are spelled out for folks. Besides, that's pretty sophisticated wordplay for mass commercial appeal."

Don shrugged. "No matter. I'm not sure I'd use the word around anyone else but you. It'd be a bit brazen. And I don't want to give the enemy too much easy ammunition."

"I'm still stuck on the fact that you've been to forty-seven states."

"That's because New Yorkers only give a shit about four or five of them. I'm not so sure you guys don't seriously wonder if the other forty-five actually exist."

"You're not entirely wrong."

"I'm not even partially wrong. And now that I've lived out here awhile, I have to say, I sort of get it. But it's a pretty amazing spectacle of a mosaic, flyover country. I mean, look at all of this," Don said, gesturing with sweeping arm to all the scenery around, the quietly gorgeous array of small mountains covered by dense woods, an occasional glimpse of a waterway, sometimes shallow, sparkling and white, sometimes deeper and dark, a greenish black. "And this is just one tiny slice of a state with Philadelphia in one corner, a city stuffed to the gills with history, Pittsburgh on the other end, a city redolent of one of America's defining industries for years and far more beautiful than the decaying smokestacks most people associate with it, and a major university planted right smack in the middle of the two. And that doesn't even begin to touch the multitude of tiny details—the stone barns, the Amish, a major Civil War battlefield. Hell, Jimmy Stewart is from some tiny town in the middle of the state. Try talking about the heart of cultural America without bringing up Jimmy Stewart. *Rear Window. High Noon. It's A Wonderful Life.* And Dwight Eisenhower retired to P A and finished out his life here."

"You are damn near gushing, D. You sound like a commercial."

"I'm a patriot, Steph, in the deepest sense. I find it hard not to gush for the U.S. of A."

Don *was* a patriot. He loved not only the ideals that were America, if not all of its practices throughout the years, he also had a primal love for the land in its many-splendored forms. And he *had* seen a great deal of it, which was a remarkable feat for anyone just a touch over thirty, really, but even more so given how restricted in monies he'd been his whole life. His father was an elementary school janitor, his mother a cook in the cafeteria of the same school, and money hardly burst out the walls of the tiny, old house Don grew up in near the edge of his tiny hometown. But Don learned early that you didn't have to be rich to see America. In some respects, it was better not to be because then you experienced the land and its people more intimately—you ate at affordable restaurants that were unselfconsciously suffused in the local flavor (as long as you avoided fast foods and chains), and you didn't stay in hotels which, once you stepped into the lobby, were exactly like hotels everywhere else in the country. Even during his financially-strapped upbringing, he got a pretty good head start on his deep and complex relationship with America. His parents were campers, largely because that's what they could afford, but also because that's what they preferred. They were young when they married and had Don, so all during his childhood they were thin and active, not yet burdened by the potbellies and aches of middle-age, and every summer they took a camping vacation to a different spot within an easy day's drive—the Ozarks in Missouri, the Ozarks in Arkansas, a lake in Wisconsin or Kentucky, a campground called Turkey Run in Indiana. Only three times did Don stay in a hotel during his first seventeen years—a weekend jaunt one July 4th weekend up to Springfield to catch all the Lincoln sites, another weekend jaunt over to St. Louis for a Cubs/Cardinals game and day at the Arch, night on Laclede's Landing, and an intoxicating three-day trip to Nashville to do the Grand Ole Opry thing when he was twelve, by far his family's most elaborate and expensive vacation complete with a day at the amusement park and one Saturday night at the Opry where he got to hear Tom T. Hall and Barbara Mandrell. When Babs did "You Can Eat Crackers in My Bed," Don's heart sang. And when she slowed it down for a sultry, "If Loving You Is Wrong, I Don't Want to Be Right," Don was putty. That weekend at the Opry was one for the ages.

Once Don left for college, he continued to pursue his relationship with America. He attended Grinnell in Iowa, courtesy of a few hefty scholarships he wrangled because of his parents' low incomes and his own fantastic test scores and

grades, and from there he took many trips home with friends—
a Thanksgiving in Minnesota, a wedding in Nebraska, a few
long weekends in Kansas. During his entire matriculation, he
never returned home for any appreciable amount of time. He
loved his parents, but he'd grown too big for the confines of his
upbringing, too interested to return to its familiarity, too
restless for its settled ways, even too proud for its provinciality.
His first summer he stayed on campus like an international
student and worked in the physical plant. His second summer
he joined his roommate, a skinny, blond violinist named Paul
Jackson, in a small town on Lake Michigan in upstate
Michigan, a tourist town whose population quadrupled every
year from the middle of May to the middle of August. Paul's
dad owned a landscaping company, and Don worked for him
all summer. He spent his days digging holes of various sizes to
plant bushes, flowers and trees. Already heavier than most of his
peers, he shed some pounds that summer. In the evenings, he
preferred to sit on a dock not far from Paul's house and watch
the sun set on the water. Don had seen plenty of lakes in his
life, but he decided you couldn't really understand why these
suckers were called "Great" until you stood on their shores and
told yourself over and over, because you had to, that it really
was just a lake. He'd often bring a book along for those solitary
sunsets, but he'd rarely be inclined to read, unless it was poetry.
He made a couple of new friends, and by the end of July he was
bedding down a chunky young divorcee, a local girl Paul had
gone to high school with. Their fling had the otherworldly
intensity of a summer camp romance, and he would always
associate Michigan with evenings on the shore and nights with
her. Her name was Trudy. Back at Grinnell, he wrote her one
letter, got no response, and considered the entire wonderful
interlude completed.

The summer of his junior year he got a job with another
friend, Colt Beatty, out in Fort Collins, Colorado. It was Don's

first foray into the Rockies, and he was predictably awed. You couldn't go from a lifetime of cornfields and modest hills to the Rockies without being wowed, but within a couple of weeks Don was already more interested in the culture of the West than he was the landscape. His job wasn't at all taxing. Colt was upper-middle class and Marlboro Man handsome, and his mom owned an ice-cream parlor on Main Street where Don and Colt worked the afternoon/evening shifts behind the counter, really a perfect job for a college kid, although Don, having gained back the weight he'd lost in Michigan over the previous school year, gained another ten pounds he'd never lose again. He still didn't have enough money to buy a car, even a cheap old one, but Colt loaned him one of their three vehicles whenever Don wanted to explore. He drove to Cheyenne, to Laramie, down to Colorado Springs. His exploring usually wasn't rustic; it involved museums and sightseeing from behind the wheel and strolls through the different towns. Though a camper, Don was not much of a man of the outdoors. Hiking was completely out. He tried a day of fly fishing on the Poudre River but got so bored that he smoked a joint and sat on a boulder to watch the physical poetry of Colt, a lifelong fly fisherman. The constant loops and waves of the fishing line, the bounce and play of the water, the tall trees and piney sunlight—Don knew how blessed he was to be sitting in that clear air that smelled so heavily of pine needles. That vision was topped in July when Don and Colt went camping down in New Mexico. Their first night on the high desert happened to be a meteor shower. Dumb luck there. The first streak of light across the impossibly vast sky got a "holy shit," from Don. But when the streaks became frequent, literally one or more every minute or so, sometimes simultaneously, he knew he was witness to something that called for silent reverence. At the meteor shower's peak, he thought that if God struck him down right then and there, he could not cry foul. It was the highlight of the summer. At summer's end, they left a week before the semester began and took a northerly route home to see Little Bighorn and Mt. Rushmore. An odd, odd sight, those big faces in stone. And a hard thing to completely embrace after the grassy silence at Little Bighorn. Few spots were probably more redolent of the white man's slaughter of the natives for their land than Black Hills, South Dakota, and it was hard not to see those big stone faces as a whitewashing of history, even a mega-sized taunt by the victors.

A few weeks before Christmas break his senior year, he called his parents to tell them he'd be joining his friend Tom Mayle out in Seattle for the holiday instead of coming home. "You ever coming home again?" his mother asked curtly. The last time he had seen them was a year before, during a Christmas break that was agonizing in its tedium. This year, not only was he going to get to see Seattle, but Tom's family owned a place in Ketchum, Idaho, where they were all going to go skiing for a week after New Year's. Don, of course, was no skier and had no intention of even attempting, but he'd never before seen the Pacific Northwest, and he could hardly resist a junket to where Hemingway offed himself. In a college of some pretty smart kids, Don had emerged as *the* star of the English Department, and already he'd begun devoting spare hours to writing some atrocious short stories and a novel that a hundred thousand words later still wouldn't be finished but nonetheless served the purpose of teaching him how to write a good sentence, how to develop a character, how to move a plot along.

"Come on, Mom, don't be that way. You should be happy I'm getting this kind of opportunity."

"I'd be happy if you ever wanted to see your parents again."

"Of course I want to see you again."

"If you wanted to see us, you would."

"It's not that simple, Mom. Nothing in life is."

"That's a stupid thing to say."

"Put Dad on."

It was a brief pause before Don heard his father. "Hello, Donny."

"Dad, I'm not coming home for Christmas, and it's rattled Mom. Could you help her out a little?"

"What do you mean help her out?"

"Console her a little. Let her know I'm working toward a better future for all of us."

"What the hell does that have to do with anything?"

"Dad, could you just—tell you what; I'll find some time this spring to come home."

"Do what you want, Donny. We're doing just fine."

Don didn't find some time that spring to come home, although he could have swung by the house for a day, or even a couple hours and a meal, on his spring break. His first spring break freshman year, he did the typical spring break beach and beer thing down in Texas. He was bored blind. Though he did enjoy getting high now and then, he never was much of a drinker, and the whole party scene, even on Friday nights, never appealed to him. He was earnest and driven, always trying to catch up to the private school kids he was now surrounded by, and Friday nights he preferred watching foreign movies in the student center or plays or even just reading. And that spring break was just one prolonged party. After his first four hours on the beach, he failed to see its lasting appeal. He was too pale to relish long bouts in the sun, he liked the water and waves but not five uninterrupted days of it, and all those beach games like volleyball or football or hitting that little rubber ball back and forth with wooden paddles—forget it. Some days it was strain enough to transport his thick carcass on solid ground; playful sport on shifting sand made him overheat just thinking about. He was also aware that his was probably one of the ten worst physiques in the vicinity. He tried to read on the beach, but there were simply too many distractions. In the end, he spent his days doing little more than stealing glimpses at the overwhelming array of taut and tan girls, trying not to get caught staring at any one girl too long. He knew there was something pathetic about fat guys ogling beautiful, skinny women. He was never not fully aware of himself.

That spring break had been such a bust that he resolved in the future to have only "learning" spring breaks. The following year he went to Chicago, spending full days in the major museums, spending nights with a friend whose family lived in Oak Park. His junior year he did the D.C. thing, hitting all the national museums, getting physically, emotionally, intellectually and metaphysically lost in the Smithsonian. His visit coincided with the blooming of all those cherry blossoms, something he just didn't see back in the Midwest, and he was awed by the profusion of soft pink and white trees. The Lincoln Memorial was pretty amazing, he thought, but he was actually more moved by the Jefferson Memorial, its modesty in scope, its off-to-the-sideness. For the Vietnam Wall he steeled himself, wanting not to get overly emotional, but he failed: so, so many names for a war every president for twenty years had been told would be impossible to win, so many graveside tokens along the bottom of that black wall—flowers with notes, a bottle of Jim Beam with a note, a picture of a black teenaged girl with a letter to the father she never knew. It was quiet at the wall, despite the decent number of people, more than a few making a pencil-rub over an engraved name. One muscular, gray-haired biker with a chain necklace and leather coat cried silently. He had one hand on a name while, with the other, he covered and wiped his eyes. Don wanted to console him somehow, pat him on the back, rub his shoulder, something, but he was pretty sure the guy just wanted to be alone. Don thought that whatever that guy had gone through, whoever he'd lost, everyone who was rather gung-ho about war should have to sit and listen to his story first.

For his senior year, he and three friends traveled through the South to visit Civil War battlefields and other major sites. It was a particularly warm early spring day when they visited Shiloh, and there was something eerie about the heavy silence of the place, as if haunted by all the bodies felled there. Given how small Bloody Pond was, it was pretty easy to see how it had gotten so bloody. Don was no Civil War maven, but he'd read enough books to know a few things beyond the basics, and he was simply incapable of even the smallest bit of sympathy for the Southern position. Which was why, when he got to the tree against which the revered Southern General Albert Sidney Johnston leaned as he bled to death, he was more inclined to spit on it than offer respectful silence. Much as the foursome would have liked following the route of Sherman's March, they knew they didn't have time, but they did stop off in Atlanta long enough to visit the MLK Center and be tipped off on a restaurant called Fat Matt's Rib Shack where Don ate a barbaric amount of ribs. In Savannah, which smelled pungently sour from the paper mills, Don thought there couldn't be an American city more beautiful, but he stood corrected the following day when they pulled into Charleston, South Carolina. The antebellum mansions on the red brick streets with the cherry trees and dogwoods in pink and white bloom—it was perfect enough to be a movie set. The hour-long boat ride out to the tiny island of Fort Sumter made him sleepy, and when he stepped into the small Fort Sumter museum and was greeted by pictures of Abe Lincoln and Jeff Davis side by side, he wondered if anyone else had ever noticed how much the two resembled each other, at least in those pictures. They were, he knew, both born within miles of each other on the same hill in Kentucky. It would be wild if they were half-brothers, but then a lot had been written on Abe, and that wasn't the kind of salacious detail that would have gone undiscovered if it were true, unexplored if even remotely possible. On the long drive back home, the foursome was, at one point on I-70, less than an hour from Don's hometown, and it would have been easy and appropriate to stop there, even just for a meal, especially since Don had promised he would come home this spring, but he kept mum, and the car kept moving.

Don didn't know if, during his undergraduate years, it was outright shame he felt about his home life, but it was some complex array of feelings akin to it. Grinnell was riddled with private school kids who had superior backgrounds in every way, and during his entire matriculation there Don was painfully aware of the disadvantages inherent in his limited upbringing. In many respects, Don's four years of college were a feverish pace to narrow the gap between himself and his peers. One reason he was the star of the English Department was that he read so much outside of class, and while he did love literature, he also saw knowledge as a realm where he could balance the ledgers, overcome deficiencies, even take the lead. By the time he graduated, he'd not fully rid himself of this shame. It's why he told his parents not to come to graduation.

"What do you mean don't come?" his mother said over the phone, his father also listening in on the call.

"I don't mean don't come," Don said, backpedaling. "I just mean you don't *have* to come."

"*Have* to come. You make it sound like boring piano recital or something."

"It *is* boring, Mom. It's these long boring speeches and bad music and two-hundred-plus names being read off."

"And one of those names is my kid," she said, "and I've worked my whole life to hear his name read at a college graduation."

Ever since he was in grade school, Don was so intelligent that, as he got older, he never doubted he was going to college.

In his perspective on everything, it was just a given, like the fact that his hair was orange. His parents, however, had never been to college, nor had anyone in their family, so it was just as difficult for Don to understand how big a deal for them it was that he was graduating college as it was for them to understand how big a deal for him it wasn't. Don's graduation for his parents was a goal; for Don it was merely the next step to he knew not what. A Bachelor's degree was small-time, penny ante. He was already enrolled at the University of North Carolina for his Master's, where he'd be headed right after graduation. Intellectually and emotionally, though, he'd already left. Not one for ceremony (largely because every ceremony, it seemed, compelled him to wear ill-fitting clothes and sit on chairs that were too small and too hard and usually in a room that got hot in a hurry), Don wasn't even looking forward to graduation. That, in fact, was the tack he took when his father neared the truth. "Donny," his dad said over the phone, "do you not want me and your mother at your graduation?"

"Of course I want you there, inasmuch as I want me there."

"Inasmuch, huh," his mother said, clearly suspicious of the word and of Don's use of it.

"What I'm saying is that graduation isn't such a great day. If it's sunny, you're out on the football field with the sun bashing at your face, and if it's rainy, everyone's crammed into the humid gym with hundreds and hundreds of people where the feeble little air-conditioner doesn't stand a chance. And that's just the ceremony. There's only a handful of restaurants in town, so it's impossible to get a table anywhere for any meal. And as for hotels, well, the closest place you're probably going to get one this late is in Montezuma or Newton. You might even have to go to Pella or Oskaloosa, which are forty miles away."

"Donny," his mom said, "if bullshit were music, you'd have enough for a brass band right now."

"Mom, what would I be bullshitting you about?"

"You tell me."

"Doesn't matter," his father interjected, "we already got a room."

"You do?"

"Days Inn. Booked it two months ago."

"Oh," Don said, "great. Why are we even having this conversation then? I was just trying to spare you two a lot of trouble."

"Won't be any trouble at all," his father said. "See you in a couple of weeks."

And it wasn't any trouble at all, not remotely the horror Don envisioned it could be. Graduation was on Saturday, his parents arrived Friday night and left Sunday afternoon, after Don and his father loaded all of Don's stuff into his car. (A few months before, knowing he'd reached a point in his life wherein he could really go no longer without one, Don got a pretty good deal on a used Grand Marquis, silver with a few dents.) During the giddy bustle of the weekend, only a couple of times did Don, with his parents, encounter some of his friends with their parents, which had largely been Don's greatest fear, but those meetings were little more than big smiles and brief introductions, most of them right after the ceremony. His parents were respectably dressed—Dad in an old but not tattered blue suit, Mom in a knee-length, yellow, flower-print dress Don could tell she'd bought for the occasion—and they were so obviously proud of him that all reservations he'd had had been cast aside by a joy in their joy. When they ran into his favorite professor on the sunny field crowded with graduates and their parents, Don introduced them. He was a Melville scholar built much like Don. "Mr. and Mrs. Bollinger," he said, "in all my years of teaching, I've had only a couple of students as intelligent and eager and curious as your son. I hope you're very proud, and congratulations on raising such a fine young man." His dad nodded and said, "Thank you, sir." His mother cried. Don was glad they'd come. He was disgusted with himself for having feared their presence. He couldn't believe he'd actually considered not having them attend.

On his way to Carolina, he stopped off at home for what he thought would be a day, maybe two. After a late evening dinner featuring barbecued pork steaks, Don sat with his parents on the back patio, a cement slab just large enough to fit their three lawn chairs and a small table. The back yard had a decent-sized garden, all vegetables, beyond which the lawn sloped down to a modestly-wooded ditch—maples and oaks and underbrush. It was too early in the season for fireflies, but not lilac, and the evening air, with only the occasional hum of a mosquito, smelled insanely wonderful. All three were eating pieces of a peach pie his mother had baked, using lard for the crust, which was why it was the best pie crust Don had eaten in four years. She rose in the increasing dark of a dying sunset and cleared the saucers and forks and took them inside.

"Your mom and I sure had a nice time at your college," his father said with his shoulders relaxed in his lawn chair, so much smaller than his son. "We're sure proud of you."

"Thanks, Dad. I'm glad you came."

"Are you?" He stared at Don. Don knew immediately where this was headed. He had made this mistake before, assumed his father was rather daffy on a thing or two when, in fact, the old fox wasn't missing a beat.

Don turned to face him. "Yeah, Dad, I am. I couldn't have done anything in the world without you and Mom and your endless support." Don had gotten some sizable scholarships, but he still had to take out some pretty hefty loans that he'd begin paying back as soon as he finished graduate school, loans that his father had to sign for. But he was referring to more than just money. He was offering thanks for a deep, stolid stability they offered on the home front, allowing him to flit about without major concern for four years. Plus there was the upbringing. In his senior year, he lived with two other guys in a dingy though serviceable apartment less than a mile from campus, an experience that made him realize just how much parents do for you in covering the basics.

"Just so's you realize that," his father said, "and really know it."

"I do."

His dad nodded. Don thought the conversation was over, point made, but it wasn't. "It wasn't because we weren't smart enough that your mom and me didn't go to college ourselves. You know that, don't you?"

"Yeah, Dad. I know that."

"I'd have been real happy to go to college. It would have been fun. I always thought that I might have been a half-decent engineer, maybe tinkering on little things, maybe working on some major projects like dams or irrigation systems." Don studied his father, a slight man with only slightly graying hair at the edges, a face hardly beset with any signs of age. He wasn't, after all, even fifty yet. There was a side emerging from his father this evening that he never knew was there, a side his father had been withholding, a side he felt the need to reveal tonight. Don knew why. He wasn't oblivious, and he erred in ever thinking his father was.

"Your mom and I didn't go to college because things just didn't work out that way. That's all. We were plenty smart enough, and we probably could have found the money somewhere, if someone in our lives had been thinking in that direction. But no one ever was. It's just the way things were." His mother returned to the patio and silently resumed her seat; she had put on a sweatshirt. "I'm so glad you went to college that I get dizzy thinking about it," his father continued. "And

I'm so proud of you for being a good student, but frankly, I expected that from you. I don't see the sense of going to college if you're not going to be a good student. But don't you ever forget that you went to college because you were raised by two people who spent your whole life thinking in that direction."

"I won't, Dad."

"And when you come across folks who didn't go to college, don't you ever forget it's usually because they just weren't fortunate enough to have someone in their lives thinking in that direction."

"I won't, Dad."

"As long as you don't forget those two things, ever, chances are good you'll be able to grow up without being an asshole. Don't get me wrong. There's assholes all over the place, not just in college. Some of the biggest assholes I know are the people who didn't go to college and feel so damned inferior about it that the only thing they can do is make fun of college people, saying they got book smarts but no common sense. That's just jealous bullshit is all that is. But the college assholes, they're the ones who never realize it all could have been different. They're the ones who don't know that if they were born in a different house, it could have just as easily been them pushing a broom. So don't you ever forget that, and don't you ever become one of those college assholes, Don."

"I won't, Dad."

"No, I don't believe you will. Not now. But just so's you know, that's exactly where you were headed up until a couple days ago. And don't think for one minute your mother and I didn't know it. And don't think that just because we knew better, our feelings weren't hurt."

It was strange to realize he had the ability to hurt his parents, but here his father had just admitted that that's exactly what he'd done. He turned to his mother to get some kind of reassurance that everything was okay, a rub of the knee or pat on the back that indicated no harm done, but she just nodded with a sad smile, as if loath but compelled to confirm everything her husband had just said. Don shook his head, disgusted with himself. To atone, he stayed a few extra days at home. There really was no need to rush out to Chapel Hill. He already had an apartment, and his summer job in the English Department didn't start for another eight days. Each morning, his mom and dad rose and went to work early, and Don set his alarm to rise with them for coffee and conversation. He wanted to make them breakfast, but his mother wouldn't hear of it, so he kept her company while she fried the bacon, and that made her every bit as happy. He did insist on doing dishes, which she didn't fight. After they left, he wouldn't read, and he pretty much avoided town or any friends he had in high school; he'd lost all real contact with them. He'd clean the house or clean the patio or do the laundry, his and theirs. He also spent some quality time in the garden, weeding and picking the strawberries, which were perfect. He baked a shortcake for dessert one night and ran to the store for whipped cream. Don hated gardening. Ever since he was twelve years old, other than those summer jobs elsewhere during college, he'd spent many a summer hour detasseling corn or walking beans or mowing lawns or landscaping. There was, therefore, no joy whatsoever in outdoor work for him. He wanted to get as far away from any of that as possible. And yet, for five days, the focus was his parents, their happiness. He embraced, fully, their lives, and in so doing he embraced, fully, them. His father had done a masterful job of making sure that Don would never again ignore the circumstances of his childhood or feel ashamed from whence he came.

At Chapel Hill, Don never became so entrenched in academia that he lost sight of the working class. To custodians, secretaries, cafeteria workers, etc., he always said hello and was unfailingly deferential and polite. Gregarious and witty by nature, he often took to joking with those he saw most frequently. At restaurants he tipped well, and if, for whatever reason, he suspected his waitress was a single mother, his tip bordered on the outlandish. He wasn't flush with cash himself, but he did have a decent loan for the first year as well as a good job in the English Department (his second year he was a TA, complete with tuition and stipend). It really was all about priorities. If you had fifty bucks a week for beer, which most students did, then you had fifty bucks a week for someone who needed it more than you. It helped that Don just wasn't much of a drinker. He was, of course, a sizable eater, but it didn't take long for him to find the all-you-can-eat barbecue joints in town. For breakfast, there was always the breakfast bar at Shoney's where he would routinely decimate the pile of bacon.

The bulk of his time, though, he spent with his words, binging and purging, reading just obscene amounts of literature and, late at night, writing bad stories and an even worse novel. Writing, he decided, was his future. He did make a couple of close friends, but his four years at Chapel Hill (he stuck around after graduating, continuing to teach some freshman comp courses and picking up other odd jobs, supplemental income— a stint at Kinko's, a parking garage attendant, an after-hours custodial job at some downtown offices; he considered writing a letter to his father to tell him specifically about the job, a gesture of solidarity, but then realized there was no way to do that without sounding condescending) were the most solitary and driven of his life.

And he continued to explore America, the southeast portion of it. He popped in on a few more Civil War battlefields—Chickamauga in northern Georgia, Stones River in Murfreesboro, Tennessee. Stones River he happened upon accidentally, and until he had, he never even knew the battle had occurred. The day he was there, he was the only person there, other than the park ranger, who told him that of all the major Civil War battles, it had the highest percentage of casualties on both sides. Don was deeply disturbed to consider that thousands had died on those acres, and almost no one even knew that the battle had even occurred. He walked among the thousands of small, white headstones, just processing the magnitude of death. He stopped before one to commit the name to memory—Lafayette Bartlett, grave number E-1947. He was from Michigan. Don recalled his own summer there and imagined Lafayette in his stead, landscaping, getting laid, both of which he'd probably done back in his century anyway, although the landscaping was bound to be of the far more rigorous clearing land variety, not digging holes to plant lilac bushes, azaleas and chokecherry trees. Lafayette Bartlett. Poor sap probably wasn't even twenty, and he was probably poor. How many rich people could Michigan have even had at the time? It wasn't the rich who headed west. They had no reason to move. And how many of the rich even go off to fight, then or now? Hell, in New York, they hired the poor to go fight in their place. Lafayette Bartlett. Don came close to tearing up. As long as he was alive, at least one person would never forget the name of that fallen soldier.

One weekend in early spring, Don went camping by himself down in Florida, just outside of Pensacola. He ate at a pizza place in town where he nurtured a fantasy about his waitress, who was skinny and blond and looked to be in her mid-thirties. "Whatch ya readin'," she asked in her happy twang.

"Wallace Stevens," he said, holding up his paperback copy of poems.

"Never heard of him," she said. She had time to stand and chat because it was a Wednesday night and there were hardly any other customers, just an elderly couple over in the corner.

"He's a poet," Don said.

"Oh yeah?" she said, instantly more interested. "I write poems, too. Is he any good?"

"Yeah," Don said, "he's pretty good." Don's tone wasn't remotely snide. His father's caution was too indelible, and he knew how privileged he was to devote a couple of years of his life to things like the study of Wallace Stevens, something that Don had to confess really didn't benefit the world in any real or tangible way.

"I'll have to check him out," she said, turning the book toward her so as to better display the cover, which had a picture of Stevens, white-haired, wearing a suit. "He's an old guy," she said.

"Actually, he's a dead guy, but he was, in fact, old before he died."

"God willing you and I will be, too." She walked off to take care of the elderly couple, and Don nursed a handful of fantasies, one that had her in his tent with him that night, one that had him at her place for the rest of the week, the two having sex and reading poetry she didn't understand, both of them knowing that the idyllic tryst would go no further than the rest of the week. But the fantasies didn't feel right. Her last line to him was such a guileless and sincere wish by a stranger to a stranger, and Don was so touched by its kindness that his carnal thoughts only sullied their interlude. After he paid, she was busy with two tables of small families that had just entered. Don left her a tip that equaled the price of his pizza and a note that said, "May you have a long life of poetry and songs."

The following October, when he was no longer a student, he went camping Columbus Day week down in Hunting, South Carolina. The campground was a woodsy place just a few hundred yards from the beach, where he went every day for sunrise and sunset. He again was camping alone, and neither the campground nor the beach was crowded—off season. He made a few friends in graduate school, but nothing too lasting or deep. He was simply too immersed in his words to be interested in much else. Ditto, girls. He had a few one-night stands, somewhat amazed that there were girls out there who found his pale, fleshly carcass appealing in that way, and one girl he even dated for a month, a well-read undergrad with a pierced eyebrow and a penchant for science fiction, but mostly he just found it easier and less time-consuming to masturbate and get back to what he was reading. At Hunting Beach, he spent his days in a lawn chair reading Faulkner. Spanish moss dropped thick and gray as the beard of Tolstoy from the palmetto trees, and he wished he'd have brought *Anna Karenina*. He was camped near a burly pair of bikers in their fifties, a couple of graying, heavyset guys with their graying, heavyset wives, and at night he joined them for whiskey and beer around the campfire, although he limited himself to no more than two beers. One biker, Lou, used fallen palmetto branches to fuel the fire, and whenever he dropped a fresh set on, the flame propulsed eight to ten feet in the air. Feeling himself getting drunk halfway through a second beer, Don backed his chair well away from the flame.

It was the following spring break, when he was a teacher but not a student, that he finally visited New York. He went because he'd never before been, and the trip was made sweeter by a Grinnell friend living in Brooklyn who offered Don free floor space, but Don had always longed to go to New York and had always so deeply suspected that New York was going to be the place he pulled up stakes that he intentionally delayed visiting there, saving it for last, sensing that nowhere else would be quite so appealing and satisfying once he'd been there. And his instincts were right. He loved the complexity and variety of his own past, but no sooner did he drive over the Verrazano Bridge onto the Brooklyn-Queens Expressway than he knew where his future lay. Nine hours he'd been behind the wheel that day, driving north, and on the BQE he had no idea where he was, no context for anything, but there was just something about the place—the pulse, the energy, the buzz, part of the concoction fueled by reality, part of it fueled by the national narrative and myth of the place, part of it fueled by his own personal myth developed through its writers, its movies, even its sitcoms. He felt that tingle and verve the moment he was in it. It didn't hurt that it was night and so his first vision of the city was in lights. When he turned left and caught Lady Liberty all glowing in green, he gasped and gave a hearty chuckle. He could scoff all he wanted about the shallow patriotism of loving such a symbol, but having grown up in deeply rural America and having heard so much about a symbol so central to the myth of the republic and the myth of this major city, he couldn't help having emotions upon first seeing it. That giddiness was also what he felt the following night just north of Times Square when he saw the giant blue marquee for the Late Show with David Letterman. The whole city, everywhere he walked, was the glamorous and mythic world of the Great Big Other finally in the flesh. New York was omnipresent in the lives of Americans. Don knew firsthand that they may say they hated it, but it was everywhere they turned, and they embraced it. Millions upon millions began their days with its morning shows and finished their days with one of its late-night shows. They watched its crime shows and reality shows and kept tabs on Wall Street and watched its evening news. Every day in a myriad of ways it was a central presence in their lives, and the fact that they accessed it through their screens only added to its mythic quality—screens create myths. Don fully understood the urge, the compulsion, the almost religious need when someone from his metaphysical part of the world visited the city and insisted on waking up extra early to stand along the thick velvet ropes at the *Today* show in all kinds of weather merely for the chance to be seen waving at the folks from home:

it was their chance to show that the myth was real and they were now part of it.

But it was more than that that drew Don to the city. Don Bollinger was a large man with large appetites, and New York was the first place he ever visited that he didn't feel larger than. He had a large intellect that had grown too restless for classrooms in small towns and smaller cities. He needed different foods, different movies, different art, different faces, different ideas, and a lot of each. He was a ball of thunder that needed a place that thundered louder. He had a bellicose wit and needed a place that could absorb it, appreciate it. He traveled so much and read so much because he was always searching, always digesting, never quite satisfied, a gnawing hunger in his soul that required more and more of sometimes he knew not what. And from the very first minutes he drove in New York, he knew that he'd finally arrived at a place where he could always have whatever he needed whenever he needed it no matter what and when it was.

So Don *was* a patriot. He did love America in ways that flag-waving hicks who never left their home states could never begin to understand. He loved her deeply, completely and wide. And yet, he did love New York best of all. Nothing compared with the humid, verdant air of the Ozark Mountains, but he wouldn't feel deprived if he never camped in them again. He was speechless before the peaks of the Rockies but wouldn't weep to never see them again. He relished the dogwoods of Carolina, the desert moon of New Mexico, even the mundane miracle of ripening corn in his own hometown, but it was only at the thought of never being in New York again that he grew short of breath.

Back in the Hyundai, though, driving through Pennsylvania, he was flummoxed by how to explain the complexity of that love for both country and city to Steph, and how to verbalize the preference of the latter to one who had no real comprehension of the former.

Steph pressed him on that point. "I mean, those redneck patriots out there in flyover country don't even think New York is really America," Steph said. "Not sure why. Maybe we've got way too many immigrants. Although when those towers came down I noticed all those rednecks were quick to embrace our city. But even that made sense. New York got attacked by a little group of brown men, so the city gave all those rednecks the chance to be a victim. They love that victim shit. Seriously, I think those rednecks got a test to belong to their clubs, and if you ain't found enough to complain about in your life, you don't get in. Especially those rich Southern boys. No one, I mean no one, can bitch about being a victim quite like those rich white Southern boys. Those people squeal like pigs the moment you even look at one of their toys."

"Some good material there," Don said, driving. "This off the top of your head?"

"Don't slow me down, D. I'm just getting started. The second reason those rednecks hugged New York after 9/11 was that it gave them another good reason to go shoot some brown people. Whether or not those brown desert folk had it coming is irrelevant—some of them did, some of them didn't. My point is Whitey loved New York because it gave him a reason to hunt down some sand niggers. And now that Whitey's been doing it a while, you notice he's back to hating on New York again."

"Wow," Don said. "From whence sprang that outburst?"

"Just reading the paper," Steph said, flicking *The New York Times* in his lap. The front page had a couple of articles on the war in Iraq.

"I gotta say, Steph, that was the blackest I've ever heard you."

"Yeah, well, I slip into it now then. I am black, after all. Meanwhile, I have found absolutely nothing of 'religious interest' in this paper. I'm still not entirely sure what you meant by that phrase."

"Me neither. Think of 'religious interest' like that famous line on pornography by that Supreme Court Justice. We'll know it when we see it."

"Potter Stewart."

"That's his name. I didn't expect much on religious interest from the *Times* anyway, pagan rag that it is. Just think of religious interest as any story with any clue on where I could possibly take my ministry."

Steph laughed. "I am simultaneously tickled and spooked by this prophet thing, D. I still can't tell how serious you are and how far you're running with it."

"All the way to the finish line, and make no mistake about that."

"Yeah, well, you'll get no help from this paper," Steph said, folding it up and tossing it onto the dashboard.

"I'll catch the next exit and we'll get some Pennsylvania papers. Besides, I'm getting a bit peckish."

"You got a cooler full of snacks."

"All salty stuff. Hankering for something sweet."

"I need to buy a toothbrush anyway. I get a little restless whenever I think I might be traveling without one. Same with deodorant."

"Still think you ought to just check your suitcase."

"Too much trouble. Besides, there are worse fates than having an extra toothbrush."

Don could have responded, but he'd mentally begun to saunter down a trail of sweet things to eat, scanning the possibilities with his mind's eye. "A shame they don't have more Cracker Barrels out east. They've got shelves of incredible candy. I could go for some of their peanut brittle or golden crumbles about now."

"You never did answer my question about why you moved to New York."

"Oh," Don said, exhaling in a major fashion. "For everything there is a season and a time for every matter under heaven. It was just time to come to New York, and it's been time to stay."

Steph laughed and shook his head. "Don Prophet," he said, and Don turned to him and winked.

The church elders voted unanimously to recommend Pastor Paul be the new minister at the First Assembly of God Church in Tuttle, Pennsylvania, and the congregation voted unanimously to accept their recommendation. "I can't believe how lucky we are to get him," Brianna said to one of her mother's friends during coffee and punch fellowship following the October morning of the vote, which came in a special congregational meeting held directly after the service. "You're confusing luck with the Lord," the woman said reproachfully, lips pursed. Brianna was simply too excited to feel chastened.

The Tuesday on which Pastor Paul moved his family to town the following February was the coldest day of that winter—five below zero and a whistling wind strong enough to belong to March. It hadn't snowed since the end of January, so only a couple of inches of a dirtied, hardened crust lay on the ground, and all the sidewalks and driveways and streets were clear. A crew of twenty or so men from the church were on hand to help the movers unload, and because the day was too cold to be in a house whose doors would be consistently opened, Pastor Paul's wife, Julie, and their two-year-old son, Gabriel, waited out the move in the home of Gerry and Georgia Schlepper, parishioners with a toddler of their own.

Brianna couldn't help burning with envy at the Schleppers. She knew her envy wasn't Christian, but she just couldn't help it.

Her own big night came Thursday, the Clays' third night in town. The congregation had arranged for different families to bring a meal to the parsonage for each of the first five nights, and the Culps had Thursday. The bus from school could not get home fast enough that sunny, cold day. Brianna could swear that Lou, the old bus driver, was weaving slower than usual through the frozen streets of Tuttle, taking longer than necessary at each drop-off spot. Her mom was making Swedish meatballs, rice and green beans, but Brianna was slated to bake the German chocolate cake, and she wanted to make sure she had plenty of time to let it cool so she didn't feel rushed frosting it. It was so easy to tear the surface with that chunky, coconut frosting.

"Brianna, did you even hear a word I said?" That was Colleen, her best friend, a volatile, red-headed Nazarene with whom she always sat on the bus toward the front with the younger kids so as to avoid the boys in back who always cussed and made lewd statements.

"I'm sorry," said Brianna, eyeing driver Lou's right foot, as if her stare could pressure it into a few more miles per hour. "I've got a lot on my mind today."

"Like what?"

"I can't really say."

"Nice best friend," Colleen said, crossing her arms and intensifying her scowl, which was essentially her expression of default, giving way only to outright indignation and, rarely, something approaching a smile, though one usually clouded by begrudgment. "First you don't listen to me, then you don't talk to me. Our friendship's just bound to go the distance."

"I don't mean I won't tell you. I just mean it's hard to put into words."

But Colleen, unconvinced, maintained her pout, and she didn't even turn from staring out the window to say good-bye when Lou finally reached Brianna's block. Brianna was too preoccupied to care.

Julie Clay was perfect, just perfect, but Brianna knew that Pastor Paul's wife would be, a pert and perky petite blonde—real blond, a shoulder-length golden blond with no dark roots. She wore a pink sweater and tightish green jeans and thick, gray wool socks, and her smile when she opened the door was as bright and warm as a cloudless July afternoon. "You must be Glenda and Brianna," she said, fairly squeaking, stepping out onto the porch to retrieve the basket Glenda held containing three Corningware dishes. "I am so happy to meet you." She scrunched her face and smile, as if making faces at an infant. "Come on in where it's warm." She held the storm door open with her own backside while Glenda, now empty-handed, and Brianna, carrying the two-layered, round cake on a round, glass cake dish, crossed into the home of Pastor Paul.

It wasn't nearly as laden with boxes as Brianna had thought it would be. One big one sat in a corner, bubble wrap spilling out, another smaller one at the base of the carpeted stairs, and a couple other small ones on the farmer's table in the dining room where Julie led them, but the house was otherwise settled and organized and clean. The furniture was so much firmer and fresher than the stuff Pastor Markey and his wife, Bess, had—sharper corners, brighter colors, more modern lamps. "Paul is going to be so happy to meet you," Julie said as she deposited the basket of food onto the farmer's table. "He has heard so much about you from Pastor Markey."

Julie unloaded the basket, and when Brianna, reluctant to impose her cake onto the table without an invitation, finally forged ahead and set it down, Julie said, "Oh my goodness, did you make that cake, Brianna?" Brianna nodded sheepishly, feeling so clunky and stuffed in her heavy jacket next to pert, lissome Julie. "Did someone tell you that German chocolate was Paul's favorite, or did you just happen to make it?"

"I just happened to make it," she said, gushing with joy.

"He's going to be so happy." Julie grabbed Brianna's hands like an excited big sister who just found out little sis got asked to the prom. "Jesus is so good," she said in such happy though matter-of-fact conviction. Brianna just nodded, not entirely sure at the leap Julie had just made.

Pastor Paul entered from the kitchen. "There they are," he said, wearing a freshly pressed, red-flannel shirt, crisp khaki pants and dark leather boots. Brianna had never seen a minister dressed so cool before. "The Culp ladies." He carried Gabriel, their two-year-old son with hair as golden as Julie's. Gabriel smiled and waved, the grand marshal of their two-person parade. "You must be Glenda," he said, reaching out to shake her hand.

"I am," Glenda said, beaming.

"Pastor Markey told me that if I ever wanted to guarantee that something get done, all I needed to do was put you in charge." Glenda actually blushed. "And you must be Brianna." She nodded. "Gabriel, I want you to say hi to Brianna. I have a feeling she's going to be your favorite babysitter."

"Hi," Gabriel said, clearly new to the ability of speaking.

Brianna was suffused in a heat of rapture and maturity. She was not even old enough to babysit yet, still a half year away, and even though Glenda pointed that out, her bliss was not diminished, especially since Julie quickly added, "And look what Brianna made us, Paul."

Paul looked down at the cake. "German chocolate. Brianna, you just made yourself *my* favorite babysitter for Gabriel." Everyone laughed in such a fun, happy way, and as the laughter ebbed and tailed toward silence, Julie said unobtrusively but noticeably, "Praise Jesus."

"Brianna," Paul said, "word has reached me through Pastor Markey and a few others that you are a serious student of the Bible looking for answers to some real hard questions." Brianna was shaken. She wanted to nod that she was, but she couldn't believe Pastor Paul knew about it, and she was frightened that by her questions she had done something decidedly wrong in his eyes. "Good for you," he said, immediately allaying her concerns. "Serious questions mean you're serious about Jesus, and I love it when young people are serious about the Lord."

"Prayer time," Julie said in the excited tone of a TV game show host.

"Yes," Paul said. "Let's pray." Julie reached out her hands, indicating that they were all to join hands, which they did, Glenda and Brianna fumblingly so, and the three adults closed their eyes while Brianna kept hers open. "Jesus," Paul said, his face serious, Julie's just outright beatific, "Brianna is seeking you. Let her find you. She is knock, knock, knocking on your door, let it be opened unto her, especially since it's so darned cold. A-men." Glenda mumbled "A-men," somewhat unbalanced by such quick and insouciant religiosity, and Julie gave a prolonged but fun "A-men," dragging out the "A" like the game show host's signature sign-off. And when little Gabriel offered his own "A-men," tiny and mushed, everyone laughed, followed again by a "Praise Jesus" from Julie. Brianna had no idea that chasing Jesus could be so cool and fun.

"Don't you worry, Brianna," Paul soothed. "Your questions are good, so just be patient. More will be revealed."

The second Sunday in March, Pastor Paul convened his first night of SHAGY—Senior High Assembly of God Youth— for 6:30 p.m. It was held in the fellowship room in the church basement. Even though SHAGY was intended for just high school kids, Pastor Paul tossed the eighth graders in with them. "Just because they're in the junior high building doesn't mean they don't have senior high problems." (JHAGY met at five o'clock and included grades 5 - 7.)

Brianna was ecstatic to be included among the older students. But she was also nervous. Her mother dropped her off in front of the church, and before she went inside and downstairs, she stood at the door outside, her unmittened hand around the cold knob, and took a few deep breaths. She prayed she wouldn't sound dumb in front of the high school students. "Here's my theologian," Pastor Paul said brightly as she entered the room. She blushed. "Todd, do you know Brianna Culp?" Todd was Todd Bailey, a twenty-year-old quintessence of geek, an awkward, unattractive, whippet-thin computer programming student who commuted thirty miles each way three times a week to junior college and who worked full-time as assistant manager at the local Hardee's. Pastor Paul and Todd stood side by side just inside the entrance of the room, greeting. Brianna had never seen Todd before in her life.

"No, Pastor Paul, I don't know Brianna," Todd said with a major grin, as if proud of it.

"Well you and Brianna have something in common. You are both in serious pursuit of our Lord, and experience tells me that it's much easier and more fun to walk along that path with someone at your side than all alone."

"A-men to that," Todd said, offering his hand to shake, which Brianna did as Pastor Paul explained that Todd would be assisting him with SHAGY.

"And smile, Bri," Pastor Paul said in a tone as comfortingly intimate and friendly as his reduction of her name. "Chasing the Lord doesn't have to be so serious. Besides, I know what you're thinking, and you're wrong: these high school kids are tickled to death to have you here. It lets them play the role of big brother and big sister."

The sandpipers of Brianna's nervousness fluttered up and away before the calm tide of Pastor Paul's clairvoyant reassurance. She was amazed that he knew exactly why she was so nervous, and if he was right about that, she could assume only that he was also right about how the high school students felt about her presence. He rubbed her shoulder, and Todd, in clumsy mimicry, gave her other shoulder a playful punch.

A half dozen or so of other students were already there, a handful talking over to one side near the old, upright piano, two girls seated at one of the four long tables arranged in a square, chatting. Brianna walked to the tables and took off her coat at the opposite corner of the chatting two, and one of them, Peggy Sneed, a thick and pretty, dark-haired junior who was the starting forward on the varsity girls basketball team, said, "Brianna, are you too stuck up to sit next to us?" Peggy wasn't smiling, but Brianna could easily tell by her tone that her tease was good-natured. "Get your butt over here." Brianna shrugged and grabbed her coat and moved to the padded folding chair next to Peggy's. Peggy had always been friendly before, but Brianna was surprised by this new treatment, as if she were a real friend.

Ten minutes later, when Pastor Paul began the meeting with a prayer, another dozen students had arrived, but Brianna was the only eighth grader, which wasn't hugely odd, given that there were only three eighth graders in her church, but while she was pretty sure Jeff Webb hadn't planned on coming (he played in an intramural basketball league), she did think Stephanie Price would be there. Brianna did not dislike Stephanie, but she was secretly glad she hadn't come. As the youngest there, Brianna felt profoundly special, like the youngest of the apostles must have felt.

"Good evening, folks," Pastor Paul said, after the prayer, seated at the center of one of the four tables, Todd seated next to him. "I would say, 'happy folks,' but since you're teenagers, chances are only fifty-fifty that you're happy right now." All students, save for a couple of boys in one corner, smiled. "For those of you who are unhappy, there are a multitude of reasons why, but one of them could definitely be that your parents made you come here tonight. Don't worry. I get that. When I was your age, I was a hard drinker, a heavy smoker, and a chronic school skipper, so you can bet I wasn't spending Sunday evenings in a church, and I know just how angry I would have been if someone had tried to make me." Brianna was waylaid with disbelief. Pastor Paul? A heavy smoker and drinker? But if she was waylaid, Todd was positively gobsmacked. His exuberant smile vanished, replaced by a fully-slacked jaw above sagged shoulders and motionless arms dropped like dead fish atop the table. Everyone in the room, though, was riveted.

"You heard me right," Pastor Paul continued. "A smoker, a drinker, a school skipper, and a few other things which hardly made me every teacher's favorite student in my small Wisconsin hometown. That was me in a nutshell, and believe you me, I was one tough little nut to crack. It wasn't being good that led me to Jesus. It was being bad. But we all have our own path, and no path is wrong as long as it leads to the Lord. 'It is good for me that I was afflicted, that I might learn thy statutes.' That's Psalm 119, verse 71 for you students of the Bible or students of the Bible wannabes. All of this is my way of saying if you don't want to be here tonight, believe me, I understand. Even though I'm your pastor, I may understand better than any other adult in your life. That's why when we meet again in a couple of weeks, we're going to have an 'I Get It' room—a separate room for anyone who doesn't feel like being in here. Let's face it. You'll have to come. Your parents will make you. They probably made you come tonight." A few students smiled and nodded, but not Brianna. Ever since church let out earlier that day, just before lunch, Brianna couldn't wait for evening to come, for her chance to again be with Pastor Paul and this time have him to herself, or at least without her parents. And part of her wanted him to know just how eager she had been to be here tonight, despite her nervousness, but she knew that blurting out as much would make her look like a real suck-up, and that would hardly win her friends. In fact, Todd *was* shaking his head no, vigorously, and he looked like a real idiot. Brianna felt embarrassed for him. But Pastor Paul, so astute, so synchronized with the thought processes of the young, diffused Todd's unconscious self-sabotage by turning to him and saying, "Not, of course, you, Todd. You're here because *I* made you come." Everyone laughed, even the boys in the corner. "But I didn't have to push that hard," he added gently, "because both you and I wanted you here." Todd smiled with the satisfaction of a retriever being rewardingly patted for an especially deft fetch. And Brianna marveled at how someone as cool as Pastor Paul could make someone as lame as Todd feel like they belonged together.

"But I'm very serious about that 'I Get It' Room," Pastor Paul said. "If you don't want to be here, you can be there while your parents think you're here. And in there you can do whatever you want. You guys can talk about girls and you girls can talk about guys. We might even set up a TV or a PlayStation. We'll see. I'll make it a nice room, with couches and soft chairs. My point is, if you're just not ready for this, if you're just not ready to believe or even be willing to believe, that's cool by me. After all, the Apostle Paul, in his letter to the Romans, said, 'As for the man who is weak in faith, welcome him, but not for disputes.' And who am I to argue with such a major apostle who does have, you have to admit, a real cool name?" The students chuckled. Brianna turned to Peggy, varsity star, and the two shared their chuckle with each other. Brianna gushed with gratitude.

"But before you do bail on me to play some Madden NFL or MLB Slugfest"—the mention of which caused the two boys in the corner to turn to each other and laugh, as if delightfully surprised that Pastor Paul might have known exactly what they were thinking—"I do want to make one request. Give me a chance. Give us a chance," he said, holding out his arms, palms up, in an all-inclusive gesture. "Because I was such a troubled teen, I think I can pretty solidly relate to many of the troubles you might be experiencing. And that's what SHAGY is going to be about. It's not going to be about Jesus and Moses and Peter and Isaiah, although make no mistake, those guys will come up in our conversation now and then, as will some other guys, not to mention plenty of girls like Mary and Rachel, Deborah and Esther and Mary. Wait, didn't I already say Mary? Oh well. There are two key Marys to be concerned with. But mostly we're going to be concerned with Ted and Scott and Beth and Maggie," and here he went around the table, listing the name of each person sitting at it. "Because it's you we need to be concerned about—your struggles, your temptations, your heartbreaks, and yes, your victories. This group is going to be all about addressing what you need to address in order to live the lives that Jesus wants you to live. It's going to be about the trials you encounter and the solutions we have to offer. And to prove my point, I think we should jump right into our first solution, but in order to have a solution, we have to have a problem. Now, since this is our first meeting, I was pretty sure everyone would be a little shy about bringing up any struggles you might be having, so I asked Todd in advance to bring a problem that would be relevant for us all to discuss, so ladies and gentlemen, esteemed colleagues of SHAGY, I give you Todd."

Everyone in the room clapped. Todd was surprised by the applause, quite probably the first he'd ever received for anything his entire life, and he laughed and rolled his eyes and held up his hands in befuddled simultaneity. Brianna and some others beamed some huge smiles before they all finally stopped clapping.

"Boy," Todd said, "I only hope you feel the same way about me *after* I'm done speaking." The students, and Pastor Paul, laughed. "So, I spent a lot of time this week thinking about a subject to discuss tonight. I stuck my nose in the Bible, looking for a cool problem, and when I told Pastor Paul what I was doing, he said, 'Todd, are your problems in your Bible or in your life?' When I told him, 'My life,' he said, 'Then that's where you need to be looking.' So, I kind of looked at my days to see where there were issues. The thing is, what I wanted was a cool problem. I wanted to impress you guys with whatever was bothering me. I guess that sounds kind of weird because I'm not real sure problems can be cool. I mean, whatever your problem is, if you're in the middle of it, I can't imagine it feels at all cool.

"But then I asked myself why it was so important for me to have a cool problem. And that's when I came up with my problem to discuss, which deep down I think I knew was my problem all along, only I didn't want to admit it. And my problem is, that problem is," Todd interrupted himself with a laugh and a look askance; he scratched the back of his head, the thin brown hair, and looked up, took a deep breath with his eyes closed before he opened his eyes, flashed a smile that could be called only goofy, and said, "My problem is that I'm lonely. It's loneliness." Nobody in the room laughed, which seemed to catch Todd a bit off guard. He scanned the room, eyeing a path around the square of tables with a slow swivel of his head, and after the visual journey was complete, he resumed:

"I mean, as lives go, mine's not too bad. I go to college, I've got a decent job, I've got two parents who really love me, but I still am kind of lonely lots of times. Not kind of. Really. I've never had a girlfriend. Ever. And I don't really have that many friends. My best friend from high school, he went off to Penn State, and another guy I hung out with some, well, he's really into Dungeons and Dragons, and I have to say, I find that whole D & D thing kind of weird. If a computer nerd like me thinks something's weird, it must really be weird."

The students all laughed, warmly, sympathetically, genuinely. Todd laughed with them, and it was clear he felt comforted and gratified by their laughter. To Brianna, it felt as if suddenly, everyone in the room were close, special friends. She found herself caring for Todd, and that surprised her; a half hour earlier, she'd not even known him and couldn't imagine liking him. Not hating. Brianna was not at all like that, never had been—hostile to or even dismissive of someone like Todd. She'd always wondered if geeks knew they were geeks. Some days she thought they probably didn't or else they would stop being so geeky, but other days she thought all people must have an inkling of themselves. Either way, she hated mean people and bullies, but while she would never tease anyone for being fat or ugly or geeky or dumb, and while she would always be nice to any such misfit, offering a friendly smile or hello, she never thought of any geek she knew as a friend. And now, she wondered why. Was she a snob? Or was it just that she had nothing in common with any geek she knew? But how did she know if she never took the time to get to know one? After all, Todd was a geek; he'd just admitted it to everyone in the room, and what she felt for him right now was a sense of genuine, warm friendship. But then again, she still couldn't imagine doing anything with him on a Friday night. What did they have in common? What would they do? Go out for pizza? What would they talk about? Maybe she could see herself bowling with him because then there wouldn't be the need to talk as much, but only if a couple of other people came along.

"So that's it," Todd said. "That's my problem. I'm just kind of lonely. I hope you all don't think I'm begging for friends. I'm not. I just thought that, well, maybe if I opened up about feeling lonely, some of you might also be lonely and open up about it yourselves. That's all. Thanks."

"Well," Pastor Paul said in something of a sigh, "that was truly remarkable, Todd. I knew there had to be a good reason the Lord put you on my path." Todd gave a shrug and grin that was the quintessence of sheepish. "I could say a lot, but we're not here to listen to me. We're here to listen to you, to each other, so if there's anyone who can identify with what Todd had to share, or anyone who has anything relevant to say about tonight's subject, which is loneliness, please feel free to speak."

Silence greeted that invitation. It lasted a few moments, enough so that Todd, after initially looking around, looked down at his fingers which he drummed in his lap, self-conscious, on the brink of feeling a dupe. But just as that room of silence was about to get the sign "awkward" hung on its door, a voice spoke, and to Brianna's amazement, it was the voice next to her, Peggy's. "You know, I didn't join the basketball team because I love basketball," she said. "I don't. I don't hate it, but if you told me tomorrow I could never play again, you wouldn't break my heart. In sixth grade, I didn't have hardly any friends. I was gawky and tall with braces, and I was so desperate to belong to any kind of group that I was willing to try anything. I joined the basketball team because it seemed like the smartest place for a tall girl to go, and the only reason I've played all these years is that I found I'm actually pretty good at it. But I've also stayed because I've made some friends on the team. They probably aren't the first girls I would have chosen to be friends. They spend a lot of time talking about basketball or playing basketball or watching it on TV. Still, it's nice to have a group like that to belong to. Sometimes, right in the middle of a game, my mind will sort of wander, and I'll get to thinking about how incredibly weird it is that I'm out on this court doing something that I'm not really that into, and doing it pretty good. And even though I don't love it, I have to admit that I do love after a game when I'm with a couple of other girls on the team, and we're all out getting a pizza, laughing at stupid stuff. Or talking about boys we'd never stand a chance with, even if we put out."

Some of the boys laughed, sharp little surprised barks of laughter. "Laugh all you want, assholes, you know it's true," Peggy said, sneering, aggressive, ready to take this to fisticuffs if need be and probably capable of winning. The boys looked at each other and laughed even harder while Brianna sat agog— Peggy had brought up sex, she'd loudly cussed out some boys, and she'd done it right next to her. Brianna was mortified. She was scared. She turned to Pastor Paul for guidance. The boys stopped laughing, but other people were chatting excitedly, Peggy had her arms crossed in a near pout, and all were looking to Pastor Paul.

He smiled vaguely, as if the meeting had unfolded as he'd somewhat hoped or suspected it might. He turned to Todd. "See what you started," he said. Todd, who'd been terribly worried by the direction of the meeting, laughed disproportionately loud. Pastor Paul addressed the room. "One of my absolute favorite moments in the Gospels comes when Jesus encounters the Canaanite woman. It's Matthew, chapter 15, verses 21 - 28." He went on to narrate that story, his voice gentle, lilting, his tone teasing out the details with admirable patience and pace: Jesus had gone to the region of Tyre and Sidon, and this Canaanite woman ran to him, begging him to remove the demon from her tortured daughter. Jesus ignored her and moved on, and Pastor Paul explained that Canaanites were "pond scum" as far as the Hebrews were concerned. The woman continued her plea, now to the disciples, and they came whining to Jesus to take care of her so that they could get rid of her. "There is nothing in the world those disciples didn't whine about," Pastor Paul said. "Sometimes I just can't help wondering what the heck Jesus was thinking when he picked the guys he did." But Jesus, surprisingly, told the disciples he wasn't going to heal the woman's daughter: he was sent as a shepherd for the sheep of Israel, he said, not those lowly Canaanite ovine. The woman came and knelt before him and begged again for help, "and like a real jerk," he said, looking directly but benevolently at those boys who laughed at Peggy, "Jesus actually said to the woman, 'It is not fair to take the children's bread and throw it to the dogs.' Can you believe he said that? Here this poor woman is begging for her daughter to be saved, and Jesus calls her a dog and says she's not worthy of his efforts." But the woman was not daunted. "Without missing a beat, she snapped back, 'Yes, Lord, yet even the dogs eat the crumbs that fall from their master's table.' Jesus was impressed. I have to believe he was a bit humbled and chastened, too. Whatever his problem had been, that Canaanite woman changed his bad attitude, and Jesus said, 'O woman, great is your faith.' And Jesus healed the woman's daughter."

Paul paused, allowing the dust of his narration to settle completely onto his rapt audience. "Now, I love that little story for so many reasons." He loved it, he said, because it revealed a very human Jesus, a guy not immune to snobbery or even a touch of meanness, "and to forget that Jesus was human is to rob him of his real glory." He loved the story, he said, because it concerned a bottom-rung Canaanite woman who not only had so much faith in Jesus that she kept appealing to him but also enough wit and sass to unleash "a quick smack down," when Jesus had it coming. But the main reason he loved it, he said, was that it was, "a great example of how, when we set out to do the Lord's work, we really never know what's going to happen.

"When we came here tonight, we didn't know that Todd was going to speak so eloquently about loneliness, or that Peggy was going to unpack her heart as she did. And we certainly didn't know that she was going to talk about sex and throw out a fun cuss word." Brianna joined the others in a laughter both humored and relieved. She knew now that no matter where the tracks might lead, she would always be safe on Pastor Paul's spiritual train. "But what we've had here tonight is a wonderful expression of Jesus' power. We all gathered in his name, and we learned more about each other and more about ourselves, and as a result, we will leave here stronger and better equipped to confront the challenge of loneliness, which I know you all wrestle with, *we* all wrestle with, even if Peggy and Todd were the only ones to share about it tonight." He looked at each person in the room, nodding, and said, "Let's wrap this up and eat some brownies."

Brianna ate a brownie, gooey and chock-full of chocolate chips, and she drank her Styrofoam cup of milk, as did all the others, and she joined in the rousing game of Pictionary, not much assistance to her teammates, still too distracted by the preceding hour. When it was time to circle up and hold hands for the final prayer, she did not bow her head and close her eyes as the others did, Todd zealously so, as if the intensity with which he kept his eyes shut were a spiritual test. She simply stared at the man saying the prayer, dumbfounded anew that he was in her life.

There she was, same as always, again: the blue plaid shirt, the blue-rimmed straw hat, the curly red hair, the slightly toothy grin, the white skin and cherry cheeks: Little Debbie. Or, as Don was wont to call her, "my snack-time bitch." He stood in an overly air-conditioned gas station convenience store in a lowly populated Pennsylvania town half a dozen miles from the exit ramp off the highway. It wasn't a Sheetz, the gas station/convenience store that dominated Pennsylvania (Don held the Sheetz burgers in pretty high esteem), but it was unremarkable in its similarity to decent convenience stores all over the country—the aisles of snack food and quick-cook products, the reduced-size boxes of various soaps and powders to clean your person or your clothes, the coffee station with

three pots and an array of flavored creamers, and the bored
clerk behind the counter who, if not selling soda and lottery
tickets or restocking cigarettes, usually stared longingly out the
storefront window. This clerk was a young and chubby girl,
early twenties, her hair unnaturally black, probably dyed,
eyelids dark with mascara and nose pierced—"punk" Don
would have called her ten years ago, but nowadays the term
seemed to be "alternative," although that word was applied to
such a wide array of people and things that it seemed to have
lost the oomph of its meaning. Whatever the word, Don knew
the type the moment he walked in and saw her: a bored, small
towner curious but scared who wears the costume of the rebel
but is ultimately too frightened to stray far from home. He gave
a hearty hello upon entering, and she chewed her gum and gave
a bored hello back, and Don immediately turned his thoughts
to the other girl, Little Debbie, who once again had her own
rack of individually wrapped products (though boxes of her
stuff were just around the corner in the baked goods aisle
dominated by Hostess but with a noteworthy Entenmann's
presence): Zebra Cakes, Star Crunches, Devil Squares, Cloud
Cakes, Marshmallow Pies, and Don's favorite, the Nutty Bar,
that incomparable chocolate-covered, peanut butter-filled wafer
that Don still couldn't believe he could get for a quarter. It
really did make him question the ingredients in, and labor
conditions behind, these snack products, but Little Debbie in
all her forms had never betrayed him before, and he had no
reason to think she would do so now. After a moment of ogling
and admiring the panoply, he reached forward and grabbed two
Nutty Bar packages and one of Zebra Cakes, the former out of
devotion, the latter nostalgia. Steph still strolled through the
aisles, looking for a toothbrush, and Don sauntered to the
counter where he dropped his snacks. The clerk, chewing that
gum with staccato chops, occasionally eliciting a pop, eyed the
cellophane packages, and Don, having decided earlier to

experiment, said, in an especially deep voice, "I shouldn't be eating those."

She looked up to him and said, deadpan, serious, a tone she maintained throughout her conversation with Don, "I love Little Debbie products."

"As do I, child. I love everything that little girl makes, but my life is no longer about pleasure. I'm a prophet. John the Baptist was running around the desert in a loin cloth eating locusts for dinner."

"With honey," she said, nonplussed. "Those locusts had honey on them."

"The very thought I had when I decided to go ahead and buy these."

"Who are you going to be a prophet for?"

"For whom the Lord clearly commands, child. The downtrodden. The unwashed. The poor in body and spirit."

The clerk appraised Don and slowly nodded. "They could sure use someone these days."

"Advocates for the downtrodden are always in short supply."

Steph, standing in the aisle farthest away, loudly said, "Excuse me, ma'am. Do you have any Reach toothbrushes here? Or even Colgate?"

"What you see is what we've got," the clerk shouted back.

"So all you've got are these crappy little cheap toothbrushes?"

Quietly to Don, the clerk asked, "What's your friend's name?"

"Steph."

Loud again: "We're a convenience store, Steph. We specialize in quick or emergency purchases. You want quality, go to Target."

Don reached for the day's *Philadelphia Inquirer* in the news rack just to his left and tossed it onto the counter. The clerk began to ring up his products. "You're not your typical gas station clerk, are you?" he asked.

"How many gas station clerks have you had a conversation with?"

He shrugged. "Not many."

"Then it's hardly for you to decide what's typical, is it?"

Steph came forward and dropped his generic green toothbrush, soft bristles, onto the counter, and Don told her to put it on his tab. "Your total comes to $4.17," she said.

Outside, walking back to the car, Don said, "Not really the interaction I'd expected."

"I noticed you having a good long chat with her," Steph said. "What were you talking about?"

"Oh, I was just auditioning an approach to this prophet thing, tinkering with tone and diction."

"And what type of interaction was it you expected?"

"Not the one I got."

They reached the car but stood at their respective doors. The reflection of the sun bounced with mitigated sharpness off the car's roof whose paint was as dully gray as elephant skin. "What exactly did you Don Prophetize about in there?" Steph asked.

"As it turns out, Little Debbie snack cakes, but it really could have been any number of things. A gas station convenience store is rife with prophet-worthy topics: oil companies, subsidized sugary products, even that clerk's wage, which was probably minimum, and I bet minimum wage out here is two bucks less than it is in the city. The thing is, if I'm going to pull this prophet thing off, I'm going to need to be able to Don Prophetize anywhere, anytime, on any subject. And thanks for that term."

"That poor girl in there did not deserve an interlude with you. Things are probably tough and confusing enough for her as it is."

ERIK SIMON

"Are you kidding me? Those five minutes with me were the most interesting five minutes she'll have all month."

Steph smiled and shook his head and got into the car. Don opened his own door but turned for a final look at the store before he got in. The clerk stood at the untinted glass door, arms crossed, staring at Don. She could have been daydreaming, could have been lost in some reverie that precluded her even registering what she looked at, and that's what Don chose to believe as he returned her stare, curiously rooted, transfixed. He was aware of himself in this visual interplay and aware of his ability to withdraw from it but not fully ready to do so, like knowing in your sleep that you're having a dream. Then, the clerk raised both of her arms to the level of her shoulders and pressed her hands against the glass door. She nodded at Don, once, a slow, unsmiling nod, and she held her body still but kept her hands pressed against the door. Don held her stare. He was confused. He was spooked. He got in the car and pulled away. He wondered what all just happened. He wondered what unwarranted hopes he might have unleashed in that girl. She didn't really believe he was a prophet, did she? But then, why not? That's what he'd told her, and wasn't he out here on this lark precisely because he knew people would buy it? He wondered if this ploy of his might not be more irresponsible than he'd initially suspected, and for entirely different reasons.

"Seriously, Don," Steph said, the two back on the highway now, Don driving and eating his first Nutty Bar, the chocolate melting in his warm fingers. "What message is it you plan to Don Prophetize?"

"Hell, I don't know. I think it will be more about reacting then acting, seeing what fastballs or curves the pitcher of fates hurls my way. It's like my great awakening in Washington Square with those loopy Koreans. That slider just came my

112

way, and I happened to have the bat to take it out of the park and the irrepressible urge to take a mighty swing."

"That was one impressive extended metaphor."

"You of all people should hardly be surprised by my dexterity with words."

"All well and good, but you still have to have some foundation of belief. I mean, prophets know their message before they take it on the road, and to know their message, they have to know what they believe. So what do you believe? And before you answer, just know that I find this conversation surreal. Not only that we're having it, but also the context in which we're having it, especially the fact that I'm actually taking it seriously."

"Ditto that," Don said, his own surreal feeling intensified by the lingering vision of that clerk's final pose, her hands pressed so believingly against that glass door. "Do you want the abridged version?"

"There's a long version? I was just looking for a simple credo. The highlights."

"What good is Leviticus without Genesis and Exodus?"

"That's some quick shit there, D."

"Are you sure you're even black in the city? I have seriously never heard you come close to talking like this before."

"I tend to cling to my urban Negro roots the farther I'm away from them. You should have heard me turn it on at Brandeis. I'd pull out some pro-Palestinian trash talk in my thickest ghetto dialect. It really threw the Zionist leftists for a loop. They tried to argue with me while simultaneously reaffirming how much they still really did love black people. It was sumptuous to watch, almost like I'd said, 'Dance, white folk.'" Steph laughed, a private memory. "Give me a semi-abridged version."

Don stared forward, wondering where to begin. He didn't really have an elevator pitch for his belief system—he'd always taken faith way too seriously for that. All throughout childhood, until he graduated from high school, he went to church almost every Sunday, and while he was often bored, looking back, he was glad for his regular attendance. His parents were adamant he attend every week, as well as Vacation Bible School for one week every summer up through the sixth grade and Sunday night youth group twice a month through junior high and high school. Sunday services could be dull, but by the time he was ten, he was already paying attention to the sermon, at least now and then, and he never tired of hearing stories from the Bible. Their minister, Delmar Smith, was a fat, affable guy with thin hair that Don always remembered as gray, even though he was only a few years older than his father. Delmar was a funny guy who seemed to have a sixth sense about how many jokes from the pulpit were too many and who, with a high-pitched voice and conversational style, had a delivery and sense of timing that he'd honed to near perfection over the years. He could be indelibly effective at just the right moment. Don was still stirred deeply by memories of communion Sunday when, just before parishioners were to drink their individual, miniature plastic shot glasses of grape juice, Reverend Smith, standing on the altar, held aloft his silver chalice and said, "I am the vine, you are the branches. Cut off from me, you can do nothing."

And yet, by the time he was in college, he was pretty much immersed in doubt, the usual doubts for a young, curious mind—the Virgin birth, the efficacy of prayer, the Resurrection. Reverend Smith was not a fundamentalist, so Don had not been reared in a literalist understanding of the Bible, at least not once he was past the age of eight or so. And as he got older, he never resented his early years of Sunday school. He came to understand that it was probably more compassionate not to tell a five-year-old that the story of Noah's ark was really just a metaphor for God's greatness.

What the hell does a toddler know for metaphors? But just because he'd essentially always read and understood the Bible seriously, as opposed to literally, didn't mean that he didn't have some doubts. Some of those were answered through scholarship (Virgin birth was a mistranslation, "young woman" being supplanted by "virgin"), but some lingered, chiefly one that buzzed and hovered over the thicket of just how active a role God played in our world. To argue that God was active was to confront, eventually, some pretty disturbing occurrences of favoritism: in fact, it was to confront thousands of years of it, and while God was certainly depicted to have his favorites in the Old Testament, Don just couldn't accept that line of thinking, wouldn't accept it. How could any mother with a dead infant sitting next to a mother with a squalling happy infant be asked to believe that was how God orchestrated it? And "Be still and know that I am God," was not a sufficient response. "The ways of God are mysterious," was the single biggest literary copout in the history of the Western world. "Where were you when I laid the earth's foundations?" God asked Job, as if that were any kind of answer to Job's misery. Don always wished Job would have shot back, "Who the fuck cares because I was right fucking here during your pissing match with Satan during which, just to prove a point, you saw fit to slaughter my family and destroy my life. Fucker." No, Don couldn't abide the "You-can't-understand-God's-ways" argument. He was okay with not understanding God. But it's one thing to believe in God and be confused by God, and it's quite another to accept selective destruction and wholesale slaughter as God's arcane machinations for an unknown goal. The world was random, Don finally believed. It was all about luck. Einstein was right. God doesn't play dice. The world was throwing its own dice, and God was just a pit boss dispassionately observing the winners gather their chips, the losers watching their chips yanked away.

ERIK SIMON

That didn't mean that Don didn't take the Bible seriously. Quite the contrary. He read it devotedly, slavishly, not just because it was great literature, which it unequivocally was. As someone who aspired to be a writer that mattered, he knew it was crucial that he know as much of the Bible as possible. In graduate school, he was aghast to hear peers proudly sneer that they'd not read the Bible because they didn't "believe" it. "Who gives a cockeyed shit what you believe?" he thundered one day in his Dante class at a skinny, redhead who often interjected that he was an MFA student in Poetry. "It's the foundation of Western literature. How can you not know it or not want to know it? Just because I don't believe in Zeus or Pallas Athena doesn't mean I should burn my copies of Homer." Even more galling to Don were people who claimed to believe in spirituality, not religion. Often he'd press these people to define spirituality. Only once did he get a lucid, thoughtful response, that from an Oregon girl whose parents were archeologists. Her response: "Spirituality is the belief that not only is there something beyond my physical, material self but also that it's more important," an answer against which Don could not argue. Some people would claim that Nature was their God, and he'd ask if that included tornadoes that wiped out villages and tsunamis that instantly murdered thousands. Some would claim an idea of believing in a force for good, to which Don would reply, "That's exactly what Goebbels and Himmler believed in—a force for good as they saw it." The pinnacle of arrogance in this spiritual vs. religious dichotomy he heard at an AA meeting in Brooklyn, where Gretchen's friend, Amber, was celebrating her one-year anniversary and had invited Don and Gretchen to attend. Don had no beef with twelve-step programs. They seemed to be changing a lot of lives for the better, and it was tough to argue against that. But at this meeting, held in an un-airconditioned Dutch Reformed Church on a hot July night, some middle-aged guy told his

116

story about how he stole thousands, cheated on his wife, beat his children, but claimed he was different now, not because he found religion but because he found spirituality. "Religion is for people who are scared of hell," he added. "Spirituality is for people who have been there." That line drew applause and whoops of approval, but it came close to drawing Don tempestuously out of his chair. "So let me get this straight," he said at the celebratory dinner for Amber after the meeting, an Indian restaurant where he and Gretchen joined eight recovering alcoholics at a round table. He was talking with a young guy, decimating, between statements, the table's supply of appetizers and naan. "You guys are drunken, irresponsible assholes for years, wreaking havoc on everything and everyone you touch, and one day that all finally stops, and you slowly mend your ways and repair the damage, and good for you. But because you've done that, you're now all of a sudden spiritually superior to people who have behaved decently and charitably their entire lives and who were going to church the whole time they were doing so?" His adversary had no response. Don victoriously popped another pakora into his mouth.

"Those AA folk," Steph said. "Late in life they get bit by God and they act like they invented Him."

"I actually prefer a hard-core believer who's never read the Bible to a hard-core religion-basher who's never read the Bible. They are positively the worst—proudly arrogant about not believing in what they don't even really know they don't believe in."

"Are you an atheist?" Steph asked.

Don shook his head. "I can't be."

Steph laughed. "What do you mean you can't be? Is God going to make you stand in the corner?"

"No," Don said, chuckling. His first Nutty Bar was long since consumed, and if he didn't eat the other soon, its chocolate would melt disastrously against the inside of its cellophane wrapper. He hated that. He would still eat it, of course, but the entire experience would be much less pleasant. He moved that second Nutty Bar under his seat, thinking it must be cooler in that darkness, and said, "I need to tell you about Uncle Timmy."

Uncle Timmy lived in a barn four miles outside of town. The barn was one of three on the farm of Crackers Hansen, who was Timmy's best friend back in high school. Crackers was primarily a crop farmer—wheat, soybeans, corn—but he raised some grass-fed cattle for meat for family and friends, and he had a trio of Arabian horses. Uncle Timmy lived with the horses in the largest of the three barns, and he paid his keep by tending them.

Throughout his childhood, Don saw Uncle Timmy from a distance. Every week or so, his father bought groceries for Timmy and delivered them out at the farm, and occasionally he took Don, who sat in the car or loitered near it while his father carried the sacks through the farm yard down to Timmy's barn. A couple of times Timmy, a tall, boney man with gray hair, was in the pasture, but Don never had any interaction with him, not even so much as a wave.

"Why does Uncle Timmy live out here?" Don asked his father on the drive back into town one day when he was seven, old enough to realize there was something odd about the arrangement, about his uncle.

"Because he likes it. He feels comfortable here."

"Why is he comfortable here?"

"That's a little tough to explain."

"Will I ever get to meet Uncle Timmy and talk to him?"

"When you're older, and when everything will make a little more sense, I'll have you meet him, and I'll tell you why he's comfortable living out here in the barn."

Throughout the years, Don continued to go with his father to deliver groceries to Uncle Timmy, not every time, but often, and sometimes they delivered other provisions such as clothes, blankets, light bulbs, a new coat. Uncle Timmy never came to their house, not for a birthday, not for Christmas or Thanksgiving, never. The only time Don ever heard of Timmy even coming to town was for a doctor's appointment, which he did a few times, but Don was not invited along on those trips.

When Don was thirteen and he rode out to see Uncle Timmy, his father, after he shut off the engine, turned to him. "Why don't you come with me to the barn today. Meet your Uncle Timmy." Don just stared at his father. He'd been kept apart from his uncle for so many years that the thought of finally approaching him gave him pause. "Don't worry," his dad said. "It'll be all right." Don nodded, but before they got out of the car, his father added, "When we're with your Uncle Timmy, don't say anything. Just stand there quietly." Again, Don nodded.

It was a cold but sunny January day, and Don followed his father down a slope of frozen, rutted ground to a large barnyard fenced in with two strands of electric wire. They opened the wooden gate and passed through, the sky blue, the air smelling faintly of manure, two whitish horses circumspectly across the yard. At the door of the old barn, the wood splintering and patched with paint darkly red as a bruised apple, Don's father stopped and held his hand out for Don to do the same, keeping him a few feet back. "Timmy," he shouted, his voice such a solitary, invasive sound in the vast quiet. "Timmy, it's Marcus. I got some papers for you to sign. I need to come in, and I've got Donny with me. We won't be but a couple of minutes." They stood in wait for a minute or so, and the barn door was unlatched from within; it opened on its own just slightly. Marcus held his finger to his lips, reminding Don to remain quiet, before he opened the door the rest of the way and nodded for Don to follow.

The barn smelled of winter and dust and settled hay, bales of it stacked in the loft above the pens, five in total, three on one side matted with mud and straw, two on the other completely clean. A faint reek of ammonia tickled Don's nostrils as they walked down the aisle between the pens to an area at the other end of the barn sectioned off with plywood walls, save for the wall facing the aisle, which was made of horse blankets nailed to a thick beam above. "Okay, Timmy," his father said, "I'm coming in now. Remember, I've got Donny with me." Marcus paused a moment then pulled aside an edge of the horse blanket and stepped inside.

Don was astonished to find a room. For years he'd known that Uncle Timmy "lived in a barn," but until now he was never entirely sure what that meant; he'd suspected it meant that he actually lived in a small house near a barn or even in a back bedroom in Crackers' large farm house, the bedroom with the clearest view of the barn. But no, Uncle Timmy literally lived in the barn in a room that Don was surprised to see was habitable, humane, even cozy. The plywood ceiling was unpainted, but the plywood walls were each covered with other horse blankets, not completely ceiling to floor but mostly so, wide strips of wall visible only along the bottom. The cement floor had a large oval rug that mostly covered it, and in the center stood a kerosene heater that filled the room with ample heat and a lambent glow. There was a rocking chair, a small chest of drawers, a table with a kerosene stove and a small stack of books. Uncle Timmy sat on his bed, a Depression-era wrought iron farmer's bed. Just above him, sunlight shone through a square window in the exterior wall, covered in plastic. The lantern on the nightstand was not lit.

"How you doing, Timmy?" Marcus said as he approached his older brother. Timmy sat on the edge of the bed, looking down, his face as ashen as his hair, his hands lethargically clasped. He didn't look up but did give a couple of nods. "I got

Donny over there with me. Getting bigger every day. Smarter too. Getting so smart that some days it scares me." Moving nothing but his head, Timmy slowly turned to look at Don. He stared at him for a moment with absolutely no expression. Don smiled, gave a small wave. Timmy nodded, unsmiling, wholly unemotional, but a nod nonetheless. Don felt simultaneously frightened and touched.

"I got some papers I need you to sign here, Timmy," Marcus said. He now stood on the other side of the nightstand, and he removed the lantern to the floor and pulled the papers and a pen out of his coat pocket and placed them on the empty space between him and his brother. Timmy listlessly turned toward his task. "Just some new paperwork from the government to get your medical treatment. Won't take but a minute." Timmy picked up the pen, and Marcus pointed where on the first page he needed to sign, which he did, and they repeated that routine two more times, Marcus turning the pages. "That's it," Marcus said, folding the papers and returning them to his coat. Timmy gently lay down the pen, and Marcus reached a hand to his shoulder, giving it a gentle squeeze. "That's all for today. How you feeling anyway?" Timmy nodded slowly. "I'll be out with some groceries early next week." It struck Don that no groceries were visible in the room; he must have had a separate place where he kept them, a place where small animals couldn't forage, maybe where there was an outlet to hook up a refrigerator.

His father crossed back to him. "Say good-bye to your Uncle Timmy," he told Don.

"Good-bye, Uncle Timmy," Don said, quietly. "It was nice to see you." He wondered why he didn't say, "Nice to meet you." Timmy didn't turn to Don, but he did nod again, slowly, deliberately. Don and his father quit the room.

Back in the car, Don did not initiate the conversation. He knew he didn't have to. His father had taken him to meet his

Uncle Timmy because he was finally ready, so he assumed he was going to get an explanation of sorts, which he did, once his dad had pulled out of the long gravel driveway and was bound on the unlined asphalt road, returning home.

"In 1967, your uncle fought in Vietnam. He was drafted and fought for a year. He was never the same after that."

Vietnam. Don, precocious in history and current events, was aware of Vietnam and its war from an early age. He remembered seeing nothing about it on TV, but he did remember seeing all those protestors at the Academy Awards the year *Coming Home* and Jane Fonda were nominated. It intrigued him that so many people were so angry about some war movies. A couple of years later, when Don was ten years old, WGN out of Chicago actually broadcast *The Deer Hunter*, uncut though with commercials. Don watched it on the small TV in the kitchen with the volume down low so that his parents, in the living room watching their shows, wouldn't know what he was watching. It was an R-rated movie, and they didn't allow him to watch R-rated movies until he was fifteen. Don was a little bored by the first hour or so, especially that long wedding scene, but the word "Vietnam" evoked such a dark mystery as exotic and haunting as the jungles in which the war was fought; plus, every time the show resumed from a commercial break, an announcer warned of the violent nature of the content not suitable for children. So Don kept watching, and even after it ended, he still didn't understand why that word, that war, was an electrical outlet to America's collective finger, always sending some level of voltage through anyone who dared touch it for whatever reason. It wasn't until later, in college, that he began to comprehend the many facets of the Vietnam War, especially on the home front, but when Don was thirteen and his father had told him that Uncle Timmy had fought there, he'd dabbled in the war enough to have a minimal context for what his father was saying.

"What was he like before?" Don asked.

His father shrugged. "Normal, I guess. He ran track. He was a sprinter. Didn't do so hot with his grades, but he did like science. He had a chemistry set in the basement, and he'd do experiments down there for hours. He'd let me be his assistant."

"How much older is he than you?"

"Seven years."

"Did he have a girlfriend?"

His father nodded. "He had a real serious one before he left. You know her. It's Angie Schroeder although it was Angie Heitzig back then." Don did know her. She worked at the stately courthouse building in the center of town which doubled as the City Hall; she was receptionist for the county clerk. "When they were dating, he and Angie took me everywhere. They took me swimming in the river, waterskiing on her family's boat. Summer nights they'd take me for ice cream. They treated me more like a son than a little brother." That explained the extra warm friendliness Angie always displayed whenever Don saw her. He never understood why this slightly older, heavyset woman always took such care to ask all that was happening in his life when she ran into him downtown or at the grocery store or in the gym Friday nights for a high school basketball game, never understood why she and his father held each other's hands and spoke with such sincerity when they chanced to meet, asking how everything was going, how their respective families were doing. "I'm not sure if he asked her to marry him before he left. But I know she didn't date anyone while he was gone."

"What happened?"

"You saw what happened today."

"He's been that way since he got back?"

"He tried living in town for a while, first with our mom and dad, then in his own apartment. He had a job for a while, too, out at Mundy Lumber. He just couldn't handle it.

123

Couldn't be with people. After about a year, he moved out to Crackers' barn. Been there ever since."

"What was it that happened in Vietnam?"

"He's never told me, and I've never asked."

Don continued to occasionally ride with his father out to Uncle Timmy's, the sack or two of groceries in the back seat, but the only other time he ever stepped inside Uncle Timmy's room came a couple of years later, when he was fifteen. It was an absolutely perfect spring day in the middle of May—mid-seventies, mild breeze, low humidity, colorful plants blooming. It was Don's sophomore year, and he had only a couple of weeks of school left. He sat in his Shakespeare class, which all honors English students took their sophomore year, when the office runner for that hour, a pretty freshman in a yellow summer dress, brought a note into Ms. Deatherage, by far Don's favorite teacher. She interrupted her discussion of *Taming of the Shrew* to read the note. "Don," she said, "you're wanted in the office." Don got up, leaving his books behind, and followed the cute freshman. He stared at her feet and couldn't help noticing they were probably half his own size.

His father stood waiting in the office, wearing the khaki pants and blue polo that was his uniform, "Jerseyville Elementary School," emblazoned in white over his left breast. His face was serious. "I want you to go somewhere with me."

"Okay," Don said. "I'll go get my books."

"No. We're leaving now."

Deanna Bridgewater, one of the two secretaries, said, "I'll make sure Ms. Deatherage knows you're not coming back, Don. She'll keep your books until tomorrow."

"Thanks, Deanna," Marcus said.

His father's car was parked in the waiting zone near the exit just outside the office. Don's body felt exhilarated by the playful slap of the bright midday sun and exquisitely fresh air. His mother sat in the front seat of the car, and in the back seat sat Reverend Smith and Angie Schroeder. Angie scooted to the middle to accommodate Don, the third oversized body in a back seat less than spacious. Don immediately rolled down the window, and his father drove. Don knew something wasn't right, and he knew it involved Uncle Timmy, but it was only a few minutes later, once they were on the country roads between fields of green wheat about a couple of feet high and soybeans just barely germinated, that he finally spoke.

"Uncle Timmy's dying," his father said, unemotionally.

"What from?" Don asked.

"Cancer. He's had it a couple of years."

Out at the farm, his father drove with particular slowness down the long gravel driveway, as if averse to anything that might disturb the solemnity. They ambled in a loose group to the barn, his father sort of in the lead, Reverend Smith sort of in the rear. The wind soughed sibilant as their steps through the tall grass of the pasture. Inside Timmy's room, Crackers stood at the foot of the bed looking down on his high school friend. "He's been agitated," Crackers said, short, thick, wearing a yellow T-shirt and faded jeans. "About twenty minutes ago, he started getting agitated, like something's wrong."

Timmy lay on the bed under a couple of blankets, even though the room was warm. The window above his bed was opened, but to little effect. Gray and thin as he'd always been, he was even grayer now, thinner. His eyes were closed, and his hair was wet with sweat. As much as his decimated body would allow, he wriggled and writhed, unable to get comfortable, as if lying down on a couple of thumbtacks. His brother went to him, sat on the bed.

"Timmy," he shouted. "It's Marcus."

"Marcus," Timmy said, his voice strong, his eyes now opened but with a distant gaze. "Oh, Marcus, I did some terrible things, Marcus. I did some terrible, terrible things. I didn't want to. I really didn't want to. But I did some terrible things."

Reverend Smith stepped forward and switched places with Marcus on the bed. "Timmy," he said, not nearly so loudly as Marcus had spoken. "Timmy, it's Delmar Smith."

"Reverend, I've done some terrible things." Don was surprised to hear that Timmy knew who Delmar Smith was. He wondered how long they'd known each other and in what capacity. "Reverend, I just—I don't—I've done some terrible things."

"Shhhh," Delmar said, placing a hand on Timmy's wrist. "It's okay, Timmy. It's okay. We've all done some terrible things."

"Not like I've done, Reverend. I did some terrible things." Timmy's writhe became more pronounced.

"I know, Timmy. I know. It's okay."

"It's not okay, Reverend. It's not okay. And I can't forget them."

"You don't have to forget them, Timmy. Go ahead. Remember them. It's okay. They're all forgiven."

"They were terrible things, Reverend."

"I know, Timmy. I know. They were. They were terrible things done by a child of God to children of God. But the Lord has forgiven them. And the Lord has forgiven you. Go ahead and remember them. They're forgiven."

Timmy closed his eyes and remembered. Whatever terrible things he did, he seemed to Don to recall them, one by one. At times he grimaced and winced, at times his body pitched upward as much as it could, at times he squeezed his eyes extra tight. Don had no idea how long the process lasted. Reverend Smith held Timmy's wrist throughout, and weakened though Timmy was, he visibly squeezed harder during certain moments. Nobody in the room made any motion to leave, any motion at all. Angie Schroeder cried but would not move to wipe her tears. Eventually, Timmy settled down. He ceased writhing, his breathing calmed. He breathed regularly for a few minutes, his body relaxed, and he opened his eyes. His gaze was present; all he saw he saw in the room and only the room. He turned his head to Reverend Smith, and Reverend Smith nodded. For the first time ever, Don saw his Uncle Timmy smile. Reverend Smith nodded again and smiled with him, and he gave Timmy's hand a final squeeze before he rose from the bed and moved over to the side of the room.

Don's father moved in close again, and Timmy regarded him. "I'm dying, Marcus," he said, his voice weak but clearly audible.

"I know."

"I think it's pretty close."

"I do, too."

"I'm not real sorry about it."

"Didn't think you were."

"But I feel good. For the first time in a long time, I feel good."

"About time. Got some folks here I thought you might want to say good-bye to."

Timmy slowly looked around the room. "How long you been standing there, Crackers?"

"Long enough for my feet to be a little tired."

"Rocker's empty."

"You're worth standing for."

Timmy looked at Don. "Your dad tells me you're pretty damn smart, Donny." Don shrugged, completely overwhelmed. "Someone in the family finally had to be." Timmy smiled, and so did everyone else in the room, save for Don, who didn't know what to think about anything. "Sorry I wasn't shit for an uncle, Donny. I wish I'd have given you some fun memories." Don shrugged. "But you've got some good parents. Don't you ever forget that." Don shook his head, unable to say that he wouldn't forget.

Timmy turned to Angie and smiled. "Aw hell, Cakes, what are you doing here?"

Angie was in tears. "You know what, Timmy."

"Come here," he said, smiling faintly. She came to him, sat on the bed and held his hand. "It could have all been different, Cakes." He kept smiling, calm, accepting.

"I don't know, Tim. It just was the way it was."

"It should have been different."

"Yeah, it should have. But it's all okay."

"It is." He nodded and smiled. "It's all okay now."

Timmy turned his head away, as if to look out the window above, envisioning in the clouds and sky what could have been. A few moments later, he asked Marcus to join Angie on the bed. Marcus sat beside her and put his hand on Timmy's leg. Angie and Timmy continued to hold hands. "It's all okay," Timmy said, one more time, quietly. He closed his eyes. Soon came the death rattle, that labored mucousy breathing that clicks in the throat. That lasted nearly ten minutes before it just stopped, and Timmy was dead.

"Have you ever seen someone die?" Don asked Steph in a hushed tone, somewhat choked with emotion from relating the story, unable to speak too much louder and also unwilling, as if all these years later still wary of disturbing the solemnity surrounding Uncle Timmy's death. Steph shook his head. "I've seen a couple of people die," Don said, "and I can tell you this unequivocally: man has a soul. I'm not arguing that there's a God, or that there's a heaven or any kind of afterlife, but I am arguing this: we all have a soul. The moment my uncle died, something vanished from his person, something fundamental to his being—it just disappeared. I witnessed it with my own eyes. His body was still there, and just seconds after he died, it couldn't have changed that much physically. It was the same

body that was alive a moment before. But it was empty. It had
been vacated, immediately, by something that had given it
essence, and what was left behind was truly just a carcass, a
shell. I saw it, and I know what I saw. Make no mistake: we
each of us have a soul, which must necessarily argue for some
kind of afterlife somewhere since that soul must have escaped
somewhere, unless you assume that the soul dies, too, which is
certainly a fair argument. Personally, I'm not even agnostic on
this. I don't give a shit if there's an afterlife or not. If there is,
there is, and if there isn't, there isn't, but I certainly don't base
any of my behavior on the possibility of one. I think the notion
of an afterlife has been leveraged as one of *the* greatest tools of
oppression in the history of the world. But as for me and my
house, I will serve this life."

Don took a massive series of gulps of water, the kind that
made the thin plastic of the Evian bottle crackle. It was a
mighty thirst he had to conquer, one begun by the Nutty Bar
and exacerbated by his tale and sermon. The scenery beyond
their windows was unchanged—hills and trees and occasional
forms of farmyard. Don had driven enough of Pennsylvania in
his life to know that nothing about this scenery would change
save for the names of the towns and the angle of the sun.

"And another thing," Don said, his throat lubricated, his
tone and pitch on the rise, "it's because of Uncle Timmy that I
also believe in God. I saw a transformation overcome him. I
saw Reverend Smith say to Timmy that he was forgiven, and I
saw Timmy not only believe it, I saw him know it. Now I know
the argument—that it was all delusional, that it was wishful
thinking, that Reverend Smith was no more than a placebo of
forgiveness. And by the way, it's folks like Reverend Smith who
give organized religion a good name, which is why I cannot
abide those morons who say they don't believe in organized
religion. It's every bit as dumb as those religious folks who
don't believe in science. You may not believe in everything

organized religion is doing or has done, and God knows you've got some real strong cases when it comes to those fucking Catholics, but that doesn't mean organized religion doesn't exist and hasn't had a major impact in our world. You can't not believe that any more than those religious idiots can't not believe science, which has also had its share of dark tales, although that's not even the stuff that makes the morons disbelieving. What's more, organized religion has done probably just as much good in this world as it has done bad. Even the fucking Catholics have put out their share of really good deeds, although it's usually been against the will of their leadership.

"But organized religion in the form of Delmar Smith did for my Uncle Timmy what no one or no thing else was able to do for twenty years—it gave him peace. And the reason I think that had to be God and not some placebo effect is simply that I just can't imagine a placebo mending the soul. Sure it can mend a body and make pain go away, but the soul is just too powerful for smoke and mirrors."

"Okay, but for the sake of argument here," Steph said, "let me say that I've seen plenty of tortured souls made to seem better through the miracle of drugs."

"No, you haven't."

"Don't tell me what I've seen, white boy."

"You're right. Poorly phrased. Let me put it this way. Timmy's not the only addled vet I've ever seen, nor the only troubled soul. I've seen all kinds, and I've seen them on their meds and off their meds. And when they're on their meds, they may be calm, but they're not at peace. They're dazed, they're glazed, they're stupefied or soporific, but they're not at peace. And that's what I saw with Uncle Timmy; I saw a child of God who had done God knows what to some of his fellow human beings—and I've gone ahead and imagined the worst: raped women in front of their husbands and smashed their babies against a tree—and I saw him at peace, a peace that was clear-eyed and clear-brained. It was achieved without altering one chemical in his brain. I saw it, and call me weak in faith for having had to see it to believe, but that's why I believe in God."

"But I thought you were arguing that God doesn't intervene in this world."

"Giving us the strength to endure whatever happens doesn't change what happens. It just changes our attitudes. The Jews at Treblinka could walk into the ovens peacefully or fitfully, but they were still walking into those ovens."

"That's harsh, Don."

"To my thinking, whenever you're dealing with God, everything has to be put to the Holocaust test."

"Okay. Fair enough. And that's what you believe. That's what you're coming out here with. You're going to tell folks that if they just believe in Jesus, they'll feel better. That's hardly novel."

"A: I'm not going to tell people that. I told you, I don't really know what I'm going to tell people. I'm out here to take on the charlatans and the idiots, and what comes out of my mouth will be dictated by what comes out of theirs. And B: Who said anything about Jesus?"

Steph shook his head and laughed.

At the second meeting of SHAGY, two weeks after the first, the topic discussed was sin—not its significance, not its prevalence, not even punishment meted it out for it. Dane Rhodes, one of the boys who sat in the corner for the first meeting and laughed when Peggy said "put out," was asked ahead of time to prepare a topic, and he started off by saying, "We hear so much about sin, but I just want to know what it is. Everyone always acts so sure about smoking being a sin, but does it say anything about smoking in the Bible? Did people even smoke back then? For some reason, drinking is some big sin, but *everyone* in the Bible seems to be chugging down some wine at some point. There was even that wedding where they ran out of wine, and Jesus turned some water into wine, and everyone was like, 'Hooray for Jesus,' but nowadays it's some big sin to drink, and that's why I'm confused. What is sin?" Dane continued on in this vain a little while longer. Brianna was both surprised and impressed by the intelligence of his topic and the thought he'd put into his presentation. She was also surprised to learn that Pastor Paul had chosen him to bring the topic in the first place, but then she wasn't completely naïve, and she knew the value of co-opting one of the rowdy boys. She never thought Dane was stupid; she just thought he was one of those boys who never cared how stupid he acted. She actually thought he was kind of cute, and after his presentation on sin, he became, to her, even cuter. He not only revealed a depth she never imagined he possessed, he also showed a willingness to plunge into a topic she had always assumed she might have been alone among her peers in considering.

But while Brianna had indeed spent a goodly amount of time contemplating sin, prior to this second SHAGY meeting, she'd never spent that much time wondering what might constitute a sin. She'd always assumed sin was pretty obvious. It *was* smoking. It *was* drinking. It *was* lying, cheating and stealing. But Dane had a point, which he astutely concluded by asking whether or not it was a sin to steal food if your child were starving, especially if you stole it from a bad person who possessed an excess of food because of bad actions, like selling drugs or robbing banks. No sooner had Dane finished than other SHAGY students eagerly brought forth further insightful points, questions and examples. We're supposed to honor our mother and father, but what if they're abusive? Are we not supposed to report them to the police because that would be dishonorable? We're not supposed to tell a lie, but what if a lie saves someone's life? Didn't anyone see *Schindler's List?* Or what if it doesn't save someone's life? What if it's just a small lie to spare someone's feelings, like when an ugly person asks if you think he's ugly? The examples poured forth. The discussion was lively. Pastor Paul served as referee. So many students were so eager to share that at times there was a mélange of voices interrupting and overlapping, vying for the floor. Pastor Paul called on people, maintained order, kept the conversation flowing smoothly and individually. Almost everyone spoke. The only two who didn't were Todd and Brianna. Todd, at one point, rocketed his hand into the air, but Pastor Paul placed his own hand on Todd's knee, whispered something into his ear, and Todd pulled his hand down, nodding in understanding, agreement. And Brianna, well, she simply wasn't ready to share. Not yet. Even if she hadn't been self-conscious about sounding stupid in front of the older kids, which she was, she was too overwhelmed by the onslaught of conversation. There were already too many voices, too much to think about.

"You may not believe this," Pastor Paul said after quite some while, "but we are actually out of time, unless you have no interest in the massive pan of M & M cookies my wife made for you tonight, and I'm willing to bet that's not the case at all. We don't even have time for me to say what I wanted to say about sin to wrap this fantastic discussion up. So here's what I want us to do. First, I want everyone to give a huge round of applause to Dane for bringing us such a great topic and being like Moses, leading us into the Promised Land of a terrific SHAGY meeting. Give it up for Dane." The applause was raucous, and Dane, fists clenched, raised his arms in victory, head bobbing in nod to his fans. "And here's the other thing I want you to do. Over the next two weeks, pick out the peer in your life who would benefit most from this conversation on what is sin. It could be anyone in your school, or even another school, just so long as it's someone in high school. Fill that person in on the conversation we've had tonight, then ask that person to join us here at SHAGY next time we meet in two weeks. Until then, try to spend more time thinking about sin than committing it."

"But how do I know if I'm committing it when I don't even know what it is?" shouted Dane, comedic, cocky, the undisputed champ (for the nonce) of SHAGY. Everyone laughed.

"Dane," Pastor Paul said, "I've got a hunch that you've had a fair amount of practice with sin to know when you're committing it."

"Oh, smack!" Dane's friend, Charlie Laughlin, said, and the room again swelled with laughter.

Brianna wasn't sure whom she should bring. The obvious choice was her best friend, Colleen, but Colleen was Nazarene and, as such, could be real snotty about church. She was just always so sure of her own brand of faith. One Sunday a couple of years back, Brianna's Sunday School class discussed the story of Jesus losing his temper in the Temple and turning over all the tables, making a real mess of the place. The next day, at lunch, discussing the story with Colleen, Brianna said, "Don't you think it's kind of weird, how mad he got?"

Colleen regarded Brianna as if she were the dumbest thing on two legs she'd ever beheld. "Of course he got mad. They were all doing stuff he didn't want them to do."

"But what were they doing that was so bad?"

"I don't know. Stuff. Bad stuff."

"But why did he get so mad? I mean, isn't he the one who said we're supposed to forgive our enemies?"

"Bri, being mad doesn't mean he didn't forgive them."

"I kind of think it does. You don't get mad at someone you forgive. You certainly don't go throwing his tables around."

Colleen couldn't repress her impatience. "Bri, I just can't believe how stupid you're being about this."

"How's that stupid?"

"It's stupid because if Jesus did it, it can't be wrong. Don't you know anything?"

So she was reluctant to bring Colleen. The problem was she didn't have that many other churchy friends. She had a decent number of friends, some of them pretty close, and she certainly knew a lot of people. But Colleen was the only friend she had who was as serious about Jesus as she was, so she really was the logical choice to ask. Besides, she figured it might be good for her to be exposed to Pastor Paul. It might, in some way, humble her, teach her by example that you didn't have to be so obnoxious and fierce as a follower of Christ.

The next day in the school cafeteria, Brianna and Colleen sat together for lunch as they always did. "Last night at SHAGY," Brianna said, "we talked about sin."

"The wages of sin is death," Colleen said. "What more is there to talk about?"

"Actually, we talked about what exactly sin is. Sometimes it's not so obvious."

"Only if you're an idiot."

This was classic Colleen, and it was exactly why Brianna was reluctant to ask her to attend SHAGY. Sometimes she wondered why she was even her friend, but then when they got off the topic of religion, Colleen could be very funny, albeit in a brutally sarcastic fashion. She was also the ideal friend to have if you really needed something, anything from help on homework to a cough drop in class, a ride to some event or just a shoulder to lean on. Her confidence didn't stop at religion. Colleen was simply not susceptible to a sliver of doubt about anything, and in the volatile world of high school, that degree of surety was a comfort to have around, even on the occasions it eventually proved to be wrong, which was usually long enough after the fact that right or wrong no longer mattered. And in times of emergency, accident, mishap or need, there was no one better to have at your side than Colleen. Her ability and willingness to take charge were unparalleled. That's why she was president of her class student council, despite her abrasive tendencies. She sacrificed so eagerly that it didn't seem a sacrifice. Every year, she offered up her family's garage for the week it took her class to construct the homecoming float, and she was happy to do it. Need to raise funds? Put Colleen in charge. At a car wash she organized to benefit an elementary kid suffering from leukemia, Colleen was out in the street, stopping traffic and fairly accosting drivers. "I don't care if you just got your car washed," she told one poor motorist, "and neither does the kid whose life we're trying to save." Or, to another motorist in suit and tie, "So basically you're saying it's more important not to be ten minutes late to work than it is to save someone's life. Nice attitude." That car wash cleared a thousand dollars.

"Actually, sin can be kind of complicated," Brianna said, timid, but willing to go a bit further.

"Prove it." Brianna used the example of stealing food for your starving child, and Colleen, after swallowing her bite of meatloaf sandwich brought from home, said, "Thou shall not steal. Period. It's one of the ten commandments. Remember those things?"

"Of course I do," Brianna said. "But if my child is hungry—"

"If your own child is hungry it's your fault. You don't make somebody else pay for your mistakes. Ever noticed that people getting in trouble for stealing aren't the hard workers and straight-A students of the world?"

Brianna conceded to her initial instinct and decided it was best not to invite Colleen. She was confident Pastor Paul could handle her, but she feared Colleen's ability to dominate a conversation, and she didn't want everyone in SHAGY to resent her for bringing such an irrepressible megaphone to the meeting. Nonetheless, she did think Colleen made a pretty good argument. The Bible *was* pretty clear about stealing, and

Jesus certainly didn't advocate the practice. He did tell rich people to give their money to the poor, but he never told the poor it was okay to sneak into the houses of the rich and take it.

She opted not to ask anyone, but she didn't feel good about that decision. She wondered if she were letting down her SHAGY peers, letting down Pastor Paul. She fervidly hoped she wasn't the only one to arrive unaccompanied, but when, on the night of the next SHAGY meeting, she entered the church foyer and heard the level of noise coming from the basement, she feared that wasn't the case. She took a deep breath and said a quick prayer and headed downstairs, convinced she was going to disappoint Pastor Paul.

"There's our Biblical scholar," he said, beaming at Brianna as she entered. He again stood at the entrance, greeting all as they arrived. Todd, his sidekick, shouted, "Hooray," upon seeing Brianna.

"Pastor Paul," she said, "I'm so sorry, but I couldn't find anyone to come with me."

"Good heavens, Brianna, that doesn't matter at all. You're not the only one to come alone, and besides, the most important thing you bring to SHAGY is your heart hungry for Jesus and your brain thirsty for answers." He leaned into her and confided in a voice just above a whisper, "You've probably given more thought to what sin is than everyone else in this room combined." He leaned back and winked, and all of a sudden, everything for Brianna was just fine.

She doubted that she'd given it more thought than the others combined, but even if it were true, it wouldn't be very Christian to think so. But she had, in fact, given it a decent amount of thought. She'd considered discussing it with her mom but assumed the results wouldn't in any way be helpful. As for her dad, well, he'd never made any bones about how uninterested he was in matters pertaining to faith. She loved her father deeply. At some point during each day, usually in the evening after dinner, he committed to spend fifteen or twenty minutes with her alone and have her tell him about her day—what she learned, what she wanted, what struggles she might be having. When the weather was favorable, this session often took the form of a walk around the block. He always encouraged her and sometimes enlightened her, but on issues of faith, she knew better than to appeal to him.

She looked up sin in the dictionary: "A transgression of a religious or moral law, especially when deliberate." That was little help. It seemed to corroborate Colleen's stringent position, and Brianna simply couldn't shake the idea that stealing food to feed your starving child was not wrong. And that part about it being deliberate: the idea of being held to account for breaking a law you didn't even know you were breaking was just harsh. For two weeks she probed the essence of sin but came to no resolution. So even if she had spent more time around the tree of contemplation, she still walked away with not one fruit to show for it.

Peggy Sneed had brought a friend to the meeting, another girl on the basketball team, but Brianna went and sat next to her anyway. "There's my girl," Peggy said, clapping as Brianna approached then holding up an open palm for a high five, which Brianna felt helplessly awkward giving. "Bri, this is my point-guard peep, Luanne, and Luanne, this is my kid sister, Brianna."

"What up, Bri?" Luanne said. Brianna shrugged. She was thrilled that Peggy had just called her her kid sister; she had no idea that thick of a bond was forming between them. Stephanie Price and Jeff Webb, the other two eighth graders, were both at SHAGY that week, but Brianna no longer minded their presence. She even waved excitedly at Stephanie. They were always going to come eventually, Stephanie and Jeff, and Stephanie might someday even be Peggy's other "kid sister," but Brianna coveted the fact that she would always be the first.

Pastor Paul soon began the meeting, but not before he and Todd and a couple of other boys gathered some more folding chairs from the standing stacks in the corner. The square of four tables was crammed with people, most of whom Brianna didn't know since she wasn't yet in high school. Pastor Paul scanned the tables, taking in all the new faces, and said, "Wow. There's a lot of people here tonight. I may have to pull off Jesus' trick with the loaves and fishes just to feed you at snack time." Half of the room laughed, none more heartily than Todd.

"Dane!" Pastor Paul said, shouting his name with a sudden explosion of playful vigor.

"What up, Pastor P?" Dane shouted back, as if completely unsurprised by his being called out. (Dane had a friend next to him that he'd brought, a boy with a loose, gray flannel shirt and a faded green cap on backwards. Brianna hadn't expected Dane, of all people, to bring a friend. She didn't think he was into the church thing enough to do that.) People laughed at Dane's "Pastor P." comment, but Brianna noted that the only people laughing were original SHAGY members, which made sense. The new kids had no context for anything.

Pastor Paul also smiled, quite pleased, it seemed, with what could feasibly become his new moniker. "Why don't you say the opening prayer, get this meeting going."

"Busted," Dane's friend sitting next to him, Charlie Laughlin, said as the others laughed teasingly.

"Pastor P., I'm not sure you want me saying this prayer."

"Oh, I'm pretty sure I want you saying this prayer," Pastor Paul said, pausing before he added, "SHAGY D."

The room erupted into laughter and applause. Brianna found even herself spontaneously clapping. "Seriously, Dane," Pastor Paul said when the noise subsided, "I'd appreciate it if you opened with a prayer. You don't have to worry about it being right or wrong. You just need to make it honest, and if a prayer is honest, it's perfect. So everyone, let's all bow our heads while Dane prays us into our official meeting."

All present did bow their heads, including Brianna, who also closed her eyes. There was a pause, as if Dane were trying to discern where into the dense forest of possible prayers he could possibly take a first step, before he said, "God, umm . . . it's sure great that we've got a lot of new faces here tonight, and, umm, it's really cool that we've got Pastor Paul, so, umm, just take care of us as we talk about sin. A-men."

"A-men," Pastor Paul hastened before everyone else repeated it in jumbled echo. He thanked Dane then segued into the discussion of sin. He did not introduce new material but rather informed the newcomers that two weeks before they'd had a lengthy discussion on what exactly sin was but came to no conclusion. "The conversation was so good, so insightful, that I thought it would be a terrific benefit to any teenager. That's why I wanted our SHAGY members to invite a friend tonight, and I'm glad that so many of them did." He then revisited some highlights of the previous discussion. Brianna listened, freshly engaged as if all she were hearing was new, but she was still a tad self-conscious that she'd not brought someone. She still believed that Colleen would have screwed up the evening somehow, but there really were any number of people she could have asked. She scanned the tables and calculated that only four or five others hadn't brought a friend. Pastor Paul concluded his recap. "So that's where we left off. And tonight, before I just toss this hot potato of a subject out into the crowd, I want to begin with someone I know has been giving serious thought to the subject, someone with cool enough fingers to handle this sizzling spud. So, Brianna Culp, why don't you tell us what conclusions, if any, you've drawn on the subject of what constitutes sin."

Brianna was stunned to hear her name. She was still busy enough chuckling with some others on the "sizzling spud" phrase that it was a few seconds before it fully registered that she was being called upon to speak. She stared her doe eyes into the headlights of his cue, and she received no solace from Peggy clapping immediately upon hearing Brianna's name and shouting, "Go, Little B."

"To be fair," Pastor Paul said, "Brianna had no idea I was going to call on her, so it's more than understandable that she's a bit taken aback. But I also know how serious a student of Christ she is, so I'm sure that once she finds her tongue, she's going to tell us something worth hearing. So, Peggy, do me a favor and look under her chair." Peggy complied. "Is her tongue under there?"

"Sure is, Pastor P."

"Great. Hand it to her so we can get this thing rolling."

Peggy mimed the handing of a tongue to Brianna, who surprised herself by holding out her hand to receive it, and after everyone clapped, Pastor Paul nodded reassuringly to Brianna, who took a breath and jumped into the waters of her monologue.

"I couldn't get past the example about stealing food for your starving child," she began. "I just couldn't see how that could be a sin, even though the Bible says not to steal." She informed everyone about how she looked "sin" up in the dictionary, and she related the definition, verbatim. "And that confused me even more." The Old Testament, she continued, says that we should honor our mother and father and that children who don't should be stoned to death. "No way," a couple of boys shouted, rattling her, but Pastor Paul came to her defense by calmly stating, "Deuteronomy 21: 18 - 21," and those boys, as well as some others, shook their heads in disbelief. Brianna, newly confident, continued. "And what really confused me is that there are a bunch of different religious laws." The Jews, she explained by example, think it's a sin to eat pork, "but we don't, so is it? Heck, some churches don't even think abortion is a sin, and I can't think of anything more evil than abortion, but if having one doesn't break their religious law, then are they committing a sin if they have one? I think they are, but they don't." Brianna shook her head. "So you see my problem. I did all this thinking on what sin is, but by the end I was more confused than ever. Anyway, that's all I've got. It probably doesn't help much, but like I said, that's all I've got."

A hand across the room shot up; it belonged to one of the guests, a girl with streaks of neon green and pink in her blond hair. Pastor Paul pointed at her and said she could speak only if she gave her name. "Josie," the girl said. "Josie Chollet." Then she spoke about divorce. Her parents were divorced, which she said was a good thing since her father was a drunk, but their family was Catholic, and ever since the divorce her mom was not allowed to take communion. "Am I the only one to think that's really effed up?" Other hands were raised. One girl said her grandparents always warned her that it was a sin to talk in church. One boy had a brother fighting in Iraq and wondered if it was a sin to kill in battle. Another boy with a father in the Reserves in Iraq took it a step further, wondering if it was a sin to kill an enemy soldier but a greater sin to kill an innocent civilian. "I worry about Dad," the boy said. "I worry about the things that might happen to him and the things he might have to do." The conversation flowed; the students were vivified and engaged. One even said, "Man, I'd give twenty bucks for school to be this interesting." Some students made a point, some students asked a question, some students felt compelled to try to answer the question. A wide variety of examples continued to be brought up for debate, and while the conversation generally avoided sex, one boy did say, "I've got a problem with that thing Jesus said about it being a sin if I lust in my heart. I mean, hey, I can't help what I think, especially if she's in tight shorts and a tiny T."

"Praise Jesus," Pastor Paul said after the conversation had gone nearly an hour. "I am amazed by the insight and wisdom that has come out of your mouths tonight and by the intelligence of your questions. It's never wrong to question your faith, question your religion, question your God. After all, it was on the cross that Jesus himself questioned God when he said, 'Why have you forsaken me?' So questioning is fine, but the trick is that you need to be prepared to live with the answers. Once you know the right answer, or the answer to righteousness, then it becomes a sin not to live by it. Which brings me to the answer to tonight's question: what is sin?"

Pastor Paul said it was very simple. He said that sin was absolutely anything that pulls you further away from God. That's why it is said that when we're born, we're born into a life of sin. He explained that we are closest to God when we're in heaven after we die but also when we're in our mother's womb. Therefore, when we enter this world from that womb, we're pulled further from God. That sin is not our fault, but it's still a sin. And we enter a world where it is very easy to do things that might pull us away from God. "That, in general, is sin, but of course it gets trickier when you get into specifics. For instance, our friend Josie brought up divorce. The Catholic Church does consider it a major sin, but if you read the Bible closely, you will see that divorce is permitted. In Matthew nineteen, Jesus does say that what God has joined together let no man tear asunder, but that doesn't mean that God can't tear it asunder, and how is any mortal to know for sure whether or not someone else's marriage has been torn asunder by God? If you've married the wrong person, someone who beats you or someone who steals the children's lunch money for drugs, God can certainly tear that marriage asunder. In chapter nineteen of Matthew, verse nine, Jesus explicitly permits divorce because of unchastity, and it's pretty clear that chastity is more than just a sexual issue."

Pastor Paul also addressed Brianna's question of other religions. He said that yes, Jews don't eat pork because they abide by the laws of the Old Testament, and one of those laws does forbid it, but for Christians it's different because in the book of Acts, God clearly tells Peter that it's okay to eat pork henceforward. "And while it's true that Jews may go to Hell after dying because they never accepted Jesus as their messiah," he said quite casually, matter-of-factly, as if going to Hell were no more eventful than heading to the store because you ran out of bread, "it's important to note that God, in the Old Testament, made his covenant with the Jews, and nowhere in the New Testament does he break it. What's between God and the Jews is between them, and while it's always good to help others find the Lord, you need to be most concerned about *your* relationship with Christ. You need to be obsessed with how near or far *you* are from God."

"But how do you know what's right?" blurted one student, an original SHAGY member, a short-haired, healthy boy with a chiseled, square chin and an untucked blue Oxford shirt. "If sin is moving away from God, how do we know we're moving away? When I was born, I didn't have any idea I was moving away. I'd just been born." Everyone laughed, but the boy's earnest expression, even through the laughter, made it clear that his humor was inadvertent.

"This," Pastor Paul said, holding out his arms, palms down. "This is how you know. Through study and discussion. After all, because of tonight's discussion, you now know why it's okay for a Christian to eat pork."

"But if I didn't come here tonight," the boy followed up, "I wouldn't have known that."

"Bingo," Pastor Paul said. "That's why I wanted you here, and that's why I wanted SHAGY members to bring a friend. Because they are here, your friends, they now know what sin is and how to avoid it. You know, sure, but you were going to know anyway because you were already coming. That's why it's so important that as many of you as possible come to church, come to SHAGY. The more you come, the more you'll know how to avoid sin, and the better the world will be.

"And one more thing. At the risk of sounding boastful, which is the second-to-last thing a Midwesterner ever wants to be. (The absolute last thing a Midwesterner wants to be is late to a potluck dinner.)" Modest laughter on that. "Tonight also highlights the importance of your pastor. In the twelfth chapter of Romans, the Apostle Paul tells us that though we are all members of the body of Christ, all members do not have the same function. Some of us are here to be teachers, some deacons, some members of the choir, and some to collect the offering or administer to the day-to-day needs of the church, which are vital and many. After all, even church toilets get clogged, and God may be able to move mountains, but I have yet to see Him answer the call for plumbing."

Again the group laughed, mirthful but not raucous. They were all in thrall. Not one was disruptive, not one slightly fidgety. It was as if they were watching a great movie, but not a thriller, for the mood was calming and calm, as was Pastor Paul's delivery. It was the type of calmness that could be borne only of deep certainty, and by her pastor's tone, Brianna knew that what she was hearing was the unimpeachable truth.

"Let every person be subject to the governing authorities," Pastor Paul continued on, pleasant, pleasing, quiet and sure. "That's also from the Apostle Paul, the next chapter in Romans. 'For there is no authority except from God, and those that exist have been instituted by God. Therefore, he who resists the authorities resists what God has appointed, and those who resist will incur judgment.' In other words, as your pastor, I have been instituted by God as your authority on faith. I didn't seek this job. It just happened as God wanted it to happen. And to resist my authority in faith and the scriptures will, according to God, incur judgment. That's just the way it is."

Pastor Paul gave the room such a warm, generous, beatific smile, and because of that smile, coupled with the logic of his argument, Brianna had no choice or desire but believe with all her heart all that he'd said.

Steph wanted to know what Don's beef with Jesus was, but Don said that would have to wait for later. It was almost two in the afternoon, and they were already nearly halfway across Pennsylvania. "That's too fast," Don said. If he was going to give himself a chance of encountering something, anything, of religious interest, he had to slow down. "Can't change the world if it's just a blur outside your window."

"So what's your remedy? Drive slower?"

"My remedy is to stop."

"For lunch?"

"For the day. Saw a billboard for a campground ahead. Should be just a few more miles."

"The closer we are to actually camping," Steph said, "the less appealing the idea of it is becoming." He looked out the window, up into the ancient, blunt green mountains. "There's got to be some cougars and bears up in those hills."

"You've never done *any* kind of camping before?"

"Who was I supposed to camp with? My seventy-year-old grandma? All my Bed-Stuy friends who barely wanted to go into Manhattan let alone the woods?" Steph was raised by his grandmother on his mother's side. According to his mother, his father was a petty thief back in Port-au-Prince where he spent life in and out of jail, but her credibility was severely limited. When Steph was six, she abandoned him to go live with a boyfriend in Tampa who said he didn't want a kid around. Once he became old enough to understand fully what she'd done, he resented her ferociously for a couple of years, and while the resentment, like malaria, never completely left him, he found a way through force of will to keep the ferocity episodic. Ironically, that battle was made easier by the fact that every six months or so, she would still phone him just to see how "her baby" was doing. (After he spoke with her, he realized how much better off he was not having her around.) "Can you believe the audacity she had to call me 'her baby?'" he said to Don on a cold March night a few months after they'd first met. They were the only two in Steph's shop while he closed up. When Steph put that question to Don, his tone wasn't angry; it was conversational, factual, as if he'd just said to Don, "Her eyes were brown." For the most part, he overcame his resentment of her because he realized his entire neighborhood was rife with parenting situations gone askew; what's more, because of the steadfast devotion of his grandmother and the regular attention and assistance of an uncle out on Long Island, he knew he still fared better than most in Bed-Stuy in the upbringing game. "Besides," he told Don toward the end of that March conversation, "even as a teen, you can spend only so much time pissed off, and then it just gets tedious, not to mention clichéd." His Long Island uncle was an engineer, graduate of SUNY Binghamton, and he'd focused Steph's gaze on college and career from a pretty early age. Angry black teen didn't fit into that game plan.

"What about Brandeis?" Don asked. "No weekend getaways into the Berkshires? No camping spring breaks?"

"The outdoorsy Jews weren't really the ones I was hanging with."

"You'll be fine," Don said. "These campgrounds are actually a lot less remote than they appear."

"For a few years now I've been reading in the news about bears strolling onto Main Street in Jersey and Westchester towns. Remote no longer seems to be a requirement for wildlife."

Don waved off his concerns. "It's all about food. If they can't smell it, they won't come, and they won't be able to smell it locked away in the car."

"Maybe. But I vote that two nights a week, we find a hotel."

"Hotels ain't cheap. Even the cheap ones."

"I'll pay. And they're cheaper than funerals."

Don laughed. "Relax. I've camped in spots all over this country, and nothing has ever happened to me, not even a spider bite."

"You ain't black. Bad shit just has a way of finding us."

"You're on a mission from God now," Don countered. "You're protected. Yahweh's not about to let some four-legged creature interfere with His work."

Five miles of divided highway, one exit and three miles of two-way highway later, they were at their campground, a KOA. Don had pitched his tent at KOAs across the country but never did learn what the letters stood for. He hoped it wasn't Kampgrounds of America but never pursued the truth for fear it might be. Don had long admired Walt Whitman's ability to embrace, seemingly without judgment, everything and everyone, and he figured he'd be a better person if he at least tried to do the same. If nothing else, he thought he'd get a lot less riled a lot less often, but then he came to appreciate an agitated state now and then, which often led to bursts of energy and commitment, and such an open-ended tolerance like Walt's would have included abolishing certain pet peeves, such as cute misspellings, which he found so galling that when he lived down South, he could never bring himself to enter a Krispy Kreme, no matter how strong his craving for a pastry or how convenient a store's location. During the day, any grocery store had a bakery section open, and those more than met his needs, especially those apple fritters, crispy on the outside, doughy on the inside, that were the size of a football. But in the wee hours, when the urge struck and those stores were closed, he could be sorely tempted to compromise his principle and probably would have had it not been for the succor of a Waffle House. He didn't pursue the truth behind the letters KOA because campgrounds were simply too few to risk having to forgo.

The campground office was a small, wooden building, white, in need of a fresh coat of paint but not chipping, just dingy. It was surrounded by a copse of pines and fronted by an abbreviated gravel parking lot. Don was pleased to see that the campground itself was wooded and not the unshaded expanse he was wont to get in the Midwestern and Plains states. An aged air-conditioner unit hung in one of the windows, but it wasn't turned on. Inside was cooled by opened windows and fans, a small plastic, oscillating fan on the front counter, a massive, institutional-sized metal fan standing in the corner, blowing the gale of a beach breeze.

"'And when you see the south wind blowing,'" Don said in stentorian tones just inside the old wooden screen door, "you say, 'There will be scorching heat.'" He stared at the fan, rather amazed by how hard it blew, but no papers were flying about, and the room was comfortably cool.

"Luke, chapter twelve, verse fifty-five," came the voice from the young man behind the counter, trim, handsome in a bucolic way, disheveled hair, skin with some color, faded jeans and a purple and green checked shirt. He continued: "You know how to interpret the appearance of the earth and sky, but why do you not know how to interpret the present time?"

"A man who knows his scripture," Don said, moving forward, Steph in baffled tow.

"Not really," the kid said. "I was a meteorology student at Penn State. I had an uber-Christian prof who always used to throw that quote out at us. Then he'd tell us never to forget

149

that no matter the condition of our skies, the everlasting skies were always more important."

"Surprised he got away with that."

"He was tenured."

"Surprised students took his class."

"Climatology 101. It was required for us meteorology students. And a lot of the Christian students took it for their science elective. They were worse than him. He'd want to get back to actual weather, and they kept wanting to discuss the everlasting skies. One kid even wrote his paper on what he thought the weather would be like in Paradise."

"Takes all kinds."

"You are not shitting there." The kid held up his hand in apology. "Sorry if I offended you."

"No offense taken, son," Don said, wondering, again, where exactly this tone and diction sprang from. He'd not intended to come in spouting the Bible. Since that spooky encounter a few hours earlier with his Little-Debbie-fellow-traveler clerk, he'd privately resigned himself to easing up on the Don Prophet routine a bit, at least until he had a better grasp on a given situation. Now, he was a bit unnerved by the minnow of a gospel quotation that had slipped so quickly through the fingers of his intentions. A student of literature, he was prone to frequent bouts of allusion, usually just quietly kept to himself, and upon seeing that fan, he could have just as easily come forth with, "Western wind, when will thou blow." He was getting a bit nervous. His mouth seemed to be operating with a will of its own.

"So what can I help you guys with?"

"Looking for a spot to camp for the night."

"Believe I can accommodate that."

"You still a student?"

"Graduated a couple of years back."

"What are you doing here?"

"World's not running short of meteorologists right now. Campground belongs to my mother. Helping her run it till something pans out. Maybe graduate school."

Don stuck out his hand to shake. "Name's Don Prophet. This is my friend, Stephan. We're pleased to stay here."

"Name's Danny Rogers. Here's a key to the restroom. And I'm pleased to have you here. Twenty-nine fifty, please."

Danny told them to pick any spot and come back later to let him know where they'd chosen. Don drove the car over the large, gravel loop of a road that circled within the campground, campsites on either side, and at present there were only two other occupied campsites, both with motor homes, but their residents were nowhere to be found. The restroom was a square, brick building in the center of the campground. He chose the site furthest from the office, got out of the car and went to the trunk where he removed the tent tightly wrapped in its nylon bag. He stepped onto the dusty ground of campsite twenty-eight, denoted by the number painted on its standing outlet, and he looked for the flattest spot of the packed, grassless soil covered heavily by pine needles and some leaves. The air smelled fully of pine. Don dropped the tent which landed with a tinging thud and took a massive nose inhalation.

"Smell that," he said. "You don't get that in Brooklyn."

"You don't get cougars and bears, either," Steph said, still standing directly next to the car, looking circumspectly out into the trees beyond the tall pines under which they camped. Don did think Steph looked helplessly out of place, but that probably had more to do with his clothes than anything else, the black jeans, green Oxford, loafers, not exactly travel clothes and certainly not camping clothes, but Don had never seen Steph be anything but dapper, and he'd no doubt change into something a bit more appropriate for bedtime.

Don set up the tent in short order and opened its flaps to air it out. He proposed that they relax there a little while and walked to the office where he told Danny the number of their campsite. He asked if there were a couple of lawn chairs he could rent, and Danny told him just to take two of the metal folding chairs there in the lobby. "You'll have only two left," Don said.

"No sweat. We're past peak season, and it's a weekday."

"I'd also like to buy a small bundle of that firewood out front."

"Ten bucks. It'll be plenty to get you through the night."

Don returned to the campsite carrying the folding chairs in one hand, the wood in the other. Steph still stood next to the car, stiffly, looking out into the deeper woods. Don dropped the wood next to the circle of ash surrounded by stones and set up the folding chairs. He grabbed his *Philadelphia Inquirer* from the car and sat on a chair and opened the paper, and Steph did move tentatively towards the other chair but constantly looking out into the woods, keeping watch.

"Bring anything to read?" Don asked.

"I'd prefer not to."

"Suits yourself, Bartleby, but if an animal sneaks up on us, it's probably not going to be during daylight hours."

"Not very comforting, Prophet."

"A prophet's job is to speak the truth."

"I may be nervous, but it's also mesmerizing for me to just sit and stare into the woods—an intoxication of new surroundings."

"When I first moved to the city, I used to sit in Washington Square for hours, just watching, agog."

An hour later, Don folded up the paper and suggested they head into town for dinner. "Small towns shut down pretty early, and besides, we didn't really have lunch." Steph asked if Don found anything of religious interest in the paper, and Don shook his head. On the slow drive out of the campground, Don stopped and popped his head into the office for a restaurant recommendation. Danny said that if they didn't want Dairy Queen or Pizza Hut, the only other option was a diner at the end of Main Street. "Pretty good. Standard diner fare. Avoid the souvlaki. Not sure why it's still on the menu."

Don ordered the chicken fried steak with mashed potatoes, all of it smothered in a white gravy, none of it standard fare in any New York diner. Steph kept it to a burger and fries although he did order a salad and was disappointed when he was served a chilled plate topped with iceberg lettuce, carrot slivers and two slices of tomatoes pink as salmon. "I can get a better salad on an airplane. I'm out here in the heartland. Why can't I get some fresh romaine?"

"Your not in the heartland, city boy. That doesn't really start until Ohio, and even then not until Columbus, or at least Zanesville. As for the lettuce, supply and demand. These folks don't want romaine. They want iceberg."

"Why would anyone prefer iceberg to romaine?"

"Too much flavor in romaine. In rural America, bland is king. Go to Minnesota and you can get entire meals that are white—boiled whitefish, boiled potatoes, iceberg lettuce with some kind of white dressing, Ranch or Creamy Italian. Even the dessert will be a Lady Baltimore cake."

"Speaking of white," Steph said, gesturing to the room with a few other customers.

"Yeah, you're probably not going to see many of you out here, especially in the real small towns."

"At least they're not staring."

"They've seen enough of you on TV not to be wowed."

"Or burning crosses."

"They don't break those out until after nightfall."

It was approaching nightfall when they returned to their campground, the eventide sky pink and blue, like an Easter outfit. Don loved October more than any other month, save June, but he did regret the shortening of days, especially at the

end of the month when those clocks were fallen back, an act
Don had no idea why we still did anymore. A few more
campers had pulled in, one with an actual camper behind its
truck, a couple of others with tents, but none had taken a
· campsite nearly as far back as Don had. He parked and
immediately got out, but Steph was a bit more circumspect
about the process. He returned to standing near the car, as if a
quick getaway might be in order.

Don grabbed a lighter from the car and used it to burn the
twine holding the wood in a bundle. He built a fire using sheets
of his *Inquirer* balled up under some of the thinner logs. He
commented on how the paper was at least good for something.
Steph still hung by the car. "You'll be safer over here by the
fire," Don told him.

"Are you saying there's an issue of safe and safer?"

"You're going to make this an awful long night for
yourself."

"I'm just out of my element."

"And yet I do marvel that you feel safer walking down
Bedford Avenue at three a.m. than you do here tonight."

"First off, Bedford Avenue's got streetlights. And secondly,
don't go throwing that Countee Cullen shit at me. Every time I
hear the words 'Harlem Renaissance,' and then I hear his name
being tossed out as a primary example, I always think that if
that's the best they could do, that was no renaissance."

"That's it. Find yourself some dudgeon. That'll get you
relaxed."

Steph, smiling now, walked toward the fire where Don,
small logs catching, threw on a larger log. "Langston Hughes,
too," Steph said, sitting in the empty folding chair near the
growing fire. "'Dream Deferred' and 'Negro Speaks of Rivers'
my black ass. Back in the day, when we didn't have *any*one's
literature to brag about, okay, fine, use his stuff to make our
case for literary relevance. But since then we've had Rita Dove,

Thylias Moss, Yusef Komunyakaa, Toni Morrison, David Bradley, and on and on. Hell, we even got kids getting in on the act now: Edwidge Danticat, Colson Whitehead, Z. Z. Packer. So let's go ahead and say it: Langston Hughes' poetry is little more than childish, simplistic aphorisms with random and irrelevant line breaks. His shit reads like a Hallmark card for ghetto kids. From fifth grade to twelfth, not a school year went by when I didn't have to read his tripe, and by the time I hit my senior year, I even told the teacher, 'Langston Hughes shows just how slim our black poetry pickings were. He's an example of how good we weren't.'"

"Did you get in trouble?"

"Absolutely not. Teacher was white, and he didn't dare scold me for hating on one of my own. But he did ask if there were any white authors I thought were similarly overrated."

"What did you say?"

"I said *To Kill A Mockingbird* was the most ridiculous book that white folks kept trying to fob off on us as adult literature. Seriously, D., that shit is childish. First off, if those white folks thought nigger Tom raped little white Mayella Ewell, his black ass isn't even making it to a trial. It's some strange fruit swinging from a southern tree. And then that scene where those little kids turn away an angry mob. Come on, man. It's a mob. Mobs don't give a shit who's in their way. I'm not saying it's not a decent little story . . . for third graders, but can we stop treating it like a great piece of literature? It's no more than a sweet little sermon to make white folks feel good about being progressive for liking it."

"What about *Things Fall Apart*?"

"Same shit, different continent, and bor-ing. But enough of my rant. Time for you to tell me about your problems with J.C. because I'll tell you right now, Mr. Prophet, I'm a fan. He told some hard truths to some people, and he stuck his neck out for the downtrodden and oppressed, and that shit goes a long way for a black man in America."

"You religious?"

"I don't know about that, but every Sunday growing up, I got dragged by my grandma to St. George's Episcopal Church on Marcy Avenue, and never once did I hear anything I disagreed with. And I knew a lot of black folk who had some real tough lives get what they needed to get from that church in order to get through one more week, so there was something real going on there. Hell, I was a pretty easy kid to raise, didn't get into any trouble at all, but raising me still had to be one tough job for my grandma, especially since it was her own daughter who just up and walked away from me, and yet I never saw her as anything but peaceful and calm, so something profound was happening at St. George's."

Something profound probably was happening at St. George's; Don didn't deny that. In fact, something profound and real was happening at churches all over the country, all over the world: Don said that was the point he was making with his Uncle Timmy's deathbed story. But still, there was a real problem with Jesus as he saw it, and it had to do with, "the shamelessly transparent marketing of the Gospels." Start with the virgin birth. By the time Jesus was born, enough prophets in the world had been borne of virgins that the success of that narrative detail was indisputable, so of course if you're going to have a messiah, he has to be borne of a virgin. "Not with the Gospel of Mark, though. That was the first one written, and there's no talk of a virgin birth in there. Mark doesn't even deal with Jesus' birth or childhood; he cuts straight to John the Baptist. It's only with Matthew and Luke, which were written once they all realized that maybe the world wasn't going to end in a few months, that we get the elaborate birth stories, and clearly that's a marketing ploy to appeal to the masses. It's like

Mark was the Gospel they ran by a test audience before they started making some changes."

Then there was the wholesale kissing of Rome's ass, everything from "Render unto Caesar what is Caesar's" to pinning the death of Jesus on the tail of the Jews. That execution was strictly a Roman affair. The Gospel of John makes it look as if the Jews wanted Jesus killed for blasphemy but had to fob the actual execution off onto the Romans for legal purposes, which Don said was historically bullshit. "When it comes to books that were just flat-out bad for the Jews, the Gospel According to John, historically speaking, rivals *Mein Kampf,* and at least Hitler didn't sugar it all up with poetic language." No, clearly those early Christians knew their politics. They knew Rome was tolerant of all other religions as long as they didn't make Rome look bad, and since Rome *did* look bad by killing Jesus, smart politics dictated that blame needed to be placed elsewhere. And of course the Jews got pegged with it. "They got pegged with everything until you guys came along.

"Next comes the issue of everything Jesus says. Basically, he takes both sides of every coin." He says he comes to make peace, and he says he comes to make war. He tells one group he's come to uphold the Law, he tells another group he's come to abolish the Law. He scolds one disciple that he who is not against us is with us, he scolds another that he who is not with us is against us. "No matter what you believe, it's in the Gospels. If you want fire and brimstone and folks consigned to everlasting hell, it's in there. And if you want peace and love and feeding the hungry, clothing the naked, helping the poor, it's in there." The genius of Jesus, Don contended, wasn't so much the fact of who he was; it was the fact of his being a mirror to whomever you were, you are. "Who do you say I am?" Well, that's the point, and that's the problem. "It shouldn't matter who I say you are. What matters is who the fuck are you?" The ploy was Politics 101. Don had read that the genius of FDR was that no matter what position you held, whenever you had a meeting with him, you left the room convinced that you and he were in agreement. It was the same with Jesus, and all across the world were millions of followers with vastly different beliefs who were convinced they were on the Lord's side, the Lord was on their side, and they had the scripture to prove it. How else to achieve such a vast and diverse popularity but with a top-notch marketing campaign? Dozens of gospels were written. Even Judas had one which, like Faulkner and Joyce, had its small band of advocates. But you're not going to sway the masses with Faulkner and Joyce, and so the Gospel of Judas, like that of Thomas and Mary and dozens of others, didn't make the final cut. And what did make the final cut was an assortment that had a little something for everyone—a sampler platter for the faithful.

"And it all became ridiculously obvious to me one day when I was reading the Gospel According to Luke. I was reading chapter six, which basically has it all. It starts with some sly anti-Semitism, cuts to some warm and fuzzy beatitudes to make the poor feel okay with being fucked, then rounds it all out with a tidy message of personal doom if you do not heed Jesus." Early in the chapter, in the Jew-bashing verses, Jesus enters a synagogue where, lo and behold, there's a man with a withered arm. Jesus then challenges the Pharisees on what humans are allowed to do on the Sabbath before he casually heals the man's withered limb. And the Pharisees, of course, are furious and launch into a discussion of what they might do to Jesus in retribution for performing such an act on the Sabbath. "And it was on that day that I figured out I was being lied to in order to win me over. That was my own little bolt of lighting on the road to Damascus, and in that bright light of my awakening I saw the commercial for what it was: a commercial. How did I know I was being lied to? Look, I know plenty of tight-assed folks who get a real hard-on for making us follow the rules. Those Pharisees aren't strangers to me. But even the tight-assed fascists I know, every one of them would be a bit amazed to see someone's arm healed in an instant right under their fucking noses. And when a story tells me that a group of guys watches someone turn another man's arm from a raisin into a grape and then tells me that not one of those guys said, 'Holy shit, did you see that?' but rather, 'Hey, he can't do that'—when a story tells me that, I know I'm being lied to and that, as with all lies, there's a very specific reason why.

"And that's why I struggle with Jesus. If he were really the messiah, then it seems to me that the writers and canonizers of the gospels shouldn't have had to resort to such obvious marketing ploys to convince the rest of us. Say what you will about the Old Testament, but Yahweh never goes out of *His* way to make you like him. It's His way or the highway, and if you don't like it, too fucking bad. And that the Old Testament never tries to hide the fact that fifty percent of the time, Yahweh is a real dick—frankly, that makes Yahweh a bit more plausible to me."

Steph stared into the fire. Night had fallen fully, and the darkness in the surrounding woods was seamless, thorough, resolute, but throughout his monologue, Don fed logs to the fire, making it, and him, a substantial giver of light and heat, the latter of which wasn't that vital that night. The other campsites offered their own idle, spaced semaphores—lanterns, campfires, fluorescent bulbs shining from within the motor homes. Steph slid his reflective gaze from the fire to Don. "That is quite possibly the most air-tight argument I have ever heard against Jesus as the messiah."

"It's not my goal, debunking Jesus."

"I didn't say it was."

"Hell, I'd love to take a seat on the Jesus party bus. It's just that, well, for years I stood in awe at the spread of the Gospel. I mean, the Mormons and Jehovah's Witnesses and every other missionary may be a bit kooky, but there's still something pretty impressive in their effectiveness, even if I do think mission work is a rather hostile fruit of a colonial mind-set. And I've spoken with ministers and theologians I deeply respect about this spreading of the Word, wondering how it could be possible. And to a person (or a parson; sorry, bad pun) they all said it was the Resurrection. Even the ones who don't read the Bible literally, who are the only ones whose opinion I would respect, even they took the actual Resurrection and Ascension as literal fact, and that's their argument for the effectiveness of the spread of the Gospel. But Islam is spreading much faster right now, and other religions are certainly growing in number, and they don't believe in the Resurrection, so I figured something else had to be going on, and I could only conclude it was the operative ethics of Hollywood: give the people what they want, even if, collectively, what they want is rife with contradiction."

"I'm not arguing with you, D. I'm applauding your logic."

"Yeah, well, the only downside is that faith and logic are on opposite sides of the ring."

"That could be," Steph said, slowly rising, "but I've had enough of God talk for one day. Hand me the keys."

"Driving to a hotel?"

"I'm getting my pillow and blanket out of the trunk." Steph did not own a sleeping bag, and Don had told him that a couple of blankets would be just fine given that the weather was still warm. Steph pulled Don's sleeping bag and pillows out of the trunk and carried them to Don before he gathered his own bedding and walked to the passenger's side of the car.

"What are you doing?" Don asked.

"I'm reclining this seat and sleeping in here where no cougar or bear stands a chance in hell of accessing my black ass. And nothing you say can persuade me into that tent, so don't even try."

Steph got into the car, and after awhile, Don crawled into
the tent where he zipped himself in and unrolled his sleeping
bag and lay on top of it. He could see the fire through the
screen and hear its crackles and pops. The air smelled of
woodsmoke and pine trees and the faint aroma of the tent's
musty nylon, and normally that olfactory combination would
be a deep comfort to him, but not that night. He could not rid
himself of two vivid memories from the day: his quoting of
scripture upon entering the campground office and the face of
the gas station clerk as he drove away, especially her nod, which
struck Don as disturbingly similar to a head bowed in prayer or
allegiance.

There was a pronounced spike in the numbers at SHAGY.
Dozens of students came and went over the weeks, but one year
after SHAGY began, it contained a solid core of nearly forty
members who attended regularly—the ten or so from the
original meeting plus thirty others coming from various
corners, some enticed from a churchless life into a churchy one,
some poached from other church youth groups, some attracted
by word-of-mouth from neighboring small towns, largely
because their parents had heard of the new pastor and had
come to investigate and were wowed into commitment. (Which
was why there was also a commensurate spike in the numbers at
the First Assembly of God in Tuttle, Pennsylvania, in general.
One of the more fervent new families was that of Josie Chollet,
the blond SHAGY guest with pink and green streaks in her hair
whose divorced mother was banned from communion in her
Catholic Church. Her mother, Betsy, was so energetic that
some said she was on the fast track to becoming a deacon, but
Betsy said she wanted no part of it, she was just pleased to
finally be accorded, by her church, the respect and dignity she
thought all human beings deserved.) All in the congregation
agreed that Pastor Paul appealed so much to young people

because he focused on what they needed to hear. He led discussions on *their* problems, not pretending they didn't exist. They talked about pressure to perform in the classroom or on the field of play, pressure to get into a good college, pressure to succeed. They talked, also, about the pressures of Satan that could come via peers—alcohol, drugs and, of course, sex. Some parishioners voiced concern at the pastor discussing sexual issues with their children, but other parishioners were quick to ask who else they might prefer addressing these topics with their children. The former were swayed.

But it wasn't just meetings. Pastor Paul actively engaged SHAGY in serving others. On one Friday night, parents in town who needed a break from their children but couldn't afford babysitting were encouraged to bring those children to the church where, for four hours, the teens of SHAGY watched over and played with them. That event was so successful that it became a regular occurrence—the third Friday of every month. Single parents from all over Tuttle were especially grateful. For Thanksgiving, Pastor Paul helped SHAGY organize food baskets to be delivered to underprivileged families; they held a series of fundraisers to buy the food and surreptitiously gathered the names of the needy from friends and neighbors in the know. There was also a school-supply drive, a new clothing drive and a Christmas gift drive, but the gifts had to be what SHAGY deemed "Jesus-approved," thus articles and toys that encouraged Christian values—not tight-fitting or gangsta clothing, no needlessly violent video games, no books or DVDs of subversive messages such as *Harry Potter* or *The March of the Penguins.*

For herself, Brianna had never been so spiritually satisfied. She was not only getting answers and strategies to help her contend with the growing issues of being a teen, she was also getting, slowly, solid responses to her own theological concerns. Not all of them, but then as Pastor Paul told her, no one among us will ever have all the answers to our questions about God, which is why we refer to our religious activities as faith-based and not knowledge-based. "If we knew everything," he told her, "there'd be no need for faith and therefore no need to rely upon Christ." She also derived great spiritual gratification from the hours she committed to serving others. She was so fortified by this component that away from SHAGY she constantly sought smaller ways to serve others—tutoring peers who struggled in math (she was a math whiz), volunteering on weekends for Meals on Wheels, bicycling once a month to a local nursing home where for a couple of hours she sat and visited with the lonely elderly. She was delightfully surprised by how fascinating it was to converse with them, especially Bill Martin, a veteran of the European theater in World War II who was there the day they liberated Auschwitz. In school, she'd always found the study of WWII rather dull. No longer. Now, because of her time with Bill, all those words—Normandy, Patton, *blitzkrieg*—came to dazzling life.

And yet, there was one thing that nagged at her: she'd not yet brought a new person to SHAGY. At the end of every meeting, just after Pastor Paul had asked everyone to join hands but before he'd called on someone to give the closing prayer, he'd say, "Always be on the lookout for someone who might need us." And over the year, every member of SHAGY had brought at least one visitor, except Brianna. Even former visitors who became members brought a guest, and some members had brought multiple guests. Not all of them stayed, but at least they'd come courtesy of another. Initially, Brianna had not brought a guest because what high school group wanted another eighth grader around? But once she became a freshman, her excuse became that she was so busy doing so many service projects that she really didn't have time to seek out a visitor. Yet as the year progressed, she got honest with herself; in the quiet of her room, in the deepest corner of her thoughts, she admitted what she'd known had long been the truth but which she'd successfully repressed: she'd become very popular in SHAGY as a hard worker and humble intellect who wouldn't constantly blurt out correct answers and penetrating insights but would rather wait to be called upon by Pastor Paul or, more thrillingly, SHAGY peers, and she didn't want to damage that popularity by bringing the wrong person to a meeting—someone loud and obnoxious, someone geeky, someone no one wanted there.

She was ashamed that rainy night in April when she admitted this truth to herself. She got out of her bed and got on her knees and prayed, asking God to forgive her pride and vanity before asking God to help her be willing to bring the right person to SHAGY, someone who needed SHAGY, someone who would likely appear to be the wrong person—the geek, the bully, the obvious sinner. After all, didn't Jesus ruffle feathers precisely because he consorted with those icky people—prostitutes, thieves, tax collectors? And didn't Pastor Paul tell them every two weeks not to look for someone whom the group wanted but rather someone who needed the group? Brianna couldn't believe she'd gone so long missing that obvious distinction, ignoring that fundamental criterion. More, as Pastor Paul said would happen, *was* being revealed, but she still refused to ask Colleen.

Toward the end of April, the weather, at long last, finally turned nice, became springlike if not yet full-fledged spring. Nothing beyond forsythia was in bloom, and most of the trees were just barely budding, if at all, but all the snows from a heavy winter had been melted for a couple of weeks, and the lawns, though soft, were green, and people everywhere were visibly happier. But not Brianna. Her conscience still nagged.

It was the time of year when, unless it was raining, she and Colleen walked home from school, even though it was a couple of miles to their houses. And because the weather was warm, in the sixties, they were walking home from school. Colleen was pleasant enough as they talked of lesser matters—homework, teachers, movies they'd like to see—and Brianna put on what she thought was an effective charade, but Colleen finally asked, "What's wrong with you?"

"What do you mean?"

"I'm not an idiot, Bri. I can tell something's bothering you."

"Honest, Colleen, nothing is bothering me."

"You've been awful quiet. I'm the one doing most of the talking here."

Brianna was tempted to say that was often the case, but she didn't want to take her bad attitude out on her friend. She had admitted her wrong to God, and she'd prayed fervently to be released from her vanity and pride, but it was all a toxic sludge of a secret that still made her soul feel dirty, and she knew she would not be rinsed of the sludge until she admitted her faults to someone else. But it wasn't going to be Colleen. She didn't want the lecture that would inevitably ensue. "I'm just really enjoying this warm spring day," she said.

"Like hell you are, but it is way too nice a day for me to fight you for the truth. You're getting more and more secretive with me, Brianna Culp, and I really don't appreciate it."

Like most people caught in a lie, Brianna clung to it even tighter, taking on an angry, defensive tone: "Colleen, why can't you ever just believe what I tell you?"

"I do believe you, when you're not lying to me. And right now, I can tell you're lying."

"Have it your way," she said, surprised by how resolutely she embraced the falsehood. One sin *does* beget another, she thought.

They reached the block where they parted ways, Brianna to the left down the quieter, tree-lined street to her home, Colleen straight a few more blocks before she turned right toward her home's cul-de-sac. "See you tomorrow," Colleen said, "when maybe you'll be a tad more interested in being honest with your best friend."

Brianna was so beset by her private remorse that she barely even registered Colleen's farewell scolding. She walked a couple more blocks toward home before she turned around and started on the two-mile route over to Pastor Paul's. The last thing she wanted to do was bother him, but she could reside with her secret no longer. On the walk, she was glad she encountered no one she knew, for she didn't want to get involved in any kind of conversation, especially one addressing what exactly she was doing in this neighborhood. She kept her eyes focused on the sidewalk before her, looking up only now and then, as if loath to acknowledge a sky whose bright blue and fun-puffy clouds seemed a mockery of her mood. In a half hour she reached their home, the wooden colonial with the large front porch. She'd been to the house only a few times, all brief errands, but she gained the sidewalk to their house with no trepidation or reserve, so eager to be rid of her shame that she no longer minded that she might be bothering him. She climbed the steps and rang the doorbell, and a moment later, when Julie Clay opened the door and smiled widely and said, "My gosh, Brianna, what a pleasant surprise,"—it was then that Brianna could no longer hold it in, succumbing to a spring torrent of tears that had been waiting all afternoon, perhaps all month, to be unleashed. She cried the cry of a child whose best friend had just moved away, a cry the likes of which she'd not had in years. "My gosh, Brianna," Julie said again, though this time in an entirely different tone, sympathetic and concerned though still unable to completely keep that bright, sunshiny quality from her voice. She opened the door and enfolded Brianna in her taut, smooth arms. "What's happened to you? What's wrong?" But Brianna could not speak. She could only stand there and blubber, and Julie could only stand there and hold her, consoling for some little while before the severe sobbing had subsided and Julie was able to get her inside.

"What can I get you?" Julie said. They stood in the spotless dining room, having crossed the spotless living room, and Brianna still had her backpack slung over her shoulder. Her eyes, though not fully dry, were clear enough for her to see how perfectly dressed Julie was again, the J.Crew blue chinos, the white button-down blouse, the blonde hair glistening more like a model's than a minister's wife.

"Oh, I don't need anything."

"Come on, don't be that way. I've got cookies, I've got milk, I've got fresh grapes, I've got mint iced tea, I've got lemonade. And you just walked an awful long way, so I know your little temple of a body needs *some*thing."

"I guess I could use a glass of water."

"Water it is, one of the Lord's greatest gifts. Just sit down and make yourself comfortable, and I'll be right back."

Julie went into the kitchen, and Brianna didn't move. She felt bulky and awkward just standing there, a hamster in a mouse's cage, but in no way did she feel prepared to just take her backpack off and sit down wherever she wanted, as if she were a frequent guest. Where would she put the backpack? On the dining room table? The floor? The house was so immaculate that anywhere she put it would immediately make it clutter, a blemish. Julie returned carrying a clear glass of water and said, "Well my goodness, me, Brianna, sit yourself down and rest those weary legs."

"I don't know where to put my backpack."

"Hand it to me." They made a swap, the backpack for the water, and Brianna took a sizeable gulp, hoping it wasn't too loud, while Julie carried the backpack to the front door and deposited it at the base of the tall, wooden coat rack. Julie, returning, said, "For heaven's sake, Bri, would you sit down?" She did sit down on a chair at the dining room table, and Julie

848

sat catty corner. Brianna's mood was lightened by Julie calling her Bri.

"So what happened to you?" Julie asked. "Nobody hurt you, did they?"

"No, nobody hurt me."

"Praise Jesus. But you were a real mess on my doorstep."

"I know," she said, all of a sudden feeling real stupid for having arrived at their house in such a state. "But nobody hurt me. It was something I did to myself."

"You didn't hurt yourself, did you?"

"No, it's nothing like that. It's just that, well, I did something awful. I've been doing something awful, and I just need to tell someone and get it off my chest."

Julie smiled, relieved, knowing. "I know all about that. Before I found Jesus, I spent a few years doing something awful on a daily basis."

"You did?" Brianna was surprised. She'd assumed that Julie was as squeaky and pure as she'd always been.

"I sure did. I was a bad, bad girl for a few years doing just about everything you'd expect a bad girl to do. It was only after I was born again and took the Lord as my personal savior that I finally started living the way a daughter of God should."

"So you were just like Pastor Paul?"

"Heavens, no," Julie said, laughing. "Paul has been nothing but a saint his entire life. He's always been just as good as the day you met him."

"But I thought Pastor Paul was a bad kid."

"Whatever gave you that idea?"

Brianna almost said that it was Pastor Paul himself who gave her that idea, but she kept mum. She was rattled. Did Pastor Paul lie to them at that very first SHAGY meeting over a year ago? Amid the muddle of processing that he, in fact, did lie, Brianna searched for some kind of response to Julie, who sat there smiling so brightly. She took a drink of water to bide for time, but just then there came some fumbles and thuds from the front porch followed by Pastor Paul walking through the front door, carrying a leather satchel like a briefcase. "Look who's here," he said in a happy voice. "What a pleasant surprise."

Julie stood, and Brianna followed her lead. "Paul," Julie said, "Brianna is having a really lousy afternoon."

"Oh no," he said, moving forward. "What happened?"

"I have to run and get Gabriel from day care, so I'm going to let her get into all of that with you."

"Sounds like a plan," he said. There came a flurry of activity, Julie kissing Pastor Paul good-bye before she grabbed her purse from the table near the stairs, pulling the car keys out and leaving the house, Pastor Paul, meanwhile, removing his blue blazer and draping it over a dining room chair before he went into the kitchen, saying he needed some water. He returned, and they sat, Pastor Paul now occupying the chair formerly filled by his pert wife. "So, Brianna, why is this beautiful spring afternoon so lousy for you?"

She was wary about confessing. Since she'd learned of his lie just a few moments ago, she was no longer sure how to approach him, what to say, what to believe. He lied. Granted, it was a small lie, but if he lied about that, what else had he lied about? True, his lie was certainly useful, and it began a foundation upon which a substantial SHAGY edifice now stood, but what good is a successful church youth program if the foundation is less firm than she'd thought? Still, she had to confess. That's what she'd come to do, he was expecting it, and she wasn't about to lie herself. Besides, it would still be good to be freed of this secret. So she told him everything, and he kept quiet as she spoke, nodding now and then and taking a drink of water. She did not look him in the eye. She couldn't, and she didn't know if it was because of shame or the betrayal of trust she once thought secure. When she finished, she did not feel the relief she'd hoped for; was that his fault or hers? She finally looked at him to gage his reaction, and he gazed upon her with a comforting, beatific smile.

"Brianna," he said, "I think you are wonderful, truly a gift from God." She had no idea how to respond and so didn't. "Let me ask you something. How many guests have you seen *me* bring to SHAGY?"

She shrugged. "You brought Todd."

"Todd doesn't count. He was referred to me through someone and was there when SHAGY began."

"Then I guess none."

"That's right. I haven't brought one guest. And do you know why?" She shook her head. "Because that's not my job. Remember when I talked about the Apostle Paul saying that each of us has a role? Well, my role is to be the pastor, not to bring guests, and your role, clearly, is also not to bring guests because if bringing guests were your role, you'd have done it by now. In fact, you're so diligent in your devotion to the Lord that if your role were to bring guests, we'd have had to get a second church by now to fit them all in."

She smiled, but the smile was false. Last week, last night, that kind of compliment from him would have made her gush, but something was broken between them, and she was wary of everything he said now; she wondered if it were all just an act. "But what is my role?" she asked, knowing she had to continue the conversation but also curious what he thought.

"Funny you should ask me that, today of all days, and I'll get into that in a moment, but let's be clear about something first. Yes, you suffered from some pride and vanity, but that's the point: you suffered. Therefore, your heart is already a good heart because if it weren't, you wouldn't have felt this guilty. And because you suffered, and because you came to me with that suffering and acknowledged it, you have moved even closer to the Lord. Understand?" She did understand, and she nodded. That's what was so tricky about Pastor Paul; everything she'd ever heard him say *seemed* so right, so decent, so accurate, so Christian. "Now, as for your role."

He opened his leather satchel. He told her that her primary role in SHAGY was as its "thinking center," that is, her peers respected her so much for her thoughtfulness and intelligence that even though she was just a freshman, one of the youngest in the group, they invariably sought her opinion on weighty matters, looked to her for validation or contradiction or sometimes the outright answer to a question that had been plaguing them. This, he noted, took nothing away from the enormous amount of service she performed; in fact, her role as the thinking center was strengthened by the amount of service she performed for others. That said, more than anything else, the group turned to her for opinions, for knowledge, for ideas, and every great movement, from Christianity to the American Revolution, started with the spark of an idea.

"Which brings me to this," he said, tapping a document he pulled out of the satchel, a thin stack of pages with a blue cover page and a Mylar cover and red plastic binder. "Brianna, what do you know about Intelligent Design?" She shrugged and said she knew nothing. "Don't feel bad. That's what most people know, although in six months, God willing, that won't be the case here in Tuttle." He went on to inform her that I.D. was a scientific explanation for our creation and existence that not only refuted Darwin's theory of natural selection but also went "much, much further," toward explaining why the world is the way it is. He slid the notebook in front of Brianna. Across the top of the light blue cover page, in large letters, it read: INTELLIGENT DESIGN. A few spaces below that, in smaller letters, it read "What You Need To Know About I.D. and About How to Get It Into Your School." At the bottom it read "Compiled by Todd Bailey."

"Todd wrote this?" Brianna asked.

"No. As it says, he compiled it. None of the ideas in it are his. He just did a lot of research to figure out everything we needed to know and then put it all together, mostly cutting and pasting. He's been working on it for months. Now that it's done, we're getting ready to go public."

Pastor Paul elaborated: a group of local ministers had been working together to find the best way to make sure I.D. was taught in the local high school. They'd been meeting once a month for almost a year, and next week they were going to hold a press conference to announce what they wanted. In June, at the only school board meeting to be held over the summer, they would demand a public forum the following October during which all in town who cared could come and debate whether or not I.D. should be taught. "This gives us a deadline to shoot for, but it also gives us a few months to educate the public and prepare our forces. That's where you come in. Young people in SHAGY, young people in general, will be looking to you for answers, and you need to have them ready. So I want you to take this notebook home and educate yourself fully on the subject. As the battle unfolds, I'll have more specific instructions for you, but for now, Christian soldier, I need you to arm yourself intellectually. And for now, I also need one more thing. Absolute secrecy. You can't even tell your parents, not yet. If this gets out before we're ready, it could ruin our entire strategy. So, can I count on you for that?" he asked her with deep seriousness. She was a little creeped out; she was also dubious. If this were all that important, why was he entrusting her? Sure she was somewhat smart, and she guessed maybe the others in SHAGY looked up to her, but she was just a freshman in high school. Did she matter that much? Still, she nodded, and he reached across the table and grabbed her hands. "Good," he said.

Pastor Paul drove her home, but he dropped her off a few blocks away so that her parents wouldn't see him and begin asking questions (his idea). Her mom was in the kitchen cooking dinner, and Brianna said hello to her before going upstairs to begin her research. She didn't get far, however, before being called downstairs to set the table, but after dessert and doing the dishes, she returned to her room, claiming she had a test for which she needed to study.

She had never given much thought to evolution before. She knew about religious opposition to it, but she'd not given much thought to that, either. She'd always been inclined to think that the religious opposition was correct, but since she'd never studied either side, she never took part in any debate on the issue, which was pretty easy to accomplish since no one in her circles ever discussed it. As a freshman, last fall, she took life science, and next year, as a sophomore, she would take chemistry, and as a junior she would take biology before rounding it out with physics as a senior—the college prep route through science. It was in biology that she would learn about evolution, taught by Mr. Coyle, who was also her life science teacher.

The first thing in the I.D. document was a brief introduction, written by Todd. "There's no need to lay out *all* of the evidence against evolution. That would take hundreds of pages. However, let me make three key points.

1. An evolutionist would argue that the world began with a Big Bang and is constantly evolving toward something better. However, the Bible informs us that God created the world perfect and that man is constantly moving away from God, which is the definition of sin. Therefore, the world's not getting better, it is getting worse and 2 Peter 3:11 tells us that it is at the end when the Big Bang will come: 'But the day of the Lord will come as a thief in the night; in which the heavens will pass away with a great noise, and the elements shall melt with fervent heat, and the earth also, and the works that are therein shall be burned up.'

2. Taking into account the Big Bang theory, it would follow that evolutionists believe the Earth was formed after the galaxies, but the Bible clearly states in Genesis that the Earth was formed first, before the heavens.

3. Evolutionists claim we humans are all descended from apes, but the Bible explicitly states that we were made in the image of God. Therefore, the evolutionists can be right *only* if God is an ape."

The remainder of the folder consisted of a handful of pages explaining I.D. It was a pretty tough slog for Brianna. The basic proposition wasn't so rough, essentially that all the organisms in this world were so complex and so perfectly designed for the environments in which they lived that there's no way such perfection could have been formed through random agents. An "intelligent designer" had to be behind it. The paper went on to discuss some key concepts and terms, and it was then that Brianna struggled. For instance, "irreducible complexity," the idea that "a single system which is composed of several well-matched interacting parts that contribute to the basic function, wherein the removal of any one of the parts causes the system to effectively cease functioning." That notion was posited by some scientist named Michael Behe, and Brianna could make no sense of it until she read the offered example of a mousetrap, which was composed of many parts, but take away one part, and the whole apparatus ceases to function. She also read about "specified complexity," the idea that when something is specified and complex, one *must* infer that it was produced by an intelligent cause. Again, she was thoroughly baffled until she read the example: A single letter of the alphabet is specified without being complex. A long sentence of random letters is complex without being specified. A Shakespearean sonnet is both complex and specified. "And as we know," Todd added, "those sonnets didn't write themselves any more than this world created itself. They're both too intelligent."

Brianna couldn't argue with the science of what she read. The world *was* complex. She learned that in her life science class. All across the Earth were 1.7 million species of animals, plants and algae, and that was only what scientists knew for sure. Most of those were insects, but nearly five thousand mammals existed, everything from humans to polar bears up north and tree kangaroos in the tropics. "Think about it," Mr. Coyle told her class. (He was a slightly overweight teacher with a black mustache who was a favorite of many students and every year was voted "the best-dressed teacher." Every day he started class by saying, "News, sports, weather," which was an invitation for the students to talk about any current event, which he unfailingly related back to science and its crucial role in the world.) "There are some mammals out there deep in the jungles that we don't even know exist. Just seven years ago, in 1997, we discovered something called a Barking Deer in Vietnam, and last year it seems we discovered a new mammal in the jungles of Borneo, something with red fur that looks like a cat."

"If we don't know about those undiscovered animals out there," one student asked, "then how do we know they exist?"

"We don't," Mr. Coyle said, laughing with his class. "But since we keep discovering them, it's short-sighted to think that that won't continue to be the case."

It was incredible to think about, the idea that there lurked beasts and creatures in our world that we didn't yet know existed. And when Brianna thought about how diverse they all were and how diverse were the environments in which they so perfectly lived, well, it did make sense that that wasn't all random, as Darwin contended. Still, the fact that Intelligent Design was being supported by Pastor Paul made it suspicious, and she couldn't help feeling that way.

The remaining two pages of the document discussed the best strategy for getting I.D. into the school. "Never give a name to the Intelligent Designer behind everything," Todd wrote. "*We* know it's God, our Christian God, but if we just refer to it as an intelligent agent, no one can argue against us on religious grounds." That was problematic for Brianna. If they were so sure of their rightness, why were they trying to sneak I.D. in? She continued reading: "Also, it's important to note that while we know I.D. is absolutely right, we are asking only that it be taught alongside evolution. In other words, we need to argue that a free range of ideas is key and that we should 'Teach the Controversy' of these competing ideas." Brianna didn't disagree with that. After all, if I.D. was a valid theory, it *should* be taught. That conviction aside, she wasn't sure how involved she wanted to get in the upcoming fight.

Two weeks later, Pastor Paul went public. Alongside four other ministers (one of them Colleen's), he stood on the stone steps of the small, purple-brick Fellowship of Christ Church and made the announcement about their intentions. Not much of a press contingent was present; there simply wasn't much of a press contingent in the area. Pittsburgh was almost two hours to the west, Philadelphia was five hours southeast, and smaller city papers, like those in Altoona or Harrisburg, weren't near enough or rich enough to cover such a small matter. Only two papers were present for that first salvo: the *Tuttle Tattler*, a weekly, and the closest daily, one from a small city about thirty miles away, the *Cropsey Pantagraph*. Each minister made a brief statement, but it was Pastor Paul who did the bulk of the speaking, contending that some of the country's top scientists believe Intelligent Design has a legitimate place alongside evolution in our classroom and therefore we are doing a great disservice to the education of our students by "not exposing them to all that we know about the origins of their very own existence." A small crowd of supporters was on hand, Todd among them, and he led the applause throughout. (Brianna was not there; even if she had known about the conference beforehand, which she hadn't, she would have chosen to skip it.) After his final remarks, Pastor Paul opened the conference up to questions, and the Cropsey journalist asked what the agenda of action was. "Simple," Pastor Paul said. "This summer we're educating the public, and next fall we're educating the school board." Todd whooped with approval.

Brianna learned of the press conference the following morning at breakfast with her parents. Her father, reading the Cropsey paper, said, "Dumbass," before folding it and setting it down on the table. The headline read, "Churches to Fight School," and there was a picture of Pastor Paul gesticulating, pontificating, in front of the other four ministers.

Brianna and her mother both glanced at the front page before Glenda said, "I hope you're not referring to our pastor."

"Of course not," he said. He flipped the paper over where, on the bottom of the front page, was a picture of Secretary of Defense Donald Rumsfeld. Brianna's parents were ardent Republicans, but her father never had been keen on the Iraq War, and he often said that Rumsfeld was particularly well endowed with an arrogant stupidity. "I was referring to him," he said, pointing at the picture of Rumsfeld. Glenda nodded then rose to clear her plate, but Brianna and her father stared at each other, she curious, he bemused, and they broke that stare only after he winked.

At school that day, nobody talked much about the press conference, except for Colleen, who was already fired up for battle. "Jesus is coming to the classroom," she said to Brianna when they first saw each other on the bus. Her eyes were simultaneously glazed and enraged. "Finally, Jesus is coming to our classroom, and Jesus never loses." Brianna gave an almost sickly smile, and Colleen was peeved. "What's wrong with you? Aren't you excited?"

"Of course I'm excited," she said unconvincingly.

"Then act it!"

"Colleen, the public forum isn't for six months. If I get that excited now, I'll be dead from exhaustion by then."

Over the summer, the fight was largely waged in isolated skirmishes throughout the community, both sides gathering support for the school board showdown in October. Brianna was aghast by how vicious it got; some parents of students on one side forbade their children to play with children of parents on the other side, edicts that most students from both sides ignored, although a fair number of the I.D. students willingly went to verbal battle with evolution kids, and friendships were ended. Brianna was sick to her stomach watching it happen. She continued to attend SHAGY, and she continued to voice support for I.D., and she did answer questions of peers throughout the summer, but she strove to make sure she lost no friends over this, and she'd privately decided that somehow Pastor Paul was wrong. She didn't know how, but she knew he was.

She was surprised by the clergy who came out opposed to Intelligent Design, a group of half a dozen ministers led by the Presbyterian minister, Paul Frazier, who argued about the importance of the separation of church and state. Brianna did not know Reverend Frazier, other than by name and face, nor did she know any of the other ministers in the opposition, but seeing so many clergy arrayed against I.D. buttressed her own doubts about Pastor Paul.

She was also surprised by the caliber of the scientists from outside of the community who came to town and weighed in on the controversy, one from Penn State who attended a meeting hosted by the Presbyterian Church and, according to the *Tuttle Tattler*, dismantled the argument of irreducible complexity: "Just because a piece of a system is necessary now doesn't mean it's always been necessary or always been there. We know through research and experimentation that evolution often alters preexisting parts or removes them from the system."

Another professor, this one from Carnegie Mellon, spoke at a meeting hosted by the Methodist Church and explained why specified complexity was wrong. She read about that meeting in the *Tattler* also, and the science of it all again eluded her comprehension. She considered calling Mr. Coyle to ask for clarification, but she felt stupid about calling a teacher over the summer; plus, he was on summer break, and she didn't want to impose.

For his part, Mr. Coyle remained largely silent throughout the battles, though the papers often sought a comment from him since he was the teacher who taught evolution. Only once did he enter the fray, and that with a letter to the *Tattler* editor:

> As a teacher in the Tuttle school system, I have the job of educating our students in accordance with the policies determined by a school board that was duly elected by the citizens. And as a teacher of science, I am always excited to teach any theory, new or old, that has undergone the rigorous process of validation required by all scientific theories, namely, that it has offered a testable hypothesis that has been tested and proven to be true.

Brianna didn't fully understand that statement, either, and having nowhere else to turn for elucidation, she finally consulted her father during their evening session together as they walked around the shady block one August night that was warm but not oppressively so.

"What exactly did Mr. Coyle mean in his letter?" she asked, knowing her father had read it in the paper the day before.

"I don't know the full process," he said, "but before any science is accepted, it has to be tested and then submitted as an article for peer review, and then I guess others start testing the hypothesis to further prove it either true or false. From everything I've read, Intelligent Design either hasn't been tested, or some of its components have actually been shown to be false."

"Okay, but what does *that* mean?"

"Ultimately, it means that as science, Intelligent Design isn't any more valid than the theory that Martians brought us the pyramids of Egypt."

Brianna thought about that for a long while before she said, "I just don't know what to do, Dad."

He stopped, made his daughter face him, and put his hands on her shoulders. "I know you don't know what to do, honey, and that's okay. But here's what I want you to understand. What's going to happen is going to happen, and it doesn't really matter what you do." He gave her shoulders a squeeze, as if he'd said something wonderfully consoling, but neither his words nor that squeeze gave her comfort.

Did it matter what she did? She didn't know, but that seemed like a pretty lousy attitude to take through life. If nothing mattered, why do anything? More to the point, her father's words didn't speak to her problem, which was trying to figure out what was right. And not who was right in the terms of the science. She conceded that she just didn't know enough about science to take a definitive stance on either side. For her, the issue was faith. How was a person of faith supposed to greet this confrontation? There had to be something in the Bible somewhere that let her know how, as a Christian, she was supposed to proceed. And yet, the only relevant passage she could think of was the creation story, which unequivocally stated that God created the world, so what it really came down to was whether or not she was supposed to read that passage literally.

She took her conflict to the only person she knew to take it to: Pastor Paul. She wanted there to be someone else she could ask, but there simply wasn't. And besides, she rationalized, sure he'd lied about that one thing, but you couldn't argue against the effect it was having, the numbers he was drawing. And as she noted before, what he said about the Bible always *seemed* to be right. It was a Sunday late in August when she went to him, during refreshments after SHAGY, banana splits. Brianna didn't like bananas, so she opted for a simple caramel sundae, and after she finished, rather than join her peers in games, she went and sat next to Pastor Paul.

"Hi there, Bri," he said happily. She tried to match his buoyant attitude but couldn't fake it. "What's wrong?" he asked. She unloaded, telling him how confused she was by the whole battle, not the science but the faith underlying each side and how it all led her to question whether it was best to read the Bible literally.

"I have no idea what to think or do," she said.

"I know exactly what you should do," he said. "On this issue, for two weeks, do absolutely nothing. Stop thinking about it. Then, at our next SHAGY meeting, everything you just told me, say it again to the group. It'll be the topic that night, and it'll be an especially relevant and good topic since school will have just resumed. We'll be nearing the finish line of this fight, and I'm sure your friends here will all hear from you something they need to get them across the line."

September came, hot and dusty, and school resumed, and students on either side verbally confronted each other in classrooms and hallways. Teachers did their best to maintain order, and for the most part they succeeded. All teachers were forbidden to address the issue, and they in turn forbade the students, when possible. Colleen was wild-eyed with fury and delight. "I love being persecuted for my righteousness," she told Brianna one day. "Makes me feel like I'm rubbing asses with the disciples." Brianna couldn't begin to fathom what that meant.

At the next SHAGY meeting, Pastor Paul gave her a glowing introduction, saying how he'd waited some while for asking tonight's speaker to bring a topic because he wanted to be sure that when she did, it was for an issue worthy of her intellect and faith. "And so I kept searching and searching, waiting for the right time, and I completely forgot that it wasn't about what I thought I wanted and when I wanted it. I forgot it wasn't me in charge, it was God, but I was reminded of that when, two weeks ago, this person came to me with a question, and no sooner did she ask it than I realized it was God telling me, 'Paul, it's high time Brianna brought the topic to SHAGY.' And so ladies and gentleman, on orders from God, I give you Brianna."

A mighty roar followed that introduction, a combination of the nervous energy hovering over every aspect of the lives of those involved in the I.D. struggle as well as the affection and respect SHAGY members had for Brianna and her unique role in the group, the scholar/mascot combination borne of her being the smartest, religiously so, and the most visible of the youngest members. Brianna was disgusted by the introduction, but once she had the floor, she shared, one last time, her questions and concerns, embellishing on details, speaking free and easy and without any nervousness, not because she was confident but rather because she was so emotionally and mentally entwined with this topic that she was eager for guidance, answers and feedback. When she finished, though, she was greeted by a square of blank stares, blinking eyes and silence. She became self-conscious. She feared she'd not made any sense. Finally, across the room, Dane said, "I didn't know there was more than one way to read the Bible. I mean, isn't it like any other book? You just read the words and pay attention to what they say?"

Many in the group nodded their heads in befuddled agreement, and Pastor Paul interjected early. "Actually," he said, "there are two different ways to read the Bible. For instance, the story of Jonah being swallowed by a whale. You can read that literally, that is, it actually happened, or you can read it as just a made up story that's trying to convey a message."

"Isn't it conveying a message if it's literal?" Peggy Sneed asked. "I mean, there's still a message to be learned if Jonah got swallowed by the whale, and if he didn't actually get swallowed by the whale, then what's really the point of having the story?" Again, many heads nodded in agreement.

"I agree with you, Peggy," Pastor Paul said, "but many so-called Christians don't, and it's these Christians who are on the other side of our I.D. fight. In the Gospel According to Matthew, chapter eighteen, verse three, Jesus quite famously says, 'Truly, I say to you, unless you turn and become like children, you will never enter the kingdom of heaven.' Now, how would a child read the Bible? Would he read it literally, taking it at face value, or would he try to offer deeper interpretations? I think we know the answer to that. A child would read the Bible literally. A child is simply not mature enough to read it any other way. And remember, Jesus clearly tells us that in order to enter the kingdom of heaven, we must be like children. In other words, we're not supposed to be like mature adults who can bend and twist words to make them mean whatever they need them to mean. And here's why that's important. When Jesus came to this world, he came for everybody—the young, the old, the sick, the weak, the smart, the dumb—everybody. But if you think the way to read the Bible is not literally but interpretively, you're saying that Jesus is interested in speaking only to intellectual adults, which is the exact opposite of what he said and did. It's an elitist attitude, and Jesus, frankly, was fed up with the elites. It was the meek, he said, who would inherit the earth, the meek in body and mind. The strong had had their day, and Jesus wasn't about to let them keep the weak from coming to him through rules the strong made just to keep them out. On the football field, it's the strong in body who prevail. At exclusive country clubs, it's the strong in money who prevail. In the halls of Congress, it's always the elites who prevail, Ivy League graduates who create all those crazy rules to make sure they stay in charge. But in the game that matters most, the game of faith, Jesus changed the rules. He said the strong no longer get to be in charge. And to do his work, we have to make sure their rules don't apply. And that's why we're fighting evolution in our schools. By teaching only evolution and not Intelligent Design, the elites are trying to stack the deck, make the rules in their favor. And as I said: Jesus is fed up with them, and so am I."

An eruption of applause. Everyone there, except Brianna, was prepared to do battle that moment, but Pastor Paul told them to relax, there were still six more weeks before the big meeting and plenty of work that remained. After SHAGY adjourned with a closing prayer, Pastor Paul went to Brianna and told her how great a job she'd done. She smiled and thanked him, but neither sincerely, and she wasn't convinced by his words. That week, in the *Tattler*, a local doctor wrote a letter to the editor noting that across the world, there was a lot of fear over a potential outbreak of the avian flu, which is an evolved descendant of previous forms of flu. "We make our vaccinations based on our understanding of that evolution," he said. "Therefore, it seems to me that all opponents of evolution, in order not to be hypocrites, should refuse any avian flu vaccination if, indeed, there is an outbreak of that flu." Intellectually, Brianna was not scientifically smart enough to argue with the doctor in the same way that she wasn't religiously smart enough to argue against Pastor Paul, but she'd reached a point wherein she was convinced it was Pastor Paul who was wrong on this issue.

"Look, Brianna, I was over at the Nazarene Church last week for its youth group meeting, and I met your friend, Colleen. She's a real firebrand. That red hair suits her well. Anyway, she told me you two were best friends, and she said you'd join forces to make a bunch of posters for the school board meeting. Does that sound like something you'd be interested in doing?" It didn't, but Brianna was even less interested in incurring Colleen's wrath. So she nodded assent. "Great. Her group's having a bake sale to raise funds for the materials. I'll leave all the details up to you two. Something tells me that when Colleen takes charge, things get done."

Colleen orchestrated not one but a series of bake sales, raising hundreds of dollars by selling cookies and brownies and cakes and pies not only at her church but also in front of grocery stores, on Main Street and at other churches. She wanted not only posters but also T-shirts for all I.D. students to wear, bright yellow shirts with a picture of an ape on the front, underneath which was written, "Not My Ancestor."

Two weeks before the meeting, Colleen had a couple dozen students in her garage to make the posters. The poster board used was all different colors, and the messages were varied along a similar theme: Grandpa's Not an Ape, Evolution is Just a Theory, Darwin was Wrong, Darwin=Satan, etc. There were art students to beautify the posters, glitter to sprinkle on. Brianna showed up and made one poster. Colleen also told everyone she'd ordered dozens of shirts in varying sizes, and they were currently being made, and each person needed to show up at her house the day of the meeting, after school, to pick up a shirt and grab a poster or two.

On the morning of the day of the meeting, Brianna woke up feeling tired and sick to her stomach. She'd not slept well. Her mother was bright and cheery at breakfast while her father, his usual taciturn and remote self, read the paper, the headline of which read, simply, "Tonight's the Night." At school, the mood was kinetic, its population on edge. Students refrained from any confrontation, but only because they all knew the main event would be later that night. Brianna went through the day in a daze, preoccupied by concern but also fatigued from the past five months. She was so worried by what might happen that night even though she couldn't say what she wanted to have happen, and she was tired of worrying about that night. In all her classes, she was unable to pay attention. After the final bell rang, she went to her locker, put away her books and slung her empty backpack over her shoulder: teachers were considerate enough not to assign any homework for that night. She went to the foyer in front of the gym, where she'd agreed to meet Colleen so they could walk to her house and pass out the posters and shirts. In the gym, the janitors were pulling out the bleachers. Normally, school board meetings were held in the cafeteria, but expected attendance demanded this one be moved to a larger venue. Colleen came racing to the lobby. "Let's go," she said.

Colleen moved briskly on their walk, and Brianna had neither the energy nor desire to keep pace. "Colleen, people aren't coming to your house for another hour. Can't we slow down?"

"What's wrong with you? We've worked months for tonight, and you don't seem at all excited."

"I don't know. Can I ask you something?" This was against her better judgment, she knew, but she had to ask. "How confident are you in Preacher Brine?" That was Colleen's minister.

"Now's not really the time to be airing doubts, Bri, especially from the co-chair of the posters committee."

"I don't doubt God, Colleen. I've just got a few doubts about Preacher Brine." She couldn't bring herself to admit she doubted Pastor Paul. "I mean, he was really wrong about the world ending on New Year's 2000."

"Bri, he thoroughly explained how the Y2K scare was a trick of Satan."

"I know, but that hardly helped those families in your church who sold everything they owned and flew to Israel to greet the Second Coming."

"Preacher Brine says we all have free will. *He* didn't go to Israel."

Brianna shrugged. "I just don't know how you can be so sure Mr. Coyle's wrong for teaching evolution."

"For crying out loud, Bri, Mr. Coyle is a Methodist!" Colleen shook her head. "Look, Bri, I've already got enough on my mind for tonight. Just promise me I can rely on you."

Brianna did promise, and she went to Colleen's house and dutifully helped pass out the posters and T-shirts. And though she promised Colleen she'd meet her at the gym later and sit with their group of student supporters, she had no intention of doing so. She'd already decided that she would sit with her parents near the door so they could make a hasty exit if things either got out of hand or, more likely, became redundant and dull. And she also wasn't about to wear that stupid yellow T-shirt. That, too, she'd decided a couple of weeks back. Instead, she was going to wear a pretty pink tank top she'd bought over the summer because she just knew the gym was going to be stifling hot.

For Don, there were some definite negatives to living in the city: the noise, the inability to see the stars at night, the multiplication of summer's heat by all the asphalt and cement. Water pressure was another, rather the lack thereof. Shower heads didn't trickle in the city, but they didn't gush, either, and Don had been washing his carcass under their tempered flow for so long that he'd forgotten what pressure in the country could be. He was astonished by the force of the flow at the campground. It was, after all, a campground a few miles from town, so the water probably came from a well, and those didn't typically offer impressive pressure. And yet, here was the campground shower, shooting, pressing, driving, fairly massaging Don's shoulders (which were a tad stiff from a night spent on the ground), reminding him of just how wonderful a rural shower can be. He reveled. He luxuriated. He cleansed.

Steph, too, was impressed by his shower experience in the square, brick bathroom at the center of the campground. The actual facility itself was problematic—the old stone floor, the rusted drain, the spider webs in the corners—but the shower was a dream. "Daaaaaamn," he said when he first put his body under the strong, warm flow, elongating the word in pure appreciation, much like when he saw a woman so beautiful he could find nothing much else worth saying. "Daaaaaaamn," he said again when he put his head and neck under the gush, feeling some relief from a night of sleep that had been better than he'd expected but still felt well short of one he'd call good. He stayed in the shower almost a half hour. Don had told him not to rush. They both slept late, Steph because it wasn't until the sun rose that he finally felt safe enough to shut both eyes resolutely and give in to the possibility of REM, and by the time they did shower, all of the other campers were clearly gone for the day, so they didn't have to worry about using all of the hot water. What's more, there was no plan to be anywhere specific that day; and because he'd said, the day before, that he wanted to slow his destination-less trip down a tad, he was in no hurry to get back on the road. Thus, Steph showered in unrestricted, uninhibited and unabashed delight. "Daaaaamn," he said intermittently throughout. "Daaaaamn." He was almost sad when he turned the water off.

Back at the campsite, freshly dressed in khaki pants and a dark green polo, sitting in a folding chair beside the cold ash,

Steph said, "If I were a poet, I would write a poem about that shower. I had no idea a shower could be so good. I don't get showers like that in Brooklyn, and I didn't get them like that at Brandeis. It sort of makes me wonder what else I'm missing by living in the city."

"Affordable rent. Affordable utilities. Starry nights, cars that aren't constantly being honked, and that extra twenty dollars at the end of each day that, no matter how many times you calculate the day's spending, you just can't account for."

"Little down on the city, D.?"

"You kidding? That place is my salvation. But I've never been blind to its shortcomings, which pale in comparison to its bounty."

"This is pretty nice, too." Steph surveyed the landscape and breathed deeply of the air. Don had rolled up his tent and was shoving it into its nylon bag, always a challenge. He wore tan cargo shorts, a blue plaid short sleeve sport shirt, gray wool socks and his brown hiking boots. "I can see why folks get into this whole camping thing," Steph added. "This morning air is like candy."

Don loaded everything into the trunk and grabbed the folding chairs and told Steph to drive the car up to the office and meet him there. Steph asked why he didn't just put the chairs in the car, and Don said it was too much of a hassle to shove them in and take them out for less than fifty yards of light transport. Besides, the air *was* like candy, and Don wanted to spend some more time with it, in it, revel in its taffy. At the office, an especially attractive blonde in jeans, T-shirt and a red fleece vest stood behind the counter. "Just returning these chairs," Don said.

"Danny said you had them."

"My hunch is you're Danny's mom, but you don't look nearly old enough to be."

"Aren't you a silver-tongued devil," she said, smiling. "I am, in fact, his mom."

"Then congratulations, Mom. That's a fine son you've raised."

"He is a fine son. I appreciate your saying so."

"Give him my best."

"And my best to you in your travels."

They returned to the diner for breakfast, Steph driving. Inside was virtually empty of customers, just one table with a couple boys in their late teens or early twenties, but it was mid-morning on a weekday, which meant most people were already off to where they needed to be for the day, or at least until lunch. Things got going early in rural America, Don well knew. It took him some getting used to the schedule of many professionals in the city, people strolling into the office at ten or eleven but then staying until eight or nine. They headed for the table next to the front window where they ate the night before. The waitress behind the counter, a woman in her fifties, hollered to see if they wanted her to bring some coffee, and Don said, "Unequivocally. Could I also get change for a dollar?" She brought two cups of coffee, two menus and four quarters for which Don handed her a dollar. Steph sat, and Don headed back to the entrance where he pumped fifty cents into the newspaper box and pulled out a copy of the Harrisburg *Patriot-News*.

At the table, Steph scanned the menu while Don read the paper. "You know what you're ordering?" Steph asked.

"I knew last night what I was ordering. Getting my fill of chicken fried steak while I can."

"Is that stuff chicken or steak?"

"It is what it says it is—steak fried like chicken, and it's one thing you cannot find in the city, although my arteries are likely to eke out an extra five years because of that."

Don ordered his chicken fried steak with eggs and hash browns, all of it smothered in gravy, and Steph ordered some pancakes and sausage. Steph took out his cell phone and checked for messages, either for him or Don. Don did not have a cell phone. He refused. Most phone calls he viewed as an intrusion into his life, which was why he rarely answered his home phone. "Just because it's ringing," he always said, "doesn't mean I'm obligated to answer, especially if I'm in the middle of something." He saw no sense of bringing that potential for intrusion everywhere he went, but then he also knew he was lucky in that his work, thus far, never required him to have one, which wasn't the case for most people. Steph turned off the phone, set it down.

"Any messages?" Don asked.

"Just my manager saying the store is fine. And grandma, wondering if I'd been eaten by a bear."

"It wasn't that many generations ago your ancestors were cavorting with lions and zebras."

"Not cavorting. Avoiding or eating."

Don turned the page of his newspaper and scanned. Steph stared out the window, fascinated by just how empty a Main Street could be at this time of day. He wondered what could possibly be the economic base of towns like this all across the country. The two young guys sitting a few tables behind Don laughed at something, and Steph turned out of curiosity but couldn't see past Don's paper. Then, Don slowly lowered his paper to where Steph could see just his eyes, which twinkled, before he could see the rest of his face, which beamed with a knowing, satisfied, almost smirking smile. "All right, D. I know that smile. What do you know that I don't know?"

"I'll get back to you on that." He raised the paper and continued to read, his face shielded behind the newsprint, and when the waitress appeared a few moments later with their breakfasts, Don lowered his paper. "Ma'am, how far is Tuttle from here?"

"It's not that far as the crow flies, but you're no crow, and there's no quick or easy way to it." She explained the highways they'd have to take, a semi-circuitous route that wove around some mountains. "If you go the speed limit, you can get there in three hours. Can I get you fellas anything else?"

"Just a little more coffee please," Don said, and she walked off.

Steph pointed to Don's breakfast. "That much food smothered in gravy is barbaric."

"Where I'm from, we refer to a breakfast this size as hearty." He ransacked his mountain of cholesterol, calories and carbs with salt and pepper.

"All right. Enough of the mystery. What do you have?"

Don folded up the paper and leaned it slanted upright against the window. He pointed to the headline: "Tuttle School Board to Debate Evolution Tonight." Steph read the first paragraph, which stated that tonight, at seven o'clock, in the gymnasium of Tuttle High School, the school board was hosting a public forum to debate whether or not Intelligent Design should be included in the biology curriculum, taught as an alternative theory to our own origins in conjunction with Darwin's theory of natural selection.

Steph looked to Don and smiled. "You crashing this meeting?"

Don smirked. "The Lord has spoken to me through *The Patriot-News.*"

The waitress returned and refilled their empty mugs. "You fellas headed up to Tuttle?"

"Believe we are, ma'am."

"Maybe you can talk some sense into those dumbshits," she said. "Next thing you know they'll be wanting to outlaw gravity from the classroom, and that's a lifelong Methodist who ain't missed a day of church in ten years talking to you. Dumbshits."

She walked off shaking her head, and Don said, "The Lord has spoken."

In the car, on the highway, Don, driving, was giddy and restless. Tonight's meeting was a fantasy come true, and he could not believe his luck. Steph asked him what he was going to say. "I haven't the foggiest. That depends on what's said before me. But I know what I think." Which was that Christians who opposed evolution had, paradoxically, a weak faith, so weak that it couldn't withstand scientific revelation and so must blot it out. "It's like all those right wing politicians who want to outlaw homosexuality. Show me an anti-gay crusader, and I'll show you a gay man in the closet. That's why they seek these laws. They're aware of their homo inclinations, and they're so fearful of that reality that they think legislating against it will improve their own chances of not acting out on their tendencies. Same with these fundies and evolution. Though they profess to believe in this strong, almighty, powerful God, and though they profess to believe with an unshakeable faith, the truth is that the edifice of their belief is so rickety that pull one pillar out and the whole thing comes crashing down. They not only can't handle scientific revelation. They can't stare lots of forms of reality in the face. In the event of trauma or disaster, they're never the ones calmly in the center seeking solutions and offering assistance. They're the ones on the fringes running back in forth in panic hollering like Ethel Merman. Someone pulls out a gun, these folks hide behind their children." Don was no Ph.D. in biology, but he knew the basics of evolution and kept somewhat abreast of current findings by reading Stephen Jay Gould's books. Over a hundred years of science and scientists continued to prove that for the most part, Darwin nailed it, and who was he to doubt all of that, all of them? It'd be a bit like doubting the polio vaccine, even though, for almost sixty years now, that very vaccine had eradicated polio from the face of the Earth. "Speaking of vaccines, the religious fundies aren't the only idiots; the secular branch has its share, too; case in point, the anti-vaccine crowd." Smallpox and polio banished from the planet, measles, mumps and rubella struggling to survive, and some Hollywood tarts who have read six books collectively their entire lives all of a sudden wake up and know better about vaccines because they've borne a couple of children.

"I'll tell you what has always gotten me," Steph said. "Of all the scientific theories out there, why is evolution public enemy number one with those fundamentalists? It may be simple, but it's not *that* simple. It took some thousands of years before Darwin figured it out, and from Plato to Galileo to Copernicus, there were some pretty heavy hitters along the way who completely missed it. Besides, if those fundamentalists think evolution is crazy, they should check out some of the shit quantum physics is saying."

"I cannot make heads nor tails of that stuff," Don said.

"I struggle with it myself."

"Could be why the fundies don't go after it. With evolution, they at least have the illusion of thinking they get it."

Steph nodded. "Hey, after you've had your fun tonight, you think we might be able to catch some sights? Some real America stuff?"

"Are you kidding me? You can't get more real America than tonight's meeting."

"I want some tourist shit. The Rock and Roll Hall of Fame or the College Football Hall of Fame in South Bend."

"We'll see. Depends which way the wind blows."

"I'd even take a drive-by of Three Rivers Stadium in Pittsburgh. Some legendary shit has gone down in that place the past three decades."

They arrived in Tuttle around four o'clock. They should have been there two hours earlier, but Don, busy talking, blew right past the junction with the highway he needed headed west, a small junction that would have been easy to miss even if he'd been paying strict attention. Only after he realized he'd gone too far north and turned around and, on the return, saw the sign did he realize how poorly it was marked. Bad enough to be a New Jersey road sign, he thought.

There were two signs as he entered Tuttle, a green one with white letters giving the town's name, and one right below it that said **Home of the 1998 Girls State Softball Champions**. "Some ballplayers in Tuttle," Don muttered as he slowed the Hyundai quickly so as not to be nabbed in a speed trap. Steph mentioned the obvious, that they had three hours before the meeting, and Don said he wanted to cruise the town for context, pinpoint the high school's location, and "Grab some sustenance. Big night ahead."

"Can't believe that breakfast isn't serving the purpose. It's not as if we've been out jogging since then."

"Quiet, son. You'll make me self-conscious."

Unlike Don's hometown, and probably every town in Illinois, the sign upon entering Tuttle gave no indication of its population. But Don found Main Street, drove its commercial district from one end to the other and, having encountered four stoplights, calculated the population to be about twelve thousand. He'd developed an equation that he'd formulated, tested and honed over the years: on average, three thousand people per stoplight, not counting those newer ones on the edges of town to accommodate for the recently constructed strip malls and, more usually, Wal-Marts. To Don, twelve thousand was sizeable. Raised in a town of seven thousand and exposed to so many towns of two thousand or less, he still thought of anything over fifty thousand as a city, even after having lived in New York. Tuttle, to him, was a "good-sized town." And it was a nice town, too, clean and calm with century-old brick buildings along Main Street, a few stretches of cobblestone roads here and there, lots of old houses and tree-lined residential streets. Picturesque, too, surrounded as it was by the mountains. The tall, white, pointed steeple of the Presbyterian Church, one of the dozen or so churches he saw, reached in solitary, spectacular relief against the forest green of one mountain's round-edged triangle. The school was an old building near the center of town, not one of those vast, characterless rectangles built the past twenty years out on the edge.

"Nice town," he said, having spent an hour driving through it. "It's a lucky child who's raised here."

For dinner, he drove to the strip mall he'd scouted earlier. He'd made a mental note of the fast food joints there, and he parked in front of the KFC, supposing his luck had been running so good it probably was too much to ask to score a Popeye's. He wanted dinner to be a hasty affair. He predicted a large crowd at the meeting, one that came early, and he didn't want to risk being shut out. After they ate (Steph not much at all, Don as if he hadn't in three days), Don grabbed some green Dockers from his suitcase and changed in the KFC bathroom. "I suspect it will behoove me to appear a bit more professional."

It was 6:15 by the time he was back at the high school, and already the parking lot was filled to capacity, as were all the spots for two blocks either way in front of the school, both sides of the street. It reminded Don of the homecoming football game back home. He parked on a side street four blocks away. He could have parked a tad closer, but he thought the extra block or two of walking might do him some good. He was getting nervous. This thing he was doing, the Don Prophet routine, all of a sudden it was real, imminent and real, and he wondered just how crazy it was, he was. In New York, it was a lark of a stunt to get himself published, and back there it seemed less bizarre as bizarre things there often do. Out here, though, in tranquil Tuttle, away from a milieu where nothing seemed implausible, the entire scheme felt as outlandish as he knew it to be. But in a strange way that increased his nervousness, it also felt right, as if he were supposed to be doing this. He closed his eyes and took a massive breath and exhaled volubly. "Prepare ye for the way of the Lord." He got out of the car and moved to the school with strides purposeful, determined, resolute.

The line of people entering the gym was more of a pile, but it wasn't long or wide, and it moved quickly. The gym itself, already warm, was three-quarters full, its noise a dull hum of variegated chatter. At one end was a stage on which sat two long tables with seven empty chairs along one side, a microphone in a short stand on the center of the table. In the center of the gym, atop the painted head of a blue panther, stood a microphone on a tall base. All range of people were present, but on one side, in the center, sat Colleen and her minions, fifty or so students in bright yellow shirts with a picture of an ape and words Don couldn't make out. They had their signs, too, with anti-evolution messages, some of the students already holding them up, waving them. Don sat in the front row, right next to an entrance. He had no idea yet what he was going to do, but he knew he couldn't be trapped high on the bleachers behind an unmovable mass of spectators.

After they sat and scanned the gym, Steph said, "I trust you notice that I'm the only Negro present."

"You won't be. Town this size probably has five or six black families, four of them related. A few will show up."

"I'll be interested to see which side they're supporting."

When the meeting was called to order at seven o'clock, the bleachers were filled, the school board members had taken their seats, two policeman stood in each of the three exits, and Steph had spotted exactly three other black people, a mother and teenaged son combination, and an older, white-haired man who didn't sit with them. The chairman of the school board, Michael Mark, gave his name and told everyone his title, lest they not know, and Steph, down low, on the sly, held out three fingers for Don to see. Don leaned over and whispered to him, "That's still two more than have been hired at Goldman Sachs this year."

Mike asked everyone to stand and say the pledge of allegiance to the large flag that draped vertically above the stage. When all were again seated, he described the ground rules of the debate: it would last two hours, eight speakers from each side had already been chosen by their respective leaders and their order of appearance already arranged, each speaker was allotted five minutes. He asked the leader of the evolutionist side, a guy named Harris Dulaney, to stand, which he did, and he asked Intelligent Design's foreman, Pastor Paul Clay, to stand, and Pastor Paul did to raucous applause from that student section. Mike reminded everyone that no decision by the board would be made until the following week at the regularly scheduled board meeting, and that tonight was just a specially-convened forum for each side to make its case. "With that," he said, "I'll introduce the first speaker, a member of the evolutionist forces, Reverend Paul Frazier."

Don was not surprised that the first speaker in favor of evolution was a minister; it was a shrewd move whose brilliance was too obvious for team evolution to have missed. Paul was a middle-aged man, portly, a heavy beard, and Don didn't pay attention to what he said. He was strategizing. He could wait until the end of the meeting to do or say what he did not yet know he was going to do or say, but then he risked a tired audience no longer paying much attention, some of whom would have probably left. Given that no new insights or arguments were likely after the first two or three speakers of each side, he doubted the efficacy of waiting even until the middle of the meeting. That said, he still had no plan of attack whatsoever, and he began to feel a pressure on his chest, a weight that comes of not meeting a potential goal, not fulfilling a plan, not beating a deadline. He listened as Paul Frazier, concluded, " . . . which is why, as a man who has dedicated his life to faith, I think it is vital that in our science classrooms we teach only science. Thank you."

A decent amount of applause accompanied Reverend Frazier as he returned to his seat, but so, too, did some jeers from that student section. Colleen even stood and snarled and gave Reverend Frazier a thumbs down. That one's trouble, Don thought.

"Okay," Michael Mark said after the noise subsided. "Next, speaking in favor of Intelligent Design, we have—"

"Next we have me," Don stood and shouted. He hadn't planned to. He'd decided he needed to speak early, but he'd not committed to this early. It was some instinct that compelled him to stand and shout, the same instinct that compelled him to stride forcefully toward the microphone in the center of the gym, even though his voice projected sufficiently without it. Everyone in the gym turned to him, watched him as he strode across the waxy veneer of the gym floor, his hiking boots squeaking with each step.

"I'm sorry, sir," Mike said. "Who are you?"

"My name is Don," he shouted. "Don Prophet."

"Well, Mr. Prophet, we have the order of speakers already set."

"Sir, I answer to a Higher Order." Don wasn't at all intimidated. In New York, the police would have gang tackled him by now, but he knew small towns intimately enough to know that here, his only real threat was an overzealous Barney Fife itching to use that taser gun. None of the six police really moved other than to stand straight, no longer leaning against the wall. And he wasn't worried about the crowd, either; they were so unused to unexpected outbursts that none would dare move until they'd processed exactly what was happening. His only challenge now was to secure that five-minute slot.

"If you were to speak, Mr. Prophet," Mike said, "what side would you be speaking for?"

Don now stood at the microphone, and he leaned his mouth toward it to say, "I speak for the side of the Lord." The I.D. supporters went spastic with applause.

"Pastor Paul," Mike said, "you were due to speak next. Do you want to defer your five minutes?"

Pastor Paul, sitting, sized up Don, and Don stared intensely at him. "Don't blow this, Pastor Paul," Don said into the microphone, knowing an amplified voice would be tougher to refuse. "The Lord has called me all the way from New York City to come speak at this meeting tonight."

Pastor Paul continued his appraisal, and Don did not relent on his stare. Nobody in the gym spoke as Pastor Paul rose and walked to the microphone, the click of his hard-soled shoes the only sound. He stood inches from Don, inches shorter than Don, and he spoke into the microphone. "Mike, I won't defer my five minutes, but I will let Mr. Prophet speak for our side right now." Frenzied applause from his supporters—they just knew Don was a ringer sent from God. "I will speak last for our side, and I will strike from our roster Brenda Edmands, who was set to speak second."

"That's fine, Paul," Mike said. Pastor Paul gave Don one last, long look before he returned to his seat. "You have five minutes, Mr. Prophet."

Don freed the microphone from its stand so that he could walk around and naturally address all corners, both sides. "First of all, we can dispense with this intelligent design nonsense. If my design is so intelligent, why do I have an appendix and a blind spot? Blind spots are responsible for thousands of accidents each year. Granted, if God created us, He did so long before automobiles, but He's God, so he should have known they were coming in a few thousand years. And as for the appendix, it can accomplish only two things: make me violently ill or kill me. Tell me, what's so intelligent about that?"

The room was still silent, and Don sensed how complete his command of the crowd was. "Let's just call this what it is, folks. God would want us to. What we're really talking about here tonight is creation. Now, what I'd like to know is, by a show of hands, how many of you in here tonight believe in creation as it's recorded in the Book of Genesis?" Approximately half of the crowd raised its hand, most of them scattered and interspersed save for the solid cluster of students in their yellow shirts. Pastor Paul, Don noticed, did not raise his hand; his arms were crossed; his stare pensive. Don assumed Paul was smart enough to realize he'd made a mistake, but there was no stopping it now. "Let me ask you folks with your hands in the air. Which creation story do you believe in?"

Don paused to let that sink in. There was some murmuring, some muttering, and people sporadically dropped their hands. "In the book of Genesis, there are two creation stories. Two. And they contradict each other. In Genesis, chapter one, God creates the heavens and the earth, then all the plants and animals next, and then he creates Adam last. Last. Then, two paragraphs later, in Genesis chapter two, we have another telling of the creation, although this time the Bible explicitly says that before God created any plants or animals, he created Adam first. First. So for those of you who claim to believe in creation the way it's laid out in the Bible, which version do you believe—Adam last or Adam first?" He scanned the entire room as if waiting for someone to answer, and the murmuring became more voluble. "You want to know which creation story in Genesis God believes in? Neither."

Grumbling came with that statement, and Pastor Paul stood up. "Mike, I'd like to—"

Don turned angrily upon Pastor Paul and pointed at him, "You sit down and hold your tongue, Preacher! You deferred these five minutes." Pastor Paul did sit, grudgingly, and the grumbling and murmuring became louder, but for Don the transformation was complete—he'd become Jeremiah proclaiming to Jerusalem, Ezekiel declaiming on Gog of Magog, Isaiah chastising the children of Israel; he was sound, he was fury, he was form and content, medium and message: all his years of righteous indignation were a shaken bottle that had reached this moment, this night, and the lid, finally, was off: he was a prophet, and he felt that to his very core. "Wake up, people!" he shouted. "The first book of Corinthians, chapter fourteen, verse twenty, tells us, 'Do not be children in your thinking; be babes in evil but in thinking be mature.' It's time for you creationists to grow the hell up on this issue. If God really wanted you to believe in creation as it's depicted in the Bible, He wouldn't have included two contradictory versions."

The noise everywhere rose. Pastor Paul sat paralyzed with chagrin, and Colleen's nostrils were literally flared. It was her coterie of students where the noise was loudest, but Don bettered them. "Even if we're to accept that we're all descendants of Adam and Eve, how did we end up with so many different colored people all over the world? All right, Adam and Eve account for the whites in Europe, and Ham accounts for the blacks in Africa, but how to account for the yellows in China and the browns in Italy and Greece and even deeper browns in India and Mexico? Huh? Doesn't that suggest that somewhere along the line some of us have been changing? Evolving? Or am I wrong, and have some of you white creationists been spitting out some brown and yellow babies?"

"Kill him!" That was Colleen. She stood and shouted it. Mike banged his gavel on the table, but to no avail. People were now talking loudly everywhere, many of them all over the gym, and Colleen was in motion. "Kill him!" she shouted as she leapt from the bleachers and led a charge at Don with a dozen of her yellow-shirted comrades.

Don cast aside the microphone and bent his knees, squatting in something of a wrestler's stance, and as Colleen and her disciples charged, and the police came from their respective posts toward the imminent melée in the center of the gym, Don, smiling, wondered two things: how aggressively should he defend himself (they were, after all, just kids), and were there any journalists taking pictures and getting all of this down?

*　　　　　*　　　　　*

Chief Bey was a Bed-Stuy legend, a black American of Dominican ancestry who became a performer of note throughout the thirties, forties and fifties. By the nineties, he'd restricted himself to jazz drumming at neighborhood clubs on weekends and private parties in brownstone backyards. Steph met him through a cultural after-school program offered to gifted black students, funded by a local millionaire and held at the YMCA on Bedford Avenue. Steph was a sophomore.

He was a beautiful man, Chief Bey—thin, muscular, bald, skin a deep, rich brown. Steph could not believe that he was in his eighties; his arms were veiny ropes, and he moved with a dancer's grace, but then he'd been a dancer most of his life, a song and dance man. That's why he was visiting the program. The cultural coordinator had arranged for Steph's program to go to City Opera and see a production of *Porgy and Bess.* Chief Bey was there to talk to the class because he'd been in a traveling production of the show back in the 1940s.

"How you all doing?" he said, sitting in the front of the room, a poster of Malcolm behind him, Langston to his left.

"Good," the students said. They were high school students, freshman through senior, fifteen total, but they were not cynical and wisecracky with Chief Bey. They did not disrespect him. They all knew he was a Bed-Stuy legend, and they felt lucky to have him addressing them.

"How you all doing in school? You studying hard?" His voice was as smooth as cocoa butter.

"Yes," they said.

"Good. You know why that's good?"

"No," they said.

"Because there is nothing in this world worse than a dumb nigger."

Steph was neither surprised nor taken aback; none of the other students seemed disturbed, either. Steph knew that whatever Chief Bey said was the truth. Chief Bey went on then to tell the class about his time with *Porgy and Bess*. He talked about the show, the music, and he broke into, "A red-headed woman makes a train jump off the track," and his cocoa butter baritone was loud and smooth oozing over the room. One student asked about the difficulties of being a black man traveling all over America in those days, and he said, "That part of my story doesn't interest me." He spoke about Cab Calloway, whom he met, and Duke Ellington, whom he knew, and Lena Horne, with whom he dined. "She was the most elegant human being I've ever known." The students knew who all these people were because in order to attend the show, they were assigned to give oral presentations on various jazz figures from the day. Steph did his on Hoagy Carmichael—"Stardust Melody," "Georgia on My Mind," "Ole Buttermilk Sky." Steph became a fan.

One week later, Steph ran into Chief Bey at night. Steph was out later than he'd intended, and as he walked home, he spotted the old man sitting on the stoop of what he presumed was his brownstone on Throop Avenue. He sat alone. Steph crossed to him.

"Good evening, Chief," he said.

Chief Bey started at Steph's feet and slowly scanned his eyes upward to his face. "Youth is golden. Don't ever forget that."

"I won't," Steph said, sensing Chief might be high, but he couldn't be sure. "I was in that class last week, the one where you talked about *Porgy and Bess*. You've been places, haven't you, Chief?"

"I have been places, yes."

"And seen some things."

"I have seen."

"And you know."

"I know."

"I want to see," Steph said. "I want to know."

"Know everything then. Know everything you can."

And that's when Steph first set out to know everything he could. He was overwhelmed by *Porgy and Bess* when he saw it three days later, and for the next three years, before he left for college, he snuck away for opera matinees throughout the year at City Opera and the Met. He saw Pavarotti sing Rodolfo and wept during "Che Galida Manina." He was more moved by Juan Pons singing "Di Provenza" than anything else he'd ever heard in his life. He was seduced by Denyce Graves' Carmen. He never told anyone in his neighborhood where he was going when he went to the opera. He saved lunch money to pay for tickets, but it cost only ten dollars to stand at the very back of the house, where the acoustics were astonishingly good. His legs never grew tired; his feet never got sore.

He also surreptitiously visited the art museums—MoMA, the Whitney, the Guggenheim, the Met. The Met he visited most frequently because it was the cheapest. For hours he stood before the works of Monet, Degas, Pollock, Klimt, Lichtenstein, Dali and O'Keefe. He was disturbed by the obvious longing and loneliness of Hopper's people; he was spellbound by Gertrude Stein's eyes in Picasso's painting of her.

He felt the pulsing muscle of Benton's laborers. He wanted to sleep with Gauguin's Tahitian women on Gauguin's Tahitian beaches.

And he read, read constantly, read everything he could get his hands on, read lying on his bed at home—Frost, Dickinson, Whitman, Steinbeck, Hemingway, Cather, Ellison, Wright, and on and on. He worked his way gleefully through what he didn't even know was the canon. It was a librarian at the branch on Grand Army Plaza, an attractive recent college grad, who guided his reading.

But by far his most favorite activity was the movies. "Don't see stupid movies," the Chief told him. "You don't have enough time for those. You're already way behind. See the movies that matter."

"Which movies are those?"

"You'll figure it out."

He did. He went and saw movies at Film Forum—the foreign movies, the runs of old black and whites, the Fellini and Bergman and Kurosawa festival films, the Beatles movies, the Marx Brothers. The assassination of the wife in *The Conformist* wrecked him for days. Donald O'Conner's acrobatics during "Make 'em Laugh" in *Singing in the Rain* left him speechless. He was never so aroused as he was by the young Joan Crawford in *Grand Hotel*. Rod Steiger was the most marvelously versatile and convincing actor he'd ever seen. He spotted his old subject, Hoagy Carmichael, playing the piano in *The Best Years of Our Lives*. He knew it was heresy, but he preferred Warfield's "Ole Man River" to Robeson's. But of all the movies he saw, no moment was so indelible as old man Bernstein in *Citizen Kane* telling the pushy journalist about the little girl he happened to see on a boat when he was a little boy seventy years before. Steph was waylaid by the power and mystery of that monologue. He tracked it down in the library and committed it to memory. "One day, back in 1896, I was crossing over to

Jersey on a ferry, and as we pulled out, there was another ferry pulling in, and on it there was a girl waiting to get off. A white dress she had on, and she was carrying a white parasol, and I only saw her face for one second, and she didn't see me at all, but I'll bet a month hasn't gone by since that I haven't thought of that girl."

There were a lot of things that Steph would remember from the hot gym in Tuttle, Pennsylvania, that October night. He would remember how nervous he got when Don charged out into the middle of the gym, thinking that if Don got in trouble for it, somehow he, too, would be assigned some guilt. He would remember the shriek of the redheaded girl as she led the charge to attack Don, a melée that was pretty minor by the time the cops had broken it up and escorted Don out of the gym, more for his safety than anything else. He would remember the clump of chewed green gum stuck to the black baseboard near where he sat, and he would remember the thrill he felt when he watched Don transform so convincingly into a prophet. But nothing he would remember as indelibly as the girl who grabbed his arm. She was a pretty girl, blonde hair, young, and she wore a bright pink tank top.

"You're with him, aren't you?" she said, still holding Steph's arm, all around them, all around the gym, a frenzy. She'd been sitting behind him the whole time, but he didn't notice her until this moment. Steph did not answer her. Like Peter regarding Jesus after the cock crowed three times, he was scared to align himself with Don at the moment. And her eyes—there was something there, something that alarmed him: a conviction, a depth, a gratitude beyond compare. "Thank him," she said. And then she started to cry, tears from someplace deep, a cry from a level of joy and relief he'd never seen before and thought likely he'd never see again. "Thank him for me. Tell him he matters. Tell him not to stop."

And she let go his arm, and Steph rose to exit the gym and go out where the police had taken Don, and he knew that as Old Man Bernstein never forgot the girl in the white dress on the ferry, he, Steph, for as long as he lived, would be haunted by, and would never forget, the grateful girl in the bright pink tank top that warm October night.

THE MIRACLE

ERIK SIMON

Terry Poland's mother, Betty, always told him that in this lifetime, every person gets to experience one bona fide miracle. "And I'm not talking childbirth or love or anything like that. Childbirth is a beautiful, beautiful thing, but there are four billion people on this precious mother of a planet, so it seems childbirth stopped being a miracle quite a while back." She was always a pretty woman, Betty, and she always looked younger than her years. Sounded younger, too. In her late teens and early twenties, she was something of a lost hippie type, and even though she returned to the earth and became a pretty standard blue-collar mother and wife, her voice never lost that ethereal soprano, as if one element of her, just for nostalgia, needed to remain back in the clouds. "What I'm talking about is a miracle, a real miracle, something supernatural that when it happens will fill you with wonder and awe and maybe a little fear. And it will be yours, just yours. And you'll know it's your miracle. And everyone walking on the face of this earth will get their very own miracle too."

Terry's mom gave him this line, or some variation of it, throughout his childhood and even into his adulthood. She didn't bring it up every night, tuck him into bed with a reminder of it, but not a month passed by that she wouldn't mention it at least once. And sometimes the message was significantly abridged, something along the lines of, "It's coming, sweetheart; your miracle's coming." But she never failed to refer to it, and she never stopped believing it, enough so that even as he grew older, Terry couldn't quite shake half-believing it himself, even though reason told him otherwise.

"How will I know it's a miracle?" he asked her once, when he was eight, the first time he pressed her for more details.

"You'll know," she said. "There won't be any doubt."

"How will I know it's mine?"

"Because it couldn't possibly be anyone else's."

"Have you had your miracle, Mom?"

"Maybe. Maybe not. My miracle is my secret."

"Is everyone's miracle a secret?"

"Not everyone's. It's all up to that person."

"And everyone gets one?"

"Everyone."

"Even little babies that die when they're babies?"

"Even them."

So of course Terry went through childhood believing he would someday be the recipient of a major miracle. He didn't walk around looking for his miracle behind every tree or under every bush. He didn't enter every game of cowboys and Indians, baseball or hide and go seek with divided attention. He didn't lie down at night and silently pray that tomorrow would be the day for his miracle. And yet, the idea that one was forthcoming was always on the shelf of his mind, ready to be grasped no matter how long it might have sat there, ignored. And there were certain times when it was hoped for, wished for, immediately—the cold March night he and his mother went to the VFW to sign up for Little League only to discover it cost fifty dollars she didn't have; the third-grade school Christmas party when there was no money for the gift exchange so Terry had to wrap a jar of homemade jelly (which itself had been a gift given to them just three days before) in the Sunday comics and hope no one would see him slide it into the grab bag. But even as he longed in those moments for his miracle, he knew it wouldn't come. Not then. Grab bag anonymity or fifty bucks for baseball—those would have been nice, but they weren't the stuff of the supernatural. Even if he had found fifty bucks lying on the ground, fifty bucks was no once-in-a-lifetime find.

But as Terry got older, he realized that his mother, while lovely and wonderful and, eventually, a good mother, wasn't the most reliable font for wisdom and advice. Of course she didn't think giving birth was a miracle; she'd done it five times with three different fathers. (When Terry's wife gave birth to his two daughters, he found it the most explosively fantastic event of his life.) His mother's first two children, a boy and girl, lived with their father out in Omaha, where she abandoned them to move to a commune in Oregon. That's where she met Terry's dad, a relationship, according to Betty, that didn't even survive the duration of the pregnancy. Terry never met his own father, never even saw a picture of him since cameras weren't allowed in Harmony Village, the name of the commune. His mother never told him much about his father other than to say, "He was a miracle of a boy just trying to find his own square of beautiful earth to give his heart and soul a home." She was still capable of that flighty kind of language even after she settled into her standard blue-collar existence.

His older siblings, the ones back in Omaha, he met once. He was six, still with no younger brother or sister, and his mother had loaded up their baby blue Pinto with what belongings she could fit in order to move them from Elko, Nevada, where they'd been living as long as Terry could remember, to Stony Point, New York, a small town on the Hudson about an hour north of the city where one of her friends from the commune, who also got out, said they could live with her until Betty got a job and could afford her own apartment. (Terry didn't know what her job in Nevada was, but later in life he deduced it was at least stripping and hoped it wasn't also prostitution, though it probably was, at least some limited form of it; she always left in the early evening heavily made-up with glitter on her cheekbones and eyelids, and he was fast asleep before she returned home.) On the drive across country, she stopped in Omaha to see her first two children.

The house wasn't large, a single-story ranch that sat on a steep hill of a residential street of small, older ranch homes that were neither dilapidated nor first-rate. Three wooden steps led to the front door where his mom knocked; she was a skinny blond, immensely attractive even as she wore no make-up, had disheveled hair and wore a floppy sun dress yellow as a sunflower and likely older than Terry. Nobody was home, so she looked at her wrist to check the time (she never wore a watch; it was just something she always did) then looked up at the sun and said, "My guess is three-thirty. So they gotta be home soon."

It wasn't soon, but Terry didn't remember it being agonizingly long, either. They sat on the steps, the sun not beating too hard, the day not unpleasantly warm, but Terry did get thirsty, having eaten the final peanut butter sandwich his mom had made in the motel that morning in Cheyenne. He strolled in the front yard while she leaned her head back against the aluminum screen door and nodded off to sleep. In the backyard, he found a rubber ball, and the sidewalk out front was on such a steep gradient that out there he could toss the ball uphill and bounce it back to himself. That's what he was doing when the father of his mother's first two children pulled up in a white Buick with Terry's half-brother and half-sister. Terry didn't know that's who it was, not at first. It was the end of the workday, so a few cars had returned to the street, the passengers all some variation of parent/offspring combination, and it was only when the father got out of the car and looked to his house and saw Betty and said, "Aw, shit," that Terry realized the two kids with him were his siblings.

"Betty," he said, "what the hell?" He was young, dark-haired, handsome, and though he wore a dark suit, it was an old suit, faded, a tad short in both the arms and legs; the collar of his white shirt was soft, and his red tie had no sheen, like a piece of cloth left weeks in the sun.

"Larry," she said, her voice groggy from her nap but still trying to be enthusiastic, "is that any way to speak to the mother of those two beautiful children?" The two children stood by the back seat passenger door out of which they'd emerged, both of them dark-haired, the girl a few inches taller than the boy.

"Wait here, kids," Larry said as he moved toward the house.

Terry stood about ten feet away, uphill, holding the ball, self-conscious about having been caught playing with their toy. When the boy turned to him and pointed and said, "That's my ball," Terry came forth with the only defense he could muster: "I'm your little brother." And when the girl, hearing that, turned to him with an expression of obvious disdain, he buttressed his defense with, "Yours, too."

The exchange near the front steps was heated on his end, placating on hers, but too low in volume to be fully intelligible to Terry. After a few minutes, she gave a nod of some kind of agreement, and he turned and said, "Kids, come on inside and meet your mother." The children edged forward, reluctant, and when she gave each of them a big hug, neither reciprocated, just stood there with arms to their sides, faces turned away. "You're both so beautiful," Betty said, crying, and only after she stood there admiring them for a moment before their father led them past her into the house did she say, "Come on inside and meet your brother and sister, Terry."

His name was Jack, Jack Phillips, and her name was Judy. They all four sat around the circular Formica table in the kitchen while Larry leaned against the portal, arms crossed. Betty bombarded them with questions about themselves, but she was unable to elicit any response beyond a few sullen words. Larry kept checking his watch. Judy was in fifth grade, Jack in third; Judy liked reading and social studies, Jack didn't really like school; Judy wanted to be a nurse, Jack wanted to play football for the Nebraska Cornhuskers. Occasionally, Betty would volunteer information on Terry, but his siblings seemed no more interested in that than they did in answering her questions. After an hour of this desultory charade, Larry said, "All right, Betty, you've got to go."

"Are you sure I can't stay just a little longer?"

"Don't do this, Betty. She's going to be home in fifteen minutes."

"Can we use the bathroom real quick?"

"Real quick."

It was in the bathroom where Terry drank out of the faucet, finally slaking his thirst. He'd been far too shy to ask Larry for a glass of water in the kitchen.

Back outside, Betty told Terry to wait by the door while she and Larry walked out to the Pinto. Muted tones again, Larry shaking his head. Judy remained inside, but Jack stood out on the wooden steps next to Terry, and the pressure of his brother's nearness was as if Jack were standing on him. "I always wanted a big brother," Terry said, which was true, he did long for an older brother, thought it would be fun to have one around the house, especially in the evenings in Elko when his mother went off to work and left him home alone with the TV on and doors locked, but he'd surprised himself by blurting this so suddenly. Jack said nothing in response.

For whatever reason, though, he did, throughout the years, send pictures and letters to his mother. Not a great deal of either, but it was something. The letters never said much beyond the basics—how he was doing and what was happening in his life—but they obviously meant a great deal to his mother, who cried whenever she received them and eagerly shared them with Terry. And the letters always said to say hi to Terry, which was the reason, his mother conjectured, he was writing them in the first place. "He really wants a little brother." Through the years it crossed Terry's mind to write back, and a few times he actually sat down and eked out a couple of lines, but he never finished a letter and never came close to sending one. Just something about the idea, the project, seemed wrong, as if it were so destined not to be that even if he did mail a letter, it would have gotten lost in the system.

And yet, despite the distance of fifteen hundred miles, and despite his inability to respond with a letter of his own, Terry fantasized about life with Jack. He'd lie in bed at night and quietly talk about his day, his desires, his dreams, as if he were sharing them with Jack. At night, walking the streets in summer, he'd hide behind trees and jump out at imaginary beings, as if he were playing a prank on his brother. Eventually, Terry came to worship his big brother. Jack did evolve into an exceptional athlete, football and baseball, and along with his infrequent letters he took to adding newspaper clippings and photos of his exploits. One picture showed him leaping to make an interception, his arms reaching, his face not particularly distinguishable under his helmet, his dark jersey saying BENSON in block letters across the top, just above his number, 49. The caption underneath read, "Jack Phillips makes the second of three interceptions in Benson High's major upset of Creighton Prep." Betty showed the picture to Terry, as she did all the photos, and this one he deeply wanted to keep; he'd come to worship his big brother. Betty consented to letting him have it, and he carried it to his room as carefully as if he were carrying a sheet of thin glass. He placed the picture between the pages of a hardbound, oversized, illustrated edition of *The Jungle Book*. Where the book came from he never did know; like his mother or his fingers, it was simply a part of his life for as long as he could remember. He never actually read it, not even one story, but he did look at the pictures now and then and lose himself in a flight of Asian jungle fantasy. From that day forward, though, that book housed the apotheosis of his fantasies with Jack—little brother of the football hero. He kept the book between his box spring and mattress and, whenever he wanted, or needed, pulled it out, removed the pictures, and imagined an upbringing with Jack in Omaha.

It wasn't that his life was terrible and that he needed some kind of escape to survive. It was more that while things were always okay, they were also always short of being good, and he was firmly convinced that life with Jack would close that gap between okay and good. There was the little brother, Marlon, and the little sister, Kayla, but Terry was nine when the former was born, eleven when the latter, so he developed no strong bond with either. Ditto the stepfather, Brice, a bald, thin, muscular union construction worker who married Betty when Terry was eight. He wasn't a bad stepfather at all. Sure he popped Terry pretty good a couple of times, but Terry did start a pile of autumn leaves on fire that did almost burn down the neighbor's garage, and Terry did, in fact, tell his least favorite junior high teacher to go fuck herself, so he couldn't claim the pop was unfair. Fact was Terry always had a roof over his head, always had decent clothes, never went hungry, and Brice treated him almost like a son—took him canoeing on the Hudson, helped Terry build his pinewood derby car for Cub Scouts and, immediately after Terry graduated from high school, got him a job with the union. You couldn't really ask much more from a stepfather. It was just that, with Brice, Betty had created a second family, and with Larry, she had created a first family (which, admittedly, she'd bailed on), and Terry always felt stuck between the two, unable to call either his own.

The final picture Jack sent was of him among a group of four Omaha boys who'd all signed letters as scholarship players for the Nebraska Cornhuskers. The four years that Jack played there, Terry and his mother watched the games whenever they were broadcast in the northeast. Only a few times did Terry see Jack on the field, actually playing, and that after Nebraska had established a sizeable lead, which it often did. On New Year's night, 1984, Terry and his mom sat and watched the Orange Bowl game against the University of Miami for the national championship. Nebraska was heavily favored but lost by one point. Terry, a sophomore at the time, was crushed, and he almost wrote Jack a letter saying how awful he felt, but he decided not to. It would be pretty stupid to make a gut-crushing loss the pretext for a first letter. After he'd been working in the union for a year, he decided it was time to move into his own apartment. He bought his own new bed, leaving the old one behind for Marlon, but he took out his *Jungle Book* and removed the picture of Jack's interception. He couldn't bring himself to throw it away, but he also felt foolish taking it with him. He left it under his mom's pillow on her bed. She never mentioned a word about it.

His apartment was small—the only thing he could afford on the salary of a union apprentice. It was in Haverstraw, a village attached to Stony Point but less affluent, and it was a few blocks off of Main Street, the top floor of a ramshackle Victorian in a neighborhood heavily populated with Latin American immigrants, who comprised probably sixty percent of Haverstraw's population. His mother visited him often, especially in the first few weeks when she brought him dinner every other night. And she usually visited without Marlon and Kayla, giving Terry and herself time alone that they'd not really had for almost ten years. "I'm so proud of you," she said the first time she visited, walking through the place largely empty save for the secondhand recliner and TV in the kitchen/living room area and the new bed in the tiny bedroom where his clean clothes lay folded neatly on the floor and his dirty clothes sat clumped in a laundry bag. "All off and out on your own and making your own way."

"Ma, what are you talking about? The place is a dump."

"It's not a dump," she cheerfully reproached. "It's your own, very own, very first home, and you should be super proud."

She'd become so conventional, Betty had, arriving unfailingly through the years at her nurse's aide job in an assisted living facility, picking up Marlon and Kayla from their various after-school activities, even taking pride in the material possession of her house where she tended a small garden and had a picket fence placed around the front yard, but she still retained remnants of that lost and hippie past. She never removed a necklace with a small crystal pendant that she insisted was imbued with protective powers, and often when she visited Terry in his new apartment, she still spoke to him of the miracle he was destined to someday receive.

The miracle was not, she made clear, Irma Guzman, the American-born Guatemalan that Terry married when he was twenty-two, she nineteen, "but that's not because love isn't one of the greatest gifts on Earth," she clarified. "It is, but it's always there, in the spheres, ready to be embraced by anyone. It's swirling through the air, between the trees, over and under the clouds, constantly, and you'll always have it for Irma just so long as you keep your heart open."

For their first date, he took her to a popular Mexican restaurant in town, and out in the parking lot, before they entered, when he asked if she'd ever eaten there before, she said, "My father cooks here." They laughed, and he reignited his truck and drove to a burger joint instead. By the end of that first date, he had a hunch that at some point in the following year, he was going to ask Irma to marry him. She was gorgeous, sure, the petite body and long, black hair, but it was more than that; he'd dated enough women to recognize that there was something special she had that all the others didn't have. It was basically just love Terry was experiencing, but it was a first for him, and while it didn't feel supernatural, it did feel incredibly once-in-a-lifetime, and every time he held Irma in his arms, he found his fortune nearly impossible to fathom.

Seven months later, on Christmas Eve, in his apartment in the evening before joining her family for dinner and midnight Mass, Terry asked Irma to marry him. She wept with joy and said she would, but only if her father consented. "Do I have to ask him?" Terry asked.

"Who else is going to?" Born and raised in America, Irma spoke impeccable English with no accent, but she was also fluent in Spanish.

Terry liked Irma's father about as much as you can like someone who doesn't speak your language. Terry had joined Irma's family (mom, dad, two little sisters) for dinner a few times over the previous seven months, and her father was a terrific cook. Latin Americans, he noticed, had a tendency to cook the holy hell out of steak, keeping it over the fire long enough to make sure all of its juices are gone by the time it reaches the plate, but Irma's father, a master, like many immigrants, at juggling two cultures, knew how to cook a steak brown enough for his old countrymen but juicy enough for the new. He was a short man, thick but not fat, and he was still young enough not to have a trace of gray in his black hair. Two days after Christmas, Terry sat in the small kitchen of the apartment where Irma still lived with her family, sharing a room with her sisters. It was a Sunday, and Terry had joined them for Mass that morning, a largely inscrutable experience both because he'd not been raised Catholic and because it was all in Spanish. He then treated the entire family to lunch at an Italian restaurant overlooking the turbid Hudson. Now he sat in the kitchen, nervous, Irma to his left, her father directly across from him. Irma's mother, a short, fat woman, had removed herself and Irma's sisters to somewhere in the apartment, and though the place wasn't large, Terry could not hear them at all, not even the faintest rumble. His stomach was all aflutter, and he wished he'd not eaten so much pasta primavera.

"Mr. Guzman," Terry said, his throat constricted by nerves and his tie, one of two he owned, both which he rarely wore, this one metallic blue. "With your permission, I would like to marry your daughter."

Irma, in a purple dress and off-white cardigan, translated, and her father, in a black suit jacket and yellow tie, listened and nodded as she spoke, betraying no emotion. Terry had no idea what all she said, but she spoke so long that he knew she was telling him far more than his own single sentence. Perhaps she was tossing in her own thoughts and wishes. She finished, and her father stared deeply into Terry's eyes, as if divining his true character, before he spoke a Spanish paragraph back to his daughter, which she translated for Terry.

"My father says that the first time he met you he could tell you were an honest and decent man. He said that back home, in Guatemala, you were exactly the kind of good and hardworking person the army would have killed because you would have never submitted to their corruption and abuse. He says that in America, a lot of the young men he meets do not have character that strong even though they are blessed to live in the greatest country in the world. Many of the young men he meets, he says, also lack manners and respect for their elders, and you do not. It is for these reasons he is filled with joy," and here Irma started to cry, and she had to pause a moment to wipe her cheeks and gather her composure—"it is for these reasons that he is filled with joy to give his daughter's hand to you in marriage. But he does want your marriage to be sanctioned by the church."

"What does that mean?"

"It means you have to become a Catholic."

Terry thought about that, looking into the eyes of his probable father-in-law. "What all does that entail?"

"Not much. Some classes. An acceptance of Jesus as Christ and his mother, the Blessed Virgin."

"Am I going to be expected to go to Mass every week?"

"That will be an issue for our house to settle, Terry, not his."

Terry melted at her saying, "our house." He nodded. "I'm in."

Terry reached across the table to shake her father's hand, and shortly after, Irma's sisters, one a teenager, the other almost, came squealing into the kitchen as if they were right around the corner, listening the whole time, which Terry wasn't convinced they weren't. They hugged their big sister, all of them laughing, and Irma's mother enveloped Terry in a flabby-armed hug, weeping as copiously as if at a funeral.

When Terry took Irma to his own mother's house to announce the engagement, Betty cried and hugged Irma and said, "You two have taken our world one step closer to peace and harmony." His stepfather shook his hand said, "You're going to like this marriage thing." Marlon and Kayla were too involved with their video game on TV to be pulled away, and Terry didn't care.

The conversion turned out to be a minor affair. Irma's priest, father Javier, was a young, handsome Puerto Rican from Chicago, an avid jogger who Terry figured could probably be banging everything from here to Wrigley Field if he hadn't become a priest. "Do you plan to attend Mass every Sunday?"

Father Javier asked. The two sat in the priest's office, and Irma was out in the sanctuary, praying to the Virgin.

"We haven't fully discussed that yet, Father. Her family kind of sprang this whole Catholic thing on me. It's a whole new world to me."

Father Javier smiled warmly, knowingly. "I understand. Do you accept Jesus as Christ?"

Impossible as it seemed, Terry had never given Jesus much thought; all through his childhood, he never once went to church, not even for Christmas and Easter. But he was open to the idea of Jesus, what little he knew—he didn't see how it could hurt or even change much in his life—and he wanted to marry Irma. "Sure."

"Are you willing to be baptized?"

"Sure."

"And will you be raising your children Catholic?"

"Absolutely on that." Irma had told him to be definite when that question came up.

Father Javier said the conversion would be no problem. "We can even fast-track it," he said. As soon as Terry was baptized, he just needed to make his first confession, focusing on the mortal sins ("I'll explain those later") and then he could take communion, after which he could be confirmed. "Everything else about the church you can learn as you go along."

"What kind of time frame are we talking?"

"When would you and Irma like to be married?"

"This coming summer. June or July."

"We can accommodate that."

"Let me ask you something, Father. You seem sort of causal about this, a lot more so than Irma's father."

"I'm a realist, Terry. I don't expect you to pursue sainthood because you want to marry Irma. Your guarantee that you're going to raise your children in the church is what matters to me most."

Terry respected that kind of honesty; it made his conversion easier, less fraudulent. It wasn't that he didn't believe what the Church was asking him to believe—he was certainly open to all of the possibilities; but he felt now that he didn't have to fake a sincerity and devotion that it was impossible, at least for now, to possess.

The baptism was a quiet Friday afternoon affair with Irma, her parents and Father Javier. Terry did not feel significantly altered by the experience, although Irma's mother embraced him immediately after with a heightened vigor. That first confession was one of the more surreal events of his life, though. His mortal sins were few—no murder, no theft beyond some petty shoplifting as a kid, no coveting except for the new trucks and better apartments of some of his friends—but he did feel stupid confessing to the number of times he'd masturbated over the years, which he could only loosely estimate, and he didn't like admitting the number of women he'd slept with ever since he'd lost his virginity to a divorced waitress when he was sixteen. It wasn't an outlandish number—in the high teens— and though he didn't give the names of the women, he felt that even identifying them by number was a betrayal. He hated when he heard guys bragging about a sexual conquest. He didn't begrudge them speaking with satisfaction in general terms, but the moment they put a name to it, he thought they violated a basic decency. Talking about his own number, he felt guilty of the same violation, and that's why he kept the number one shy of the actual tally. Only he needed to know that he'd slept with Irma, the future mother of his children. He wasn't her first, but neither was she his, so he harbored no jealousy.

The wedding took place on the kind of day in early August that every bride dreams of—mid-eighties, low humidity, plenty of sunshine. Terry was nervous, but his best man, a fellow union guy he'd gone to high school with, told him that the hardest part was the standing around and waiting to begin, and he proved to be right. For the rest of his life, Terry only vaguely remembered the service. The most salient detail was the priest's mouth because that's what he spent most of the service looking at. The reception was at the restaurant where Irma's father was the cook, the same restaurant that was almost the site of Terry's and Irma's first date. The parking lot was cordoned off to all save invited guests, two large tents were raised in front of the restaurant, a Latino DJ played a mix of Latin and American music, and the food in the buffet serving trays was mountainous. Knowing that Irma's father could not afford this kind of reception, Terry had contributed a good chunk of his own money to help, and his mother and stepfather pitched in, too. "What's the point of a wedding if there's not a decent party afterward," his stepfather had said.

The reception had upward of a hundred people. The wedding was late afternoon, so by the time the dancing got started, it was almost night. Terry and Irma's first dance as a married couple was exquisite—pink sky, soft breeze, the song a slow ballad by Pablo Milanes, a Cuban singer that had long been Irma's favorite. But for Terry, that dance wasn't the most indelible memory of the night. That distinction belonged to his dance with his mother. Night had fallen, a clear night with an opulence of stars. The DJ played Sinatra singing "I Get a Kick Out of You," and while Irma danced with her father toward one end of the asphalt makeshift dance floor, Terry danced with Betty at the other end. For the first part of the song, she said nothing to him, just stared smiling at her son before she started to cry. After the song's first verse, the DJ said other couples could now dance, and a handful did come out, including his stepfather with Irma's youngest sister and Marlon with Irma's mom. That's when Betty spoke.

"I wasn't stupid, Terry," she said. "I knew what I'd done."

"What are you talking about, Ma?"

"You. How alone you were. How alone I made you. For a few years, I actually tried to find your father."

"Ma, it's okay. Really, I was fine."

"Then that time we stopped in Omaha. Remember that?"

"Of course I do. I've watched Nebraska football for fifteen years because of it."

"I tried to leave you there. It wasn't that I didn't love you. I just thought the Phillipses would give you a better home. Larry got his head screwed on straight so much sooner than me, and I had no idea what to expect out here in New York, and at the time I thought that if I couldn't be with all of my kids, at least they could be together. It seemed like such a good idea."

As vividly as anything, Terry remembered turning to Jack and saying he always wanted an older brother. He couldn't imagine how different life might have been had he stayed in Omaha and grown up with Jack. Though there were many times during his upbringing when he would have eagerly embraced that scenario, that certainly wasn't the case on his wedding night. "If I would have grown up in Omaha, I would have never met Irma. Believe me, I've got no complaints."

"I know," she said, crying. "That's what I'm trying to say. I know how alone you were all those years, never meeting your first family but just that one time, never really feeling a full part of your second family. I know it. I could see it. And now you've got Irma, and pretty soon you're going to have your own family, and you are never ever again going to feel alone like you have, and I'm so sorry I made all of your life harder than it needed to be."

Terry gave his mother a firm hug. "You did all right, Ma. You did just fine." The song ended, and the other couples all dispersed, but Terry and his mother maintained their embrace. "We both came out all right," he said, before they finally did separate.

The honeymoon was a weekend jaunt up to Foxwoods, the casino resort in Connecticut. Irma worked as a cashier at CVS, so both she and Terry took Monday off for their honeymoon, but neither could afford to take off more than one day, so they were back late Monday afternoon, when Terry and Irma's father moved the rest of her belongings into his apartment. They had already spent much of the summer furnishing and arranging it to her liking.

Thus commenced their prosaic life together, the standard life of a young couple becoming a family. Fourteen months after the wedding, they had their first child, a daughter they named Jessica. Fifteen months after that, they had another daughter, Kimberly. They moved into a larger apartment closer to the river. Day care was so expensive that continuing to work at the CVS with its minimal, if not minimum, hourly wage no longer made sense, so Irma quit that job and began cleaning houses where she could keep the children in a portable playpen while she worked. Life was more of a struggle, but they were still both happy. Irma said they always would be as long as she continued to pray to the Blessed Mother, which she did every night on her knees with her daughters when she put them to bed. It was a plastic icon of the Virgin no bigger than a teacup, Mary in profile, on her knees, praying, her head covered in a white veil that looked like a nun's habit. It was old. Irma explained to Terry that back in Guatemala, her father had kept it in his coat pocket and prayed to it constantly, and he was convinced that was the reason he'd survived the government terror that had tortured and killed so many men during his first twenty years. Terry wasn't so sure, but he felt in no position to argue with the reasoning of anyone who'd survived something like that.

But their tree of modest fortune slowly began to lose branches. First came the recession at the end of the century, and the work for Terry tapered, not dramatically, but they were

living on a tight budget even when the work was plentiful, so
the four weeks or so of work he'd been cut back that year had
an impact. His bosses said it would all turn around soon, and
he told himself that the time off gave him a chance to spend
more time with the girls, but all day with two kids under three
wasn't exactly sunshine and beer. He felt less exhausted after a
day of hauling and hanging sheetrock. And the work situation
didn't improve. After 9/11, it only got worse.

Other factors compounded. Jessica, the older daughter,
developed asthma when she was three. During the first attack,
Irma knew exactly what it was, having seen it in her own sister,
and even though she told Terry what it was and that it would
be okay, it was still a gut-punching experience to watch his
toddler daughter unable to gather enough oxygen. Kimberly
slept in her baby car seat while Irma held Jessica on the drive to
the emergency room, Terry steering the truck with one hand,
rubbing Jessica's back with the other. It took superhuman
restraint to keep from putting his mouth on hers and blowing
enough air into those tiny lungs. The asthma became a
manageable condition, but not for free. He had pretty good
insurance with the union, but co-pays for medicine and
emergency room trips added up. And no matter how many
times he saw it and knew what would be the ensuing scenario,
it never did get easier watching his daughter fight for breath.

And then he wrecked his truck. Not his fault, and not
totaled, but again, not free, even though he had insurance.
Terry fantasized that one of these days, he was going to wake
up, and insurance in America wasn't going to be the legalized
scam that it was. But then that would mean—well, he didn't
know what it would mean, and he knew that nothing regarding
insurance would probably ever change except to benefit the
companies even more.

Next, Irma lost one of the houses she was cleaning. It was a
sweet family over in Nyack—the ritzy, artsy town of the

county—and the father was being transferred to Dallas. They had a daughter a couple of years older than Jessica, so Irma not only got paid from them, she also got clothes for her own girls, toys, books. She was able to pick up a replacement house a few months later, but that was four months with one less house per week, which was a hundred fewer dollars per week, which was four hundred fewer dollars per month, which was a significant sum in a household where the father's hours had been reduced first by four weeks, then six, then eight and eventually, ultimately, eleven—almost three months of work lost. That four hundred dollars, spent carefully, was a month of groceries and diapers. It was new coats for all of them for winter. It was a big chunk of one month's rent with just a small chunk set aside for him and Irma to have one night, just one night, out for dinner and a couple of beers while his mom or her mom watched the girls. Just one night. But no. And more work never came.

"I'm headed down to Florida," his stepfather told him. The two sat at a bar one hot summer day after work, not union work, rather a two-day side job building a small deck that Brice had gotten them. "I got a friend in Tampa who has his own company. He says it's still gangbusters down there. I'm going to be one of his foremen. I asked for you, but he said he could only hire one for now."

"I appreciate it, Brice."

"What are you going to do?"

"Haven't a clue."

His mother wept lavishly the day they left. His sister, Kayla, now fifteen, was dressed like a slut with a tank top that barely reached her belly button and tight jeans that barely rose above her pubis. She sat in the car listening to her music with her earphones, and when Irma asked if she wanted to get out and hug her nieces good-bye, she shook her head no. Terry wanted to backhand her. He would not miss her or Marlon, who'd not become selfish and mean but had become fat and useless. But he would miss Brice, who had raised him well. And he would miss his mother, whom he'd seen almost every day for these first twenty-six years of his life.

"You take real good care of my granddaughters," she said, hugging Terry so tight it almost hurt, her elbows and forearms a bony collar around his neck.

"You'll see them soon enough," he said, just saying something to say something, to keep himself from crying, but still believing it was essentially true.

"No," she said, "I won't. I won't see them much now ever again, and I won't see you much, either."

"Come on, Ma."

"I know how these things work, Terry. It's how it'll be. But it'll still be okay."

But okay was a goalpost that each passing day was moved further and further away. Over the next year, Terry lost another three weeks of work, and at the end of the following September, Irma was pregnant again. They'd been so careful, taking a handful of precautions, but one broken condom dashed all of their efforts. They tried to be happy about it, and Irma tried to excite him with the idea that this time it would be a son, but any way Terry looked at it, another round of diapers and another mouth to feed was nothing to rejoice over. For the first time in his life, he felt desperate. He reached for any filament of hope. He did not go to Mass, thinking it would be kind of cheap for him to start showing up now, but one night, as Irma went into her daughters' room to tuck them in, he joined her. She kneeled to pray to the Virgin, and he kneeled with her, grasping her hand, the hand that held the icon. And that night, as he lay in bed, before he fell asleep, which the potholes of worry made an increasingly difficult destination, he had the idea, out of nowhere, to contact his big brother Jack.

It was an especially desperate act, he knew, but he was especially desperate. He'd not heard from him since that last letter just before he went to college to be a Cornhusker. He didn't even know where he lived but figured Omaha was a good place to start. The next morning, another unwanted day off, he called directory assistance in Omaha. There were four listings under Jack Phillips. He wrote down the address and phone number for each. The first he called was an old man, the second he called he spoke with the wife who said it wasn't the Jack Phillips who used to play for Nebraska, "But I sure would like to meet me that Jack Phillips," she said lasciviously. The fourth he called he spoke with Jack himself, who said he wasn't the son of Larry. The third Jack Phillips, he got an answering machine—Jack, Bess, Tom and Bo weren't home, but he could leave a message, "and be sure to thank the Lord for a blessed day." He didn't leave a message. He had no idea how to begin the conversation he knew he needed to have. And he was thrown off by the Lord comment, not merely because his day didn't feel so blessed. He opted to write a letter instead.

Jack: I know it's been a real long time, but it's your little brother, Terry. Mom is living in Florida now with Brice. He's a real good guy. They've been married about twenty years. I'm still in New York. I've been married six years. I've got two daughters and another child on the way.

This is all up and out of nowhere, Jack, but I could use some help. I'm a union construction worker, and I'm a real hard worker, but the work's been drying up something terrible. I know we hardly know each other, but since you are my older brother, I'm just wondering if there's any work out there in Omaha. Like I said, I'm a hard worker. All I've ever done is construction, but I'd be willing to do anything. Sorry to bother you. Thanks, Terry.

He considered including a picture of his daughters, just to show Jack his nieces, but he thought that might come across as playing the sympathy card way too hard. He felt a sense of humiliation when he mailed the letter but also a sense of hope. He got a response in a week.

Little Brother: The Lord God is a mysterious one indeed.

My favorite scripture has always been 1 Peter 5:6: "Humble yourselves therefore under the mighty hand of God, that in due time he may exalt you." When I was playing football for Nebraska, I said that scripture over and over to myself, especially in practice when things were getting rough. A lot of us Christians on the team would repeat that line of scripture—it was a pretty popular one with football players. To us, it meant that we just needed to shut up and keep working hard and one day we would have our moment of glory on the field.

Well, I never had any glory on the college field. I'm not complaining. I had plenty of glory in high school, and I'd rather be on the sidelines for Nebraska than on the field for any other team. Nebraskan by birth, Husker by the grace of God, we like to say. But I've never forgotten that scripture, and I've never walked away from the Lord just because I didn't win the Heisman. Maybe my day of glory will come later, I thought.

After college, I got a job here with Barber Pine, a solid company that does some heavy machinery manufacturing. The home office and one of our factories is here. I started out as an administrative assistant to the vice-president, a big booster for Nebraska football, and I have kept myself humble under the mighty hand of God, showing up fifteen minutes early every day to work and never complaining about even the most menial task. I climbed the ranks, and just last week, I was promoted to head of personnel. That night, while my wife and I were having dinner with our own children, Tom and Bo, she and I discussed why it might be that the Lord gave me this new position. And then the next day your letter arrived. And the man is a fool who tries to convince me that this was all a coincidence.

So yes, brother, come to Omaha as soon as you need. We're doing plenty of hiring, so give me a call. My number's on my

enclosed business card. My wife said she would also start looking for
a starter apartment for your family so you can move right in, get
right to work, and get your girls into school. I cannot wait to meet
my nieces. Judy, our sister (remember her?), is a high-powered
lawyer, and she's married, but she doesn't have any children. So
you can't imagine how excited I was to hear about your children.

I'm sorry things have been tough for you, but not completely
sorry. That scripture from 1 Peter I quoted, the end of that
paragraph is, "And after you have suffered a little while, the God of
all grace, who has called you to his eternal glory in Christ, will
himself restore, establish and strengthen you." Sounds like you've
suffered and like the Lord is restoring you. But had you not
suffered, you would have never reached out to me, and I would
have never been reunited with my little brother. I would have
never gotten the chance to be a real big brother. Yours in Christ,
Jack

Terry was dumbfounded. He sat and read the letter in the
local McDonald's where Jessica and Kimberly laughed and
screamed joyfully in the play palace with a handful of other
screaming and laughing kids, their mothers nearby. He read the
letter once, twice, then read it a third time. He simply couldn't
believe it. He wondered if it were a hoax, but then how could
that be? He had his brother's business card with his title,
Director of Personnel, Barber Pine Industries, in his hand.
What dumb luck. What incredible dumb luck. Or was this his
miracle? The idea to contact his brother did, after all, come
after he'd prayed with his wife to the Virgin Mary. And his
brother was certainly tuned into the whole Jesus thing. Miracle
or no, he needed to get home and give him a call. He gathered
the girls and charged out into the rainy September afternoon to
his truck.

He was nervous as he dialed Jack's number at work. A
secretary answered, and when Terry gave his name, she said
excitedly, "Oh, Mr. Phillips has been looking real forward to

your call. Wait a moment and I'll put you through." Jack answered with, "Baby brother, how *do* you do?" It was a booming, boisterous, buoyant voice that didn't even attempt to reign in its joy. "Well," Terry said, "I got your letter here, and I'm doing a lot better today than I was yesterday." Jack gave a laugh whose heartiness was buoyed by years of beef and pork products. He then explained that because he was at work, he didn't have a lot of time for catch up chit chat, but there would be plenty of opportunity for that in Omaha. He said their company constructed roadwork machinery, pavers and the like, and there were currently three positions he needed to fill on the floor immediately, "assembly but not assembly line. You can have any one of those three, but I need you out here in a couple of weeks, tops. Can you do that?" Terry said he could. Jack asked his price range for an apartment, Terry told him what he was paying for his current two-bedroom, and Jack fairly guffawed. "You can get a house out here for that kind of money." Before they said good-bye, Jack told Terry to keep him apprised of when he would arrive and to be sure to call the day before, and Terry promised that he'd be there within two weeks.

Irma wept when Terry told her the news. He asked if she was sad, and she said she was crying for a combination of factors. She was crying because she was leaving her parents and sisters, and she was crying because she wasn't sure she wanted to live in Omaha, and she was crying because the Blessed Mother had saved her family yet again, but mostly she was crying because she felt that everything might be okay after all, and for two years now she hadn't been sure that would be the case, even though she never stopped faithfully praying and telling herself it would.

Her tears were nothing, though, compared to the deluge of her mother and sisters during the warm October sunrise of departure. It was absolute agony for Terry to watch. "I'm sorry

I'm moving your daughter so far away," he said to his father-in-law, convinced the stoic brown immigrant understood his sentiment if not his words. Irma translated, and her father, through Irma, said, "As husbands and fathers, we do what we have to do. I left my country twenty years ago and have not seen my parents since. But my daughters are healthy and safe, and I know Irma and my granddaughters will be healthy and safe with you."

"And maybe your grandson," Terry said, patting Irma's belly, which had not yet begun to show. His father-in-law smiled without Irma having to translate.

And Terry loaded his family into the truck, which had a U-Haul hitched to the back, and he drove slowly out of town and over to I-80 where he headed west for Omaha.

Also on I-80, headed west, was Luella Hastings, mother of Broderick, nine years old and at her side, fervently playing his Gameboy. He'd been playing steadily for two hours, ever since they stopped for gas, pretzels and water, and he'd been largely silent about it other than an occasional groan or sigh. So for two hours she'd not interrupted his fun, not even disturbed him with attempts at conversation. She got no radio reception out here in the mountains of Pennsylvania, other than some right-wing AM Bible stations, so she'd kept her own company, placidly enjoying the scenery and fantasizing about their future. But she was ready for a bit of dialog to rattle the monotony, and besides, she was getting antsy, nervous, which she tended to do in between rehearsals.

"Okay," she said, trying to sound excited so as to pep him up—low energy was murder to any performance. "Let's run the greeting again."

"Oh come on, Mom. We just ran it."

That ticked her off. She'd been prepared to hear him say he didn't want to run it, which she could have accepted—she wouldn't have, but she could have—yet she was in no mood for him to dodge the pursuit of excellence with an untruth such as they'd just run it. "We most certainly did not just run it, young man. We haven't run it for almost four hours."

"Can't we just wait a little longer?" he pleaded, though not with a whine. He was not a whiny kid. Bit of an asshole at times, but not whiny. He was implausibly handsome with sandy blonde hair and ridiculously blue eyes and the two largest, most obvious dimples she'd ever seen on any human being, adult or child—long fingernails stamped into uncooked dough. Everybody said he looked like a mini-Brad Pitt, and while Luella always smiled and thanked them for the compliment, she thought they always said that because they were too stupid to know better. Brad Pitt, hell. He was no legend. Where was his Oscar? Redford. Her child looked like a mini-Robert Redford, but then most of the parents of Broderick's friends probably had little idea who Robert Redford even was. Those yahoos knew nothing pre-Schwarzenegger. Pre-Jim Carrey. Pre-Julia Roberts, that horse-mouthed no talent.

"We cannot wait just a little longer," she snapped. "What possible good does waiting a little longer do anyone for anything? Especially in the car? Wait for what? Right now, you're just sitting there doing nothing, and in a little longer, you'll still be just sitting there, doing nothing, so just give me the goddamned greeting, and then you can go back to your goddamned game."

Broderick shook his head and turned off the game. He wasn't nervous; he'd seen her worse. And he'd been here before often enough to know that acquiescence was his only recourse. "Good afternoon, Mr. Spielberg," he said with all the dazzle and snap of a wet sock.

"And what, young man, was that? You greet *any* director with that sort of tone, you won't land an extra role in a pissy, small-town production of *A Christmas Carol* let alone the lead in Steve's next movie. So, give me the greeting, and give it to me like you mean it."

Broderick's transformation was sudden, his performance seamless. He sat the Gameboy on the seat between him and his mother, he manufactured a smile that was wide but not so much so as to hint of a lack in sincerity, his ridiculously blue eyes sparkled with warmth and delight, sunrise on the Mediterranean, and he said in his mellifluous boyish tenor: "Good afternoon, Mr. Spielberg. Before I begin, I wanted you to know how profoundly moved I was by your use of color in *Schindler's List*. It was, quite simply, art of the highest caliber." And then he closed his eyes and gave that brief, slightly devotional nod of his head.

And Luella, though she'd seen it countless times before, could not refrain from marveling. "God, you're good," she said. But then he ought to be. She'd done everything humanly possible to prepare him for this opportunity, or one like it, since the day he was born.

Luella Hastings hailed from Goodland, Kansas, and she always claimed it was the most inappropriately named town in America. "Nothing good about it unless you're partial to boredom and wheat." But that wasn't true. Her father was a mailman, her mother a homemaker, and Luella had a near perfect upbringing out in the vast plains of western Kansas, and she knew it. She just repeated that boredom and wheat line because it took her a good six months to stumble upon it, and she knew it had pep and punch. It was not only witty, it also conveyed a certain jaundiced urbanity that she didn't have when she first left Goodland straight out of high school.

Goodland was small, approximately five thousand souls, but it was large enough to give her a major sense of accomplishment when she landed the role of Anne Frank her junior year of high school, competing against nearly a dozen

other girls, some of them seniors, all of them with "real talent."
"Not for one moment did I not believe that this daughter of a
mailman wasn't a tragic little Jewess trapped in an attic,
confined by the cruelest circumstances of our century's greatest
tragedy," wrote the reviewer for the local paper, the *Goodland
Star-News*. Her senior year she was cast as Adelaide in *Guys and
Dolls*, and the same reviewer wrote, "Last year a Jew; this year a
joy. Apparently there's nothing on the stage that Luella
Hastings can't do with soaring ability." Luella concurred.

She attended McPherson College in the small town in
central Kansas named after Civil War General James Birdseye
McPherson, and she did not surprise herself when, after
auditions just two weeks into her first semester on a hot,
September day, she landed the role of Nora in *A Doll's House*,
the school's first production of the year. A string of triumphs
followed: Mother Courage in the Brecht classic of the same
name, Laurie in *Oklahoma!*, Karen in *Speed the Plough* (a racy
production that went largely unappreciated in the sleepy college
town), Laura in *The Glass Menagerie* (of course), Nina in *The
Seagull*, and perhaps her greatest performance, Puck in *A
Midsummer Night's Dream*. "Made us forget that the role had
ever been played by a man," wrote the co-ed reviewer, an
awkward though not wholly unattractive kid from Missouri
whom Luella slept with, largely to secure the solid review—
she'd read the Hollywood histories; she knew how the game
was played. "Made us forget that there ever was a Mickey
Rooney." That was a line Luella had to feed him. He, like
probably most on campus, had no idea what he was referring
to.

After college, she beelined to L.A., bursting with
confidence. Her parents weren't thrilled about her decision.
They'd been to McPherson and had seen some of her
performances, and they readily admitted how talented their
daughter was (though for the life of them they could not

imagine from where the talent came; they hardly ever watched movies let alone thought about performing, and they were both such awful singers that even for their most cherished hymns in church, they just hummed along). But Los Angeles was so far away, and it was such a, well, sinful town, and the movie business could be so . . . contrary to solid, family values. "Couldn't you just stay here in Goodland and get some top-notch community theater going?" her father asked. "Or what about doing some shows in Kansas City or Denver first, something a little closer?" Privately, Luella scoffed. Kansas City? Denver? Those towns weren't nearly big enough to contain her charisma and talent. At best, they were whistle-stops for has beens and second-raters touring in shows best left forgotten. But outwardly, to console her parents, she played the role of cautious, pragmatic daughter. "I know you'd like me to remain close," she said. "I know to you I'm still just daddy's little girl. And if nothing turns up in a couple of years, I'll be happy to come home. But I have to give this a shot. I just have to." Of course she never dreamed something wouldn't "turn up." Was it really just a fluke that she happened to have the same first name as the great Luella Parsons, even though it was spelled differently? In fact, as she left for the west coast in the shiny white Ford her father bought for her, she couldn't decide if it would be six years or seven before she was able to buy a home in the Hollywood Hills large enough to comfortably accommodate herself, her director husband and her parents. She'd be like Elvis sharing Graceland with his folks.

In L.A., she became a cliché—a buxom, wholesome-looking Midwestern girl who, even after she'd gone ahead and succumbed to the casting couch three years after cattle calls and auditions had landed her nothing more than some extra roles, was still unable to land anything better than a couple of lines as a waitress in a B-grade horror flick. ("Those fries good?" she asked the gruesome murderer. "Got any ketchup?" he asked.

"Let me check," she said. "No," he said, "let me," before he immediately slit her throat with a steak knife and let her blood spill all over his fries.) So four years after she moved to L.A., she did it—she turned to porn. Soft core.

She figured she couldn't degrade herself any more than she already had. And she was still young, taut, attractive and wholesome-looking, that Midwestern bucolic fulsomeness not yet fully given way to the gaunt cheeks and hollow eyes of a life whose dreams were crushed. She ended up with a sizable role in three soft-core pornos, although everyone in the business simply referred to them as "films." She wasn't sure how much the producers liked her after her first movie, so she took to dating the director to secure the next two. Colin Gray. He was a handsome but overweight blond Irish guy from New Jersey, and Luella was attracted to him not only physically but also emotionally. He wasn't a jerk, like a lot of guys in that business tended to be. He had a naiveté which she found endearing: he genuinely believed that art, even in the porn world, was still the goal, and he was convinced if he made a few real quality gems, it would open the door to a nice studio deal for a legitimate film. She dated him steadily, happily, over the course of a year, essentially moving in with him though keeping her own apartment, just in case, and it was near the end of the shoot for her third film that she became pregnant with Colin's child.

"You can't have an abortion," Colin told her, still dripping with the residue of his childhood Catholicism immersion; his attendance at Mass had fallen off, but he was still wont to go after a particularly hard party where he snorted what he considered to be an unseemly amount of cocaine.

"I can have whatever I damn well want," she told him, "but it just so happens that I want to have this baby." The moment she learned she was pregnant, she'd begun transferring her dreams for herself onto her child.

"Do you want to get married?"

"No."

"You don't want to marry me?"

"I don't want to marry anyone." She knew that nurturing and raising a performing prodigy was going to be a mighty task that tolerated no divided attention.

"What do you plan to do then?"

Pretty good question, that. Even had she wanted to return to Goodland, she couldn't. Only one week after her first movie was released on cable, she got a call from her father. "Oh, Luella," he said in a heartbroken voice soon after she answered. "What did you go and do?" "I'm sorry, Dad," she said, sincerely so about the pain she'd caused him but not about the choice she'd made. "I only did what I had to do." "You didn't have to do that," he said. "Not that." He would never understand, she thought. He couldn't. But she was still their daughter. She knew they would welcome her and their grandchild into their home if she had absolutely no other alternative, but she was not about to return to Goodland, not because she was such an obviously fallen angel but rather because she was such a publicly grand failure. Those people never understood her aspirations and were therefore bound to feel superior; they said they loved it when the youth of their town went on and succeeded, but she knew they always privately resented those who were too uppity to stay home. And that mentality, coupled with her movies—she was not about to return to endure the stares of condemnation from the eyes of such complacent mediocrities.

She ended up moving in with Colin's mother, Clancy, back in Elizabeth, New Jersey. It was, to Luella, a godawful, smelly, overcrowded, factory-belch of a town, but Clancy had an old, spacious house right across the street from a park with massive trees and a playground. Colin was the youngest of seven siblings, and his father had died twenty years back, but he'd been successful enough in the banking business to have paid off the house and provided his widow with a nice pension. Had he lived longer, their sunset years would have known opulence, but Clancy wasn't complaining. She'd been able to be a full-time mother for a sizable brood that never had to worry about food or clothing, she could enjoy her grandchildren now, all scattered about the tri-state area, and she could even take a nice trip once a year and catch a few shows on Broadway. When Colin phoned Clancy to tell her he was giving her another grandchild, she said, "What about another daughter-in-law first?" Colin laughed it off, and after he explained the situation, it was she who said, "Send the little vixen out to me. There's plenty of room. Tell her she'll never have to see me if she doesn't want to."

"You don't mind?"

"Colin, if my seeing this grandchild is dependent upon you coming home, I'll never see it. If I minded, I wouldn't have made the offer."

It wasn't Luella's first choice, but financially the move made the best sense. She wouldn't have to pay rent, she wouldn't have to pay utilities, and she might not have to pay that much for food. She did have a tidy sum saved from her movies, and there were going to be some modest residuals for the next few years, but that money wasn't going to last forever, and even though she let Colin know she'd be making damn sure that through him their child never experienced even a dram of deprivation, she still thought it made too much sense to save her money as much as she could not to do so. Besides, she didn't want to have this baby alone. She would never admit it to anyone, but she was scared. It was hard enough raising a regular child. How much harder to raise a star? So many things could go wrong. And since she didn't have her own mother nearby to coach her on the basics of parenting, allowing her to concentrate on the child's career, she was pleased to get Clancy as a surrogate. Seven kids—she'd seen it all. Besides, if the kid was going to get the training it needed for its stellar career, it was going to have to be in L.A. or New York, and since the West Coast option wasn't proving viable, the East Coast one was a must.

Colin arranged for a livery driver to take Luella from the Newark airport to his family home. It was a cold, slate-sky day, and Luella, standing on the spacious, elevated porch, waited until her chauffeur had her four bags of luggage on the porch and had driven off before she rang the doorbell.

Clancy was a thin, white-haired woman more stylishly dressed than Luella had been expecting—tan slacks, white blouse and red sweater, all Brooks Brothers, some smart Stewart Weitzman shoes. Her pretty face was admirably free of wrinkles. "You must be Luella," she said, not with a brogue but with the cadence of one. There was no faint hint of a smile or twinkle in her eyes.

"I am," Luella said.

"You don't look like a tramp."

"Because I'm not."

"Well let's add this up. You're carrying my son's child even though you're not married to him. And you spent however many years in Hollywood doing God only knows what, only to wind up starring in one of those whore movies my son seems to think is going to lead him to an Oscar someday. By my tally, that makes you a tramp."

With the past five years of her life pared down to such stark, undeniable statements, Luella got her first clarion glimpse of just how degenerate she'd become. Out in L.A., where everyone in her milieu was willing to do whatever it took to get to the top, the only acts that merited pause and discussion were those of *not* selling out. "What do you mean you wouldn't take it up the ass? His show is slated for HBO!" But now, standing before someone so matronly on such a wholesome porch (porch swing, welcome mat, wicker table and chairs) of such a homey home, she saw with piercing clarity how far she'd fallen. And she wept. That's when Clancy opened the screen door and wrapped Luella in her arms. "That's okay, dear. Even the worst of tramps can turn things around."

But Luella wasn't crying because of what she'd done to her person or her reputation. She was crying because none of it had paid off, for that was the moment she'd also seen with bone-crushing insight that all her dreams for herself would always and ever more be just that—dreams. She wiped her tears, took a deep breath and climbed the stairs inside four times with her luggage. Sitting on the twin bed in her new room with the door shut, she swore an oath that all the things she had had to do to try to make her own dreams come true, she would be willing to do that and more for her child.

She was so relieved the child was a boy; it really did stand a much better chance at succeeding in the business. And as a boy, maybe he wouldn't have to do the casting couch gymnastics she'd had to perform. She named her son Broderick. On phone calls home, Colin had voiced his hopes that Luella would give their son a nice Irish name—Seamus or Liam or Guilwellen— but Luella had made it clear early that that would not happen.

"What have you got against Irish names?" Colin asked.

"Nothing. It's the Irish I have a problem with."

"And what would that be?"

"Every Irish guy I've met is either stupid or a pussy."

"Well which am I?"

"You figure it out." (It was the latter, but the longer she had to deal with him, the more she thought the former applied, too. He'd been in the porn business now for eight years, and while he'd directed almost a dozen movies, he had yet to produce one, and it was eminently clear that producing was where the money was.)

She named him after Broderick Crawford. She loved *Born Yesterday* and happened to catch it on Turner Classic Movies the night before she gave birth. She brooked no discussion that Bette Davis in *All About Eve* was robbed of the Oscar that year. Judy Holliday was flawless, and Broderick Crawford was so virile in the movie—domineering, bellicose, decisive, a real man. He barked orders at everyone from maids to senators, and things got done. That's the kind of strong Luella wanted her son to be. She fantasized about little Broderick calling the shots and all the producers and directors scrambling to meet his demands. (It did strike Luella that Crawford's character wasn't overly bright, but for brains she'd just watch him in *All The King's Men*, which was the role, after all, for which he won an Oscar.)

But Luella well knew that her own Broderick would have to be more than just strong to make it in the business, more even than just strong and smart. He would have to be handsome, he would have to be sensitive, he should have a ready wit to quickly unholster in any situation; and it wouldn't hurt him to be able to sing and dance, either. So the moment she brought him home from the hospital, she did everything humanly possible to make the complete perfect package. She bathed him only in organic soaps free of all chemicals and dyes, she bought him clothing made only with organic cottons and wool, and she used cloth diapers delivered every week by a high-end laundry service that used eco-friendly detergents. She used organic cleaners to keep the house diligently free of germs, and when little Broderick did get ill, she refused to taint his body with baby Tylenol or any other non-holistic medicines. Once, he had have a fever of 104°, and she gave him a sponge bath with washcloths dipped in cold Evian water. The fever subsided.

Of course she breast fed him, and to guarantee the quality of her own milk, Luella ate a strictly organic vegetarian diet. And when he was old enough to eat, she made him an organic vegetarian, too. "What's wrong with giving the boy a little meat?" Clancy asked.

"Your son ate meat, and look what happened to him."

"You're starting to lose your sense, missy."

Colin, for his part, did an admirable job as a father, at least as much as Luella would allow. He paid all the hospital bills and for everything else—food, clothing, even some rent to his mother. He sent toys, which Luella always donated, unopened, to charity, not wanting Colin to gain any kind of foothold. He even gave two hundred dollars each month to a college fund he started for Broderick, despite that Luella had made it clear that college would be beneath her son. And all he ever asked in return was the chance to see Broderick; Luella, however, was relentless in her refusal.

"Why not? He's my son."

"You're filthy, Colin. You're a filthy man in a filthy industry surrounded by filthy people and filthy ideas. I'm not going to let you near my little temple, and if you try to visit, I'll slap a restraining order on you, which won't be too hard, given your occupation."

Luella wasn't completely heartless. She did send Colin pictures, copies of the same pictures she sent her parents. They wrote a note, expressing their desire to see their grandson some day. Luella wrote that that could be arranged once he was a tad older. "But it'll have to be out here." She wasn't about to subject her temple to the silent judgment and scorn that would be heaped on him, on them, in Goodland. The tidal wave of negative vibes would be devastating to his psyche. It would open him up to a future of all talent and no esteem, a Sal Mineo or Gary Coleman.

He was six months old when she took him to his first audition, a modeling gig for a magazine ad selling baby clothes. He didn't get it, and she was livid. She called the casting agency and excoriated them for making such a poor choice, but when the woman on the other end of the line asked her name, she hung up. She knew better than to start burning bridges. She calmed herself and resolved that for the sake of Broderick's career, until he had some real clout, she would have to take an entirely different tack, one that was pleasant, congenial and, if need be, accommodating in every way possible. Which was how she did land Broderick his first job—a magazine spread for baby food that included an Asian baby and a black baby. Luella invited the representative in charge from the baby food company to her house for "a private conference and consultation." She'd lost all of her pregnancy weight, she wasn't yet even thirty, and she knew damn well how good she still looked. The rep was in his mid-forties, fit, and didn't look so bad himself. When he left the house, he guaranteed Broderick the job.

"I'll not have that behavior in my home," Clancy told Luella. "You can whore yourself to ruin all you want, but you'll not sully my grandson's life under my roof."

"Don't you lecture me on morality, you shanty bitch. Your precious flesh and blood is one of the kings of the porn world."

Life with Clancy was no longer possible, and Luella moved into her own apartment in Fort Lee, which was just a quick drive over the George Washington Bridge into Manhattan for auditions. She made Colin pay the rent and buy her a new car, a silver Toyota Corolla. She couldn't wait until Broderick signed some major contracts, securing their financial independence. And given how beautiful, how perfectly adorable, he looked when she opened the magazine and saw him in that baby food ad, she just knew the days of the major contracts would be sooner rather than later. In addition to the two thousand dollars for that job, Luella also received ten complimentary copies of the magazine. She sent one to her parents and kept all the others for herself, as well as twenty more she went out and purchased at various newsstands and drugstore magazine racks. She used a razor blade to cut his ads neatly out of each magazine before she attached one each to Broderick's head shots, saving one that she had laminated for the scrapbook she was compiling of his career. He was going to be bigger than that little asshole Macaulay Culkin; she could just feel it.

When he was four, she took him to see *Les Miserables* on Broadway. She'd prepped him by having them listen to the soundtrack together for weeks, and she'd also read him the script. (Ever since he was a baby, she read to him constantly—Shel Silverstein, P.D. Eastman, Margaret Wise Brown, Dr. Seuss, yes, all of the standard children's authors, but she also read Tennessee Williams, Eugene O'Neill, Beth Henley, August Wilson, and on and on, including movie scripts. Luella believed greatness was a multifaceted achievement arrived at by many means, one which included something akin to osmosis. "You think Drew Barrymore understood what the hell she was doing in *E.T.?* Of course she didn't. But she didn't have to. Just growing up in a Barrymore home with the Barrymore name—legendary talent swirling like birds all around her, constantly pelting her with the birdshit of greatness. She was destined. It was in the house, in the name. She couldn't give a bad performance if she tried.") She especially focused on the lines of little Gavroche and his song, "Little People," a cute ditty if not exactly a showstopper (although when Broderick had that role—and she swore he would have it—Luella had some ideas to punch up the song a tad; She also thought she might pursue getting Gavroche a second number). They attended a Saturday matinee, but inside a Broadway theater it is always night—a time of darkness and bright lights and a stardust of dreams sprinkled in the air. It wasn't only Broderick's first time at a Broadway show; it was Luella's, too. When the houselights went down and the music began, Luella wept. She'd come a long way from that high school stage in Goodland, Kansas.

Granted, she wasn't performing, but it was still a long way she'd come to sit in this seat where most in Goodland never would. She was flabbergasted by the quality of the production—the lights, the scenery, the singing and choreography (the acting was of a level she knew she could still match, even exceed). Broderick, for his part, sat wide-eyed through the production, full of wonder and awe. When little Gavroche climbed over the barricade and was shot and killed in his elaborate, minute-long death scene, Luella turned to her own son and, with tears in her eyes, said, "Oh, Broderick, don't you want to die like that every night?" The look her son gave her could be described only as blank. She left the theater that afternoon with a renewed vigor for her commitment to his excellence.

She enrolled him in a dance class at a local studio, focusing on tap and jazz. "What the hell good is there in ballet? Take away *The Nutcracker*, and there's no role for Broderick for the next twenty years." She also started him in voice class with a mid-fifties homosexual who had his years in various Broadway choruses and minor roles as well as some leads in a handful of traveling shows. Luella preferred gay teachers for Broderick because her looks and wiles were irrelevant to them, so there was never anything ulterior at work in those lessons. For his acting, she was in charge. Together they did scene studies on a regular basis throughout his childhood, plays and films that involved children but also, to improve his range, quality adult works. When he was seven, he absolutely nailed the final Russian roulette scene from *The Deer Hunter*. He had the De Niro role.

Amid all the work, the lessons and the auditions, Luella strove to give Broderick as normal a childhood as possible—school, play dates, birthday parties, slumber parties, trips to the amusement park. Colin eventually stopped pleading to see his son, as she knew he would. He was always preoccupied most with his career, and that achieved greater heights in the porn world, which required more of his focus. And as for Broderick, he seemed to embrace, or at least accept, his mother's dream for him. Sure he loved playing with his friends and appeared happier doing that than anything else, but what child didn't? He was a dedicated student who never whined about his lessons and only occasionally groaned or sighed at a demand. All of it had been such an integral part of his life for as long as he could remember that he never perceived any of it as any more optional than eating or sleeping. "When you grow up," his mother would tell him, "you're going to be so rich, famous and powerful that no one is ever going to tell you, or me, what to do ever again. Doesn't that sound like fun? Doesn't that make all of this work worth it?" And Broderick would smile and nod his head, not fully grasping what she was saying but seeing how excited she was and wanting to share that excitement, if only to please her.

His first big break came when he was seven. By then there was the string of modeling gigs, but nothing else thus far. He'd auditioned for a number of plays and musicals around town but had never gotten more than a chorus extra—a nameless orphan in *Annie*, a child villager in *Fiddler on the Roof*, ditto *The Music Man*. And all of those productions were off-Broadway. He'd also auditioned for a handful of tiny movie roles and a couple of nice-sized roles for TV pilots but had never been called back. When he was seven, though, he was called back. Luella shrieked with ecstasy after she hung up the phone. She charged into Broderick's bedroom where, with a friend (a little Chinese kid—Fort Lee was full of Chinese), he was putting together one of those high-tech Legos, this one some futuristic ninja bird. She wrapped him in her arms and squeezed him violently. "You got a call-back, Broderick."

"Mom," he said, almost angry, holding his Lego safely aloft, "you're about to break my Ice Ninjago." His Chinese friend rescued their half-built construction.

The pilot's director, its creator, and a handful of producers were present at the call-back, as was the original casting agent. They sat on metal folding chairs in a large, plain studio in a building on Thirty-fourth Street. One end of the room was set up like a half-hearted attempt at a living room—a couch, two slipper chairs, a coffee table. The pilot was a police drama of a single-father cop (wife was killed in a bank robbery) with a son so handsome that every time the father brought a girl home, she would be utterly smitten with the kid. Broderick was in the running for that kid. He ran scenes over and over with three different actors, all of them obscenely gorgeous and perfectly lithe, and all of them "fun" for Broderick. But there was one actor in particular that he meshed with, another sandy-haired guy who, before he even ran a scene, came onto the mini-set, picked Broderick up, slammed him on the couch and tickled him mercilessly. His name was Sam, and Broderick fell in love with him. He'd been getting tired of the tedious process, but the tickle attack was just what he needed to bring some fresh vivacity to his audition. Sam was no fool, either. Broderick would grow bored with running the same scenes over and over, repeating the same lines, but with Sam there was a familiarity, a rapport, and an obvious energy that was lacking with the other two, almost as if they *were* father and son, or at least close cousins. Watching them, Luella felt a twinge of guilt for keeping Colin out of Broderick's life, but then he would have never been as cool and clean as Sam, so she exonerated herself just as quickly.

It was impossible for Luella to discern what the show's brass might have been thinking, but she didn't need to. The chemistry between Broderick and Sam stuck out like a quarter in a stack of dimes. Nonetheless, when they left the audition, she didn't brim with confidence; she knew from experience that over the next few days, a handful of other boys would be doing what Broderick did today, and maybe one of them would be even more spectacular with another of the older actors. And so she waited, but she was calm. Something about this one felt guaranteed. And when she got the call the following week, and the show's creator told her they wanted Broderick, she wasn't surprised. And when she asked who got cast as the father and was told that it was Sam, she was, again, unsurprised.

The following three months were the best in her life. As they filmed the show's first five episodes, she was consumed with her duties as mother of the child star—getting him to the set, making sure he ate well, tutoring him in schoolwork, helping him memorize lines, and best of all, watching him perform. He really was a natural, at least in this role, but that was in part because Sam made their scenes together so fun that the spirit in them was genuine. After three months of shooting, Sam told Luella, "Broderick's got it. I've worked with kids before, but none like him. He's really got it."

But as high as she flew during the filming, she descended that low when she got the call that the series had not been picked up. "Not even by some pissy little second-tier network like A&E?" she asked, incredulous. Nope. Not even them. Nobody. She hung up the phone and dropped to the floor and sobbed. Broderick came to her and hugged her and asked what was wrong. She told him. "Does this mean I don't get to see Sam again?" he asked. She gave her adorable son a hug. Of course it was all about Sam for him. So they phoned Sam a couple of times, and he promised he'd come out to Fort Lee to play with Broderick, but he never did, and Broderick returned to his normal routine, but Luella, having gotten a real taste, having come so close, could never be the same. Her obsession became Faustian. She pushed Broderick even harder, doubling up on the dance lessons to include hip-hop, lengthening the voice lessons, driving even harder in the nightly scene studies. Broderick started to push back, resist, complain about the workload, but Luella would have none of it. "I know what's at the end of this road, little man, and you don't, so just shut up and do as I say, and believe me, believe me, when this is all over, you will thank me with every fiber of your being." So Broderick kept his mouth shut, kept his smoldering resentment in check, at least with her because he was scared not to. With others, though—friends, teachers—he began to display an unlikable streak, began to solidify his reputation as a bit of an asshole. And all for naught because no work came. For the next two years, despite all the auditions, nothing came to fruition beyond the steady modeling gigs.

But the moment Luella heard Spielberg was holding auditions in Chicago for his next movie to be shot on location there, she knew this time would be different. It was a feeling in her gut, a deep certainty that something big was about to break their way. And she wasn't about to blow this through laziness or stupidity. Which was why, driving in their silver Corolla on I-80 in Pennsylvania toward Chicago, just a few miles from the Ohio border, she slipped into a bout of irrational fanaticism borne of paranoia, something she was wont to do. She'd had an interlude of mental solitude to replay in her head the past nine years of her life with Broderick, and she turned to him toward the end of the long internal monologue and finished it ferociously aloud: "But a woman who has the innate brilliance to name you after Broderick Crawford knows how to strike when the iron is hot, and I'm telling you that right now, in Chicago, the iron is blisteringly, scaldingly, mercilessly hot. So give me your goddamned monologue, and give it to me like you goddamned mean it."

Broderick had become accustomed to these random outbursts. "The one from *Jaws* or *The Color Purple*?" he said, slyly turning off his Gameboy.

"*Jaws* goddamn it, *Jaws!*"

And Broderick delivered his monologue while his mother drove them toward his stardom, drove him toward his destiny.

And a few miles in front of Luella, also headed west on I-80, were Don and Steph, Steph at the wheel. They'd slept late that morning and had gotten on the road moments before lunch, having only just finished breakfast. They spent the night in a hotel, a Days Inn they found an hour north of Tuttle, near Clarion, a decent-sized town with a traveler's hub of hotels and restaurants just off of the interstate. They had their choices of hotels—Hampton Inn, Days Inn, Best Western—but once Steph declared he wanted separate rooms, prudent economics guided their choice along with an assist from nostalgia—a Days Inn is where Don stayed with his parents while vacationing when young. (Toss in the marquee boasting of the free breakfast buffet, and the Days Inn became a slam dunk.) It was a little early in their journey to be succumbing to the wiles of a hotel; the money would go fast if hotels became a habit on only their second night away. But Steph was close to pleading in his tone when he made his request. "I really need a good night's sleep, D. And that will not happen if we camp tonight."

"Thought you said you slept all right in the car."

"No. I said I slept all right *for* sleeping in the car, which does not mean the same thing. I had low expectations, exceedingly low in fact, and they were met."

"These little foreign seats are pretty lacking. If I owned a Buick or Lincoln, you'd be able to spread out and sleep the sleep of the dead."

"It wasn't the seats as much as it was the mountains. Lovely during the day, but nighttime's a different game. I'll probably be better in the Midwest. What's the worst thing that can get me out on the prairie?"

"A serial killer. We seem to have been blessed with an inordinate amount of those in the heartland. Also a klansmen, but that's mostly if you're in Indiana. Ohio and Illinois you'll be fine, especially if you trend north of Columbus and Springfield."

Truth was, Don was in a hotel state of mind himself—a nice bed, a few Diet Cokes, some cable TV: that was the award he thought he deserved. He was in a decidedly celebratory mood.

It took the Tuttle police a few minutes to remove him from the gym. He offered no resistance, but it took some serious effort to extract those kids from his person and keep them at bay long enough to shuttle him out. Even as he left with the escort of two cops, each gripping a bicep though not roughly, the other six policemen were still at the center of the gym where they'd formed a circle around the rabid Colleen and her zealous cohorts. Those kids were shouting, but the gym was otherwise relatively quiet, a low murmur of chatter. It felt, to Don, that he had them rattled, the bystanders of Tuttle, and that felt good. During his police escort he tried to make sly eye contact with Steph, but he could not do so without turning his head, and he thought it best to stare forward.

Once outside, the two policemen let go of their grip on Don's arms. "Thanks, guys," Don said. "I wasn't sure I was coming out of there in one piece." Which was an exaggeration, but he did feel like he might have just dodged a drubbing. High school kids aren't kids, after all, and a couple of his attackers looked meaty enough to be on the football team. Don did well defending himself, though. Only one person got a decent lick in, but it was to the shoulder blade region, so little damage was done, little pain inflicted. It was mostly a lot of shoving and a hugging kind of wrestling, the type that can lead to pulled hair and a scratched face, so Don used his arms to protect the head region—those scratches can have a nasty sting for a good couple of hours. His other goal had been to remain on his feet, and his girth served him well there.

"What's your name, sir?" one of the policemen said, the younger of the two, although they both looked to be young, one a contemporary of Don in his mid-thirties, the other in his late twenties. The officer's voice wasn't hostile when he asked Don's name; just curious, conversational.

"Don," Don said before he paused, wondering if he should go with Bollinger or Prophet. He didn't want to risk the trouble that might accompany lying to a law enforcement official, but the night had been such a roaring success, and he didn't want to stymie his momentum. "Don Prophet." He kept the dream alive.

"That your real name?" the other, older officer asked.

"What's real? Judy Garland's real name was Frances Gumm, but to the world she was real only as Judy. Say Frances Gumm, and most people still won't know what you're talking about."

"Let me see your license."

"It's Bollinger, Don Bollinger. But in public I go by Don Prophet." Don fessed up in something of a panic, but he immediately regretted it; if he was going to do this thing and make it work, there could be no lapse, no breaking of character; something was just compromised, something lost.

"That's fine," the officer said, "but I still want to see your license."

"Have I done something wrong?"

"Beyond lying to a law enforcement official? Probably not, but we haven't decided yet."

Don pulled out his wallet and handed over the license, and the walkie-talkies on the officers' hips said, "Where do you guys have him?" The younger cop unhooked his radio and spoke into it. "Right out front, Sheriff." The other officer used his flashlight to scrutinize Don's license, and a moment later out on the street a police SUV rolled up and was double-parked. The sheriff turned on his flashing blue lights but not his siren, and he got out. The other three stood quietly waiting, and Don kept glancing at the doors to the gym, wondering why no journalist had followed them out. If they were going to write about the incident (and how could they not if they were covering the meeting?), it seemed to him that they'd want a little back story on Don Prophet, some pertinent details on the outsider who descended upon Tuttle and caused such a ruckus.

"Evenin', Sheriff," the officers said almost in unison as their boss approached, a chubby guy in his late fifties wearing civvies—dark slacks and a short-sleeved plaid sport shirt.

"What do we have?" he asked.

"Don Bollinger," the one holding the license said. "From New York."

"Where in New York?" the sheriff asked Don.

"The city."

"Which city? There's more than one."

"New York City. Brooklyn specifically."

"That doesn't come as a walloping surprise. My wife's from Buffalo. They get a little tired up there of New York City being referred to as 'the city,' as if it's the only one."

"Never been to Buffalo," Don said.

"You're not missing much." The sheriff reached for Don's license, which the officer handed him. "Give me some light, Jim." The officer shone his flashlight on the license. The sheriff studied it, studied Don's face, and returned his license to him.

"Was it your intention to cause a public nuisance?"

"Furthest thing from my mind, Sheriff. I came to Tuttle because that's an important meeting you're having in there. How your school board ultimately decides on this could have ramifications that affect far more than just Tuttle. The impact could be national." Don knew that the more he elevated Tuttle's importance, the more, by association, he elevated the sheriff's. He briefly considered complimenting the efforts of the officers in protecting him and maintaining order in the gym but thought that might have been pouring it on just a bit too thickly.

"Well from what I hear," the sheriff said, "you caused a bit of a scene in there."

"With all due respect, sir, I only rose and spoke my piece according to the rules of the debate. It was the group of teenagers who physically assaulted me who, if I may say, caused the scene."

"That true, Jim?"

"That's pretty much how it happened, Sheriff."

"Where are the kids?"

"They're being held out back till we find the parents."

At that moment, Steph came out of the building, loudly, pushing the long metal handle on the blue metal door with a fierce urgency, as if he were being chased by a mob. He saw Don with the police and immediately adopted the tack of pretending not to know Don: Steph knew better than anyone that at that moment, having a black friend would do Don no favors. He walked calmly, normally, down the sidewalk, bubbling out into the grass to give Don and the officers a wide berth then back onto the sidewalk. He considered waiting nearby though out of sight but thought it prudent just to keep walking calmly and normally back to the car.

"Well," the sheriff said, "I got nothing to hold you on and no real reason, either, although something about you coming all the way out from New York City just doesn't settle quite right with me. Why don't you just go to your car and drive on out of Tuttle, never to return, and we'll pretend tonight's incident never happened. Sound good to you?"

"Sounds fine to me, sir."

"And you weren't considering pressing charges on those kids for attacking you, were you?" the sheriff asked with a hint of menace to his tone, guiding Don's response.

"Absolutely not, sir. I wish all of our children were so passionate about issues that matter."

"That's enough, son. Jim, why don't you escort Mr. Bollinger to his car, make sure he gets there safely. There may still be some angry teens out there, waiting behind some bushes for one last shot at our guest."

The older officer smiled. "Yes, Sheriff. Where you parked?" he asked Don.

"A few blocks that way. Over on the street."

Jim and Don walked back to Don's car. The autumn night was gorgeous—warm, quiet, redolent of sweet decay. Jim's footsteps against the sidewalk clacked decidedly louder than Don's rubber-soled steps, and they made an unavoidable noise, one hard not to register, even focus on, in the insect-riddled night. Don was doing his level best not to smile. Once he would be delivered to his car, the night's victory would be complete, but he wanted to maintain a straight face so as not to appear gloating or condescending.

"So what's it like in the city?" Jim asked once they were beyond the reach of any lights from the school, out of earshot and eyeshot, Don noted, from his boss and colleagues.

"Pretty amazing place," Don said. "Always something interesting happening."

"Are people as rude as they say?"

"Not even close. And look, I'm no native. I'm from a small town in southern Illinois, so when I moved out, I had some of the same expectations of the city as you. But I've found people in the city to be the friendliest, most helpful people I've met anywhere. You just have to ask is all."

"What about crime? Is it as bad as they say?"

"You hear about it, but frankly, the thing about crime is if it's not happening to me, it's tougher to be aware of it."

Jim nodded. "I've always wanted to visit. Go to a Yankees game. Catch me a Broadway show."

"You should."

"Maybe someday. Just hasn't worked out yet."

They turned a corner, and Don's car was now in sight. Steph stood leaning against it, but when he saw Don and Jim approach, he stood straight, and while Don wasn't positive, he was pretty sure Jim moved his hand to his belt—his gun, his taser, his club, something. "Know him?" Jim said.

"One of my best friends and one of the finest people I know. He owns a great cigar shop in Brooklyn. When you visit, you should come on out and have one, on me."

"I don't smoke."

"It's never too late to start. You're really missing out."

At the car, Don introduced Steph to Jim. The two shook hands, and Don told Steph to pull out one of his business cards. Don asked Jim if he could borrow the pen in his shirt pocket, and he wrote his home number on the back of Steph's card, telling Jim to give him a call when he came to the city and he'd be happy to show him around.

"I appreciate it," Jim said, putting the card in his chest pocket, along with the pen, and shaking Don's hand. "Hey, let me ask you something if you don't mind."

"Shoot."

"What you were saying in there tonight about the Bible, those two conflicting stories—that's true, isn't it?"

"Yes."

Jim slowly nodded his head. "It does make you think, doesn't it?"

"That's the hope."

"That Pastor Paul," Jim said, "I never have trusted him. He's a little too smooth for my tastes. I prefer my preachers to have a wart or two and not look like a game show host."

Don and Jim said good-bye, and in the car, as Don drove cautiously out of Tuttle, he remained quiet, keeping his ebullience in check. Steph started to speak, but Don held up his hand. "Not yet," he said. He drove on the highway north, leaving the lights of Tuttle, entering the outer dark, the mountains darker shapes against the dark night sky. His headlights on high beam shone an indication of a gravel pullout up ahead, and he slowed his vehicle onto that gravel and stopped. He put the car in park, raised his clenched fists, and said, "Yes. Yes, yes, yes," pounding the air with his fists each time he said it as if pounding on a door. His joy was too much for the Hyundai to contain. He unfastened his seat belt and got out, leaving the door opened wide as a frozen yawn. "Yes," he shouted to the night sky, thrusting his fist toward the dim stars, which he felt convinced he could reach. He went in front of the car for more freedom of movement and did a dance, a sort of touchdown celebration, some shimmies, some shakes, some butt-shaking turns. He pressed down on the hood a few times, bouncing the car enough to make Steph instinctively put his hand on the dashboard. "Yes," he shouted again before shouting it one last time then returning to the car and fastening his seat belt, almost winded. "Unbelievable," he said. "Unfuckingbelievable. I was on fire in that gym tonight. *En fuego*. I was the burning fucking bush spontaneously combusting for all to see, and the good people of Tuttle, P. A. were a collective Moses wondering what the hell it was that came storming into their meeting, storming into their lives. I. Was. Great."

He drove, and the wonder was that he drove so calm amid the tempest of his joy: it was the exuberance of a game long prepared for and won, a production perfectly performed on

opening night. Granted, Don hadn't been *that* long in
preparing for the night; the idea of becoming a prophet, after
all, had struck him only a few days earlier. And yet, for such an
outlandish idea to have come to fruition not only so soon after
its inception but even at all—Don simply couldn't believe it.
Things didn't work out for him like that. Things didn't work
out for most people like that. It wasn't his way, his path, his
life. Oh, his wasn't a bad life at all. He had, really, no
complaints. He had food, clothes, a roof, which was already
more than most in the world were guaranteed. He may not
have had a job he enjoyed, but neither did ninety-eight percent
of the rest of the working world. So his life was okay, he knew,
but he wasn't among the charmed, the people for whom
everything worked out. Don had seen them; he knew them.
Some of them were famous, some were not. They were the
people born under a lucky star, they breezed through life with
little effort and rigor, and good fortune came their way often
unbidden. Their hopes were realized before they were even
hoped for. They were the people who went to baseball games
and caught a foul ball, people who went to the beach and it
never rained, people whose car never broke down. They were
the people who got great jobs they didn't even interview for—
they just happened to meet the boss at some bar or happened to
sit next to the boss at some dinner party, and the boss really
liked them. They weren't plentiful, but they were ubiquitous.
They weren't mean. Mean people were those who had
absolutely no idea how blessed they were in this life or who
thought all of their blessings were not the result of some dose of
luck, small or large, but rather the result, solely, of their efforts.
The mean people weren't the charmed ones, and the charmed
ones weren't mean because they were too happy breezily
enjoying the moments of their lives, not giving too much
thought about tomorrow. When the mean ones happened to
get great seats for that Broadway show that had become

impossible to get tickets for, they could think only of the handful of people who had better seats that night or think only of how hard they'd had to work to put themselves in a position to get those great free seats. The charmed ones simply enjoyed the show. The charmed ones were not most of us, and yet, we never resent the charmed ones because they enjoy the show so thoroughly that their mere enjoyment becomes an act of unadulterated gratitude. Life unfolds exceptionally for the charmed ones without any planning on their part. Don was not one of the charmed. Things turned out well for him, he knew, but not exceptionally, and never without toil. And that's why his level of excitement was stratospheric that night—it was propelled by fiery surprise and the fuel of exceptionalism.

"It was incredible," he continued in the car. "*I* was incredible. I was filled with a purpose and the purpose poured forth." He shook his head, reliving, disbelieving. "Through me," he said, gesturing forward with the hand that didn't steer the car. "Through me. That's what D. H. Lawrence said about what he wrote. He said he was a channel, that his work did not come from him but through him. I've had a similar experience when I write. I'll be on a roll, in the zone, and I'll come out with this word I didn't even know I knew, and then later, when I check the definition in the dictionary, it turns out to be the perfect word, *le mot juste*. That's how it felt tonight. It just came through me. I mean, that scripture from Corinthians: where in my big old roomy ass did I pull that out from? I didn't even know I knew it. But then I do have a superlative memory, I'll give myself that. And when you read the Bible as much as I do and give those evangelists the time that I give them, you're bound to be absorbing more than you realize." Don shook his head, amazed. "Damn." He thought about it all a little further and said again, incredulous, "Damn." He was so consumed with himself that he didn't even think to ask Steph what he thought of the night. In fact, it was only after Steph poked the finger of his voice into the bubble of Don's self-reverie with, "It *was* pretty amazing," that Don even registered the idea that there might have been perspectives that night other than his. But even that poke Don received as a nudge into deeper self-reflection. "Wasn't it?" he said. "Wasn't it precisely that? Amazing?"

Yes, it was, Steph thought; amazing and more. For him, it was something bordering on the alarming. It wouldn't have been. Normally, it wouldn't have been anything more than a choice and chance spectacle he just happened to be present for, something out of the ordinary that happened in the world every day but that we usually only read about or catch on the news— a hiker lost in the Rockies, a bank robbery, a walk-off grand slam. But that girl altered his experience. She was a variable that changed the equation, transforming the chance spectacle into something deeper. As embarrassed as Steph was to even have the thought, and as impossible as it seemed, that girl made the whole lark of Don Prophet seem as if maybe, just maybe, this wasn't a lark. He could not shake the earnestness of her face, the gratitude and relief in her eyes. He wondered what unwittingly he'd gotten himself into, what Don had gotten himself into. Through him? Don himself just admitted that that was how it felt, that he was a channel and those words came through him. Could what he said really have been inspired? And if so, from where did that inspiration come, and why? Steph sought solace by immediately changing the topic. "Look, D., what do you say we get a hotel tonight? It's a bit late to be setting up camp and I could use a good night's sleep."

They then had their conversation about the quality of Steph's night of sleep. Don did not seem surprised by Steph's sudden request. "I got no problem with that," he said. "Seems the least tonight's success calls for. I could go for a nice massage, too, but I doubt those are available."

And so they drove along the dark highway that curved through the mountains until they found the brashly lit cluster of hotels and restaurants near the junction with I-80, a garish oasis in a desert of darkness like a safe outpost in some futuristic world. Don was actually leaning toward the pricier Hampton Inn, still with a sense of celebration, the quality of his room a stand-in for champagne, but that's when Steph tossed out the separate rooms idea.

"Are we made of money?" Don said.

"I got a hunch you snore something fierce," Steph said. Don allowed that Gretchen had said as much. "Besides, I need a little time to myself. I'm going on forty hours straight with you, interrupted only by the solitude of my shower, which didn't feel so solitary in that lavatory in the woods, and I just need to be alone."

Don didn't begrudge that; he needed some time alone himself; and the need for two rooms was what pushed him toward the Days Inn. Their rooms were on the same floor, near each other though not connecting, and before they parted for the night, Steph asked Don if he wanted to borrow the cell phone and give Gretchen a call. Don said he'd call her tomorrow, and the two friends bade each other good-night.

It was amid the steam and meditative patter of a long shower that Don's sense of buoyant celebration eased toward something else, sidled into the realm of thoughts that Steph was having, though he didn't know Steph was having them. He let himself kick around the hacky sack of a notion that he might actually be a prophet. He knew it was grandiose, stupid and implausible, and yet it didn't hurt to play with the idea for a while, anymore than it hurt when he fantasized about being on the set of a movie based on his novel, consulting the director, joking with Natalie Portman or Gwyneth Paltrow in between takes. Plus, some evidence did seem to be accruing—the girl at the gas station who bowed her head, the incredible coincidence

of the evolution meeting, his inspired speech. And what about
that cop afterward who implied he'd now be taking another
closer look at Genesis? And that was just one person out of the
two he'd spoken with after the meeting who was there and
heard him. Fifty percent is a pretty solid average, and when
you're talking prophecy of the Lord, anything above ten
percent has to rank as stellar. Just to spare Sodom and
Gomorrah, Yahweh asked Abraham to scare up only ten decent
people total. Ten people is nothing. Peanuts. Don figured he
had ten people before he even got to Corinthians.

If he were a prophet, he would have to have been called.
An odd concept, that. Hear a voice calling you to serve God,
you're a mainstream minister, hear that voice often, you're a
psychopath. He watched a PBS special once on this very
subject, a low-budget set of interviews with ministers and rabbis
and imams discussing their calling into the clergy. It was men
and women, and to a person each one said it wasn't a voice so
much as it was a feeling, one of discomfort, distraction, even
slight depression because they were all pursuing one course but
had the nag of a notion that they needed to be pursuing
something else, a nag that grew stronger over time and came to
dominate their days. And it was only after they acknowledged
that nag, that calling, not just quietly to themselves but also out
loud to another, that there came a release from the discomfort.
Did Don have that? There was the despondency of having to
get a job and the cynical elation of his gimmick, its idea then
pursuit. Does that qualify as a calling? Or what about the urge
to rail against the Koreans in Washington Square? He did feel
relief after that outburst, but again, that was more the delight
and optimism of stumbling upon the gimmick. Did that
compare with the prophets of old? Well, God told Jeremiah
he'd fingered him for the job in the womb, even consecrated
the fetus, and then broke the news to him as a little boy, who
even at that tender young age knew enough to beg off the gig.

So there was an actual voice, a conversation, as there was with that little do-gooder Samuel who kept hearing his name while trying to sleep in the Temple (wasn't he at least a tad creeped out to be sleeping next to the ark of the covenant?) and going over to Eli's room and asking what he wanted before the old guy finally figured it out. "Go lie down. If you are called again, say, 'Speak, Lord, for your servant is listening.'" Again, some dialogue, and Don had nothing remotely akin to that, but the Bible did say that in the days of Samuel, the word of the Lord was rare and prophecy was not widespread, so maybe at the time there needed to be an actual voice from above, something to really grab the prophet's attention (though not to the extreme it reached with wacked-out Ezekiel, the four figures in the swirling dust, one-legged and winged, the fiery throne atop: the only time Don had a vision resembling that came after a bad batch of oysters he slurped down in Carolina). Then there was all the drama surrounding the call to Jonah, that diva, but for the most part all the other prophets—Zephaniah, Zechariah, Amos, Nahum, Habakkuk, Haggai, Hosea, even Isaiah, Mr. Perfect himself—with all those other prophets, there was no mention of their calling. It was just a leap into action in their books, a jump cut to the exciting parts, as if prophecy were no longer so rare and the calling a minor event not worthy of mention—a trip to the butcher or an evening glass of wine.

Don's "calling" certainly fit into that classification, but the logical equation he formulated there would imply that prophecy was once again widespread, and he was far from sure he wanted that to be the world's calculation, for that would plunge him into the dicey math of who else in contemporary America might be conveying God's message. No wonder these televangelists could be such a crazed lot. Some of them, to be sure, knew they were frauds and were in it for the money and were laughing (and praying) all the way to the bank. But some of them actually believed their words and their mission to shout from the mountaintops of gold. Don could see that in that glazed look they got in their eyes. But maybe some started out as frauds and became so intoxicated by their ability to captivate millions that they came to believe in a special calling for themselves. It was the very path Don was half-facetiously walking now, and that only because of one successful night in a Pennsylvania high school gym.

By the following morning though (latish morning, for he did sleep the long, deep sleep of a solider after battle), he put away the grandiose thinking of the night before and returned to a light-footed joy of celebration. He basked in a copious feeding at the breakfast buffet, paying special attention to the sausage links and the mini-doughnuts smothered in cinnamon sugar. He went through those as if they were potato chips. At the Hess station across the street, he filled the car with gas and bought three major newspapers from the state. He told Steph to drive, he had some research to conduct, and Steph asked, "Where?"

"Let's do the interstate a while."

"Thought you preferred highways."

"Any sane person does, but I am Pennsylvania-ed out. I need me a different state, some new turf. We'll find a highway once we hit Ohio."

And so Steph drove west on I-80 while Don scoured his three newspapers. But he found nothing. "Nothing" was, in fact, the word he used. It did not take him long to scan all the headlines in the relevant sections of the papers, including the op-eds, which he was especially surprised had no comment about the meeting. After reading at the third paper, he tossed it into the back seat atop the previous two and said, "Nothing." He had not lost all sense of accomplishment from the night before, but there was now a slight but certain disappointment. "Not a goddamned thing. Nothing in the *Philadelphia Inquirer,* nothing in the *Philadelphia Daily News*, nothing in the

Pittsburgh Post-Gazette. Nothing. Put aside the fact that whether or not we teach our kids actual science is a big enough deal to merit coverage, but in addition, I turn that crucial meeting into WrestleMania, and not one of these three major papers prints one word of any of it. There wasn't even an op-ed. Does no editorial board in the state of Pennsylvania have an opinion on this?"

Steph shrugged. "Maybe they already wrote their opinion on this a while back, when the issue first came to light. And maybe there's no report on the meeting because it finished too late for them to get it into today's edition."

"Late my ass. I made an eminently newsworthy event even more so, and they all dropped the ball. No wonder newspapers are an endangered species. They deserve to be. Thoreau was already onto their uselessness in *Walden*, and that was almost a hundred and fifty years ago."

"You're condemning an entire industry because three papers in one state didn't find you particularly newsworthy? You just went from prophet to diva."

"Fighting words there, son. I have more brotherly love for pedophiles and the insurance industry than I do divas. It's amazing what society tolerates from them."

"It's amazing how society abets in their creation," Steph said. "Is there anything more fragile than the Hollywood ego? These people make a handful of movies, and all of a sudden they think they matter on a major scale. I remember a few years back when Warren Beatty was considering a run for president, and everyone in the industry was taking it seriously, taking him seriously. I mean, come on. President? Warren Beatty? I thought, 'Go ahead, Warren. Run. And see just how smart you ain't and what it's like to get your white ass chewed to shreds.' For all of those stars who think they're so crucial, I've got just two words: River Phoenix. River OD'ed, and everyone was crying, 'River, poor River, oh such a tragedy,' and then six months later everyone in the industry was like, 'River who?'"

Much as Don fantasized about being a player in the entertainment industry, there were few activities he loved more than bashing it. "One of my favorite stories about Tom Cruise was his being pissed off at his studio because during a shoot they wouldn't pay to fly him home one weekend on a private jet for his sister's birthday."

"That's the shit. That's what I'm talking about. They get such a warped sense of reality, and then it colors everything. I remember watching the Oscars one year, the year everyone thought Madonna should have been nominated for her performance in *Evita*. She didn't get a nomination, but despite that she showed up at the ceremony to present an award, and after she left the stage, Billy Crystal commended her for her courage to come make that presentation, and everyone applauded as if what she'd done was, in fact, really courageous. They clapped like she'd walked through a war zone to rescue a group of orphans. Courageous? For handing out an award? Hell, the bag of goodies she got for doing that probably came with enough expensive toys and prizes to pay my rent for a year."

"I seem to recall another story about some young actress being called courageous for letting her eyebrows go bushy for some role. Didn't have them waxed during the entire shoot."

"That's the diva shit I can't stand. Now don't you go pulling it on me, D.P. You had one great night so far. You can be a prophet, but don't become my diva sidekick."

Steph smiled, and Don smiled with him. Truth was he wasn't that disappointed that the papers hadn't covered him. He was still so delighted and surprised by how well last night had gone. Even if he didn't max out on potential, he'd still exceeded expectations—not the gold, but at least a bronze when no one, including himself, expected him to medal at all. A small part of himself was disappointed, sure. He had, after all, given a remarkable performance, one that could have garnered him some attention somewhere in the national media, but he doubted it was flashy and big enough to get the level of attention he'd need to land a book deal. Last night, had it been covered, would have been no more than a good start, a definitive one, too, the event that pundits, journalists and anchors could point to in the background discussion of his coverage: "Don Prophet's first recorded public appearance came at a specially convened school board meeting in the town of Tuttle, Pennsylvania." Or something like that. Well, they could still cite that meeting as the beginning of his prophecy career, but in the absence of footage, they'd have to get some eyewitness interviews. Don had, of course, thought his media coverage through. He'd fancied how his fame would play out. Last night during the drive and also this morning at breakfast. He was American, and it was the American thing to do, especially among the younger folk—imagine your fame. He couldn't prove it, but he swore that all Americans under the age of thirty spent approximately twenty-five percent of their time acting as if they were on camera, being watched. Probably not in the history of the world has there been a society so thoroughly self-centered and self-conscious, and advances in technology had risen perfectly to meet that demand: YouTube, Facebook, blogs. Everybody had the means to further their delusions of mattering more than they do; like the stars, they had the capacity now to be viewed by anonymous millions. Initially, when Don saw how willing people were to violate their own privacy for something facilitated by the Internet, he was surprised, but eventually he was surprised by his initial surprise. Of course they felt no shame at their video of beating up a helpless nerd or performing fellatio or telling an overtly racist joke. Who cares what you're doing as long as millions are watching you do it? No such thing as bad publicity. Steph's divas were no more than the ineluctable apotheosis of a society run amok with citizens utterly enthralled by themselves and bent on doing whatever was necessary to get us to partake of their fascination. Look at the people behind home plate in a baseball game. They aren't watching the game. They're on their cell phones to their friends, waving non-stop. No experience could possibly matter unless someone else saw it. We had all become trees falling in the woods and making sure we were heard. And Don knew he was no different from everyone else. He could kid himself that he was, that the only reason he sought fame was so that it would afford him the chance to write, to make art, but strip away the grandiosity, the false nobility, and his motives were the same as everyone else's: they wanted fame so they could do what they wanted to do, be it write books, live in big houses, attend parties hosted by Hollywood stars, get daily massages, go shopping, have orgies, whatever, it was all about accessing a life of wants consistently gratified. Don shook his head. It was tough to see how those Buddhists weren't right about desire, its corrosive effect on our psyches, our selves, its ground zero status as the root of all suffering.

Just then, they encountered a large sign welcoming them to Ohio. "Hey," Steph said, "I'm in Ohio." He spoke with a giddiness as if he'd just crossed into Paris or Morocco. "My first ever bona fide Midwestern state. Looks a lot like Pennsylvania."

"Wait till we get to the other side."

"What'll that look like?"

"An endless tabletop."

"The Buckeye State," Steph said, reflective, delighted.

Don felt immediately more relaxed. He'd long suspected that something deep in his genes always sensed the homeness of home. Granted, Ohio wasn't Illinois, but it was more Illinois than New York was, part of that seven-state region lumped under the banner of Midwest, and the moment he crossed into that region replete with people and mores he understood as quickly as English and knew as intimately as his own skin, his heart eased, soul relaxed. This time, however, that ease of spirit did bring a physical challenge. "I need a rest area," he said. "Pretty fast."

"Little too much coffee this morning?"

"This is about more than coffee."

"Uh-oh," Steph said. "Code blue."

"All these states have major welcome centers just inside the state lines. Down south, the welcome centers are better taken care of than the public schools. There should be something up here pretty quick."

And there was. Just a few more miles that Steph had upped the speedometer for, and they reached it not a moment too soon. Don't hadn't moved his bowels since they'd left the city, which wasn't unusual for him. He always became constipated the first couple days of any travel. This time, though, he packed that constipation with a string of oversized portions of hearty victuals, so he knew that when that moment did strike, it was going to strike with an outsized vengeance. He was grateful it had been so near a rest area, or it would have been a roadside bear-in-the-woods type of experience. Steph hadn't even got the car to a full stop before Don was out, hot-footing it to the restroom. He wondered, not for the first time, why bathrooms were bathrooms in private spaces but restrooms in public. Yes, the private spaces did usually include a bath, but not always, and the bath wasn't the primary reason people visited the room throughout the day. And it's not as if people go to restrooms to rest. Most people, or at least most men, spent their entire trip to the restroom on their feet. He hoped this restroom was clean. It was already early afternoon, so it had probably seen a decent amount of traffic. Then again, there were presently no other cars at the rest area, and the interstate in this corner of the state was lightly traveled. Don's last thought as he entered the restroom was that it was a lovely rest area on a lovely day—trees, hills, green grass, clean air. It gave him confidence and hope for what might be inside, a hope he never had entering a gas station restroom anywhere, especially the ones where the entrance was outside. Those places were invariably satanic.

The restroom was a clean, well-lighted place. The floor tiles were small red squares, the walls glossy beige bricks; paper towel trash was not spilling out of the trash cans, and there were no wet stains on the floor, even around the toilets. The state of Ohio had every reason to be proud. He checked the first stall, saw it was immaculate so knew he was going to use that one, but he quickly checked the other three, a perverse instinct to survey the breadth of the cleanliness. He'd never been in a ladies room so didn't know if it was the case in them, and he'd never discussed this with any girl, but in men's rooms all across America, it had been Don's experience that a sizeable number of men, having moved their bowels, simply refused to flush, and Don could not fathom why. He presumed all of them flushed at home. Why not in public? Was it a germs thing? But you couldn't get any more germy than what had happened just prior. And even if it was just one brush with germs on the handle that you couldn't abide, use your foot to flush. Seriously, what was the difficulty behind flushing your own excrement? This was one of those examples of American laziness or selfishness that staggered Don (others including littering, especially out of a car, as if it would be terribly strenuous to retain that trash until an accessible garbage can at the next stop for gas; circling a parking lot for minute upon minute in search of a close space even though plenty of spots were available farther away; and microwaving popcorn). It was no badge of honor that bathrooms across the country were switching to automatic flushing urinals and toilets—a sad, pathetic mother of that admittedly impressive invention. It spoke to a widespread refusal to be responsible for one's most basic instincts. It spoke to a population of adults behaving like children. And it's why Don felt so mortified at the conclusion of his own Ohio movement. He was unable to flush it down.

The movement itself was remarkable. Like Leopold Bloom, the slight constipation of yesterday was gone. Hope it's not too big to bring on piles again, thought Leopold, and Don thought about Leopold thinking that, as he often did when on the commode, which further launched him into an oft-considered reflection of why, in literature, there weren't more bathroom experiences. There were none that Don could think of beyond Leopold Bloom's in "the greatest novel of the twentieth century," although Don, after three earnest attempts, could never make it past page 350, finding too many sizable portions of it simply inscrutable. There were a couple of fecal references in the Bible, his own favorite being the prophet Malachi threatening to strew dung upon the faces of priests who refused to honor the name of the Lord. Some heavy artillery there. Don thought a good number of Catholic priests, not to mention their hierarchy, deserved some faces strewn with dung, but those perverts would probably enjoy it. Anyway, the movement: it was big, epic, a sort of piled log that landed in a most peculiar shape, and yet, Don produced it with extraordinary haste and ease, almost without feeling. And the clean up required just one wipe, which saved the Parks Commission of Ohio a few pennies even though Don was typically frugal in his use of toilet paper, even the decidedly un-Charminlike thin tissue that public facilities always threw at you. In fact, the entire experience was nothing but delight on the highest order, which was why it was all the more dispiriting that he couldn't flush it down. It was a mechanical malfunction. He kept pushing down the handle, but the handle offered no resistance, obviously not connected to the crucial mechanism that caused the flush. "For crying out loud," he said, repeatedly pressing the handle as if one of these times it would cooperate and catch. No dice. This pile wasn't flushing, and Don was mortified. No one else was present, true, but it wasn't about being caught in wrongdoing. It wasn't his fault, sure, but he still couldn't help feeling some culpability. He approached desperation as he tried the handle a few more times, and he shook his head and stared down helplessly at his handiwork. "Doggone it," he said. He surrendered and walked to the sink to wash his hands.

As Don thoroughly lathered his soap, young Broderick Hastings entered the restroom, although Don had absolutely no idea who he was, just some anonymous kid. Initially, Broderick didn't enter far. The door was opened, bringing in fresh air and sunlight and the sounds of outside, and Don was seized with panic that he was about to be discovered, but just inside the door, Broderick stopped and said, "Whoa," and raised his hands to cover his nose. Don briefly considered claiming innocence, saying that he, too, was waylaid by the odor, implying it was someone else's doing, but such moral cowardice was simply not an ingredient in the casserole of Don Bollinger.

"Sorry about that," he said, shrugging sheepishly as he rinsed his hands, hoping that the confession might palliate his lingering guilt. It didn't. The kid resumed walking, inching forward, and as he passed that first stall, he peeked in before he turned to Don with a face of obvious disgust. "It wouldn't go down," Don said, holding up his dripping hands, but the kid had nothing but condescending accusation in his eyes. That ticked Don off. Who was he to heap such condemnation on Don, a child who understood precious little about the world? The kid continued down to the farther stall and went inside, shutting and latching the door. "Little asshole," Don muttered to himself once he was back outside, on the sidewalk, returning to the car.

"Everything come out okay?" Steph asked, in the driver's seat.

"Let's go," he said.

Steph carefully reversed out. A red truck pulling a U-Haul was coming into the rest area, and Steph wanted to be careful to avoid a collision. Steph drove on while Terry Poland parked the truck and U-Haul sideways across seven spaces, obviating the need to reverse out when he anticipated leaving a few moments later.

In his life, Terry Poland had taken few enough long trips that the novelty of them gave him a certain lightness of being. Other than the trip across the country when, as a child, he moved from Nevada to New York, there was a drive to northern Georgia with his mother and Brice a few months before they married for a week's stay in a cabin on a lake with a friend of Brice's, and there was a drive to Kentucky with a couple of his union buddies just after he moved into his own apartment. It was a spontaneous lark of a trip to go see the Derby. Terry had not a drop of interest in horse racing or even betting, but he went for the experience, for the journey with friends. Of the race there was little to remember—he stood amid the mostly drunken crush of people on the infield where he couldn't even see the race; he could hear only the loud, slurred, steady cheering of the infield denizens and, briefly as the horses passed by, the thundering of hooves. But the trip, the actual drive, was indelible: on the way out, they stopped at a Taco Bell in Morgantown, West Virginia, and the cashier who took their order had such a severe limp from one leg being so much shorter than the other that it almost hurt Terry to watch him walk. They stopped for gas soon after sunrise in Ashland, Kentucky, and Terry, fully awake and driving, thought the town was so beautiful tucked as it was in those green mountains that he drove through some of its residential neighborhoods and identified houses he'd most like to move into, fantasizing about a quiet, domestic life with no surprises. And on the drive home, the trio listened to WSM on the truck radio, amazed they were able to get that Nashville station all the way up in Louisville. By the time they were back in West Virginia that evening and the Grand Ole Opry came on the air, they were still getting the station. Terry and his friends listened with rapt attention. None of them were fans of country music, but they knew the show was legendary. They finally lost reception around Charleston.

But what Terry recalled most vividly about that trip was the airy, floating feeling that came with his push into strange lands he'd never visited before. It started in Maryland because in Maryland there was enough of a change in the topography and geography to make him feel he was somewhere different. In West Virginia, it wasn't only the land; it was also the people and their accents, the voices on the radio, the consistently different license plates, which included not only West Virginia but also a good number of Virginia, Kentucky and Tennessee. And Kentucky, with its impossibly green grass, velvet air and idyllic farms amid valleys of rolling hills, was an enchanting land out of a storybook. And that was the point. Terry knew that Kentucky, West Virginia and that jagged panhandle of Maryland were hardly exotic destinations. But they were something different from what he knew on a daily basis, and so the deeper he took himself into these lands, the further behind he left the daily Terry Poland, the heaviness of familiar roads, unstrange sights and droll routine.

He got that same feeling in western Pennsylvania and especially eastern Ohio on the trip to move his family to Omaha. Even though he was dragging a crammed-full U-Haul trailer with a truck that contained his pregnant wife and two young daughters, who had been pretty docile travelers thus far but were slipping toward restlessness and the noise that comes with it, he acquired a lightness that gained incrementally with each mile west. To be sure, he was nervous about his life ahead. He was worried that Irma wouldn't like Omaha, wouldn't like being so far away from her family; he was worried about raising his girls in a city and all the added dangers that entailed; and he was especially fearful that he wouldn't be any good at his new job and that his brother would regret having brought him out. But those were all heavy concerns of a daily nature, concerns currently left behind in Stony Point that would take some little while to fully arrive in Omaha, only after he'd been there long enough for the newness of the place to erode under the steady flow of routine. For now, there was still the lightness that came with travel, the excitement of new lands, different visions, uncharacteristic sights, the impunity of placelessness. He was even a bit giddy about pulling into the rest area. It was Ohio, a brand new state. He and the girls were going to run around and lie on different soil, different grass. They would do cartwheels and somersaults and figure eights around trees. He would stretch his legs and maybe chase the girls and then breathe deeply the Ohio air. But first he had to get Kimberly to the bathroom.

"I want to come," said Jessica.

"I'll take you, Jessica," said Irma.

"You stay out here and get some fresh air," Terry told her. She'd been skirmishing with a low-grade morning sickness. "I got the girls."

"Are you sure?"

"I don't have to go potty," Jessica said. "I just want to go with Daddy."

Terry carried Kimberly hugged around his chest, as if she were sleepy, but Jessica gamboled at his side on the walk to the restroom, and the fun of it was too much for Kimberly to abide. She clamored for Terry to let her down, which he did, and she giggled and played with her big sister as they all three continued walking. In the clear, fresh air under the cloudless blue sky, Terry had a wave of gratitude for simply being alive.

Inside the restroom, the odor was horrendous. "Oooh, Daddy, it smells bad," Kimberly whined. Jessica pinched her own nose.

"Shhh, Kimberly, it's okay. We won't be long." Terry didn't want to hurt the feelings of the kid at the sink washing his hands—Broderick. He assumed the kid was responsible for the smell; he was a small vessel to transport and unload such a powerful odor, but God knows what little Kimberly and Jessica left in their diapers back in the day could be pretty crippling. He moved forward with the girls, who now clung to his legs, and the kid at the sink turned off the faucet and moved past him to the paper towel dispenser, nodding his head in a curt, single gesture to Terry's hello. Good looking kid, Terry thought. He glanced into the first stall, Don's stall, and was appalled by what he saw. He couldn't believe the kid didn't flush. He almost said something but decided his job wasn't to police the manners of every young slob he ran into. He took Kimberly to the second stall, wiped the seat with toilet paper, even though it was already clean, and sat her down. He stepped outside the stall and shut the door just as the kid was exiting the restroom. Jessica, standing next to her father, looked into Don's stall.

"You okay in there, Kimberly?" Terry asked.

"Yeah, Daddy."

Jessica tugged on her father's hand. "Look, Daddy."

"What, sweetheart?"

"Look," she said, pointing into Don's stall, Don's toilet. At first, he didn't see it. He was too disgusted by what lay in there, too preoccupied with making sure all was okay with Kimberly, too eager to be back outside in the fresh air. But Jessica, in her sweet little voice, was just persistent enough. "Do you see it, Daddy?"

He was just about to ask her again what she was talking about when he saw; as clear and obvious as a lone tree in a meadow, a beautiful woman at an empty bar, dirt under the fingernails of an otherwise immaculate hand, he saw. He moved Jessica gently aside and stepped deeper into the stall, closer to what he saw. He stood almost directly over the toilet, staring straight down, seeing if the vision survived a different perspective. It did. He leaned way to the right, pressing a shoulder against the stall wall before he did the same thing to the left, and the vision still held, unmistakable. "No way," he said, knowing with more certainty than he'd ever felt his entire life that he was standing before a miracle, *his* miracle, the one his mother promised he would have. "No fucking way." Only later would he think to himself that cussing before such a vision was probably dangerously blasphemous. Kimberly flushed her toilet and a moment later came out of her stall, and Terry grabbed her hand and fairly dragged her out of the restroom. "Come on, girls. Hurry."

"What's wrong, Daddy?" Jessica said.

"Nothing's wrong."

"I need to wash my hands," Kimberly said.

"We'll get that later. Come on."

Outside, it was a dilemma: Terry could either reach the kid before he got back in his car and rode away or patiently wait for the small-step slowness of his toddler daughters. "Hey!" he shouted to the kid who was almost to his car but who did not turn around. Terry lifted both girls, one in each arm, and started to run. "Hey, kid. You. Wait up." Broderick turned around, but he didn't stop walking, and Terry ran faster. "Ow, Daddy, you're hurting me," Kimberly said, but Terry eased neither his grip on her nor his pace. "I'll let go in a minute, honey," he said.

Luella got out of the car. Its windows were opened, so she'd heard Terry's first, "Hey," and looked up from reading her *Variety* magazine. But when the guy shouted a second time and came running after her son, she just knew the little bastard had done something wrong, and she'd had enough of his antics and attitude. "Damn it, Broderick," she said, coming around the front of the car toward the passenger door where he stood holding the door handle but not getting in. "What did you do?"

"I didn't do anything," he said with more sass in his tone than anything else. Terry kept running, and Irma, watching from the truck the scene unfold, got out. A twinge of fear shot through her system, even though the girls looked unharmed and she couldn't imagine what such a little boy could have done.

"Kid, wait," Terry said one more time, though it was hardly necessary; he wasn't moving from standing at the door, holding the handle as if for safety.

"Goddamn it, Broderick," Luella said, now standing next to him, gripping his shoulders. "What did you do?"

"Mom," he said, his tone now a cry of confusion, the plea of the innocent, "I didn't do anything."

"Lady," Terry said, arrived at Luella's car, slightly winded, still holding the girls. "Your kid didn't do anything wrong."

She turned and snapped angrily at Terry. "Then what the hell are you yelling about and chasing him for?"

"Relax, ma'am."

"Don't tell me to relax. Do you have any idea who this boy is?"

"Ma'am, please, relax. It's all okay. I think your son," and here he paused because he couldn't believe what he was about to say and couldn't imagine how it would sound to her. He decided not to get into the specifics, just speak in general terms and let the vision speak for itself. "I think your son just performed a miracle in the bathroom."

Luella closed her eyes to the confusion of it all. She opened them, looked to Broderick, who also appeared confused, and looked back to Terry. "What the hell are you talking about?"

Terry set down the girls, who were not crying, but on their own feet they immediately clung to their father. "Come with me."

Irma came onto the scene; she wasn't breathless, but her tone was concerned. "What's wrong, Terry?"

"Nothing's wrong. I need you to run back to the truck and get our little Blessed Virgin."

"But you said nothing's wrong."

"Irma, nothing's wrong. I promise. Just go get the icon and meet us in the bathroom."

"Are the girls okay?"

"The girls are fine. They'll come with me."

At that they moved, Irma back to the truck, everyone else toward the restroom, Terry leading the way. The girls still tried to hold his legs, but that made walking nigh impossible, so he grabbed each by her hand and walked slow enough to accommodate their gait. Inside the bathroom, Kimberly again commented on the stench, and even Luella, upon entering, said, "Holy Christ." Terry walked her to the stall, stood to the side and held out his hand, presenting the toilet. Luella saw immediately what he was talking about. Broderick tried to speak, "Mom, I didn't—" but she held up a finger to shush her son and stared threateningly at him.

"Not one word," she said. "Trust me. Not one word."

She turned back to the toilet, and Irma came rushing into the bathroom. Terry held out his hand, and she gave him the icon. He stepped forward and held the icon up between his fingers, facilitating visual comparison, and he gestured for his wife to look. She did, and she instantly saw what Terry had seen without the icon and what Luella had seen without even knowing the icon existed: Don Bollinger's bowel movement was a dead ringer for the Virgin Mary, even down to the few blocks of tissue paper lying on top, so perfectly resembling the white veil of the plastic icon.

"Ay dios mio," Irma said, bringing her hand to her mouth before she dropped to her knees at the toilet, made the cross with her hand, bowed her head and launched into a torrent of prayer in Spanish. Luella was disgusted with herself for not having thought to do that. She needed to come up with something quick. From the moment she looked in the toilet and saw what she saw, she knew that what lay in there was their ticket to Broderick's fame, their path to glory, but she was caught by such surprise that she'd had no idea initially how to utilize it. And here the little immigrant had beaten her to the punch. No. Not *the* punch. *A* punch. There were other punches out there, roundhouses, jabs and uppercuts waiting to be landed just as soon as she knew where to throw. Think, Luella, think. This is the moment for which you've prepared. Rise to the occasion. Rise. Rise. WWTBVD? What Would The Blessed Virgin Do? Weep. That's what she'd do. That's what she did, right? She wept? Or maybe that was Jesus who was caught weeping on some cross somewhere in the world, and Mary just appeared to people without tears. No matter. Weep. That would be convincing, although these two hardly seemed to need any more convincing. The little beaner was already on her knees, but of course she would be. Those people were kookier about Catholicism than the Irish, and they were way nuttier on the whole Mary thing. Surprised the white husband is already in so deep on this, but God knows how wifey might have poisoned him on all of this stuff. Beaner must be a hell of a lay. All right, Luella. Concentrate. Focus. Weep.

Luella brought all of her acting skills and experience to bear on the head of this golden pin. The little girls asked their daddy what was happening, what was wrong, but she was able to ignore them and run through a mental reel of awful highlights—dead puppies, abused children, teen virgins gang raped. She settled on her first rejection as an actress out in L.A., a brusque dismissal by a piercing casting agent so soon after

Luella nailed what she thought was a perfect reading that she thought the shrew must be talking to someone else. She relived that lonely walk away from the audition, the soul-sucking weight of dejection, and bingo: a tear emerged from each eye, slowly descending the cheeks. She turned to her son and, convinced she could not be seen by any of the others, gave him a wink and pursed her lips in shushing fashion before she dropped to her knees, took her son's hands in her own, kissed them and bowed her head. He started to say something, but she gave his hands a crushing squeeze and kept her head bowed. Broderick remained mute.

It became too much for Terry—one mother worshipping her son, the other mother, the mother of his own children, praying before a full and foul toilet. He became spooked. Something bigger than he could comprehend was happening smack in the middle of his life. "Irma, get up," he said. But she continued her torrid praying, eyes firmly closed. "Irma, come on, get up." His voice contained enough of his spook that his daughters looked up, some alarm in their eyes. "Irma, for Christ's sake, get up would you?" That got the girls crying, and they pleaded with their mother to get up, Luella all the while still holding Broderick's hands and praying to him, knowing that this family would finally be gone any minute now and she could begin her real work. Terry finally got physical. Irma was in a trance, and there was no other way. He stepped forward and reached under her armpits and lifted her to her feet. She still kept praying, eyes closed. It was only when he reached around to grab her hands that there came a struggle, some resistance. Terry dropped the plastic icon, which bounced violently on the tile floor over toward the sinks, and he grabbed Irma's hands and used a decent amount of physical force to pull her away. "Come on, girls," he said. They obeyed, and once Terry had Irma out of the stall, she became peaceful, following her husband's lead as calmly as a sedated patient follows his nurse.

Finally, finally, the guy got his wacko wife and kids out of the bathroom, but when the door shut behind them, Luella said, "Don't move." She held her own position, too, waiting, listening, looking at the door. After a couple of minutes, she rose and went to the door herself. "I'm going to go out there and see if they're gone. If someone else is here, I'm going to have to put on a show, pretending you just did this, so if I'm gone for more than thirty seconds, you need to lie down on the ground near the toilet and act real, real tired, like you're sick."

"Mom, that's disgusting. I'm not going to lay down on this bathroom floor."

"Don't you blow this, Broderick. This is our ticket, and it's a bigger ticket than I ever could have dreamed of. Don't you dare fucking blow it."

"I won't blow it," he snapped, "but I'm not laying down on a skuzzy bathroom floor."

She couldn't fight him, not now. Any moment someone could drive up, enter the restroom, and the whole charade would be shattered if they weren't in place, in character. She spotted the plastic icon under a sink and hurried to it. She placed it on the front edge of the sink directly opposite Don's stall. "Here," she said. "Kneel down in front of this. You don't mind kneeling, do you?"

"No."

"Kneel with your hands on the sink, and the minute you hear that door open or you hear footsteps approaching, drop your head in prayer and close your eyes and wait for my command. And no matter what anyone says, do not say one word. Got it? Not one word. I'll just say your own miracle struck you mute. Okay?" He nodded. "Okay, get on your knees." He did, and she went to the door from where she checked his position once more before she transformed her own self, gave her face and eyes a shock and glaze as if she'd just watched Lazarus rise from the dead, and stepped outside.

Back in the brash and clang of the sun and its bouncing glare, she slowly lifted her head to survey the area, not altering her glazed expression. Empty. The family had left, and no one else had arrived. She hastened back into the restroom. Broderick stood. "No," she said. "You have to stay on your knees."

"Mom, I've got to get out of here. It stinks."

"That stink is going to make you famous. It's the final payment on your dues, and smelling shit is a whole lot better than eating it, which is what most of us in the business have had to do. Now get back down on your goddamned knees and be ready at the drop of a hat to look worshipful."

Broderick did as he was told, but he couldn't disguise his resentment. She wondered how much longer he was going to tolerate all of this from her, especially if there continued to be no payoff beyond the pittance he was making for modeling. He was old enough now to have a will of his own, and she knew that if she pushed him far enough into waters he just didn't want to swim, he would exert that will in ways more major and perhaps ruinous than these minor strokes of rebellion. And yet, he was still just young enough to allow himself to be cowed by her at least a little while longer. And if they could arrive at a payoff with something soon, then he would see how all of her stern guidance had been worth it, and he would return to full malleability again, trusting her, obeying her, at least until he'd been a star for some little while and, like Macaulay Culkin, would lawyer up for a fight with her. But she'd deal with that when the time came. For now, she had to figure out how to get people out here to see the vision and how to get the miracle irrevocably ascribed to Broderick.

"You didn't do this, right?" she thought to ask.

"Do what?"

"What's in the toilet."

"No," he said, offended. "The fat guy who was in here before me did."

"Just checking."

She'd figure out how to handle the fat guy later, if it came to that. She went back to the toilet to check the vision, keeping focused on the sounds at the door, ready for any entrant. She looked at the toilet and at the icon. It *was* uncanny. Now, think, Luella. Think. She could call local news herself, but who would she call? Newspapers? Too small, too slow: their story wouldn't come out until the following day, if it was a daily, and God knows when if it was some little piss-ant weekly. Besides, what town would she call? She had seen plenty of signs for Sharon, Pennsylvania, just before she crossed the border, as if it were some great destination, but she'd never heard of it. Youngstown lay just ahead, as did Akron, but she didn't know how far, and from everything she'd heard, those places were just graveyards for factories and the people who once worked them, hardly springboards for a glamorous career, although it could feed a rags-to-riches narrative; and if anyone was susceptible to miracles, it was the denizens of a dying town. She could make a 911 call, say her son had terrible stomach pains and had collapsed on the floor, but then an ambulance would arrive, and the medics would whisk him away, and she couldn't risk having Broderick separated from the vision, not so early in the process. Besides, the police would likely come out, and that was the last thing she wanted. Authorities always took charge, and they were the last to give credence to possible miracles—too many years on the job had jaded them to a healthy suspicion of everything. Think, Luella, think.

She already knew what she'd do once Broderick had been identified for his miracle. She was going to call Wolf Glazer, that Jew superagent who seemed to be representing everyone worth a damn. Last spring she read an interview with him in

Variety. Question: "What drives you? You're not even fifty, you've got a stable full of Hollywood's top money getters who have won every award there is to win, and you've accomplished everything there is to accomplish in the business. What keeps you going?" Answer: "The unseen," he said, the pompous ass. "The unexpected. The never seen and never expected. Somewhere out there is a talent that hasn't even crossed our minds, hasn't even entered our imaginations. That's what drives me. I'm waiting for the chance to represent that talent." Well, now Luella had that talent. Nobody imagined this. "How'd you like to represent a saint, Wolf?" That's what she'd ask him over the phone, and he'd be on his private jet to Ohio quicker than she could say, "I'd like to thank the academy." But first, she had to get people in here to see the vision and link it to Broderick.

"We have to wait," she said. "There's no other way."

"Wait for what?"

"For someone to come in here and see this. We can't force this. It has to be organic."

"How long will that be?" Broderick whined.

"I don't know, but it can't be that long. It's an interstate rest area. People stop at them all the time."

"Come on, Mom," he pleaded. "Can't we just go to Chicago?"

"Chicago?" she said, aghast at his shortsightedness, but then he was young, and her vision of the possible was, she had to admit, unsurpassing. "Chicago is nothing anymore. Spielberg is bush league. This thing is so big, Broderick—if we play our cards right, we're talking the O.J. trial, even the Lindbergh baby." She was losing him, she could tell, and of course she was: he had no idea who O.J. and Lindbergh were, father or son. She took an alternate, softer tack: "Look, Broderick, I know you're frustrated, and I know you're tired. So am I. But we have worked our fingers and toes to the bone for years, years, and we're almost there. I don't know how much longer we'll have to wait, but I'm betting it's just an hour, tops. *Tops.* So if you can give me just one more hour, then I guarantee all the thankless toil will be behind us, and all the fun will begin. Can you do that for me, honey?" she asked in the sweetest, most cajoling voice she could muster, and he nodded that he could. "That's my temple," she said, noting now the irony, or serendipity, of having chosen that name for him so long ago, allowing herself to wonder if the prescience of that choice didn't signal that today was fated.

They didn't have to wait an hour. They barely had to wait ten minutes. It was a trucker who came through the door, mid-fifties, orange beard, soiled two-toned Kent Feeds trucker cap over his bald head, the front of the cap blue, the back white and mesh. His stomach was a massive ball under a pale blue T-shirt stretched as tight as his skin. He stepped inside and saw Luella, who had positioned herself behind the kneeling Broderick; she was not inside the stall but did face the vision, head bowed, on one knee. "You two okay?" the trucker said, his voice high-pitched and pleasant, concerned. "This isn't the ladies room, you know."

Luella placed one hand on her heart, turned to the trucker with an ethereal gaze, and pointed to the vision. "What the hell's going on in here?" he said. She gestured with her head toward the vision, and he came forward, confused, leery. He moved his hands into an aggressively defensive position, but short of brandishing an automatic weapon, it was difficult to imagine what those two on their knees could do to harm him. That didn't mean a third wasn't waiting in the stall. He inched forward, keeping his stare on those two, and at the stall he slowly peeked around the divider. It took about ten seconds to fully register. A squint and wince of skepticism slowly transformed into a wide-eyed bafflement at what lay before him. He turned back to the kid. He reached for the plastic

Mary poised on the edge of the sink but at the last moment pulled his hand away, as if frightened of touching something so obviously sacred. He looked down at Luella who was still on one knee. "That your son?" he asked. She nodded. He pointed to the vision. "Did he do that?" She nodded again, solemn. "The amount alone is a miracle. I wouldn't have thought he was nearly big enough to have all of that in him." Luella nodded again, slow, reverent. "That your statue? Where'd that come from?"

Luella thought it best not to lie—the statue being their own was a hefty dose of coincidence, and too much coincidence will pulverize any story, especially one already so tenuously credible. "Some couple," she said, speaking in a high-pitched, airy voice, trying to sound as ethereal as she looked—she was going for a Melanie Griffith sound. "The husband was the first to see it. He saw it before me. He came and got me in the car and had his wife get the icon from the car. The resemblance would be frightening if it weren't so . . . comforting. Blessed."

The trucker looked back and forth between the toilet and the icon. "It is bizarre. Your kid religious or something?"

"No more or less than most kids his age. Would you like me to move so you can pray?"

"No. I've never really been the praying type. Seems an odd time to start."

"Any time is a good time to come to the Lord."

"I hear what you're saying, but no thanks." He turned to Broderick. "How long's he been praying like that?"

"I don't know. Earthly time has lost all relevance and meaning."

"Does he talk?"

"Not since it happened."

The trucker nodded. "What's your name, by the way?"

"I'm Luella Hastings. And this is my son, Broderick."

"Well Ms. Hastings, I believe you have a bona fide miracle on your hands in here."

At this she rose, which was a relief to her knee. There was no give to these floor tiles, and she knew she needed to get Broderick on his feet soon. A groan or admission of pain on his part wasn't going to further their miracle claims. She placed her palms on the trucker's chest in a damsel-in-distress kind of way, and she widened her eyes to give them an air of naivete, spicing the sauce of her plot with a few dashes of cleverly disguised seduction. "I have no idea what to do in the face of a miracle," she said in her most helpless voice. "Do you?" He began to breathe more heavily, and having him where she wanted, she offered a means to allow him to derive an answer. "If it really is a miracle, it seems a shame not to make it available to others. Lots of people could always use a little miracle in their lives."

"You are right as rain there, Ms. Hastings. I should go out to my truck, get on my radio and let folks know what's happened here."

"Do you think that's the right thing to do?" she asked, playing an ersatz devil's advocate to lure him into solidifying his devotion to the cause.

"Like I said, miss, I'm not really the praying type, but keeping a miracle like this to ourselves, well, it seems to me like that would be pretty selfish." Luella nodded a slow agreement, easing her charade toward the light of his unimpeachable truth. "Let me get out to my radio."

"What should I do with Broderick?" she asked.

"I don't know. What do you think? He's your kid."

"I think his knees must be getting tired and sore, but I'm reluctant to move him."

"Why's that?"

"Clearly it was my son who was chosen to perform this miracle, so I don't think there should be any confusion about that, and I'm worried there might be if I pull him away."

"You got no worries there, Ms. Hastings. I'll make damn sure the world knows it was your son who was responsible for this."

"You're a kind soul, Mr. . . . . "

"Squat. My name's Benny Bazzelle, but my friends call me Squat. And I can't say I've ever been accused before of being a kind soul, but I've got a hunch some things are about to change for me."

"Thank you, Mr. Squat."

"No mister. Just Squat. I'm pretty sure you and I are going to be friends after all of this."

"Yes," she said. "I'm pretty sure we already are." This is almost too easy, Luella thought, but then as a Hollywood failure she was a student of the world's toughest school of hard knocks, and even if she didn't graduate, she still walked away with an elevated amount of savvy.

Squat said that there were some nice benches outside and that while he was on the radio, maybe she should get Broderick out to one of them. "Don't rush it, though. Take it at his pace. Kid's got to be overwhelmed. Fresh air won't hurt him none, either."

Luella nodded, and once Squat quit the restroom and had been safely gone for a few moments, she told Broderick it was okay to stand up. "I don't know about this, Mom," he said, on his feet, flexing his knees.

"Shut your mouth. I do."

"What if we get caught?"

"The only way we're going to get caught is if you don't keep your mouth shut." Which she knew wasn't entirely true. In the endless blue horizon of her dreams hung the lone gray cloud of the person who actually did have this bowel movement. When the time was right, she would get a physical description of that guy from Broderick so that she could recognize him immediately if he re-emerged onto the scene. She was confident she could handle him. After it had been established in the public that Broderick was responsible for the vision, it would be awful easy tarnishing some adult interloper trying to horn in on the credit. For now, it was important to get Broderick away from the rest area and safely ensconced in an undisclosed location, before the press arrived. She knew how savvy she was, but part of that savvy was knowing her own limitations, and if this thing went national, as she was sure it would, she'd need Wolf Glazer to handle those hawks. Hell, even the low-rent hacks at the Cleveland *Plain Dealer* were probably pretty apt at sniffing out a fraud. But before she got him ensconced, she needed to get a picture of Broderick into Squat's hands. Those TV folks loved their visuals, and there had to be no doubt whatsoever of the face atop the body responsible for this miracle.

"Here's what we're going to do. We're going to go outside and sit on a bench for as long as we need."

"How long will that be?"

"As long as it needs to be. Then we're going to find a hotel and wait until our agent gets here."

"We don't have an agent."

"The hell we don't. He just doesn't know it yet. But for as long as we're on that bench, I need you to keep absolutely quiet and look shocked and serene."

"What's serene?"

"Peaceful. Just look that way for a little while, and pretty soon we'll be at a hotel where you can watch TV and play your Gameboy and do whatever the hell you want."

"How long will that be?"

"Broderick, I don't know. Just stop asking questions and do as I say."

"Mom, I'm scared. I really don't think this will work."

"It's already working, Broderick, so enough. Enough with the doubt and pessimism. You've got to believe in yourself and believe in this. Now, give me a shocked and peaceful look and put everything you've got into it. And hurry." Broderick took a breath, closed his eyes, and in an instant gave his mother the face she sought. "Perfect," she said. "Absolutely perfect. You have no concept of how talented you are. Now follow me out, keep that look, and please, no matter what happens, don't speak."

Outside, another bit of serendipity seemed to be under way. A Trailways bus of senior citizens had pulled into the rest area, and Squat was in the grass in front of the bus talking to a semicircle of a half a dozen or so variegated old men—white hair, gray hair, no hair at all, all of them in some stage of obesity save for one tall, skinny guy at the end. Luella spoke softly to Broderick, told him to keep walking toward the bench under the tree not far away and to keep his shocked and serene expression. Squat turned and caught a glimpse of Luella and Broderick, and he waved, but Luella did not wave back, a gesture too common, profane. Squat pointed at Luella and Broderick while he spoke to the old men, and the latter turned to view the mother and her miraculous son. Once the two were seated comfortably on the bench, leaned back against the wooden slats, relaxed, Luella holding Broderick's hand, Squat led over his commission of the aged.

"How's he doing?' he asked Luella, nodding at Broderick.

"As well as can be expected," she said. "Just stunned. Overwhelmed."

"I'll bet. Look, Luella, I told these gentlemen all about what's in there, and they're itching to take a look. You think that'd be okay?"

"Squat, this isn't up to me. Just because the miracle happened through my son doesn't mean it belongs to us. To my mind, it belongs to the people now, all the people who want it, who need it."

"That's mighty wise of you, ma'am," one of the older men said.

"I think we just need to make sure that the miracle isn't somehow harmed or disturbed," said Luella.

"You can take it from me," Squat said with deadly seriousness. "As long as I'm here, nothing, absolutely nothing, will come to harm, alter or disturb what's in that toilet."

"Thank you, Squat," Luella said, solemn, meek.

"And ma'am," said another of the older men, "you can rest assured that if what Squat here says is true, he won't be alone in making sure this miracle is protected for pilgrims."

"These folks are from Canton, Ohio," Squat said.

"Billy McKinley's hometown," one of them piped up.

"They're just coming back from some religious retreat in upstate New York. Catholic."

Luella could not believe her luck. She'd thought this group was awfully credulous, even for Midwesterners. Were they at a rest area in New Jersey, Luella could have never pulled any of this off. Nobody would have stopped long enough to listen let alone believe a word she said, and even the vision now would have been flushed or, more likely, shat on top of. Twice. But not in Ohio, which was so much like the Kansas of her upbringing. Midwesterners were preternaturally disposed to give anyone a fair hearing, and no group could have been less surprised by a vision of the Blessed Mother, even a fecal one, than a group of geriatric Catholics fresh off of a retreat. Squat turned and led the men into the restroom, and within ten minutes, he led most of them back to the bench. A couple had peeled off from the group to go inform all the others who, over the next few minutes, slowly made their way toward Luella and Broderick.

"Is everything okay?" Luella asked. "You seem to be missing a few."

"Some went to tell the others. A couple stayed behind in the bathroom to keep guard. World War II vets."

"So you saw the Blessed Mother?" Luella asked with that wispy, innocent voice.

"Ma'am," one of the older men said. "We saw. We believe. A vision like that . . . " he was too overcome to finish.

"Do you think we might be able to touch the boy?" the skinny older man asked in a scratchy voice.

"I'm not sure he's ready for that," Luella said. "It's still so soon." They all nodded agreement at her eminent good sense. By now, many more geriatrics had made their way to the area of the bench, but they kept a respectful semi-distance. "You can, however, take a picture."

Luella didn't have to say that twice. A handful of old folks broke forth with cameras at the ready amid an arthritic flurry of a collective geriatric bustle—people conferring, people chattering, some headed back to the bus for their cameras, some already on cell phones calling friends. The ball was rolling. Luella almost lost her composure when she saw that two of the cameras being used were Polaroids—the press would now have its photo instantly. She was glad none of the old folks appeared to have cell phones with cameras—that would lead to too many pictures and too wide of a dissemination.

It was time for her to leave. She told Squat and some of the older men that she needed to get Broderick to a place where he could lie down and rest. "You can bring him on the bus," one of the men said. "The seats are huge, and they recline real nice." Luella thanked him but said she thought she should take him somewhere more private. Squat volunteered to accompany them, "for protection," he hastened to clarify, but Luella told him she thought it best he remain there to make sure order was maintained. He couldn't disguise his disappointment, but her position was inarguably sensible.

"Broderick," she said, speaking to him very loudly, as if he were an octogenarian, "I'm going to take you somewhere to rest. Do you think you'll be able to walk to the car?" She was so proud of how he turned his head so slowly to her and gave just one, long, slow nod. "Okay," she said. "Here we go." She stood first then helped him stand, and as they walked a slow procession to the car, all the aged at the rest area parted to offer a path, and Broderick and Luella walked between them much as she'd imagined they'd one day walk on the red carpet between his fans and into the ceremony for the Academy Awards.

What makes something last? Don wondered. What makes it stick? What makes a sensation the kind of sensation that captures the imagination and attention of the American public and makes untold numbers want to hold onto it for a while, follow it, watch it, own and abet it? The first sensation he could remember was the Pet Rock, which came onto the scene when he was in third grade. A couple of his friends owned one, as did a number of older siblings of other friends, and all throughout the fad he felt as if he were missing out on some vital information that everyone else had gotten. It really was just a rock, a round, smooth stone set on a patch of fake hay in a small box with air holes so that it could breathe. Don did not get the appeal, the joke, at all. It even came with elaborate instructions on how to take care of your pet rock. He sat in a bedroom with a group of kids, mostly older, as one of his friend's older brother read those instructions, and Don was the only person in the room not laughing, although he was pretty sure his friend, the only other little kid in the room, was faking it. Now, all these years later, his memory of the Pet Rock actually alarmed him. That thing's popularity soared, millions of pet rocks sold across the country, perhaps across the world, and Don, for the life of him, even all these years later, could not grasp why. As a kid, he was often out of touch with the national zeitgeist (he also didn't like *Mork and Mindy*, Van Halen, Rubik's Cube and *The Breakfast Club*); if he was still that out of touch now, there was no way he could appeal to large numbers of the public. The mere fact that he thought Don Prophet was such a good idea could well guarantee that few others would. So Steph thought the idea had potential, but that hardly filled Don with confidence; Steph also enjoyed experimental theater, read obscure European novels and preferred Eritrean food to any other—how could he possibly know what might appeal to the cake-eating masses? He was a black kid from the ghetto who graduated from Brandeis. Could you even invent an experience rarer than that? It was Gretchen who thought the gimmick was stupid, and Don ignored her because he embraced only what he wanted to believe, but really, of all the people in his life, it was his second-generation Chinese girlfriend who had her finger on the pulse of American culture. She watched untold hours of TV—*Monk, Law and Order, Everybody Loves Raymond, CSI,* even *Oprah* on her days off; she watched no reality shows, and yet she always seemed to know the results of who won or lost on those dancing and talent contest shows. And because she never missed *Entertainment Tonight*, there was no bit of hot Hollywood gossip that wasn't given the chance to shack up for the evening in her brain, maybe spend a while there.

"I should call Gretchen," he said, riding along on I-80 through Ohio, Steph at the wheel. Steph reached for his cell phone on the console, handed it to Don. Don waved it off. "Just because I should doesn't mean I will. She's at work anyway." He shook his head, looking out on the landscape that was still wavy but was certainly flatter than that he'd looked out upon eighty miles east, at the border. "I'm going to lose her. I have fucked everything up."

"From whence sprang the despondence, D.P.? Three hours ago at breakfast, you were riding high, singing the body electric?"

"I don't know. Sometimes your own failure just smacks you in the face in a way that can no longer be ignored."

"Failure? Are you kidding me? You *owned* that gym last night. Your expectations for today were just too high. Plus, you're probably experiencing the emotional hangover that comes after a roaring success. It's why I never go to a play on its second night. Actors can't help feeling flat if opening night went great. And you're not going to lose Gretchen. At worst you're going to go home, get a lousy job, but still come home every night to her. She's not cutting you loose over some unemployment issues."

"Those Chinese are tough," Don said. "They've got deprivation and suffering in their genes. A little heartache is nothing compared to a history that features the Long March and the Cultural Revolution, and that's just in the past seventy years. Gretchen would take heartbreak over a return to squalor any day, and I don't blame her."

Steph wondered if, just to lift Don's spirits, now was the time to tell him about the girl at the meeting last night, the one who said to thank him, but her gratitude was so genuine and profound that he didn't want to cheapen it by using it for a quick, temporary pick-me-up. That's what Hallmark cards were for. He opted to change the subject. "What about Cleveland? We going there?"

"I cannot believe that Cleveland is a desired destination for you."

"It's Cleveland, man, home of the Browns, the Indians and the Rock and Roll Hall of Fame."

"And the problem with the Hall of Fame is that it's already almost two o'clock. It'll be past three by the time we get to the city and then another half hour, minimum, before we find the place, which gives us less than an hour to actually tour it."

"It closes at five?"

"Everything closes at five in the Midwest, except restaurants. So then in order to see the museum, to really experience it the way its curators would want us to, we'd have to come back the following morning, which means we'd have to pay twice what we should be paying for a hotel tonight, and we really shouldn't even be staying in a hotel two nights in a row, not even some cheap job on the outskirts of Findlay or Marion or someplace like that."

"Marion. Why have I heard of that?"

"Warren Harding."

"There's something we can do. We can visit Warren Harding's hometown. Must be a quirky little museum there."

"That guy was such an asswipe I wouldn't even go there to feed my occasional need for cheap and easy irony."

"Come on, Don. We've got to go *some*where. Do *some*thing. Look, I know I signed on to come along for the ride, and God knows I have gotten to experience a slice of Americana I never even could have imagined, but even with the adrenaline of last night's meeting, Americana has so far struck me as pretty damn dull."

"Because it is dull," Don said. "Beautiful and dull, like an old barn."

"Well a man can look at only so many barns and be satisfied. I need some scenes, some sites, some heartland glitter."

"You're right. You deserve better. We'll make it happen. Let's get through Ohio and into Indiana, eat an early dinner, set up the tent, and tomorrow morning, I promise, we'll head first thing to the College Football Hall of Fame."

"It's a start, but I'd like to be in Chicago before tomorrow is through, and don't back out with the expenses dodge. A night in the Windy City is on me."

Don felt so deflated that it was all one to him—there was nowhere he wanted to go, so he might as well go to Chicago. Despite Don's lethargy, Steph drove happily enough through the state of Ohio and into Indiana, marveling at how bizarrely flat the land became. "I bet you I am seeing twenty miles," he said just inside the Indiana line. There were few trees, just the expanse of land interrupted only by occasional houses and barns and small stands of trees. The crops had all been harvested for the year, so the land was even more spartan, most of it covered with smashed and broken corn stalks. "Seriously, man, this shit is almost Martian."

"You want Martian," Don said, "hit the salt flats in Utah, west of Salt Lake."

"There is something not natural about the way nature's laid out here."

"Of course it's not natural. The pioneers didn't come out here and discover a bunch of plowed fields ready to be planted. A hundred and fifty years ago, this place was all as woodsy as Vermont."

"A person shouldn't be able to see this far. It ain't right. Too much for the mind to handle."

"You can only see this far because everything's been harvested. A month ago, most of these roads were like tunnels between the corn."

"Well that shit doesn't seem natural either. Whatever happened to trees and plants? A little biodiversity?"

"Feeding you and your family got in the way."

They saw a sign for Fort Wayne, and Don told Steph to take I-69 down to it. "I want to camp there tonight." Down in Carolina, Don met a youth minister who used to break dance in public to gather attention before he then launched into his testimony, which usually scattered the crowd, some leaving while tossing a jeer or derisive comment. One time, Don stuck around to chat with the guy because he felt kind of sorry for him. The pity lasted just moments. The guy was short but intensely well-built, which was to be expected, given that he was a talented break dancer. His invariable white tank top was loose enough to reveal through the sleeve holes his especially defined ribs and abs. Don's dander rose early in their conversation, the moment the guy said, "Jesus may love the weak, but it's the strong he really likes." The guy called himself Reverend B. D. (for Break Dance), and when Don asked him where he got the credentials to call himself "Reverend," he said, "Fort Wayne Bible College in Fort Wayne, Indiana." That's why Don wanted to camp there; he hoped that merely staying within close proximity of the school might get his Don Prophet juices flowing again, both the righteous anger and the creative ones, but especially the latter.

They had dinner at a trucker's eatery off of the interstate just north of the small city. Don's current malaise did nothing to his appetite, and his spirits were somewhat revived by his fried chicken and mashed potato dinner. He wondered if his depression weren't linked to his morning's bowel movement. Emptying himself to that degree had to have some kind of effect on the system, although it was tough to argue that the effect wouldn't have been positive. No matter. He ate heartily, and he felt better, and they found a campsite just west of town.

But he still had the issue of getting the creative juices flowing again. Creativity, he'd realized during the afternoon's ruminations, was what he needed to become the sensation he hoped to become. "That's what Americans want in their sensations," he told Steph that evening around another campfire he'd made from another bundle of wood he'd purchased at the campground office. It was another sparsely populated campground, and the three other campsites being used also had tents, but again, Don had pitched his as far away as he could. Steph was mostly relaxed. They were surrounded by plowed and grassy fields, and the interstate was close enough that while they couldn't hear the traffic, they could see it in the distance, especially when darkness fell, the headlights moving from one side to the other, both ways, like video-game lights against the panorama's screen. "They want something new, something they haven't seen before. Ever. And if they've already seen it, even if it is sensational, then they're not interested. Take the Pet Rock." Don had filled Steph in on his day's thoughts. "After that there came a bunch of knock-offs, other objects transformed into pets that just sat there and did nothing, but none of it flew because people had seen it before. Or the Rubik's Cube. How many knock-offs of that were there? There was some kind of pyramid with a bunch of different colors you had to arrange in a special order, and there was some long chain thing whose colored links you had to arrange in a certain order, but again, those were old news. We've even come up with a phrase for the phenomenon. Been there, done that. So people didn't buy that other stuff. Hell, I'll even go gruesome on you. Columbine was major news for weeks—TV talking heads lingered over that for show after show, revisiting it from every angle, but how many school shootings have we had since then, and all those merit is basically a passing mention on TV, sometimes not even that, and a few paragraphs in the back pages of a paper."

"What about that Asian kid at Virginia Tech? That was headline stuff."

"The Asian factor there made that new; it appealed to people's innate fear of the other. And if you don't believe me, just look at Northern Illinois University. The classroom rampage there got a fraction of the Virginia Tech coverage because the kid pulling that trigger was just another crazy white kid. Even still, Virginia Tech got only a day or two of coverage.

Nothing like Columbine got. Even the word Columbine has imprinted itself on our collective memory. Just say the word, and everybody immediately thinks one thing. Not so Virginia Tech."

"What about reality TV? All reality TV shows are just a knock-off of the very first reality TV show. Why do they keep succeeding?"

"No fair. That's TV. Anything that lets Americans sit on their asses has a better than average chance of succeeding."

"Lady Gaga."

"She may not be new to you and me, who grew up with Madonna, but she's something new to everyone under twenty." Don rose to put another log on the fire. The two sat in lawn chairs that the campground rented to them; the actual rent was cheap, just three bucks per chair. There was a twenty dollar per chair safety deposit, but they would get that back in the morning, provided they didn't break or lose them. "Even with our biggest politicians, it's all about new. Jimmy Carter won everyone over by promising not to lie to them. Nobody'd tried that since Washington, and even Father George's promise of honesty was implied through deed whereas Jimmy's was explicitly stated. Ronald Reagan rode to town on the promise of money from the rich trickling down to the rest of us. That line hadn't been used since Hoover, so who remembered it? Didn't matter that that thesis has never proven to be true, it was new, or at least came off as new."

"Clinton?"

"I still haven't figured out how that slick son of a bitch pulled it off. Maybe it was the I-feel-your-pain stuff. It'd been a while since someone running for president even faked giving a shit about the poor. For George W., it was that compassionate conservative crap. God knows what it means, but it was new, so it did the trick."

"All right, I'll grant you your hypothesis. You have to be new. So then why are you all of a sudden so pessimistic? You *are* new—an evangelical ranting on behalf of enlightened theology."

"And that's where you're wrong. It doesn't matter what my content is—my form isn't new. I'm just another ranting evangelical. Look at the current big things in religion—Joel Osteen, Rick Warren. These guys got big because they changed the form. Rick Warren dressed like a construction worker on his day off and spoke quietly. Joel Osteen calmly stood in front of his massive audience, not shouting at them but talking with them. People were tired of being yelled at. These guys are to televangelism what *Oklahoma!* was to musical theater. Don't start with a big show number and a chorus line of leg-kicking girls. Give them a lone cowboy out on the prairie singing 'Oh What a Beautiful Morning.'" There was, of course, Barry Gladwell, but as with Clinton, Don could not figure him out, at least not fully. Osteen and Warren were good, but he could explain them, could see right through their acts back to the stage managers, techies and green room. Gladwell was pure genius, and by the very definition of genius, unknowable. Oh, Don could point to certain elements—the blend of old-time fire and brimstone with New Age comfort, the lowering and raising of his voice at atypical places, the perfectly coiffed and silver-suited appearance that somehow came across as natural and relaxed as Warren's flannel, but there was still a genius there that Don could no more define any more than he could deny. And Gladwell was new, like Warren and Osteen in their time, and Don felt that he himself simply wasn't and that he therefore couldn't compete. But Steph knew Don was new. He'd watched it all the night before. He'd heard firsthand testimony of the result. He considered telling Don about it now, but Don was too depressed, and he wouldn't hear. So they sat in relative silence around the fire until the last added log burned into small, broken embers, and then they both crawled into the tent, Don congratulating Steph on the progress he'd made as a camper.

But greater events were coming to pass in Ohio and around the country. Earlier that day, in the late afternoon, just as Don and Steph were approaching Fort Wayne, the number of people at the Ohio rest area who had either seen or were lined up to see the vision was in the low hundreds. The line snaked out of the rest area off to the side and into the grass where it weaved back and forth. It was self-policed, but Squat and his senior citizens did stand guard in the restroom, which basically meant they kept the line moving, allowing each pilgrim no more than fifteen seconds with the miracle, which caused no fuss. Indeed, each visitor seemed quite happy with his fifteen seconds. Hers too. Early on, Squat and his defenders knew they had to allow women in the restroom, and that turned out to be no problem; whenever someone had to actually use the facilities, any woman was made to wait outside until the business was finished.

The law arrived an hour or so later, a couple of state troopers who'd been ordered to the site after a call had come in that an inordinate number of people were gathered at the rest area. The two troopers arrived in separate cars at about the same time, and one immediately called for backup. He and his colleague strode the grounds, investigating the scene, and when they heard why everyone was there, they cut to the front of the line. The pilgrim at the front was happy to oblige. Inside, the two troopers shook hands with Squat, who seemed rather pleased to see them, and after they saw the vision and saw its likeness to the icon on the sink, they told Squat to keep up the good work inside while they maintained order on the outside. One trooper got back on his radio and called into headquarters and explained the situation. He said that backup didn't need to hurry, but that he was probably going to need much more of it as the night progressed. He also said they were going to need to cordon off a large field nearby for parking and maybe camping, they were going to have to direct traffic in the area, and they were going to need to set up some portable latrines. The dispatcher got their boss on the radio to have the trooper repeat everything he'd just said, which he did. The boss asked him to explain again what people were flocking to see before he said, "You mean I can end all of this with one quick flush?" The trooper on the scene said, "Sir, that call's going to have to come from the governor. I've seen this thing. Something's going on out here, and lots of people are headed this way, and I'm not sure you want to be the one responsible for ending it."

The media arrived less than an hour later, a van out of Akron with one camera and one reporter, Bradley Harrison, the first reporter on the scene, a recent graduate of the University of Akron journalism program who would use this experience and footage to land a job at WGN in Chicago in a couple of months. Within an hour of his report, which made the five-thirty Akron news, the three Cleveland stations choppered in their reporters, and while they weren't able to file full reports until the ten o'clock news, their footage was used as the teaser throughout the evening. "Find out why these people are flocking to a rest area just east of Youngstown where some say a miracle of epic proportions has occurred." CNN was on the scene by midnight, Rosalie Sanchez, a young reporter that producers thought could bring a properly sympathetic and reverential perspective to the story, given her Latina background.

By the following morning, CNN was all over the story; it was the lead for each segment, and Rosalie, who smelled a Peabody in this, had covered it from an array of angles—the history of Virgin Mary sightings, the reasons people flock to them, and the reason the people in Ohio flocked to this one. And people did flock. They arrived throughout the night, and

she interviewed many of them, asking why they'd come,
telecasting bits of the most compelling interviews, the single
mother with Hodgkin's disease who needed to stay alive to raise
her daughter of eight, the homeless family of four whose father
had lost his factory job the year before but whose two
elementary school sons had not missed a day of school despite
the fact that they lived out of their minivan, a couple of the
old-timers from the bus first on the scene, as well as Squat. It
was Squat who told Rosalie about Broderick, explaining how he
came onto the scene, what he saw, and how he made sure, as
much as he could, to take care of Broderick and take care of the
miracle. "Where is Broderick Hastings now?" she asked Squat.

"No idea, ma'am."

"You have no idea?" Rosalie confirmed.

"Undisclosed location."

"When might you think he'll come out of hiding?"

"I suspect when his mother sees fit. She's in charge."

The Polaroid photo of Broderick was then shown on TV
screens all across the country, and it was in the morning,
around nine-thirty, once the Eastern and Midwestern portions
of the United States had been awake long enough to watch
their morning shows and get a firm image of Broderick's face
imprinted on their minds, that Luella Hastings finally phoned
the offices of Wolf Glazer. She knew someone would be there.
She'd read in that *Variety* interview that he always had people
up and working in his office early because six a.m. in L.A.
meant nine a.m. in New York, so "dreams were already
buzzing." Glazer himself was often at work by six, and she
dearly hoped today was one of those mornings. She sat on her
Holiday Inn double bed with the TV muted, Broderick still
asleep on the other double bed. A pizza box with a couple of
remaining slices, cold and congealed, sat closed on the table,
next to some fruit and other foods Luella had the foresight to
buy at the grocery store, knowing that an indeterminate

sequestration was inevitable. All the snacks were healthy—granola bars, trail mix, fruit juice, water, and the ingredients for some peanut butter and jelly sandwiches, the former organic, the latter sugar-free.

"Shooting Star Agency," a perky female voice answered, "how may I direct your call?"

"This is Luella Hastings, mother of Broderick. Write down this number."

"I'm sorry, ma'am, who's calling?"

"Luella Hastings, mother of Broderick. Turn on any news show right now, dearie, and the name will mean something. Now, take down this number, and the minute Wolf decides he wants to represent my son, which will be the minute someone in that office turns on the TV, have him give me a call."

She gave the number, hung up and waited. The call came ten minutes later. She wasn't daunted at all by his status. In Hollywood, she fawned over and sucked up to the rich and famous enough times, having actually blown a couple of them to no avail, that they'd all lost their luster and sheen for her. So she was hardly star-struck while talking to Wolf. The way she saw it, she was in charge. She told him she was at an undisclosed location in Youngstown—she didn't even say it was a hotel—and that she wanted Wolf to be Broderick's agent and that she would do nothing—issue no statement, call no press—until he arrived on the scene to handle the situation. He said he'd be there that afternoon. He asked where she was staying, and she told him that when his plane landed, call again and she'd let him know. He agreed, and she hung up and turned the volume back up on the TV, but not so loud as to awaken Broderick. The amateur Polaroid shot really couldn't have been better. She was only a little bitter that she'd been cropped out of the picture.

Don awoke with a stiffish back, a renewed spirit, and absolutely no idea of all that had transpired over night. He was feeling better because, well, it was a new day. Don was cynical, sure, but he wasn't a depressive. Just because there were players far greater than him that were conning the vast majority of American people, and just because there were forces beyond even the reach of the most powerful that were determining some of the world's most decisive and influential events, never meant to Don that he had to be distraught about it. Don had often described himself as a cheerful fatalist. Things probably weren't going to work out, true, but that's no reason not to have a fantastic dinner. Okay, so maybe the Don Prophet thing didn't really set the world on fire in Pennsylvania. Today was a new day, so who knows what could happen? Besides, even if nothing happened, he was still with his friend in Indiana, they were going to hit a great museum, they'd be in Chicago later tonight, so why ruin it all with a lousy attitude? Fact was, Don had begun to allow himself to believe that the whole Don Prophet idea wasn't going to pan out. Good idea, sure, but how many peoples' good ideas ended up on life's cutting room floor? And what would be the fallout? No more than Steph had described—a job that sucked that he'd have to show up to every day. Well, boohoo. Get in line. He still had a damn good life, and rising an hour or so after the October sun on a cool morning in Indiana, he realized just how fortunate he was. Sometimes, in the midst of New York's bustle, surrounded by so many pinnacles, he could too easily lose sight of his nice life. But he was fortunate. After breakfast, he was going to give Gretchen a call, tell her how damn lucky he was to have her and that as soon as he got home, he'd get a job cleaning latrines if he had to in order to keep her.

"From now on on this trip," Don told Steph as he folded up the tent, both having showered, "you're in charge. From

here on out, we go where Steph wants to go, do what Steph
wants to do."

"What the hell happened to you during the night?"

"Must have had a dream about reality, but like most
dreams, I just can't remember the details."

Don shoved his folded tent into the trunk, and they got
into the car. The day was fine, the morning crisp as fresh, cold
water smacking in a can. Steph felt especially vivified by yet
another fantastic shower experience. "You're not folding your
hand on the whole D.P. thing, are you?" he asked.

"No, I'm not doing that, but I am taking the indirect
approach. I'll keep myself open to possibilities and
opportunities, but if it happens, it'll happen while we're focused
on your wants, not mine."

"Well aren't you the Zen Jedi warrior all of a sudden."

Don shrugged. "There is one caveat."

"There always is."

"Your desires matter only after we've finished breakfast.
I'm dying to lay my face into a Shoney's breakfast bar."

"Did you spot a Shoney's on the way into town?"

"The good people of Fort Wayne could hardly prosper
without one. The old lady in the office will know how to get us
there."

The old lady was who checked them in the night before;
she didn't have the morning shift, but her husband did, and the
old guy steered them to Dartmouth Drive, where a Shoney's lay
waiting. It was a Shoney's much like all the others—the brick
front, the comforting red letters, the red awnings over each
window. Inside was the same wooden décor, the same red
carpet, the same ample breakfast bar laden with mounds of
food, all lying helpless and supine as a drugged virgin waiting to
be violated by Don. The place wasn't too crowded, but then it
was a weekday, and for Midwestern routines it was pretty late
for breakfast, almost ten. Don approached the hostess' station,

but the hostess, a cute, young blonde, was turned around, looking up at a TV that hung from the ceiling. A couple of waitresses stood nearby, also looking up, as did a handful of patrons. They were engrossed by the news.

"What's going on?" Don asked, fearing something bad, another space shuttle crash or a particularly lethal IED bombing in Iraq.

The hostess turned around, startled. "I am so sorry. Table for two?"

"No problem," Don said. "Something happen?" He pointed to the TV.

"You haven't heard?" Don shook his head, and the hostess giggled. "It's really unbelievable."

Don and Steph stepped closer to the TV, and the hostess turned to resume watching herself. "The boy's name is Broderick Hastings," Rosalie Sanchez said into her microphone, dozens of people milling behind her in what looked to Don like an outdoor setting. The screen cut to a picture of Broderick, the Polaroid shot, and Don knew the face immediately. You can't be rude to Don Prophet and expect him to forget, especially inside of twenty-four hours. Rosalie went on to say that in the statement released by Hollywood agent Wolf Glazer, Glazer would be meeting with Hastings and his mother in an undisclosed location in the Youngstown area before they would all be making a statement sometime early this afternoon. "Meanwhile," Sanchez said as the screen returned to her onsite coverage, the camera panning away to show behind her a line of people waiting patiently to enter the rest area restroom, "the true believers keep flocking to this rest area in eastern Ohio to see something we're safe in assuming they probably never thought they'd see and never thought they'd want to see. But here they are, seeing, believing, and calling it a miracle."

Everyone around the TV turned to each other and chatted and laughed before resuming with their day. "What's going on?" Don asked.

"Some kid took a huge crap at a rest area," one of the patrons on his way out said, "and it came out looking like the Virgin Mary."

Don knew the crap was his, and now that he saw how it was playing out and envisioned how it could play out, he said the inevitable: "Holy shit." Everyone in the area laughed.

"Someone had to say it," one of the waitresses said.

"Come on," Don said, slapping Steph's chest with the back of his hand, already turned and headed for the exit. "We've got to go."

"What are you talking about?" Steph said. "I'm hungry."

That stopped Don cold, as if Steph just reminded him of who exactly he was. Suppose we do need to eat, he thought. And losing another half hour isn't going to change much. He turned around and came back to Steph. "We'll eat, but we've got to make it quick, and then we've got to get back to Ohio."

"Because it was so much fun the first time?"

Don leaned into Steph and fairly whispered. "Steph, I know this is going to sound crazy, but you have to believe me on this. That Virgin Mary crap? It's mine. That kid was in the bathroom when I did it."

Steph laughed, of course he laughed, but then he said, "You know, there are actually three reasons why I believe you on this. We *were* at a rest area yesterday. I *did* see a kid walk into the bathroom after you. And this seems *exactly* the stupid kind of irreverent spectacle your fat white ass would get us into. Are you sure that kid is your kid?"

"He was an asshole, Steph, and I never forget assholes."

Steph shook his head, laughing. "Guess we're not going to make it to Chicago tonight." Then, on their way to their table,

"I am going to get struck by lightning before this trip is through."

After breakfast, in the car, headed north on I-69, Steph driving, Don did not speak. He was busy reading the two papers he thought worth reading that were available at Shoney's, *The Indianapolis Star* and *USA Today*. The former had just a small AP story on the third page with no pictures, but the latter, God love them, had the story plastered on the front page with a huge picture of Broderick and the headline one simple word with one simple punctuation mark: MIRACLE? Don learned all about Squat, the old folks on the bus and that by nightfall last night, a couple hundred pilgrims had already visited the site and state police had already designated a large area for them to pitch their tents. "We have an area for tents near the site of the restroom and an area for campers and motor homes just a little farther away," said the trooper in charge. He went on to say that while the entire area would contain a strong police presence, they anticipated no major problems. "It's going to be like a Woodstock for believers," Don said, folding closed the paper, "minus the sex, drugs and rock and roll. Let me ask you something, Steph. You believe in God, right?"

"Not a black man in America who doesn't."

"Why is that?"

"I could be flippant and say it's because our mothers would beat the holy hell out of us if we didn't, but it probably has to do with the fact that there isn't much sense in not believing. Jesus is in our blood. We need him there. Being black in America—from the minute we step out of our homes in the morning to when we return at night, the day for us is just one clenched fist waiting to have to be used. Jesus gives us some ease and release."

"Black in America is a hell of a lot easier than black in Africa. Somalia, Uganda, Zimbabwe—those places aren't exactly peaches and cream."

"Never said they were. But I'm not in Uganda. No black in America is, and I can only tell you what it's like here."

"Fair enough. What's the nature of your belief?"

"What are you getting at, D.?"

"What I'm trying to say is—what's your take on what's happening in Ohio? I'll be honest: I'm a little freaked out. I mean, I haven't seen the crap I took—well, that's not true. I did see it. When I was trying to flush it. It wouldn't go down because the toilet was broken. But what I saw, I didn't see a Virgin Mary, but it looks like I'm the only person who didn't. Hundreds of people are gathering now at something they're all pretty sure they're seeing, and the fact that they're seeing it isn't even what freaks me out. Hell, there have been Virgin Mary sightings all over the world since God knows when, so that element of this doesn't even surprise me, although this one did come in a pretty unusual medium. What's freaking me out is that it came from me. It's all starting to make me wonder a bit."

"I started wondering before this," Steph said. It was then that he told Don about the girl at the meeting and, per her request, formally thanked him. "That look in her eyes . . . something happened for her, and you made it happen."

"That one's easy. All across America there must be thousands of smart, young Christians looking for an answer to reconcile evolution and their faith. That girl could have been any high school kid in any town. That's just the numbers at work there, the odds. Those numbers were the reason I started on this quixotic venture. I *knew* those people were out here. What's going on in Ohio, that's something entirely different. That's something that truly does seem, well, miraculous. And that miracle came through me. And it's making me really start to wonder."

"Wonder on till truth makes all things plain, D.P. I have no clue what to think, and I am frankly okay with that. Truth is, I am a little nervous heading back to Ohio for this, but this is exactly what you were shooting for, and I knew that when I said I wanted to come along for the ride. Now, granted I didn't expect this, but I had a hunch something stupid crazy would happen, and it's happening, and here I am along for the ride. And this morning's newscast, coupled with your explanation, officially marked the point at which I stopped trying to figure any of this out."

Steph was right. What was happening in Ohio was what Don had set out to accomplish, although it had all taken a turn he never could have predicted let alone imagine, and that's what bothered him. In Tuttle, he was in control. He walked into that gym with a specific plan, and even though the words that emerged from him were, for lack of a better word, inspired, spontaneously so, he did only what he'd intended to do. The response was beyond his planning and control, but responses always are, and he knew that headed in. But Ohio was different. He had generated exactly the type of media circus he'd hoped to generate, but he'd had absolutely no control over its instigation. It was something that had just happened, and he was no more than an unwitting vessel. Which made him wonder if his lark were really a lark, if he, in fact, had been chosen by God for a specific mission and if his thinking that he was coming out to America to be a prophet was no more than delusional thinking that the form of his genuine calling took. He had to be duped into being a prophet because the straight plea would have never worked. He'd have been like Jonah running away from God to avoid the duty. But that is crazy, Don thought. I can't have been called to be a prophet, and the minute I think I have been, I become no different from all the other wackos who think they've been called, Jim Jones and David Koresh and that Applewhite guy in California who had all his male cult members castrated. And yet, there was a miraculous nature to this bowel movement that did seem to defy all the world's arguments for coincidence and fluke. But then again, if you think about all the bowel movements across the world on a single day—billions and billions—and you multiply that over just a single year, or even a decade, well, just the sheer numbers argued for a probability that one of them could drop into the shape of the Virgin Mary. At least one. Hell, mine was probably one of dozens, if not hundreds, just that day that bore some resemblance to the Blessed Mother, and perhaps the only wonder was that more hadn't been spotted. Don took solace in this line of thinking. It did make the event seem more plausible. After all, the last sighting was not so long ago, her face appearing in the cement of some overpass or abutment. How many overpasses were there in America? Hundreds of thousands? Given that number, surely her likeness had appeared on others, they just weren't noticed. And why this bowel movement through Don? Hell, why not? One could just as easily ask why Michael Jordan? Why Margaret Thatcher? Why Gabriel García Márquez and Julia Roberts? Which no doubt all of them must have asked not a few times themselves, along with hundreds and hundreds of other newsmakers throughout the years (not to mention those on the other side of life's coin, the shit side, the people on planes that blew up or the gunshot victim who just happened to be in the bank when it got robbed or those poor saps walking under construction scaffolding just as it was collapsing). And what mattered with those successful examples, eventually, wasn't why them. What mattered was, okay, it's me, what am I going to do with it? And that question was the one Don had to focus on answering now. After all, that Virgin Mary crap may well be his, but at the moment, only he and Steph knew that.

Everyone else was convinced it belonged to that handsome little asshole, Broderick Hastings. Do the beautiful people get *everything*? Don wondered. What he wouldn't give for someone fat and/or ugly to win the White House again, a William Taft for the modern era. He had to get to that rest area and find a way to convince the public that that bowel movement was his, and he presently had no earthly idea how he could pull that off.

It was late in the afternoon by the time they reached the traffic jam west of Youngstown on I-80. He didn't know how many more miles it was to the rest area, but he was nervous he might not be there by eight o'clock. Earlier that afternoon, he and Steph listened on the radio to the formal statement by Broderick's agent, Wolf Glazer. Broderick was present, along with his mother. (What kind of psycho must that woman be, thought Don, going along with this massive charade? Although maybe she didn't know the truth, either; maybe the little fucker was lying to her, too.) It was held in the conference room of the Youngstown Holiday Inn where Broderick and his mother had been secretly staying. "My statement this morning will be brief," Wolf said. "First, Luella Hastings, in the interest of her son, Broderick, has agreed to my representing him. Second, Broderick intends to spend the day in quiet communion with God, and this evening he will return to the site of his miracle where, at eight o'clock, he will make a formal statement himself. Thank you." Then came the hubbub of journalists shouting questions before Wolf said they would answer no questions at this time. A while later, the radio station Don listened to reported that the Reverend Barry Gladwell had also issued a statement, calling this so-called miracle a desecration of all that's holy and saying he, too, planned to be at the rest area tonight to personally confront, "this latest gambit of Satan," and he hoped that hundreds of his followers would be there to join him. Don shook his head. Glazer and Gladwell were a doppelganger, one sacred, the other secular, and both masters of theater. It was a shrewd move on Glazer's part, pump up the anticipation for a big announcement tonight, giving all other media plenty of time to get there, Gladwell countering by saying he'd be there, too. The whole thing was tailor-made for a major indignant-Christian fundraising campaign. Douche bag. He recalled Jerry Falwell orchestrating just such a campaign around the film release of *The Last Temptation of Christ.* Jerry said he'd never before been so offended or upset in his life, and Don saw the brilliance of the line: he could use it again and again with each subsequent offense and never be accused of lying. The line, like paper towels and WD-40, could always serve a purpose. And with both Broderick and Gladwell headed to the site tonight, no wonder Don and Steph sat in a traffic jam. Don supposed he should be grateful that it wasn't worse.

"Your shit has really stirred up a storm," Steph said, inching the car along.

"If I'm starting to sense that we may not make it there in time, I'm going to get out and start walking and let you park the car."

"That may not sit so well with me."

"If you can think of something else, don't hesitate to share it."

"If I do have to drop you off, how will I find you later?"

"That's my shit over there that thousands of people are coming to see, and I'm going to make damn sure they know it's mine. I've got a hunch I won't be too tough to find."

Steph smiled. "So what do you have planned?"

"This whole thing has unfolded without me making one plan. No sense starting now."

A little over an hour later, Steph had driven five miles and reached the state troopers directing traffic, right lane to go through and keep heading east, left lane to go left across the median, across the interstate headed west where another trooper stood directing traffic, and into a large field of long grass. A number of cars didn't turn with Steph. In fact, most cars on I-80 East didn't. Nonetheless, the grassy lot Steph parked in had hundreds of cars, and by the time he and Don had gotten out, a good dozen or so more cars had followed them in and parked in their row, and more were coming. The rest area was still a mile away, and a trooper explained that they could make the walk along the interstate shoulder.

"Ohio law enforcement seems to have a pretty good handle on this thing," Don said as they walked the smooth asphalt of the shoulder, the evening air smelling of the exhaust of all the cars to their immediate right.

"Don't mind my silence," Steph said. "I'm waiting for the whole thing to become believable."

Don couldn't believe it either, but he'd realized that even with faith, contrary to what the apostle Paul said, what you believed really didn't matter compared to what you did. It was just another cliché being verified, actions speaking louder than words, but to Don they spoke even louder than thoughts and beliefs, and what he thought now was irrelevant; it was time to act. The moment he got out of the car and got the limbs moving, the blood circulating, he gained a sense of calm confidence. All these cars, all these people, all this commotion—it was all for him, even if they didn't know it, and that knowledge gave him a sense of authority.

The scene at the rest area was about what he'd expected, though maybe not as crowded as he'd anticipated, but TV always made things look more whatever—crowded, larger, awful. And if TV couldn't make it look more, they usually didn't cover the story. To be sure, the numbers were high; if Don had to guess, he's say the low thousands, but then he had no aptitude for such estimations. Still on the shoulder, which was elevated, he looked down on the scene. Over to his left was tent city where dozens upon dozens of tents had been pitched, and people were cooking over campfires, on portable gas stoves and on the permanent grills provided at the rest area for travelers. Kids were running all around between the tents, playing. At the restroom was the long line that weaved back and forth in the grass. Troopers stood guard at the door. Gladwell's protesters were there, shouting in a small group off to the side, holding up some signs, but their numbers, too, were fewer than Don expected. All in all, the scene was calmer than Don had anticipated, but he still had his work cut out for him. A makeshift stage had been constructed in the rest area parking lot (nice touch, Glazer, Don thought), complete with a couple of large kliegs plugged into a generator. The heaviest concentration of people stood before that stage, waiting for Broderick to speak, which would be soon. The pink sky was darkening fast.

"See that crowd at the stage?" Don asked Steph, who nodded. "I've got to be at the front of that."

"How you going to get there?"

"Same way anyone gets anywhere. Act like I belong."

"I'm not heading into that with you."

"See you after the show."

Don descended into the area, plunged into the spectacle of his miracle. At the restroom, he paused to view the pilgrims coming out. They didn't look visibly changed—no one walked in on crutches and emerged to cast them aside—but true change, Don knew, occurred within. The snippets of conversation he overheard were all tangential—the setting, the day, Broderick, the weather holding out. Some people standing in line were praying, eyes closed, lips moving, but most stood as benignly as if waiting to buy a ticket for a movie. Gladwell's minions were shouting, but those glazed zealots were always shouting about something. Don moved toward the stage. Broderick was due up there in half an hour.

He had little difficulty getting to the front of the crowd. All he had to do was say, "Excuse me," and push forward as if he were supposed to be up front, and people moved unquestioningly to the side. These people were gullible followers open to believing anything, so he knew they'd not give him much resistance. Catholic Church has capitalized on this sheeplike quality for two millennia, he thought. He got an added boost when, halfway to the stage, the lights came on, and people looked up and got excited and gave no more notice to Don pushing his way forward than they did a mosquito. The stage was chest high, and along the front were a dozen TV cameramen and print photographers pointing their cameras up. He looked around for Rosalie Sanchez.

When, some moments later, a wave of hushed, reverent whispering flowed from the right, Don turned just in time to see Broderick and his mother gain the stairs to the stage, led by Wolf. A marvelous quiet came over the crowd, not even whispers, and Wolf, decked out in a perfect silver suit, brown Italian shoes, shiny orange tie, continued to the center of the stage. There was no microphone. "Ladies and gentlemen, please remain silent. I offer you . . . Broderick Hastings." They did remain silent, even Gladwell's troops. Broderick, over at the edge of the stage with his mother, did not move at the mention of his name. His mother nudged his shoulder, he turned around and looked at her, and she nodded and pushed him harder. Broderick turned back around to Wolf who had his arm outstretched and was smiling, although Don thought the smile wasn't nearly so encouraging as it was menacing. Broderick walked forward, slowly, and while Don had seen this child only that one other time, he was confident in his ability to read children, for whom guile does not come easily, and Don knew that young Broderick Hastings was neither happy nor comfortable. He smiled confidently.

Broderick reached the center of the stage. Wolf put his hands on his shoulders, gave him some fortifying pats of encouragement, a reaffirming nod with a serious expression

Don again thought hinted of menace, and he walked over to the edge of the stage next to Luella, whose intense stare was that of the mother of a spelling bee finalist.

Broderick turned to the crowd. "I'd just like to say," he began, far too quiet, and some pilgrim from the back shouted, "Louder, Broderick." Broderick looked out over the crowd, he turned to his mother and Wolf, neither of whom looked happy, and he turned back to the crowd and shouted, in haste, as if he might self-destruct halfway through, "I'd just like to say that the turd you're all coming to see isn't mine."

"Goddamn it," Wolf said, turning and walking down the stage, exiting the scene in his limo, which would take him to his plane which would take him back to California, back to the more predictable and therefore easier to manage tantrums of the Hollywood elite.

The crowd was baffled; it was the calm hubbub of confusion before the roar of indignation at betrayal, and Don knew now was the time to pounce. "The boy speaks the truth," he shouted before he hoisted himself, not without difficulty, onto the stage. He stood next to Broderick and straightened his clothes. "Remember me, kid?"

"Do I ever." Broderick's relief was apparent.

"Go ahead, Broderick. Finish this thing off. Tell them who I am."

Broderick turned to the crowd, whose hubbub had grown louder, a few wondering quite loud and clear who the fat guy was with Broderick. "He's the one who did it," Broderick shouted. "He was finishing up when I came in. It was the worst thing in the world I ever smelled."

Don smiled warmly down to Broderick. "Way to go, kid. With you, the Lord is well pleased. Now why don't you go over there and take care of your mother." Broderick did as he was commanded; his mother was a sobbing, heaving lump on the edge of the stage.

Don turned to the crowd to face his destiny. They were all growing restive, and a few shouted up, asking who he was. "My name is Don," he said, stentorian, authoritative. "Don Prophet."

Back in Brooklyn, Gretchen, ever the slave to pop culture, sat on the couch in her living room watching Rosalie Sanchez and the coverage on CNN. She had just shoved the front tip of a slice of pizza into her mouth when Don rolled on the stage, and when the national telecast caught him giving his name to the crowd, to the nation, she said, her mouth full but her word no less decipherable because of that, "Unmotherfuckingbelievable." Moments later, Rosalie's voice came in over the coverage. "This has been an unbelievable turn of events, but it does now appear—wait, something else is happening. There's a small disturbance, a—I've just been told that Reverend Barry Gladwell is on the scene and is making his way up to the stage."

Don heard the same thing from random shouts in the crowd. He suspected Gladwell had been there a little while, waiting for the theatrically perfect moment to appear. Up on stage, waiting now for Gladwell, Don felt not one drop of discomfort. Gladwell's supporters started to hosanna and hooray while everyone else chatted quietly, nervously, but Don had a strange feeling that everything was going according to plan. He stood above it all, serene, suzerain. Cheers grew louder in the area to his left, and he turned to see Reverend Barry Gladwell, tanned, manicured, silver-haired with a suit of electric blue, pink tie, a bodyguard on either side, both of them big and bearded and all in black leather. To Don, it didn't look like Gladwell climbed the stairs to the stage as much as he floated, a little three-step glide in which he moved his knees merely to facilitate the illusion of walking. Don had seen famous people before. He lived in New York City. You couldn't swing a dead cat in that town without hitting someone

famous. At the Shakespeare and Company Bookstore on lower
Broadway, on his way out, he passed Dustin Hoffman who was
on his way in. Don knew the face but couldn't immediately
place from where, thought it was someone he'd met at a party
or maybe worked a temp gig for. A few steps later he realized
who it was. That's how it usually was for Don when he ran into
famous people; he saw their faces and felt like he knew them
from somewhere in his past, but his recent past. Not so with
Gladwell. As Don watched him glide his way toward him,
toward the center of the stage, he felt as if he'd known Gladwell
his entire life. You may be a genius, Don thought, feeling no
intimidation, but I know you. I know you on the deepest level
to your innermost core, and with that knowledge I shall defeat
you. Tonight, you belong to me, as this crowd belongs to me.
Thus saith the Lord. Don's thoughts were wild stallions on the
plains of his brain—fast, unhindered, beautiful and strong.

Gladwell stood inches from Don and looked up, shorter
than Don had imagined. Don had heard athletes talk about
"being in the zone," about how, when they were, everything
seemed to move in slow motion, and they saw their fields of
play with pristine clarity and were, for the duration of
engagement, constantly one step ahead of their opponents. Don
was in that zone. The surrounding night was dark, the
streetlamps notwithstanding, but he and Gladwell stood in the
center of brash, ample light, and the whole night and all in it
moved a little more slowly than Don, and he knew everything
Gladwell would do and say just before he did and said it. So he
was not surprised when Gladwell stared up at him with almost
a sneer, nor was he caught off guard when Gladwell turned
with a smooth motion to face the crowd, raise his hands in a
call for complete silence so that he may speak. Neither did one
word from Gladwell's small sermon come unexpectedly to
Don's ears. "Brothers and sisters," he intoned in that
mellifluous baritone, which became no less honeyed when he

raised it to a tenor in excitement, real or no, "I have come a long way today and all for one reason. The Lord has asked me to let everyone know that what is going on here is blasphemy, a desecration, and the Lord is not pleased." Gladwell paused to let his supporters cheer. But Don knew the pause was coming, and he knew of its end. "And as for you, Mr. . . . " Gladwell turned to Don.

"Prophet. Don Prophet."

"As for you, Mr. Don Prophet. The Lord has told me that your own salvation begins with you marching into that restroom and flushing down that abomination that has spurned all this idolatry, all this evil, all this sin." Gladwell's supporters erupted in a savage cheer, which brought to Don only comfort and ease. "Have you anything to say?" Gladwell asked.

Don turned to the crowd who belonged to him as he belonged to them. "In the nineteenth chapter of the Gospel According to Matthew, Jesus says that it is easier for a camel to go through the eye of a needle than for a rich man to enter the Kingdom of God. And in the Gospel According to Mark, when a rich man asks Jesus what he can do to inherit eternal life, Jesus tells him to sell everything he owns, give the money to the poor, and follow him. Those commandments don't seem to jibe with the lifestyle and ministry of our well-off friend, Mr. Gladwell. And so when he claims that the Lord has spoken to him, I'm not so sure. Brothers and sisters, in your Bibles, whom did the prophets preach over and over that we needed to help? The widows and orphans. The poor and downtrodden. The sick in body and spirit. And did Jesus every say, 'Blessed are the rich, the powerful, the well-adjusted?' Did he not ruffle the world's feathers precisely because he was affiliating with outcasts, with the meek and defeated, the refuse of society? In other words, those who have come to be viewed as shit? And so when a clean-smelling, well-dressed rich man tells me, tells you, that your dirty encounter here with your God, a miracle that has lifted your spirits, isn't valid, all I can say is, 'Bless him, Father, for he knows not what he does.'"

A pall swept over the land of the rest area, but Don knew that, too, would happen. Even Gladwell's supporters were mute. Gladwell leaned into Don and said, very quietly, "You and I, young man, shall debate."

"Anytime," Don said, just as quietly, "anywhere. The Lord has determined it so."

"CNN. The *Josh Weinman Show*. Tomorrow night in New York."

"I'll meet you at the studio."

"My people will call the Jew and set it up." Gladwell pivoted on a smooth heel between his bodyguards, and the three crossed the stage, fled the scene.

Don allowed Gladwell's exit to be complete before he followed his steps and descended into the multitude. The people came to him. They were not afraid. He moved among them slowly, perfectly, touching them, allowing them to touch him. He spent the night hearing their stories, not advising, not blessing, just hearing, listening, the elderly who had to designate their meager funds either for not quite enough medicine or not quite enough food, the single mothers who couldn't get the support they needed from the fathers of their children, the children themselves whose shoes were shoddy and whose socks got wet whenever it rained. He listened at length to a father of five who had never been out of work but who, in winter, hung blankets over all the doors in his decrepit living room and slept his family in there with a kerosene heater. He listened to a mother whose son had been killed three months earlier in Iraq; she said she woke every morning with a heart so heavy she could barely carry her body through the day. He listened to diabetic retirees whose pension had been abruptly discontinued when, a year and a half into retirement, the company he'd worked his whole life for declared bankruptcy.

On and on through the night he listened. A teacher who wondered every day why her students couldn't afford even pencils and paper, and why their school didn't provide them. A young married couple whose child died in infancy. An older married couple whose daughter was raped and murdered at college. He listened to people who were tired of being hungry, people who were tired of being lonely, people who were just plain tired. These weren't statistics on a graph or characters in an exposé. They were people, and they were suffering, and they were plenty. Don had previously thought that suffering in America was still better than suffering anywhere else in the world at any other time in history, that a crumbling home in Detroit was better than a tin-roofed shack in Mexico or a thatched-roof hut in Sierra Leone, and while he still thought that was true, he also thought it was irrelevant; suffering in America was as real as it was anywhere, if not as extreme. He spoke with a pudgy teen who was friendless and was constantly bullied at school, and he spoke with the boy's mother who hadn't the means to find him a friend or alter his situation. He spoke with another teen whose father beat him routinely, and he spoke with the mother of a gay teen who had committed suicide, unable to withstand the hectoring at school. These weren't clichés. They were souls in pain, and while their numbers that night may not have been large, relatively speaking, they no doubt represented numbers so great that their stories had been allowed to become clichés. And how does that happen? Don thought. How the hell does that happen?

Steph eventually did find him, and he stayed at Don's side through the night, but only a couple of pilgrims asked who he was, most no doubt thinking he was just another one of themselves. "My sidekick," Don described Steph to those who'd asked. "My friend." When Don and Steph got hungry, people fed them—burgers, hot dogs, doughnuts, apples. Not all the pilgrims were normal people having a tough stretch in life.

Some were wild-eyed Catholics who had a craze for the Virgin Mary, others were fuzzy-brained Protestants who wouldn't dream of missing a miracle, especially the particularly fringe strain of Protestants for whom this miracle was just another obvious example of the end times. And there were also some frat boy types who came to the spectacle as they would a concert. None of those people, the uber religious or tailgaters, had much interest in Don, nor he in them. Rosalie Sanchez tracked him down for an interview, but he declined. It was a golden opportunity to broaden his exposure, further his brand, but the spotlight that now shone directly in his eyes was so unexpected and of such high intensity that he feared bumping into a stupid phrase or clumsy quotation that couldn't be adequately retracted. And besides, something had changed for Don that night. He was different. His motives had become purer. "Tonight," he told Rosalie, off camera, "I just want to be with the people and listen. I've done enough talking for today."

And he listened. Through most of the night, he listened. He couldn't imagine how he might be bringing comfort to those who came and told him of their troubles, eagerly, as if he could help, but after they finished speaking, they did look relieved, as if some solution to whatever plagued them was now imminent. Or maybe the relief is just the talking, Don thought, the being heard. And maybe that's what all of this is about, just a little bit of comfort. But Don didn't want to offer comfort. What good is comfort? Comfort doesn't feed them, doesn't give them a home or a job. It doesn't take away cancer or put pencils in students' hands or bring back their dead offspring. In fact, comfort only exacerbates the problem. Prolongs it. Don was no Marxist. He was as capitalistic as they come. It's why he was out here, after all, to make money through a gimmick. He loved creature comforts as much as the next guy, Marx included, who drank those fine wines whenever he had a splurge of money, put his kids in private school, dressed them in expensive, tailored linens, fed them and himself choice cuts of meat. And yet, it was pretty tough to argue that Marx wasn't right about the opiate effect of religion. If people can find comfort even in their suffering, then they're probably a lot less likely to agitate for change. But it was worse than that, and that's when Don landed on what he suspected somewhere deep in his being he'd probably known all along: *That's* why these preachers preach about suffering so often and loud. They're playing to the crowd, their crowd. The vast majority of all humanity did experience suffering on some level. What better way to raise your ratings, enlarge your demographic, than to transform that suffering into a badge of honor? A trophy? You think suffering's bad? Hell no, it's good. It's what your messiah did. It's your guarantee for a better afterlife. It's why you're blessed. It's why you'll inherit the earth, for God's sake, so quit your complaining. Not only will you receive all of this, but you're suffering will make you a better person. So accept it, nay, embrace it. What a great ploy to keep the masses mollified, pacified. And it even exonerated the non-suffering from having to do anything about the problems of those who suffered. It's what allowed suffering to become a cliché easy to ignore. The problem was, even though the people bought it, even though they showed up every Sunday for it, it was all a lie. A goddamned lie. Nothing in the entire history of the world had given any indication that the meek would inherit it. Nothing. And there was not one shred of tangible evidence that the poor were blessed. And there was nothing, absolutely nothing, to suggest that suffering served any good purpose whatsoever. The young couple whose child was born with cancer, a child who suffered four years of a limited, painful existence before it died—what was ennobling about that experience for either child or parent? The homeless family living in its van—how was that good for their souls? What possible benefit could be derived by not having a fucking pencil for school? And yet on and on the preachers preached of the good of suffering, and understandably enough, the people kept coming to hear it, deriving comfort from it. Those preachers did no more than what everyone else on TV was doing—they gave the people what they wanted. And that's why Don just listened to people share their problems and did not speak. He did not want to be a party to that great lie.

Well after midnight, Steph returned to the car to gather the tent and sleeping bags. Don had said he'd help, but a few men stepped forth and volunteered their assistance so that Don could remain listening to the people. It was only a few hours from sunrise when Don finally crawled into his sleeping bag, next to Steph.

"You're in deep now," Steph whispered as they lay in their tent, fearful of speaking too loud, of being overheard.

"I know."

"What on earth are you going to do?"

"Haven't the foggiest."

He didn't sleep well. He'd put himself in a position from which he could see no plausible, palatable way to freedom. He'd wanted people to be smarter about their faith. He'd never wanted them to come to him for comfort and solutions. And he'd wanted to publish his books. But he was so burdened by his new reality that late the next morning, after they'd awakened and been served some Corn Flakes by campers who'd kept their milk in a cooler with ice, and after he'd spent some more hours listening to more people and their concerns, and after he'd again declined an interview with Rosalie Sanchez and a couple of other journalists who'd asked—after all of this, when Steph's phone rang and Steph answered and listened and looked surprised then bemused before he got Don's attention to tell him that his agent called Gretchen and said there were six different publishing houses who wanted to meet with him for a book deal—he was so burdened by the dilemma and responsibility of his new reality that when he heard that, heard that his gimmick had worked, that he'd gotten what he'd wanted, what he'd set out to get, he couldn't even be happy.

Governor Brad Wannamaker, originally of Centreville, Ohio, came into office on the Republican wave of 2002. Ten years before he was elected governor, he was the successful founder and CEO of a multimillion dollar home health care business who had decided to run for the state assembly largely because of his passion for the education issue. The rural and suburban public schools of Ohio were terrific, and he wanted to do everything he could to bring the struggling inner-city schools up to their level, a goal he knew he wouldn't fully realize, but just putting his brains and money behind a concerted effort was bound to bring improvements. In the Assembly, though, he wasn't able to accomplish much, so four years later he ran for the State Senate, and won, and while there got a bill passed that would allow for the establishment of charter schools in Cleveland, Columbus and Cincinnati, as well as some of the funding, the rest to be picked up through private donations and federal grants. Wannamaker had a libertarian streak, and on most issues he toed the Republican line and was okay with doing so, even if he didn't fully agree, but on education he was his own man, a renegade who worked with members of both parties. He never thought he had answers to all the questions, and he knew any solution likely wouldn't come from him; but the solution could come through him, and he studied the issue enough to be confident in his ability to identify the right ideas when they came his way, and he was firmly committed to trying any idea that just might prove effective, not worrying about whether or not it failed. "This entire country was founded upon trial and error," he said, "and I'll stop being interested in trying new things the day everything in our educational system is working just fine."

He was an affable, witty guy who was never much interested in picking fights, and he became so popular among his colleagues and associates that in 2000, many began to encourage him to run for governor. "I don't want to be governor," he told his closest friend in the Senate, a moderate Republican from downstate. "You could win," his friend said. Eventually, he did throw his hat into the ring because he was persuaded by the argument that as governor, he stood a legitimate chance of truly transforming inner-city education in a way he never could as senator, and in the light of that possibility, he saw his desire not to be governor as selfish. Basically, he didn't want to live in Columbus year around, and he didn't want to politic year around. As senator, there were reprieves from the grind. But did those wishes, he asked himself, matter more than the lives of so many of our children, not to mention the civic health of our society? Like the forefathers, Wannamaker believed that the strength and stamina of our democracy relied on the education level of the electorate. "Why do you even care about those kids?" a lobbyist asked him one day, to which he said, "Because if those kids aren't educated, our kids are doomed." And he meant it. And so he ran.

He coasted through the primary. There were two other candidates. One was an assemblyman from the Cincinnati suburbs who wanted to put the election of U.S. senators back in the hands of the legislature and who wanted gun safety to be a mandatory class for all public school students; the other was an upstate mayor from a mid-sized city who raised local taxes to pay for the construction of a boondoggle arts and culture center, the contractor of which just happened to be a large donor to his campaigns. Brad Wannamaker fit nicely in the middle of those two, and he won the primary with sixty-three percent of the vote. The general election was a bloodier tale. The Democrat he ran against was a popular secretary of state, a seasoned pol Wannamaker himself quite liked and had worked well with from the Senate. All along, pundits knew it was going to be a close race, and either side was looking for any advantage. But Wannamaker was not excited about the advantage "the boys from Washington" wanted to bring to Ohio. "Gay marriage," the D.C. operative said. "We want a ballot initiative banning it."

"What the hell for?" Wannamaker said. "Nobody out here is even talking about that issue."

"That's the problem. We want them talking about it. And voting on it. That's exactly the kind of issue of passion that will get people to the polls, our people. You could win this thing by four or five percentage points."

"That's crazy math," Wannamaker said.

"No, it's not. It's Washington math, and it's a lot more sophisticated than the algebra your yokels are computing out there. The initiative is going on the ballot, Brad. That came from the top. And if you want to be governor so you can help your ghetto chilluns, then I suggest you find some Jesus and embrace this issue."

Wannamaker didn't care about gay marriage; it was the libertarian in him. Government shouldn't be in the business of marriage, he thought. He also thought pot and prostitution should be legalized, but he kept that to himself. He was pretty convinced that the Washington body behind this brainchild belonged to a gay man because only a gay man, probably repressed, would think to make gay marriage an issue where it previously wasn't. (He was more convinced of this a few years later when it was revealed that a White House press correspondent famous for lobbing softballs to the president was discovered to be a shill who moonlighted as a gay prostitute. He couldn't believe the press didn't dig deeper on that story, which all but confirmed for him that a gay man, maybe not so repressed, was a lead player in the White House, but then maybe the press was a bit frightened about pursuing that story; J. Edgar Hoover showed just how ruthless a closeted fag could be.) And the last thing Wannamaker wanted to do was get elected in a campaign alongside Jesus. Sure it was effective, but again, he was a libertarian, and he dreamed of the day that talk of God was removed from all public discourse. He was no atheist; he, his wife and two high school children were solid members of the First United Methodist Church of Centreville. He just thought that so many people had so many different takes on God that it was wisest to make decisions without the interference of those takes, to confront problems as if we, the mortals, were going to have to find the solutions without divine guidance. And yet, he wanted desperately to do something about education, especially because, from what he saw, he was the only person in elected office in Ohio who genuinely gave a tinker's damn about the issue. And so for the sake of those kids, he held his nose and embraced the ballot initiative, hugged Jesus more tightly in public than he ever thought he would, and got elected governor with fifty-three percent of the vote, exactly the five percent margin that the Washington boys said he'd win by. And as governor, he was able to put all the religious nonsense aside, at least until the Virgin Mary incident at the rest area out east of Youngstown.

The morning after Don's confrontation with Gladwell, which the governor had watched on TV, he sat at his desk in the governor's mansion, getting briefed by his chief of staff and her top assistant. "All right," he said, "give me the rundown."

"Religious Right wants it flushed, says it's a desecration."

"They have an opinion on everything and a brain on nothing."

"Careful, Governor. They're your base."

"My point exactly. Candy from a baby. What else?"

"ACLU is in town," the assistant said. "They say the stuff is in a toilet that belongs to the government and therefore violates the separation of church and state."

"So they want it flushed, too?" Wannamaker asked, and the assistant nodded. "The Religious Right and ACLU are in agreement? There's your miracle. So where's the problem?"

"Overnight polls," the chief of staff said. "Seventy-two percent think the kid's a saint and that the miracle should be left alone, although we now know the kid wasn't responsible, the fat guy was, but we didn't know that when we conducted the poll, and we think the new information's effect on the numbers would be negligible."

The governor shook his head. He couldn't believe he had to deal with this. Attending all those fundraisers was purgatory enough, but he knew those were coming when he signed on for the job. And he knew there would be plenty of other unexpected and unwanted problems and crises, but this thing seemed unfair. He playfully wondered if it were God's revenge for his having so hypocritically embraced Jesus to get elected. "This shit is going to ruin my career," he said to the delight of his aides. He figured the longer he let the situation fester, the more toxic it would become. "All right. Here's what we do. Let the people have their miracle for one more day. Notify the state troopers and even some National Guard. Tell them at five o'clock this evening, they roll in and get rid of this thing. No press conferences, no warnings, just do it. I'll answer questions when it's over."

"Anything else?" his chief of staff asked.

"Better send in a plumber, too. I'd look real stupid whipping up a huge operation and not pulling it off because of a clogged toilet." He and his aides laughed.

The National Guard might have been overkill, but Wannamaker knew you couldn't be too soft these days, especially with the religious crowd. They arrived in two trucks and fanned out through the rest area, a few heading straight to the restroom with the plumber and some state troopers. There was no resistance from anyone; to some extent, they must have expected this, or something like it. Some people in line simply asked if the operation couldn't wait a tad longer, at least until they had a chance to see. "Sorry," the soldiers said, not unsympathetically, "Governor's orders." They marched into the restroom with the plumber who carried his plunger and tools much as the soldiers carried their weapons. Squat was still there, exhaustion writ large on his face. He was accompanied by two older men, but since their shift had just begun at five, they looked fresh. "You shutting us down?" Squat said.

"Governor's orders."

"Render unto Caesar what is Caesar's," one of the older men said, and the three stepped aside.

A soldier stepped in, looked down at the vision before turning around and looking back to the icon on the sink. He shook his head, as if thinking either people were crazy or he hated doing this, then he raised a leg and stepped on the toilet handle with his boot. The toilet, as if it had never been broken, flushed with a loud vigor, and probably all present would have been even more amazed by the miracle if they had known the truth: that Don never flushed because he couldn't. In seconds, the water was clear. Squat wept. And on his way out, he grabbed the icon, having no idea what he would do with it. Maybe he would hunt down Luella and Broderick and take it to them.

Outdoors, those in line had not moved, just in case, but when the soldiers came back out and announced the miracle had been flushed, they all slowly dispersed, back to their tents, back to their cars, back to their unmiraculous lives. The denizens of tent city broke down their tents and returned to their homes, sporadically, those who had homes. Some hung on for another day, and the authorities let them, but by noon the

341

day after, the authorities insisted everyone leave, and everyone did. A couple of hours later, after the last of the state troopers had left the scene, the rest area was, for a moment, completely empty. Soon after, though, a father and mother with three children pulled in to use the facilities, returning the sacred to the mundane.

Don was in New Jersey as his miracle was being flushed. Steph drove, and they rode through the rocky, tree-laden Delaware Water Gap, alongside the Delaware River, which flowed rugged and shallow with whitecaps like flecks of vanilla icing. They'd left the rest area an hour before noon, not long after Gretchen's call. Don needed to be back in the city for tonight's show. He said good-bye to as many people as he could in tent city. He reached to shake their hands, and sometimes they shook it, sometimes they grabbed and held it longer than usual, reluctant to let it go. A few dozen pilgrims walked with Don and Steph back to their car, carrying their tent and sleeping bags for them.

"So what do you do now?" one guy asked Don at the car, a farmer type with overalls, flannel shirt, dry and calloused hands.

"Guess I go back to New York and find out."

"Good luck," he said. "We're all sure pulling for you."

Don looked at the fifty or so people who followed him to the car. Some were waving, some held their children on their shoulders, some simply watched, sloe-eyed, unsure. Don knew that as they saw it, their fates were tied to his; whatever it was that victory in this situation could possibly be, it would be as much theirs as it was his own, as would his defeat. They needed him to go to New York and ratify the validity of what had happened here for them. They knew that what had happened here the last twenty-four hours would have no appreciable impact on their lives, and yet, they still needed it to matter, still needed it to count. At least, that's what Don assumed they were thinking, which was why, just before he climbed back into the

Hyundai, he said, loud enough for all of them to hear, "Don't worry, folks. This isn't over. And I'm not going to let you down." To which they all cheered before Don and Steph got back into the car, Steph driving them out to I-80, back to New York.

As soon as they got through the traffic jam and were on open road, Don phoned his agent. In a half hour or so, they'd be back in Pennsylvania, back in the mountains where cell phone reception would be erratic for the following five hours, so he wanted to get this call in now. "Donny, you're a star," she said, "a star. In all my years I've never had anything like this. I'm not even sure I like it, but it's something new, and it's going to pay, so what the hell."

"What's going on, Muriel?"

"What isn't going on? I got houses wooing me for you like you're John Grisham or something. They're pulling out all the stops. Any minute I expect HarperCollins to send Tony Bennett over and sing me an offer."

"My girlfriend told me we had six offers."

"That was two hours ago. Nice girl by the way. A real sweetheart. She's got some class, that one. Don't blow it there when you start making money. I've seen not a few authors shed that first wife for some little chippie once they got rich and famous, and they all lived to regret it. Anyway, I got ten houses making offers now, and the bids are all six figures for a two-book deal."

"You're my agent. Tell me what to do. I trust you on this."

"And you're not wrong to. Look, the numbers are the numbers, and there's not much difference there. Besides, whatever your advance is, you're going to make that back on your first print run, so it's really all about who you want to work with. There's a jewel of a girl over at Random House, Brett Shales, and I think you should meet with her. Normally, I'm not so keen on Random House, ever since the Nazis took them over, but this girl's sharp as a tack. I knew her mother back in the day. She was an editor at the *New Yorker*. Nice family."

"All right. Set up a lunch meeting with her for tomorrow."

"Done."

"You going to be there?"

"You don't want me there. This is all about you two establishing a relationship. Where are you now anyway? Still out in Iowa or Idaho or whatever?"

"Ohio. And we're just leaving. I'll be back in the city this evening. I'm supposed to be debating Reverend Gladwell on the *Josh Weinman Show*. Can you call and get the details? I don't even know where the studio is."

"I'm all over it, Donny, like a cheap suit. You just get back to the city and make that girlfriend of yours smile. She's solid, Donny, a real gem, and you're going to need someone to anchor you these next few months. It's all about to happen for you, kid, and I couldn't be happier. Call me when you get back into the city."

Don hung up, wondering what Gretchen could have possibly said during that phone call to make Muriel like her so much. He took a deep breath and placed Steph's phone on the console. Steph asked him what was up, and Don filled him in on the details. Steph shook his head and whistled. Don said, "I know what you're thinking."

"What makes you think you know that?"

"Because it's probably the same thing I'm thinking."

"Bet it isn't."

"What are you thinking?"

"I'm thinking this whole damned country is getting niggerfied. Idea ain't original with me. Read it from some other guy, can't remember his name, but all through last night and all through this morning, I kept thinking that slowly, one by one, one day at a time, everybody's becoming a nigger. You're never a nigger because you call yourself a nigger. You're a nigger because someone else decided you were then decided to treat you like one, and all of those people I listened to last night, they're just a bunch of niggers now, cheated, robbed, kicked out to the curb like they don't even matter, which they don't. It was such a nigger kind of scene that I was a little surprised there weren't more black people there, but then we never have been too big on the Virgin Mary thing. Mary had it pretty easy, relatively speaking, and premarital pregnancy, doesn't matter how it happened, cuts a little too close to the bone for worship in our community. Jesus is more our speed. I figured that's why there weren't many blacks there, but then niggers didn't need to come because those folks I saw last night, they're all coming to us niggers. Shit keeps going the way it's going, niggers going to be in the majority in this country in about thirty years. The only good thing about that is the place will probably be a little more fun. Slavery sucked about as much as suck can suck, but I shudder to think how boring this country would be if we hadn't been shipped over. On the whole, you white folks are D-U-L-L dull, although you, D.P., are one notable exception."

Don thought about all of that for a moment before he said, "You're right. That's not what I was thinking."

"Then your turn."

"I was thinking that if I sign a major book deal and make a ton of money off of this whole gambit, I'm really no better than, and no different from, Gladwell and his ilk."

"Oh, I was thinking that too, so kudos on the telepathy. I just found the niggerfication of America idea far more compelling to contemplate. Your dilemma is just the same old selling-of-the-soul routine that I've seen or read about too many times to be interested in seeing again."

"You don't find it more fascinating this time since it involves someone you know?"

"Nope."

"Well, it might be more interesting for you to know that I think this decision isn't so cut and dried as it seems."

"People about to choose money over principle rarely do."

But Don genuinely believed that it wasn't so clear a demarcation between choices, and he wasn't just rationalizing a justification on behalf of mammon. Almost everything he'd been taught as a child about money, and that semi-socialist crap he bought into in college, was, he realized, a lie. Money couldn't buy happiness? Maybe not, but it sure can keep a lot of misery at bay, which sure gives happiness a solid leg up. To always have the rent, to always have decent clothes, to always have ready access to good food—there was a lot to be happy about right there, or at least a lot not to sink you into dolor, and that's not even broaching the extraneous stuff, the money for a Starbucks latte anytime, for a Christmas trip to Costa Rica, a new Ralph Lauren sweater, an Armani suit or Hermés scarf any old time just for the hell of it; no, money was fun, and having plenty of it did make a lot of things better, and the idea that it didn't make you happy was an idea Don was convinced was fed by the rich to the poor to give them a false sense of superiority and thus make them less likely to do anything major about their condition other than maybe find a better job. And it was obviously why the poor and middle class cling to that line, keep it like an heirloom and pass it on to succeeding generations, a lie of superiority borne of a sense of inferiority, but deep down, and perhaps not so deep down, every damn one of them, Don thought, knows it's not true. The rich don't look any less happy than anyone else. In fact, on the whole they looked pretty damned glad about things. Sure some of them get divorced, but so do some poor people, and rich and divorced must be preferable. Sure some of them commit suicide, but that, too, is hardly confined to the top tax bracket. Don knew plenty of exceedingly wealthy people in the city, dynasty wealth, hcir or heiress wealth, and they all struck him as sufficiently giddy about life. And selling out? Who wouldn't sell out for fortune and sometimes fame? Selling out was the point. Don was amused to hear people bitch about some artist or musician or actor or whatnot selling out. Hell, all these people got in the business *to* sell out, and the only people who scoffed at selling out were those who'd never been offered the opportunity. Selling out simply meant that somebody with means thinks what you're offering will appeal to so many people that he's willing to pay you a lot of money to help make it happen, and isn't that the goal of your art, any art—getting it to a lot of people? Don sold out the moment he decided to get in the car and go west with his gimmick. The only difference between then and now was that it worked and now he had someone offering him money. And exploitative? Well, only if what he were offering was a lie, and he certainly didn't lie last night, nor did he even get paid last night. He offered no false solutions, no specific hope. He didn't have crews of women and children working twelve-hour shifts in sweat factories for a nickel an hour. He didn't have men in mines breathing lead and mercury for a grueling gig at a quarter a day. He was selling a book, a novel, which people could choose to read or not. And if they chose the former, they didn't even have to buy it. They could head down to the library.

And there was one more issue that made the whole rich/poor Marxist dichotomy a little muddy for Don, and that was that the rich really do run the show. For a few years now he'd had a sideline gig as a bartender for a catering company, and he often worked major fundraising events around the city—one for a conservation group held in huge tents in Central Park, one for a group combating rape held at MoMA, even the mega Robin Hood Foundation fundraisers, which, with his own eyes, he watched raise over fifty million dollars in one night for programs for the poor. The money was obscene, unlike anything Don had imagined. Individuals pledging a million dollars for some project or other, others bidding half a million or a quarter of a million for auction items such as a trip to Africa or dinner at some celebrity's home. One of the guys hosting an event was someone who used his money to singlehandedly preserve millions of acres of wilderness in Alaska, Idaho and Montana. And Don wasn't repulsed by this display of wealth; he was grateful for it. Environmental movements were great, and they gave people a banner to rally around, but these moneyed folks, like it or not, were the ones who were getting results, effecting outcomes. All the marches and kvetching in the world were a lot less likely to save a single spotted owl or feed a neighborhood of children or end abortion or whatever the cause might be. Sure there was Gandhi and Martin Luther King, but they really were the phenomenally rare exceptions. Even Jesus and the prophets, for all their blather, didn't change much in this world, if anything. There was war, poverty and suffering before they came, and there was war, poverty and suffering after, and there always would be. Don didn't quote Jesus on the rich because he believed it; frankly, he thought it was hooey. He quoted Jesus and the prophets only to highlight the hypocrisy of charlatans and mountebanks who used Jesus and the prophets for their own venal ends. If you really wanted to make a major difference in this world, you stood a much better chance of doing so if you were rich, and that was just the inarguable way the world was as Don saw it, "and that," he told Steph at the end of this hour-long monologue, "is what I was thinking."

Steph sucked his teeth and shook his head. "That's a formidable argument, D. Not sure if I buy it. Have to spend some more time with it, first. But it's formidable."

Halfway across Pennsylvania, they stopped for gas, and Don asked Steph to run inside, get some snacks and some newspapers. "I'd go, but I'm a little nervous about being recognized." The station wasn't crowded, but his nervousness, he discovered through the papers he read while Steph resumed driving, wasn't unfounded. His picture, while not on the front page of *The Philadelphia Inquirer, The New York Times,* and *USA Today,* was still in all of those papers, each photo showing him at some point during his sermon, an extra one in *USA Today* showing him sitting at a campfire, listening to members of the flock.

When, in New Jersey, they emerged from the deep valley of the Delaware Gap into four-lane interstate just a little over an hour from the city, he got back on the phone with Muriel. "What do we know, Muriel?"

"Your Josh Weinman appearance with Gladwell is tomorrow night. He's already got Angelina Jolie scheduled for tonight, and he's not about to bump her for you two, so take your time. Also, they want you there at three to record early. Josh has to run off and host some benefit for some kind of cancer. You've got a lunch meeting at noon scheduled with Brett Shales, down here at Pastrami and Why near my office. They make a fabulous brisket. We'll talk tomorrow. Get home and get some rest. Look fresh tomorrow. Appearance matters."

In Newark, across the Hudson River, Don saw all the lights of the city he now called home, and he was glad to be back. Traffic wasn't so bad through the Lincoln Tunnel, and riding on the Manhattan Bridge, Don ogled the stone and lights of the Brooklyn Bridge and almost grew weepy. He wished he knew a line from the Hart Crane poem about the bridge. Steph drove directly to his own apartment in a brownstone in Ft. Greene, right on the edge that bordered Bed-Stuy. He doubled-parked but left the engine running. "So what are you going to do?"

"I'm going to meet with an editor tomorrow and then go on the *Josh Weinman Show*. After that, your guess is as good as mine." Don looked around the neighborhood and couldn't believe how comfortable it all felt, as if he'd just slipped into his oldest, most favorite sweater. The place was definitely home—his heart and being declared it so. He marveled that he'd been gone just a few days.

"Well, D., it was a hell of a trip, and I thank you for that. But you still owe me a day at the College Football Hall of Fame and a night in Chicago. And I can't believe I'm saying this, but if you ever want to go back out as Don Prophet, I'd be happy to tag along for a few days. I've got a hunch you might have this gig for a while." Don couldn't begin to fathom that. He got out of the car and gave Steph that half-handshake, half-hug gesture of greeting or departure that had become standard in the ghetto and, subsequently, everywhere else, at least among the young and those who wished to be. "Do the right thing tomorrow, D. I don't know what that is, but your instincts on this whole D.P. thing haven't been wrong yet, so trust your gut and do the right thing."

Don drove to his neighborhood and parked and didn't even bother unloading the car, a cardinal sin of city dwelling and open invitation to any thief, but he was just too damned tired and preoccupied to care. The October sun was setting as he walked into his dim apartment where Gretchen sat on a stool at the island in the kitchen, reading a magazine. Don couldn't remember ever being more joyful at anything in the world than the smile she gave when she saw him. "You look like hell," she said.

"I'm exhausted."

"I was about to say you looked like shit, but that word has taken on a whole new meaning."

"Who you telling?"

"I'm not letting you near my bed until you take a shower."

"*Your* bed?"

"Remember our deal. You still don't have a job yet."

"Meeting with an editor tomorrow to discuss a two-book deal."

"We've been there before."

"No, we've never been there."

"Well, no contracts have been signed, so you're still on probation. Besides, aren't prophets supposed to be celibate?"

"God made Hosea marry a whore."

"Probably not the best thing you could have said to start winning me back over." She rose and came to Don and embraced him fervently. "Your clothes smell like smoke."

"Campfire."

"What have you gotten yourself into, Don?"

"Something I can't see my way out of yet."

"Don't get out until you've signed a contract. And go take a shower. If I weren't so crazy about you I'd probably be repulsed."

He stayed in the shower a long time, until the water ran cold. He was not trying to wash or wish away the last few days. Even though he had no idea what was going to happen or where he was going to go, he was utterly delighted about where he now stood. Life, he knew, was about to be, every day, something akin to what he'd always wanted it to be. He was burdened, and he was unsure, but it was a weight and lack of clarity that was borne of responsibility, significance. It was the price of an interesting life. He got out of the shower and toweled dry and put on some shorts and a T-shirt and went into the living room. Gretchen had containers of delivered Greek food splayed on the island, their lids opened wide as the beaks of hungry baby birds. "You trying to seduce me?" he asked.

"You wish. Want to watch the news? People have been talking about you."

"No, I don't want to watch that. I'm tired of me, and there's nothing to say." Which, Don knew, never stopped the talking heads from speaking an infinite deal of it anyway, nothingness, but he'd read about himself in the papers that afternoon, and the upshot was that nobody could yet identify who exactly he was. They didn't even know his real name yet. And he was hardly interested in listening to an array of various themes on that strain. "I want to eat, and I want to go to bed. I'm running on fumes, and I've got a huge day tomorrow."

"You need to call your parents. I promised them you would as soon as you got home."

Don had little interest in speaking with them tonight, but he couldn't wait until tomorrow because they went to work too early. Plus, they were his folks, and he did owe them some kind of explanation. God only knows what they could be thinking. He sat at the counter and methodically indulged in dinner— lamb, Greek salad, grape leaves, pita—and he got, if not a full second wind, at least enough of a breeze at his back to power a call home. His father answered. "Dad, it's Don."

"What the hell is going on out there, Don?"

"Aw, Dad, I wish I could say."

"Well if you can't, who can?"

"I'd really rather not talk about it tonight, Dad. I'd rather talk about something else."

"What the hell else matters?"

"I don't know. Is Mom home?"

His father shouted for Don's mom to get on the other phone. "Don, I hate to say it," she told him after their greeting, "but you looked like you've gained a little weight."

"That's just the TV, Mom. Cameras do that to everyone. You wouldn't believe how skinny Rosalie Sanchez is in real life." Don and his parents then talked of things mundane—the harvest back home, how his high school football team was doing, who had either gotten married or died, and other bits of hometown news too often mislabeled as gossip, Don thought. Those snippets of information about people in their community were a verbal adhesive that bonded all in that community together, even Don, who now lived so far from where they did. He told his parents he needed to go. His mom quickly asked how Gretchen was and if Don had proposed yet. He said she was fine and that he'd not proposed, and his mother scolded him for that and again lobbied for them to come home at Thanksgiving or Christmas. He thought about telling them to be sure to watch the *Josh Weinman Show* tomorrow night, but he feared that would lead to a lengthy inquiry on their part, so he left that job to their neighbors and friends, who would certainly catch the CNN promos.

"Don't you do anything stupid," his father said.

"I won't, Dad."

"And you remember everything I've told you."

"I won't forget any of it," he said, seriously. "I never have."

He went straight to bed and slept twelve hours and woke just before Gretchen left for work. He slept so deeply that he did not feel her either getting into bed last night or getting out this morning. He did not even hear her alarm. It was strange to watch her in her normal morning routine, given how unroutine his own life had become. It came as a shock to notice the whole world not dramatically changing just because his was. "There's a fresh pot of coffee. I've put out the clothes you should wear."

"The show's recording early, so I should be home to watch it with you."

"I've got a few friends coming over to watch, too."

"I hope one of them's that bitch Amber who said you should leave me. I want to gloat. She relapsed in any of her twelve-step programs yet?"

"No," Gretchen laughed, "she hasn't relapsed, and she's not one of the people coming over. But you'll get your chance to gloat some day." Fresh and pressed and looking pert, Gretchen, amid her morning bustle, came to Don who sat on the edge of the bed. She grabbed his face and gave him a kiss. "Kick some ass today, Don. It's all finally happening for you, and you deserve it."

"I do deserve it, don't I?"

"You've worked too damned hard."

She was right. He had worked too damned hard for too damned long. What was happening may have been a fluke, but it wasn't all without some effort on his part. Woody Allen had famously said that ninety percent of life was just showing up, but Don thought it was more accurate to say that ninety percent of life, if not more, was plain dumb luck. That said, you still had to be able to deliver the goods when opportunity came your way, and Don was ready to deliver. And he was confident. All doubt and reluctance had been scattered like buckshot from the shotgun of a good night's sleep. He got up and got some coffee and took another shower, a quick one, just to rinse away the physical and mental muck of slumber.

In his robe, he fixed a bowl of Corn Flakes and sat on the couch to watch CNN. He needed to know if any new developments had occurred so he could be prepared for his debate, but there was very little coverage on him or Ohio, just a brief mention of tonight's interview and a clip of Governor Wannamaker saying, "I did what I thought was in the best interest of the people of Ohio. I'm running a state here, not a circus or a church." During every commercial break, there was a promo for tonight's *Josh Weinman Show*. "Miracle or malarkey?" the bass voiceover said. "Find out tonight when Josh hosts the man responsible and the reverend incensed." After an hour of this vacuity, Don rose and got dressed, a shiny pair of navy slacks and white Oxford Gretchen had bought him on a trip to Brooks Brothers last spring to get some decent business clothes, of which Don previously had none. The fancy duds did make him feel even more confident, but he sensed they didn't alter his mood as much as reaffirm it. He was ready to tackle this town, make it his. He had a lunch with a high-powered editor then an appearance on a nationally televised show. Today was his first day of living not the American but

rather the New York dream—media in every direction. His star
was ascendant, finally among the firmament.

He thought about taking a taxi just to avoid being
recognized, but this was New York where the stars went
unmolested, so he walked to the subway. Mayor Bloomberg
took the subway every day, and during an interview Don heard
the mayor say that the only time anyone on the train had ever
disturbed him came when another passenger looked at him and
pleaded, "Isn't there *anything* you can do about the Knicks?"
The subway wasn't crowded, off-peak, and nobody on it
seemed to notice or recognize him, which didn't surprise. His
was a new face on the media scene, certainly known to only a
relative few, and while his story was pretty big, it was also
niche. New Yorkers were busy with plenty of other things to
think about, and happenings in the religious world were the
happenings they were probably least likely to be privy to.

Brett Shales was attractive—thin, dark-haired, the
muscular calves of a frequent treadmill jogger. She wore a
sleeveless, red, J.Crew dress with a sharp white sweater,
unbuttoned. She was standing just inside the restaurant when
Don entered, and he knew immediately that it was her—she
just had that smart, serious look of an editor. Plus, she knew
him, obviously from TV, and she said hi the moment he
entered, offering her long, boney hand to shake. "Great to meet
you," she said. The place was empty (still a tad early for lunch
for most), and they were taken to a table near the front
window; the table was well-lit by the sun, almost too bright for
Don's tastes. They sat and chatted, and Don was witty, relaxed.
He talked about his recent trip, about the night of his sermon,
answering her questions in detail. She looked riveted, and she
probably was. The waiter came and took their order (salads for
both—Don wanted to keep light, hungry, for his debate,
although his salad was a more substantial Cobb with bacon and
apple slices), and then she asked him about his past—his

experiences, his upbringing, what brought him to New York. It was when the waiter brought their salads that she got down to business.

"Look, Don, it's no mystery why we're here, so let's get serious for a minute." He wanted to take a bite of his salad, it looked so good, but since she had not even made a motion for her own fork, he thought the act of eating, even something as light as lettuce, would look oafish. Besides, his heart had picked up its pace a bit, and his stomach fluttered. "So, I've had a meeting with my boss and with the people in marketing, and we all definitely think the sooner we get something out, the better."

"I'm not sure what all Muriel has told you," Don said, "but I've just started a second novel, and there is, of course, my first novel, which Muriel thinks very highly of. She didn't have much luck selling it the first go around, but I think we can agree that circumstances have changed a bit," Don said with a sly smile.

"Indeed they have," Brett said, also smiling before the two shared a knowing, sinister chuckle. "I'm sure the novels are great. If Muriel loved them, then they must be. She's got one of the best eyes in the business. But I think those are something for down the road. What we're looking for right now is something to capitalize on your recent experiences in Ohio, something more about you. A memoir that combines a narrative of this past week with your own religious upbringing and spiritual development, and then a follow-up book of your philosophies and beliefs, something upbeat, a self-help guide that's as witty and forceful as you. We firmly believe that if you give us the kind of material we think you're capable of, and we package it just right, you could be absolutely huge, a Deepak Chopra or Joel Osteen with attitude and sass."

Don was waylaid. He felt lightheaded, dizzy. A memoir? A self-help guide? How did he not see this coming? How could he have been so unsuspecting and naïve? Why had Muriel not told him this was where things were headed? She was his agent, for fuck's sake, it was her job to learn this stuff and convey it. But then maybe she didn't tell him because she thought she didn't need to, it was so obvious. Or maybe she didn't tell him because then she knew he wouldn't come to lunch. But Don didn't have time to think about that. This was business, he was on the brink of stardom, and he couldn't look stupid, green. He was a rookie with a fast ball coming his way, and he needed to swing. "A memoir?" Don said, trying to disguise his disappointment, his bile.

"And a self-help book. I've watched those CNN clips over and over. You were great. So convincing and so convinced. This country's never seen anything like you before. You've got what it takes to really soar."

A memoir and self-help book. Well of course. Of motherfucking course. Nothing was more of a sure thing these days than memoirs and self-help, and people in media, people everywhere, loved nothing more than the sure thing. And they're probably not wrong to, Don thought. They were businesses, after all, and business was about making money, and there was nothing more profitable than the sure thing, that is, until it stopped being a sure thing and everyone sat around and waited for the next sure thing to come bounding along. But was there no place anymore for daring and risk, for a gamble on genuine creativity, surprise, the not-so-sure thing? Could nobody stomach the unpredictable? And yet, what was sensationalism if not unpredictable, a flash of meteor that no one anticipated, the something new that Don had theorized about at his campfire in Indiana? Something like Don now was. Who in the world, besides Don Bollinger, saw Don Prophet springing onto the scene, but even Don Bollinger didn't foresee the Don Prophet that emerged. So they were, in fact, capitalizing on the unexpected, the unforeseen, but did they have to then take it and make it so . . . palatable, digestible—unpredictable content in such a nauseatingly predictable form? Of course they did. If they wanted to make sacks and sacks of money they did. And if Don wanted to gather his own sacks, then he had to play along. It was the game these days, perhaps all days, the rules, and before he could make money by breaking the rules, he had first to make money by playing by them. A memoir. A self-help guide. He couldn't believe, but yes he could. He could believe all too easily. His contempt and disillusion was now complete, and it included himself. But he'd waited too long for this chance, worked too hard to cast it aside on principle. He did not want to return to days of mundane labor and financial insecurity. Poverty did suck, and he'd not even tasted the worst of it. He choked back a wave of self-loathing, but that didn't change the game or the smart ways of playing it. "Sure," he said, nodding, not smiling, crushing his front teeth together behind his closed lips. "A memoir sounds great. And it probably won't even take me that long to write. I'm methodical about work, and I'm very familiar with the material."

"I'll bet you are," Brett said, laughing mischievously, almost salaciously, as if Don had just tossed out some coy sexual innuendo. "Can you give me an idea of where you might head with this book?"

"I think you got that from the CNN clips, Brett. And for a further taste, I suggest you watch the *Josh Weinman Show* tonight."

"Playing hard to get, Mr. Bollinger?"

"Not at all," Don said, affable, pleasant, not backtracking, just playing. "It's just that, with the written word, I never really know where I'm going until I get there. Like any journey."

"Just so long as we can work well together. Understand each other."

"I think we already do."

"I agree."

"And by the way," he said, "I think that, for business and marketing reasons, it would be best to call me Mr. Prophet and not Mr. Bollinger."

"It probably would," she smiled, "but I think from here on out I'll stick with Don."

"Yes," Don said, "that probably would be best."

After he ate his salad, he flagged his waiter and ordered a steak, then chased it all with a chocolate mousse cheesecake and a double espresso. He didn't mind making Brett wait while he ate. Sure the extra food was a power play, an assertion of his position. It not only made her malinger when she had a multitude of tasks waiting back at the office, but it also displayed a moderate gluttony, something he was sure she abhorred. Most important, though, that morning's bowl of cereal was meager sustenance, and Don was hungry, and just a salad wasn't cutting it. But as he flagged a taxi for a ride to the CNN studios, and as he walked through the glass doors of the studios into the sparkle and shine of the marble-floored atrium, he felt a good deal more bloated and heavy than he thought optimal for his debate.

"I'm here to appear on a show," he told the security guards at the front desk, who didn't look impressed, but then they saw people appearing on shows by the dozens every day.

"Name?"

"Don Prophet."

"May I have your license?"

This posed a problem. "The name on my license isn't the name I gave you. Prophet is my stage name."

"Not a problem. Just give me your license, and I'll tell them Don Prophet is here." Don did, a guard made the call, and he hung up the phone, handed back the license. "Around the corner. Take the elevator to the third floor."

Don was a tad surprised security hadn't recognized him, but after working at CNN all day, maybe the last thing they wanted to do when they got home was watch the news, especially if (and Don was surmising here) their wages and benefits were lousy. He stepped out of the elevator on the third floor, and a skinny, effeminate young man wearing a headset and carrying a clipboard was standing there to greet him. "Hi, Mr. Prophet," he said with an exuberant smile. "I'm Shane, and I'm going to escort you to make-up."

"Hi, Shane. Call me Don."

"Sure thing, Don." He led Don down a hallway in which people came and went in and out of doors spaced evenly along the walls, quickly and diligently performing tasks in measured haste. "By the way, caught the clip of you last night on the station. Great act. This thing's got legs. You're here to stay for a while."

"Thanks, Shane," Don said, sickened to hear his earnest sermon reduced to the words "great act." But focus, Don. A mission to complete, and don't look stupid and green.

"You bet, Don."

Shane opened a door near the end of the hallway and deposited Don within. Bright lights, big mirrors. "Courtney, here's Don. Fifteen minutes and then we do hair."

"Got it." Courtney was an insanely beautiful woman of what appeared Mediterranean descent, dark hair, dark skin, Greek or Italian or maybe Lebanese. She gestured to a chair, and Don sat. She wore faded, tight jeans and a loose peach blouse. She went to work immediately, blush on the cheeks, mascara on the eye lashes, earnestly applying his make-up, the act of which necessitated close physical proximity. She smelled great, a powdery scent not too perfumed. Her face spent so much time just inches from his that Don was compelled to stare in her eyes. "Let me ask you something, Courtney."

"Ask."

"How many guys that you do make-up for hit on you?"

She smiled. "You hitting on me, Don Prophet?"

"Absolutely not. I'm too much of a slob to hit on beautiful women, and I'm nuts about my girlfriend. Just curiosity."

"I'd say about fifty percent. The politicians are my favorite. They always try to do it in a way that makes them seem like they're not doing it, and they never pull it off."

"Pigs," Don said.

"Actually, some of them are pretty cute."

It was when Don was getting his hair done a few doors down that Josh Weinman came strolling in to meet him. "So you're the Don Prophet that made such a splash out in Ohio, and pardon the double entendre." He smiled warmly, a charming man, older than he looked on screen, thin, urbane, impeccable in his suit, a real pro with the insouciant confidence of a man comfortably and securely atop his milieu.

"No apologies necessary. Given what I did, the puns and entendres are a plentiful low-hanging fruit."

"You're going to be just fine out there today, and Barry's great, too. I've had him on the show a few times. Consummate guest. You're going to be miked, so you won't need to shout. It'll be a debate, yes, but let's keep it conversational. That said, fury and indignation are great for ratings. I'll let him start, then you'll rebut, and we'll go immediately to questions from callers. I might have a word or two to add here or there, but I want to play the role of detached facilitator on this one. We'll screen the calls, so you won't get a real doozy, but if something does come in that's just too good to pass up, we'll go to a commercial then feed you the question beforehand to give you some time to think about it. Sound good, Don?"

"Sounds great, Josh."

"Fantastic. You done this before?"

"First time."

"A virgin then. Don't worry. You're going to be fine."

So that's how it works, Don thought. Everything is staged, everything choreographed. But of course. Celebrities didn't come onto these shows to risk a pitfall with a difficult, unexpected moment. And now that Don was backstage, on the inside, he was already one of them, and they treated him as such. Even Gladwell treated him as such. When Don walked onto the set and took his seat at the circular table, Barry and Josh were already there. "Safe trip back from Ohio?" Gladwell asked, friendly. Something about him looked different. It was the same Gladwell, silver hair, perfect suit, but the face looked real, the entire aura less plastic. And then it hit Don: of course. He wasn't on camera, he wasn't on stage. He wasn't performing. Don wasn't speaking with Reverend Gladwell. He was chatting with Barry.

"Not a hitch."

"Good. Glad you could make it," he said as if he were the host.

The stage manager came forward, said, "Places," then said, "five, four, three, two, one and go."

"Good evening, America," Josh said, "and welcome to the *Josh Weinman Show*. Most of you watching know the story by now. This man, Don Prophet, had a Blessed Mary bowel movement that thousands have called a miracle. This man, the eminent Barry Gladwell, vigorously disagreed, calling it a sacrilege. Who's right? That's what we're here to decide tonight. Welcome to both of you, and let's first turn to Reverend Gladwell," Josh said and literally did, angling his body that direction. Gladwell, Don noticed, had transformed, had become Reverend Gladwell, the nemesis with which he was so familiar, no longer the pleasant, genuine Barry. That relaxed demeanor had given way to one of indignation, and Don marveled at how convincing he was. A consummate guest. "Reverend, why are you so offended by Don's holy feces?"

"This goes well beyond mere offense, Josh," Gladwell said before he launched into his predictable screed on the desecration of it all. Don tuned him out. He didn't have to listen to know what was said. He was sickened by the charade of it all and his part in it. Josh and his ilk were playing off the gullibility and naiveté of the public, and that, for Don, was forgivable. But Gladwell and his ilk were playing off the public's need, sometimes desperation, and that was not forgivable. Gladwell gave them false hope, a rope to hang onto that wasn't attached at the top. They came to him for something nourishing, meat and vegetables, and he gave them cotton candy, and they liked how sweet it tasted, but it did them no good, only they wouldn't realize that until they'd eaten too much. Pray and things will get better. Believe and your dreams will come true. And so they clung to his message and called it faith, but for most people, dreams didn't come true, and life plodded along, and the people had only bellies full of cotton candy to get them through their darkest hours of spiritual hunger and need. Did he, Don, really want to be a part of this? Too late. He already was. But he didn't have to play by their rules completely. He could pull the curtain back, so to speak, and speak some semblance of the truth.

"Okay," Josh said at the end of Gladwell's diatribe. "Strong words from a strong man. What do you say to those accusations, Mr. Prophet?" Don said nothing at first, just stared at Gladwell. The loathing was sincere, but the pause was for effect. "Don?" Josh said.

"I heard you Josh," he said.

"What do you think?"

"What do I think? I think I'm so tired of these hypocritical charlatans using religion for personal profit. Do you realize, Josh, that America has so successfully fused Christianity with capitalism that most people have no idea it was Ben Franklin and not the Bible who said, 'The Lord helps those who help themselves?' The prophets and the gospels clearly show that the Lord is most concerned with helping precisely those who are incapable of helping themselves. But that doesn't jibe with capitalism, so that's why they've had to push this myth about the Lord helping the industrious, who are really just the lucky in disguise. That's why they've convinced most Americans that if a person's poor, it must be because of some inherent evil or fault on his part. The likes of Gladwell have brought to this country a messiah that is supply-side economics. They've turned religion into a commodity. Even now he's turned my Virgin Mary shit into a fundraising campaign. Whether or not my shit was evil or a miracle, I really don't know. But I do know his ministry is the work if not of Satan then at least of mammon, and the Good Book tells us explicitly that we cannot simultaneously worship God and mammon. And let me say something to you, the American people. I'm going to leave here right now and go back out into America and resume my ministry. And I do not want anyone to pay me for my work. If you want to give me a meal, it will be appreciated. If you want to pay for a tank of gas, I'll take it. But I want no extra money, no profits, for my ministry. And I challenge you, Barry Gladwell, to minister under the same circumstances."

"Okay, Mr. Prophet," Josh said. "There you have it. Both sides of the argument. Now, let's hear from you, the callers."

"No," Don said. "Let's not hear from the callers until Barry answers my challenge." Josh gave a certain smile to Don that revealed some displeasure for going off script, but Don didn't relent. "Come on, Reverend Gladwell. You going to minister under my terms?"

"I think we have other questions to answer tonight," Gladwell said.

"We do, and I'm sure we'll get to them, but come on. Tell me. You going to minister and eschew the profits? Answer me."

"Mr. Prophet, you have no—"

"Yes or no, Barry. You in?" There came silence, only a brief moment before Don, not wanting Gladwell to come up with a good response, said, "I thought not. Thanks for having me on your show, Josh."

Don took off his microphone and stood up. "We'll be right back," Josh hastened to say, and when they got the signal that the show had cut to a commercial, he said, "You can't leave, Don. You were great. Calls are coming in now, and we've got forty minutes to go."

"You and Barry answer questions."

"Don't blow this Don," Josh said.

"You've got a future in this business," Gladwell said. "Don't ruin it now."

"I'm not ruining my future, Barry. I'm securing it."

And he was. The indignation, the message, the gauntlet, the hasty exit—they were all sincere, but Don knew they'd also play incredibly well across the country. More than that, in homes across the country, those tent-city denizens who needed him to be victorious knew that he'd just won, at least this first round. He walked blissfully off of the set of the show.

Later that night, when Brett Shales watched the *Josh Weinman Show,* she smiled. "Brilliant," she said. "Totally fucking brilliant." She knew the first print run for the memoir would have to be a hundred thousand, minimum. Steph watched the show, and after Don's monologue, he simply shouted, "Yes," as if his team had just scored a touchdown. Don had gotten home to Gretchen before she could watch, and he explained that what he'd said was just his strategy, that he agreed to a major two-book deal, and not to worry, plenty of money was on the way. And it was, and Don was not sorry. He knew, in the future, he'd be able to sell those novels. If former politicos could become morning talk show hosts and land supporting roles in serious films, he could sell his novels; if an Oscar-winning actress could publish a cookbook and just about everybody who ever did anything remotely famous could publish a children's book, he could publish his novels; if senators and house speakers could publish their goofy novels, and if pop novelists could get so huge that they got to publish some new books under the rubric of "serious" fiction, then Don could publish his novels, too. Because this was America, after all, where anything was possible, especially if you had a platform. And if Don Prophet was establishing a platform by preaching to the downtrodden, well, at least he was doing it on their behalf and not on their backs. And if they shelled out twenty bucks to read his book, at least they'd not be getting a message of false hope, and they'd not be reading that they were to blame for their own suffering. A voice for the voiceless? Nothing so grandiose as that. Just the truth, at least as he saw it, and his vision was pretty damned good. And though he had no idea where this all would end, he was very comfortable with where it began, and he was looking ridiculously forward to his journey back out into the heart of America, an America where anything still was possible.

Especially if you were famous.

ABOUT THE AUTHOR

Erik Simon is originally from rural Illinois. He currently lives and works in New York.

15620987R00216

Made in the USA
Lexington, KY
07 June 2012